Out of Body

**Center Point
Large Print**

Also by Stella Cameron
and available from Center Point Large Print:

Cypress Nights
Target
A Marked Man
Mirror, Mirror
A Grave Mistake
Now You See Him
An Angel in Time
A Useful Affair

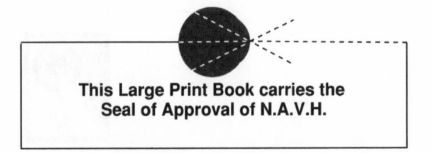

**This Large Print Book carries the
Seal of Approval of N.A.V.H.**

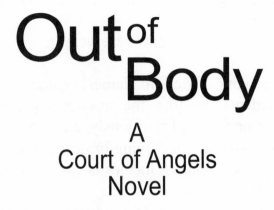

Out of Body

A
Court of Angels
Novel

STELLA CAMERON

CENTER POINT PUBLISHING
THORNDIKE, MAINE

This Center Point Large Print edition
is published in the year 2010 by arrangement with
Harlequin Books S.A.

The text of this Large Print edition is unabridged.
In other aspects, this book may vary
from the original edition.
Printed in the United States of America
on permanent paper.
Set in 16-point Times New Roman type.

ISBN: 978-1-60285-730-8

Library of Congress Cataloging-in-Publication Data

Cameron, Stella.
   Out of body / Stella Cameron.
      p. cm.
   Originally published by: Harlequin Books.
   "Center Point large print edition."
   ISBN 978-1-60285-730-8 (library binding : alk. paper)
   1. Large type books. I. Title.
   PS3553.A4345O98 2010
   813'.54--dc22
2009049740

For Philip and Lynn Lloyd-Worth
and Zara West

Prologue

If ever a man had suffered for marrying the wrong woman, it was Jude Millet.

For three hundred years.

In the attic above J. Clive Millet, the French Quarter antique shop his family had owned since their flight first from Belgium, and then London—Jude listened appreciatively to the crack of early summer lightning, the rumble of thunder, and watched flashes of white light pierce the gloom in his cluttered bower.

Three hundred years.

He raised one corner of his mouth. Time flew when one was having fun, wasn't that a saying he'd overheard when he broke his own rule and listened in on a conversation among those living in the here and now?

His poor descendants had suffered as a result of his birth and subsequent poor choices. Or one choice in particular: That wife of his.

The Millet family, an old and respected one, started their difficult journey from favor in Belgium, early in the eighteenth century.

Red-haired and green-eyed, without exception—almost—they were seen as close-knit and eccentric, but they were respected. Dealers in fine art of all varieties, they were sought after in Bruges society, even though they rarely accepted invitations to balls, soirees or other crowded, smelly gatherings they considered boring.

Then "The Event" occurred in the form of a robust, dark-haired, blue-eyed infant Millet, a male, and there was consternation.

They called the child Jude. And from time to time, a Millet has remarked on how similar the name Jude is to Judas.

Males in the family had forever chosen red-haired, green-eyed mates and, possibly through something a little beyond understanding, all subsequent males and females also had red-haired, green-eyed children.

And all went well.

Until the arrival of that dark-haired boy, Jude, that boy they at first suspected must be a changeling, an infant who didn't belong to them at all. He was no changeling, but the Millets were eternally changed by his birth.

The child grew to manhood, a tall, dark, flamboyant force filled with the other, more important element that made the family different: they all had paranormal talents, some even magical.

There was no end to their mystical potential.

The dark-haired one eventually married a beguiling woman whose true nature he could not know until it was too late and, together with the rest of his kin, he was forced to flee to London. They barely eluded those who suspected Jude's wife of causing bizarre deaths; the citizens of first

Bruges, then London, wanted to punish the Millets for "witchcraft."

That wife disappeared, but not soon enough to save her family by marriage from rejection and flight.

The Mentor, as Jude Millet became known by his descendants, moved to New Orleans in search of a way to combat the damage done by his ill-chosen wife and her kind. He considered her acts dark and hoped to find answers where dark arts are practiced.

He had discovered a great deal, but no ultimate answers.

Tonight Jude was far from peaceful. He could feel unrest seething on the lower floors of the Millet's Royal Street shop. Not surprising since a new crisis had already begun to unfold. At last he would be called upon to guide, in secret, his twenty-first-century relatives. They were a feisty lot, exactly as he would wish them to be.

So many years had passed without incident since he and the others first arrived in New Orleans that he had come to hope they were out of all danger.

Now he knew how wrong he had been.

Jude moved from his place among the shadows and approached the veil through which he must pass to be present in the world of the living. He had always known there could be those events that would require him, within the bounds of the Millet Code, to become active again.

Like now.

After his release from life, followed by ages of observing and occasionally flying into a rage over decisions he would never have made, he must take an active role in his family's affairs. The Mentor would return, not to take control, for that was not the Millet way, but to remind them of the responsibilities that came with their extraordinary powers.

Naturally, he would keep himself largely hidden from them. After all, he had never been seen by any member of the recent generations. He must introduce himself carefully, making sure they never as much as guessed that he was no farther away than the attic of their own shop, and certainly without presenting a "solid" form they might become attached to.

The actions they took would, as they always had, depend on their own conclusions and skills.

Even as he stood there, only a floor or so from some current Millets, there were a few family members looking for traces of him in London, and perhaps elsewhere. Jude, the Mentor, smiled at the thought. They not only questioned that he had ever existed, they probably hoped he had not! If they could prove he was a myth, then they could forget about dark-haired males being dangerous to the family.

Since there was, right now, another dark-haired male Millet, they desperately longed to debunk the old theory.

In front of him shimmered a weblike veil. He pointed a single, long forefinger in its direction and it disappeared.

Jude had learned a good deal about the enemy, the Embran as they were called, and their home deep in the earth.

Right now, and for thirty years past, a single member of the Embran tribe had been present in New Orleans, creating unspeakable horrors he had so far managed to hide.

No more.

Jude would oversee the beginning of the end for the one who had recently been brought to his attention. An informer had reported that for thirty years the renegade Embran had been in this very city without the Mentor's knowledge. And in the past few weeks this Embran, who had grown too drunk on having his fill of earthly delights to carry out his mission, had made a mistake and revealed himself. Panicked into action, at last he had taken up the quest he was sent to the surface of the earth to accomplish, to crush the Millets and steal the power his people believed the family had over the fate of the Embrans.

There was little time now. The madness was unfolding. And Marley Millet, a young female descendent of the Mentor's, had been placed in a position where the enemy might well use her as their route to dominance. Over centuries, the

Embran had come to the earth's surface from deep in the earth. Only one of them was allowed to come at a time and they had to fight one another to the death for the privilege. For expediency, the winner chose to manifest either as male or female—more or less. These creatures came to satisfy their greed for human pleasures. And they wreaked pain and fear without ever tasting justice.

But the Embrans' own twisted strengths had begun to fade. Had begun to fade, in fact, after the one who had ensnared the Mentor himself into marriage and caused the Millets to flee for their lives had left earth and returned to Embran. She carried with her some element that began the systematic termination of her kind.

Embran after Embran visited earth only to return without answers or help for a dying race, then the latest member arrived. After indulging himself in the perverted human sexuality to which they were all addicted, he had been betrayed by the one whom he trusted. Now he was faced with his own destruction.

Desperate to reverse his fortunes he had set a ruthless plot in motion that, unless thwarted, would make sure young Marley did not live to an old age.

The Mentor stood at the small, very high dormer window in the attic and looked down on Royal Street. His superb vision made it easy for him to see every incident, every human, in detail.

Somewhere, perhaps even very close to him, the final battle had begun.

There would be loss.

There would be terror in New Orleans.

The just order would be challenged and threatened.

The Mentor was ready and he hoped the often inconvenient balance between the human and the . . . the other, would not end in disaster.

1

A woman would die.

Unless Marley Millet could find the victim, and quickly, it would be too late. Marley was convinced this was true and that she was the only one who could help.

In her crowded workroom on the third floor of J. Clive Millet, Antiques, on Royal Street in New Orleans, Marley paced in small circles, desperate for insight that would tell her how to find and rescue an innocent marked for murder.

On her workbench stood a red lacquer dollhouse, an intricate piece of nineteenth-century chinoiserie placed in her hands by a stranger for safe and secret keeping. She hadn't and still didn't know why, except that the house was the portal that led to a place of great danger for some. Above the curvy roof with flaking gilt twirls at each corner, a whirling sheath of fathomless gray took more definite shape, like a vaporous tornado. It shifted until its slenderest part disappeared through a wall of the dollhouse and the gaping maw at the other end crept closer to Marley. A current began to suck at her like a vast, indrawn breath.

The decision to stay or give in and be pulled away, her essence drawn out of her body, was still hers.

Whispers came, a word, and another and another, never growing louder, only more intense.

Marley pressed her hands over her ears, but the sounds were already inside her head. The few whisperers became a crowd, and although she could not make out much of what they said, she knew they were begging. The Ushers, as she knew the voices, wanted her. They needed her. They were the last, invisible advocates for a life on the edge of an unnatural death, calling for Marley to witness a crime in progress. Witness, and act to save the victim.

Almost two weeks earlier, she had done as they asked and traveled away from her body to a place she did not know, and a woman she did not know. Evil had permeated the atmosphere there and Marley knew a murder was planned.

"You left her to die." This time the Ushers spoke clearly.

"I don't even know who she is." Her own voice sounded huge.

"You saw her."

"But I only saw the inside of a room. I don't know where it was."

The whispers softened and became a gentle hum. And Marley let out a long, emptying breath. Another word came to her clearly, *"Please."* A woman spoke.

It could be the victim. Perhaps it was not too late. Yet.

Marley expected the unexpected. She always had, day-by-day, from her earliest recollections.

Today was no exception, but she needed to decide what to do next without pressure from the sickening emotion she felt now.

Winnie, her Boston terrier, placed herself in Marley's path and stared up at her. Black and shiny, the expression in Winnie's eyes was almost too human. The dog was worried about her beloved mistress. Another step forward and Winnie flopped down on Marley's feet, which meant she was imploring her boss not to leave her body. The dog had an uncanny way of sensing problems for Marley.

"Not you, too," Marley said. "I need answers, Winnie, not more confusion. Now concentrate," she told herself. "You've got a major problem."

On that Sunday afternoon in June, Marley wrestled with a warning she'd received less than a week ago.

Her uncle Pascal, current steward of J. Clive Millet Antiques, had called her to his top-floor apartment. Speared by one of his most heated green stares, he had kept her there for more than an hour.

"Tell me you will do as you're told," he had said repeatedly. "I don't meddle in your affairs, but it is my job to watch over you. Certain alarms have been raised and I will not have you straying into dangerous territory. Defy me and I shall . . . I shall have to rethink my trust in you."

By "alarms," he meant that although she hadn't told him about the red house she had been given, or what had already happened, he had sensed a distance in her. He suspected she might be playing around with portals to other realities again and said so. He had not explained why he thought so. And Marley had been just as calm about not admitting she had not only encountered a portal, but it had already led her on a journey she could not get out of her mind, day or night. All she had told Uncle Pascal was that she was working hard and that long hours sometimes left her distracted. That was true, if not very helpful to her uncle. Where day-to-day issues were concerned, the Millets were in charge of their own actions, but Pascal had the final say if their powers threatened their safety.

Marley had been tempted to push him for an explanation of how he might make her regret disobedience; instead she had lowered her eyelashes and made a subservient sound.

"Good, good," Uncle Pascal had said, expanding his muscular chest inside a green velvet jacket. "You are a kind girl. You four girls make a poor bachelor uncle think he's done fairly well bringing up his brother's children safely." He smiled at his mention of "you four girls," by whom he meant Marley and her three sisters, but had then given her a slight frown which they both understood meant that her outlandishly talented maverick brother, Sykes, was not a subject for discussion that day.

That had been then, when she wanted to please someone who, unlike her parents, had always been there for her. This was now, days later, and the curiosity that came with her ability to be called away from her body, to travel invisibly into another location, was once more too provocative to ignore.

Marley crossed her arms and stared at the doll-house. The trembling cone of whirling matter sparked flashes of green, then blue. It was unlikely that more than a handful of people anywhere would be able to see the manifestation at all. Unlike aura readers, energy sentients were rarer than goldfish teeth. She was one of that elite number and her brother Sykes, hidden away wher-ever he had his mystery-shrouded sculpture studio, was another.

Marley wasn't a child. She was thirty and her irresponsible parents had been exploring the world for twenty years. The only way any of Antoine and

Leandra Millet's offspring managed to see them was by tracking them down in distant places. Marley's older sisters, Alex and Riley, were in London with their parents right now. Even if A and R, as the rest of the family dubbed them, were supposedly searching for the key to neutralize a family curse, who cared what they might think about the way their children lived, or how careful they were or were not?

But in a weak moment before his piercing stare Marley had, more or less, given her uncle the impression that if she encountered even a hint of subversive force, no matter how alluring she might find it, she would turn her back on whatever it was at once.

Boring.

Uncle Pascal was not a man to be easily frightened or to give fanciful warnings. Marley knew she could wriggle out of the *agreement* she'd made with him, but if she defied him and went too far with an experiment, her life might be changed forever.

In fact, her life could well be over.

On the other hand, the Ushers, the invisible forces that were her companions when she heeded their cries and went traveling through parallel time, had never let her down.

The Ushers and their seductive whisperings were back after only days. They never came unless she was needed, always somewhere right in New

Orleans, always immediately. On this humid afternoon, a great urgency lapped at her.

Like a whirlpool, the funnel into the dollhouse spun faster and faster. Soft, faintly vibrating, this apparition was familiar, as were the increasingly desperate waves of sensation beckoning her closer.

Apart from brushes with malignant spirits who tried to block her path, she had never encountered real danger on her journeys. But she did know of the terrible threat she faced. If she ever lost her way back, her soul could be forever separated from her life, from her living body. She would know manic terror while she searched for a way to return. If she failed, she would forever toss free, carried by the demanding currents of those on the edge of death and begging her to save them.

During each of her earlier travels she had done good things, brought about rescues for people who would never even know her name—until her most recent transfer through a parallel space, the one she had not mentioned to her uncle.

She had lied by not talking about it, and guilt didn't make a comfy companion.

Despite the cry she had heard only moments ago, Marley believed that someone in New Orleans, a woman she had been called to help, must be prematurely dead by now. Without knowing who the victim had been or exactly what happened to her, Marley was convinced she had kept company with a victim's final heartbeats, seen through her now-dead eyes.

At her feet, satiny black-and-white and giving off waves of displeasure, Winnie snuffled irritably. The dog was a barometer of Marley's moods and objected to these moments when she sensed she was not uppermost in her favorite person's mind. Winnie was ignoring her constant companion, a huge plastic bone, and this was a sure sign that she wasn't happy.

Absently, Marley used her bare toes to squeeze one of Winnie's feet.

What if the woman hadn't died? What if she was still alive and reaching out one last time for help?

Marley switched off the lights over her bench and reluctantly made her way between aged pieces of furniture and objets d'art awaiting her attention. She was known as one of the best restorers of antique lacquer and gold leaf in the city.

Her door onto a tiny landing outside was shut. Stained-glass panels, richly emerald, ruby, sapphire and amethyst, glowed, dappled faint colors on the dusty wooden floors in the dim workroom.

For some seconds, Marley rested her hand on the latch. Then she turned it, thumped the heavy bolt home. Anyone trying the handle from the outside would know to leave her alone.

She retraced her steps and stood in front of her bench again. All around her, the air buzzed and popped. Here and there she caught sight of partly formed faces, their mouths open as if calling out.

Slowly, her feet and legs heavy, Marley stepped backward, once, twice, three times until her calves bumped into her cracked brown leather wing chair, and she sank onto the seat.

"Don't go," she told herself aloud.

Too late. The separation had already begun. Luminous green brushed the funnel, spun quickly and turned the vapor to shimmering water. *Inviting.* Marley felt its warmth, its temptation. She touched it with her fingertips, drew it open wider. Its matter adhered to her skin. Her own weight slipped away and she was free, gliding through the iridescent tunnel toward a pulsing black membrane.

The membrane opened, slid apart like the aperture in a camera lens. Scents of age and dampness rushed at her.

Wetness shone in grimy rivulets on the concrete walls of an empty room. This was the room she had been in last time. Ahead of her the door to some sort of compartment—or locker—stood wide-open, a thick, heavy door with no handle on the inside.

In the opening a woman in red gradually appeared from clouds of icy mist.

Not the same woman as the last time.

Dark haired as the other had been, rather than being striking and voluptuous with a single black birthmark above her mouth, this time the facial features were pointed, the eyes large beneath thickly painted lashes. Behind her thin figure, the mist hovered around hooks hung from a slowly revolving rod, and billowed over white, rectangular boxes placed in a precise row.

Shapes, indistinct, swung heavily just out of clear sight. Marley thought they were suspended from the hooks.

She shivered. Cold struck painfully into her brain. She should go back, but she could not look away from the woman, from her pale, pleading face.

Then the woman smiled. She cocked her head to one side, listening to a deep voice as mellifluous as warm honey falling from a crystal spoon into a golden bowl. The voice said, "Come to me, child."

Nodding, the woman appeared in a trance.

The voice darkened, caressed, but with force. "Join me, child. Now. Come to me, now."

And she began to drift away, back into the space behind the heavy door.

"Wait!" Panicked, Marley moved her presence forward. "Let me help you. Come with me." From experience, she knew she couldn't be heard and that only if she managed to bring help from the real world to this place would there be any help for the woman.

But there were no clues as to where she was.

The door began to close and Marley could scarcely breathe. She thrust herself forward, clawing at air as if it would help her move faster, and she collided with the creature in red. Instantly she felt consumed into rigid flesh, bone-cold flesh, and she cried out, "I must go back."

The wrench to separate again sapped her consciousness. She could not slip into sleep here, must not. The Ushers mumbled very close and Marley focused on their sounds. She gathered strength and once more she heard the thump, thump, thump of a heartbeat that was not her own, and saw through eyes that didn't belong to her. This woman wasn't yet dead.

She struggled, staring ahead, willing herself to break free. And as she did she cried out to the woman, "Hold my hand. Come with me now." While she talked, she searched around for any clues to her location. Nothing.

Her fingers, repeatedly reaching for the woman, came back empty each time.

A man stood with his back to her, a tall, dark-haired man, with wide shoulders and a straight, unyielding spine. He had a different substance and dimension from both the woman and their surroundings.

Marley had started to shift. Faint warmth entered her, and she caught sight of the funnel regenerating, its direction switched so that the large opening faced her again. Still vaporous, it took on the green tint.

Thrusting forward like a swimmer with the pool

wall in sight, she made to pass the man and he looked at her over his shoulder. For one instant she cringed at the directness of his gaze, the hardness of a mouth that should be beautiful, despite a thin white scar through both lips and upward across one cheek in several slashes.

But he couldn't see her, could he? She must be imagining that he was staring at her.

Marley gave a last, horrified look to where the woman had stood, only she had disappeared. A last thought as she felt a familiar, dragging pull, was that she knew why the man seemed out of place: She saw him not in color as she did the rest of her surroundings, but in the gray shades of a black-and-white photograph. And as she stared at him his face changed again. The corners of his mouth tilted up and the scars faded.

2

As soon as she felt steady enough, Marley ran down three flights of stairs and left the shop through French doors that led to an enclosed courtyard behind the building.

Gray-tinged light creeping between the fronds of palms and oversize ferns shouldn't have bothered her. This afternoon it burned her eyes. Wet heat dampened her skin.

Her experience with the woman in red had deeply shaken her. Each breath she took barely touched her lungs and came out in jagged puffs. She hugged herself tightly and tried to hurry toward her apartment on the far side of the courtyard.

She couldn't hurry. Her legs were still heavy and cold. Tremors racked her in waves. This was the first time she had returned from a disembodied journey and not stayed in her workroom until she had eaten, usually voraciously, and rested in her chair. But this had also been the first time she had been truly afraid for her life. If she had not been strong, she would never have shaken herself free of the icy body she had unwittingly entered.

The shock of a new and scary experience had sapped her energy.

The woman hadn't drawn her in, had she? Surely not. Surely her own dash to reach the other one before she disappeared had caused a collision.

Marley could find no believable explanation for her absorption into another being.

Most disturbing of all was knowing she had been unable to help that woman, that she remained in that place and Marley still had no idea where it was. Her responsibility was to follow up and search for a way to get to that room. Only she didn't have the luxury of talking openly to the police, or to most people, since she was likely to be laughed at.

Uncle Pascal. Much as she quaked at the thought of his reactions, once she had collected herself, she must go to him.

She needed food. Chocolate. As always she craved chocolate and sugary food.

Winnie stayed in front of Marley, her much-chewed plastic bone sticking out each side of her head like a magnificent handlebar mustache, but she stopped frequently to check out her buddy. The dog's glossy, bulbous black eyes managed to look worried again.

Marley paused by the fountain in the center of the cobbled courtyard. The sound of water tipping from a shell held by the statue of a young angel calmed her a little. Each breath she took felt like thick, perfumed steam, but her hands were cold and she looked at the pads of her fingers. They were white and ridged and tingled slightly as if circulation were slowly returning.

Why would the coldness in that mystical place follow her when she left? Her own body hadn't been there, but on her return she had obviously brought the alien sensations back with her. Again, something that had never happened before.

She chafed her arms and sat on an upturned stone pot. On each of three sides of the court-yard, one of the oldest in New Orleans and known as the Court of Angels, four stories of red brick walls with random-set windows hemmed her in. Green-painted metal staircases crisscrossed the walls. The back of the shop made up the fourth side of the courtyard.

Granite cherubs reclined on door and window

26

lintels, peeked from alcoves beneath rain gutters. Statues of angels, worn smooth by the years, stood where they had for well more than a hundred years in corners and among lush old flowering shrubs. Here and there a gargoyle seemed out of place. The gate between the side of the shop and one wing of flats showcased a griffon.

This was where Marley had been born and had lived ever since.

The fourth of four uniquely gifted siblings, a brother followed by two sisters—then Marley—there was a fifth Millet offspring, another sister who celebrated "her limitations." Marley shared a telepathic connection with the first three. Independently, each of them had his or her own otherworldly talent. Except for Willow, of course. The youngest of the brood, Willow, did her best to dispel any notions that her family was *unnatural.*

"You are all perfectly ordinary. Got that?" was Willow's often repeated reminder. *"People won't hire me if you go around talking about being psychic."*

Marley rolled her eyes at the thought. Willow's interference was a waste of time. They never discussed the fact outside the family, but the Millets *were* unnatural, thank goodness . . . or whatever.

They *were* psychic.

Hallelujah!

Sykes had the gift of invisibility, a rare and priceless gift. He was also psychic and read minds with ease. Like Marley, he was an energy sentient, picking up unusual disturbances in the atmosphere. And Sykes had mastered the art of paranormal martial ability—a discipline used for both attack and defense. This was so potentially dangerous that it must not be used unless there was no other alternative. Marley was quite adept at PMA, but had so far used it only as a means to cause a diversion so that she could retreat into peace and control. She feared hurting another.

Alex, also psychic, could commune with those on the other side more or less at will. Of all of them, she was the least sociable and seemed to consider herself above the rest.

The next sister up the line from Marley, Riley, was, again, psychic and she saw the future with often alarming clarity—if she chose to. Riley read auras with disturbing accuracy.

After Marley, with her penchant for out-of-body experience, her paranormal martial art ability, energy sentience and effortless mind reading, came Willow, supposedly the only "normal" one. Marley didn't believe she was without power and neither did the rest of the family. Too often she had shown quickly masked signs of hearing her siblings' thoughts and they all discussed the mystery of what other secrets Willow was hiding.

They answered, supposedly, to the Mentor, an entity about which or whom they knew little other than this was the guardian of family rules and the one authority they must never cross. Not that any of them had ever seen this oracle or had any proof of his or its existence. She had guiltily admitted to herself many times that she suspected this Mentor had been invented to keep them all in line.

Today she would welcome the appearance of the Mentor with a brilliant answer that would solve her problems.

Winnie plopped her front paws on Marley's knee and panted, her tongue hanging out the side of her mouth.

Marley scratched the dog's head. "You're the best. You've got the prettiest ugly face I know."

Her stomach turned over and over. Now there were two faces glued in her mind, two faces, two women, both of whom she was convinced had unwittingly called her forth because they needed her to get them help. They needed her to save them.

That meant the dollhouse had come to her not only to be kept safe, but because it held a cipher, a key to a code that could unravel a mystery. If the signals were aligned, then when she touched the toy she became the path between two places, the possible guide to someone's escape.

Marley knew how these things were supposed to work, but one element had been removed from the equation and without it, she was useless. She needed to know the location of each victim.

The sky darkened, kept darkening until it turned

to the color of wet ashes. White lightning crackled overhead. These electrical storms had come with semiregularity in the past week or so.

Winnie leaped into Marley's arms just as thunder rumbled and crashed.

Marley pushed to her feet and Winnie jumped to the ground again and snatched up her bone. Large drops of rain fell hard enough to sting the skin.

Moving as fast as she could, she climbed green-painted iron steps to her second-floor flat. A ringing sound echoed from her footsteps. As she went she checked windows in the other flats, but there was no sign of anyone at home, not that they were likely to be since Sykes rarely showed up here and both Alex and Riley were in London with the parents. Willow would almost certainly be working. Uncle Pascal lived in an opulent flat over the shop, but that had been closed when she left and there was no sign of Pascal. Marley took out her keys, but she needn't have bothered. Her door stood open an inch.

Before she could react, other than with a big thump in her chest, Winnie barged onto the stone-tiled floor of the hallway and disappeared into Marley's sitting room. The television was on and the volume too high.

Sister Willow's own set must be "on the fritz again" so she'd come to borrow Marley's. This was a regular event. The whole family knew that in all probability Willow's TV was fine, but she was often lonely if she wasn't working and made the excuse to hang out with one of them.

"Oh, there's my baby, Winnie," Willow cried out in the voice she used only for the dog. "Come to Auntie Willow and have a cuddle. Marley?"

"Hey, Willow," Marley said. "Give me a few minutes. I'm wet."

She passed the sitting room and went directly into her bedroom where she shut the door and opened one of the built-in cupboards that flanked her bed. Her curly hair was barely damp and she wasn't at all wet enough to matter.

She had to eat.

The DeBrand of Indiana Connoisseur Chocolates, or chocolate pralines from Aunt Sally's on Decatur in the French Market?

They weren't big boxes. She took them both, crawled into her bed and sat against her pillows. With the goodies open on her legs, she inhaled. The mouthwatering scents alone were enough to start the trickle of new strength into her weakened muscles.

Willow would think she was changing clothes.

A chocolate praline melted rapidly away in Marley's mouth, followed by another, and then one of the exquisite little DeBrand chocolates, this one white chocolate passion fruit ganache dipped in milk chocolate with a piece of candied ginger on top.

Marley ate the entire contents of both boxes too

fast and considered returning to her well-stocked cupboard for more.

There wasn't time. She'd already dithered for too long. Where could she find some help in tracing two women who must be missing?

Her first step would be to track down Uncle Pascal and ask if he could suggest a way to locate someone without knowing their name—or anything else about them. How would she do that without making him even more suspicious about her activities?

"I saw someone and I'd like to talk to them." She needed to practice a more conversational tone. Marley cleared her throat and tried again. *"How d'you think I'd find a person without knowing their name or where they live?"*

She groaned at the thought of risking what he might say after outrageous questions like those. And she must make sure he didn't find out about the dollhouse. He would want to take it away if he discovered the danger it had got Marley into.

When she tried to call him, his phone rang and rang. "If I can help you, I will. Leave a message." He might not be out, but his voice on the answering machine meant he was unavailable.

Could be lifting weights.

"Marley?" Willow called.

She gave her stash cupboard a longing glance, but got resolutely out of bed, quickly changing her clothes, and went to the sitting room.

All she could see of Willow were coppery-red curls as unruly as Marley's own dark red ones, sticking out over one arm of the rust suede couch. "I was just feeding the toads," Marley said loudly to be heard over the television. "I like 'em fat when I pop them in a spell."

"Hah-hah," Willow responded. She sounded distracted.

"Have you seen Uncle Pascal this afternoon?" Marley asked.

"Mmm, he and Anthony went out."

Anthony was Uncle Pascal's trainer. Frustrated, Marley hurried around the couch and sat on the edge at Willow's feet. "I really need to find him."

"I don't know where he is," Willow said, her voice sharp and rising. "Shh. I can't hear with you talking."

Television was Willow's addiction.

Winnie-the-traitor sat in the curve of Willow's diminutive body, eyes closed, pretending to be deeply asleep.

"Didn't they say where they were going?"

"Nope." Willow hauled a turquoise-and-gold cushion onto her hip and stood it up to form a screen between them.

"Uncle loves to chatter about his outings." Marley wrestled the cushion away. "Are you sure—"

"Shh!" Willow hugged Winnie close. "The police conference is starting."

Frustrated, Marley gripped one of Willow's ankles and gave it a shake.

"Stop it," Willow said, waving her aside. "This is important. It's horrible . . . and scary. We all need to know about it. Haven't you heard what's happened?"

"I guess not."

"They found a woman dead in the river. They think she was thrown there. And she got mauled by a gator."

"In the river?"

"I don't know if she was mauled there or somewhere else, then put there," Willow said. "And don't tell me there aren't any gators in the river 'cause I already know. They're pretty sure it's murder."

Marley shuddered. "Horrible."

"There's a panic because there are three other women who have gone missing. They're saying they're all singers in the Quarter. The police are going to hold a press conference. It should already have started."

Marley looked over her shoulder at the television. On a split screen, a podium crowded with microphones stood vacant on the right side. On the left there were several photographs. An announcer's voice, female and strident, rushed along, "We'll bring the conference to you live the moment it starts. Meanwhile, here are photographs of the missing women and Ms. Cooper. Shirley

Cooper, whose body was found this afternoon, is in the larger picture."

"Nobody even knows when they went missing," Willow said. "Not for sure. It's horrible. It could be someone's targeting singers."

Four women.

Marley had seen two of them.

Neither of those two had been Shirley Cooper.

3

"This is a fucking mess," Detective Nat Archer said, staring at a crowded whiteboard on his office wall. "I get a floater in the river at noon—I hate floaters, the water messes up evidence. And it looks like an alligator tore into this one. A gator attack in the Mississippi. You ever hear anythin' like that?"

He didn't wait for an answer. "Now everyone thinks three missing singers are connected to the body we found in the river, and they'll wash up in bits and pieces, too. They got an army down there by the river lookin' for a damn gator."

Gray Fisher watched Archer's back, the broad, tensed shoulders, long fingers shoved into his pants pockets. "So you could end up pulling three more bodies out of the river—give or take a few missing pieces," Fisher said, grateful that he wasn't on the force anymore.

"Goddammit, Fisher, I'm not laughing at this."

35

Archer gave him an unflinching, almost black-eyed stare. "You do know you're the closest thing I've got to a suspect?"

"Because I came in for a friendly chat?" *Well, hell!*

"A chat about supposedly looking for a missing woman. One of *our* missing women. You haven't told me how you knew about the vic."

Even creased from a long day's wear, Archer's white shirt gleamed. It made his dark skin look even darker. Fisher didn't like the way the other man looked at him.

"I didn't know about the . . . You're pissing me off. I didn't know Shirley Cooper. I never even heard her name until I came to this office today. I came looking for information about Amber Lee. I thought you and I were friends and I could do that. When I got here I hadn't heard there was a search on for several women."

"Journalists are journalists and they're mostly a pain in the ass. You're an investigative journalist." Archer's eyes moved away from Fisher's. "That's worse than any other kind."

"I've been a journalist for years. It hasn't stopped us from being civil—until now."

The office was beneath street level and muggy. Throughout the subterranean warren of rooms, old cigarette smoke tainted the air. Fisher sat in a metal folding chair with his legs stretched out and his heels on the piece of orange carpet that spread from beneath Archer's desk. If you stood still on that carpet a little too long, the bottoms of your shoes got sticky. Maybe it was soaked in nicotine from years of service.

Windows along one wall overlooked the corridor. Mangled blinds hung at random angles and didn't stop anyone outside from seeing the entire room and whoever was in it.

Archer let out a long sigh and drew his lips back from his teeth. Dimples, there whether he smiled or not, were out of sync with his big frown. "We're friends," he said. "Until you give me a reason to be somethin' else. You were a great cop, just like your dad. I wish you'd stuck around. You would have been my partner after Guy Gautreaux left for good. I'd have liked that. But you had to write *stories* for crissakes."

Fisher had been a good enough cop, but he had wanted to write about the kind of people he met on the job every day. He knew the Quarter like the back of his hand—the clubs, the bars, the strip joints. Shops and their owners. And the everyday work force: portrait sketchers, palm readers and card readers, folks who hung out with bags of grave dust, rodent droppings and chicken feet in their pockets; dancers, singers, musicians, pushers, pimps, pavement princesses, pickpockets and crackheads—both the zombies and those who still had a few gray cells left to fry.

There was a lot of humanity existing on the very

edge, people with rich or crazy histories, and often crazier here-and-nows.

"When will we know exactly how the vic died?" Fisher asked. "If it was before or after the gator?"

"The autopsy should be going on now, if Blades got to it."

Fisher grinned with half of his mouth. "Blades is a first-rate M.E. I still say he chose the profession to fit his name." He made a note about the autopsy in his notebook.

"I don't think you'll risk asking him about that one again—if you ever see him." Archer jotted several more lines on his board.

"It's not my fault if he doesn't have a sense of humor," Fisher said, and had a mental image of the tall, stooped man with his cadaverous face. "What's your best guess on this woman?"

"She's dead."

"Ha-ha."

"Let's get back to where we were," Archer said. "You weren't finished spilling your guts when the press conference came on."

"I wasn't *spilling my guts.*"

"Seemed to me like you had a lot to say."

Fisher let it go. "You ever see gators in the river?"

"Nope. Heard of one a time or two."

"I don't believe it." But Fisher supposed they could get there somehow. "I guess Katrina could have caused just about anything." The hurricane continued to get blamed for most things and it was often guilty.

Archer began a fresh round of pacing back and forth, picking up crime scene photos from his desk in one direction and peering at them through slitted eyelids; dropping the grisly images of Shirley Cooper down again on his return. The body looked as if it had been in an outsize blender. He had held the photos up for Fisher to see when her name was mentioned on TV a while earlier.

"You could have been going to say just about anything." The detective hadn't forgotten his previous line of questioning. "What would you have said if you hadn't found out we had a body?"

"I didn't think about a body at all. Not one way or the other. Did I know I was going to walk in here in time to watch a press conference and hear about a bunch of missing women?"

Archer scowled. "The chief couldn't wait to get in front of the cameras."

After another detective had interrupted them to tell Archer to turn on the TV, Fisher had watched Chief Beauchamp's press conference. He learned the case was Archer's and that he'd begged off being on camera, not that reporters wouldn't get to him soon enough. And that was the burr up Archer's ass.

"You know the press will be all over this like white on rice. That's why you're so mad. There's probably a posse of 'em hanging outside right now. And the calls are going to start. Get used to it."

"Now you're a mind reader," Archer said through his teeth.

"I know you," Fisher told him. "I know they rode you like a rented mule in the Cassidy case and you're still sore from it." Benton Cassidy, a rich, spoiled kid with a father who could hire any hot-shot lawyer for sale, had almost walked even though everyone was convinced he'd killed his young stepmother and the son she'd had by Cassidy's father.

"Cassidy's going to rot in his cage until he croaks," Fisher went on. "Your side won in the end."

Archer grimaced. He lifted a slim, frosted glass bottle of Bong Vodka out of his bottom desk drawer and pulled two paper cups from a dispenser on the wall beside his personal water cooler.

"Every crime's public property now." Vodka gurgled into the cups.

"It's always been that way."

"They didn't used to expect every detail." The vertical crease between Archer's brows had become permanent. "What they want most is what you don't have and may never get."

"The guy from the *Times* brought up the seven other women who disappeared and never showed up again."

"Yeah," Archer said. "But they were spread out and the type that make themselves vulnerable."

"Weren't they all on the street?" Fisher asked.

"I think so," Archer said. "Can't remember. And it stopped a couple of years back."

"But the cases were never solved. And they weren't singers."

Archer's frown darkened even more and he shook his head.

"There could still be a connection," Fisher said. "The perp may have waited until he felt safe to start again."

"Thanks, Sherlock," Archer said.

Fisher felt deeply morose. "I don't know how you afford this stuff on a detective's salary." He looked into the soggy cup he'd been given. "Can't you get some crystal glasses to drink it out of? On the arm—"

"Fuck you," Archer said, then he snapped open a smile. They both knew he was too straight to be on the take. "The only things I take on the arm are expensive dinners, and women, of course."

As far as Fisher knew, Archer continued to have only one woman in his life. She lived out in Toussaint on Bayou Teche and was an off-limits topic unless Archer brought her up.

The booze blasted Fisher's throat. It might not be his favorite treat, but this stuff packed a wallop. It was good. He thought he'd finish the drink before he revealed a new detail. This one might turn out to be part of the case that was currently eating Archer's hangnails.

41

"Bucky Fist's still at the scene," Archer said of his current partner. "He's probably got an audience he'd like to feed to a goddamn gator. I thought Lemon would be slamming tips at me already. I reckon there's so many it's takin' him a lot longer than he likes to weed them out."

Lemon was a semiretired cop who worked phones on this type of case. He was good at pinpointing what was worth passing on and where it hung in the pecking order. Five years ago he'd lost the use of his legs in an ambush. By some miracle, the bullet he took didn't put a crimp in his connubial bliss— Lemon made sure no one thought otherwise.

The way Archer talked, as much to himself as to anyone else, made Fisher think the other man had as good as forgotten he wasn't alone.

"We'll know soon enough if Shirley Cooper was killed somewhere else—Lake Pontchartrain for instance—and taken to the river afterward," he said.

"Yeah," Archer said. "We haven't found the spot where she went in the water yet. The body could have traveled a long way. There were no signs of a struggle near where she got hung up."

"Hung up?"

"On a motorboat's propeller. It was moored, thank God. The owner felt a thump and found her."

"Nice surprise," Fisher said.

He sucked in a large swallow of the firewater and contemplated the prospect of dropping a new bomb. Archer had suggested, most likely in jest, that he suspected Fisher because he'd come in to ask about Amber Lee.

Things could get worse.

He drained the vodka. "I know Liza Soaper, too," he said, expecting the blank look he got. It took only moments for blank to be replaced with angry disbelief.

"I interviewed her, but I didn't know she'd gone missing. That happened after I worked with her."

Archer pointed a very long, blunt finger at him. "Shut up, and answer me when I ask a question. Whatever game you're playin' here is about over. Are you serious about knowing both Soaper and Lee?"

"Absolutely. Can you check to see if Lemon's holding up anything useful? He could be . . ."

"Can it," Archer said. "I told you I'm asking the questions."

"You need tips and I want you to get them."

"Why did you know those women?"

"I interviewed them for a piece on making it in New Orleans. As jazz singers. I'm working on it now."

Archer might as well have told Fisher he didn't believe a word he said. The message was clear in his eyes. "How many other singers have you *interviewed?*"

Letting out a long breath, Fisher finally said, "None. Just the two."

"You got more singers on your list?"

"I've got some prospects."

"You sure Shirley Cooper wasn't one of them?"

Fisher sat up straighter. "Is she a singer?"

"I don't know yet. Do you?"

"No," Fisher said. "I told you I didn't."

"She lived with a boyfriend. He'd already reported her disappearance when we found the body. How about the fourth one, Pipes Dupuis?"

Fisher put his forehead in his hands and leaned over his knees. "Yeah, Karen Dupuis, she's the next one after Amber Lee. She *was* the next one I intended to talk to. It's a tough world, y'know, trying to make it as a musician or singer here. Talent pours into the Quarter. Only a few ever make it big."

"Save the informational announcement." Archer appeared to consider his next move. He checked his watch, then reached out a hand to hover over his phone. "Looks like you'll be working a different story real soon. I should put you in an interview room."

Fisher buried a rush of anger. "Whatever you say. You're the boss. How did you find out about Liza Soaper and Amber Lee? How did you link all the women together?"

Archer looked as if he'd refuse to answer, but he shrugged and said, "Liza's landlady said her lodger went out to work one night and never came back. That was about ten days ago."

"You've known she was missing that long without making it public?"

"Yeah." And Archer's hard eyes warned Fisher not to have any opinions about that. "The case didn't come to me then. They were hoping to get some leads before any suspect got frightened out of the area. Amber's been gone a few days. Pipes dropped out of sight last night."

"Who reported them?" Fisher asked.

"Sidney, that's Amber's singing partner, reported Amber missing. She didn't arrive at Scully's for work one night and hasn't been seen since. Pipes took a break between sets at Caged Birds last night and we can't find anyone who saw her afterward. Or her daughter . . ." Archer paused, staring at Fisher. "Erin. The kid's five or six and she wasn't mentioned in case it put her in more danger. If she's still alive, the killer might decide she's too much of a liability and get rid of her.

"While her mother sang, she slept in a dressing room. They didn't go home—or they didn't get home. The band Pipes sings with is sure she and the kid were snatched. No husband or lover on the scene."

Fisher winced. "Too bad about the kid."

Archer gave him an exasperated look. "I don't like it that you may be part of the problem. Not at all."

"If you thought I was a problem, you wouldn't be answering my questions."

"If you already know the answers, what difference does it make?" Archer pushed around the mess of papers on his desk. "We'll get through a few preliminaries right here. If you're willing to do that? Informal?"

"You'd better record everything, hadn't you?" Fisher said, unflinching.

"I'm not accusing you of anything—yet. Just having that chat you wanted. Who did you meet first?"

"Liza Soaper. Maybe I need a lawyer."

"There's the phone," Archer said, nodding at his desk. "How long ago did you hook up with her?"

"Around six weeks, give or take."

Archer wasn't taking notes—or recording anything. "How did you find her?"

"I asked around. Who was an up-and-comer? Did anyone know someone who was making it, but had a rough story to tell about getting there? Most of them do, but you've got to think through how you approach them."

Archer kept his mouth shut and waited.

"Then they sleep most of the day and they work nights. A lot of the singers do, anyway. Makes it difficult to interview them. Takes time to get a story together. Mostly we talked between her sets. I like Liza."

"That's nice," Archer said. He did pick up a pen to jot down a few words on a yellow pad. He drew box after box around what he'd written.

Fisher smiled, and enjoyed the irritation Archer showed. "Yeah, it is nice," Fisher said. "There's only one body, and neither of us knows if the owner was a singer. These people come and go. They get an offer or a hint of an offer that appeals to them, and they're gone. That's probably what's happened to Liza—and Amber." Fisher didn't think so, but he wasn't going to tell Archer that, not unless he had to.

Archer could be more right than he knew about Fisher needing a new story.

"And Pipes—and her kid?" Archer said.

Shit.

"Okay." Archer scooted his chair away, crossed his heels on the desk and tipped back. "Shirley Cooper is the only one I'm working on for real until I find out if she was a singer or knew any of the other three."

"You could have four for one," Fisher said. He wouldn't let himself think about the possible fifth victim, the child.

Archer laced his fingers on his flat belly. "You're tryin' to goad me into something. Damned if I know why."

"I'm not. Just stating the obvious. Amber Lee sings with a woman who calls herself Sidney. She showed up for work one night, but Amber didn't. I was there that night. Sidney told me she'd be in touch, but I haven't heard from her and neither of them has been at work since. Are you working on any theories about what could have happened?"

"This Sidney's probably scared out of her mind," Archer said, ignoring Fisher's invitation to share the information he had originally come looking for.

"Or dead. That could make five for—"

"Don't go there," Archer snapped.

"If the vic can be connected, to even one of the others, people will fill in the dots and unless human nature has changed, the phones will ring. There'll be dozens who heard them sing and can't wait to spew anything they know—or think they do."

"They'll call anyway, you know that."

Fisher moved his shoulders around. Prickling showered the middle of his back. He looked at his damp, empty cup. His fingers felt cold.

"Someone walking on your grave?" Archer said. "You shivered."

And Fisher shivered again. "I wouldn't be surprised," he said and grinned.

He didn't feel like smiling. His gut was hot and jumpy. It had happened before, many times, starting when he'd been a kid. In the past year the episodes had come more frequently and with increasing discomfort. He might as well face it and hope whatever it was this time would move on quickly. He got these feelings before something happened, something unpleasant.

"Tell me something about Liza Soaper?" Archer said.

It wasn't a pretty story—although it got better recently—and he didn't feel like sharing much of it. "She's a loner. No friends she mentioned or that I saw. Country girl with guts and drive. Her family never wants to hear from her again. They're convinced she's a prostitute or a stripper, and New Orleans is sin city."

"Sounds like they know our little burg."

"Yeah." Fisher snorted. "She lived on just about nothing for the first months, until someone noticed she's got a big, rich voice."

"That matches what we know," Archer said. "There isn't even a record of her having a car."

"I don't think she did—or Amber."

Archer rocked a little, then jotted a note. "Probably doesn't matter, but we'll find out how these women got to work."

Fisher wanted to rub his back and walk around, but he stayed put, and still. The heat inside him cranked up. This time was different from the others, exciting rather than unpleasant. Muscles in his back bunched so tight he rotated his shoulders.

The phone rang. Archer swung his feet to the floor, picked up and barked, "Archer."

Silence, except for the occasional grunt, went on for a while before he got off and said, "You were more or less onto something. Everyone who ever heard Liza or Amber or Pipes Dupuis sing, or think

49

they did, must have called in. I'm going up to Lemon and take a look." He stood, but hesitated. "You'll be here when I get back."

The order wasn't subtle, and Fisher didn't like it. "Not if you're up there long. I've got to keep on doing what I'm doing. I've got a living to make."

"I'd like you to wait."

"I can give it about ten. After that, you've got my cell number. If I intended to make a run for some reason, for any reason at all, I wouldn't be here now."

Hands on hips, Archer studied him.

Fisher's teeth locked together. He looked over his shoulder at someone standing outside the windows—looking in. Breath left his lungs as if he'd been winded.

"Who the hell is that?" Archer said.

Someone for me. He could feel it. Fisher didn't answer.

"Civilians aren't supposed to wander about down here—on their own," Archer said.

A woman, a bit shorter than average, stared at them through spaces in the warped window shades. She had very curly, dark red hair that burst out in ringlets to her shoulders, and eyes green enough for the color to be obvious at fourteen feet. She was suddenly even shorter. Apparently she had been standing on tiptoe to get a better look at the office.

The door opened slowly and she stepped

partway into the room. Fisher heard a whine from the corridor and the woman turned and looked down. "Don't embarrass me, Winnie," she said clearly.

Fisher realized he'd mashed the cup to a pulp. "Dog," he said, hoping Archer wouldn't notice the cup.

"Why not a dog?" Archer said. "Or a damn performing monkey? Fits right in with the way this day's been going."

"Detective?" the redhead said.

Archer cleared his throat. "What makes you think I am?"

"One of you probably is. There's a name on the door."

Forest-green. That was the color of her eyes. Fisher couldn't have met her before or he would have remembered the instant he saw her. A little woman with a big impact—on him. For the first time he understood exactly what was meant by raw nerve endings.

"Who are you looking for?" Archer said, but Fisher noticed he didn't sound angry.

"Detective Archer," she said with a puzzled frown. "I already said that."

"Ma'am, how did you get down here?" Archer asked. "The public isn't supposed to wander in off the street and poke around."

"Why not? The public pays for all of this. We pay your salary, too."

While Archer watched, his lower jaw slack, she came in and shut the door.

Again Fisher felt a slam to his diaphragm, this time even harder. This was it. The closer the redhead got, the more excited and riled up he felt. She was part of something to do with him.

"I'm Detective Nat Archer. This is Gray Fisher —he's a journalist friend of mine."

After nodding at her, Fisher balanced the notebook on a knee and wrote words, just words. Later he'd take a look and see if they said anything. For now he didn't care as long as she didn't get a look at the effect she was having on him.

"I'm Marley Millet," she said. "I wanted to talk to someone about what was on that press conference earlier. Upstairs they told me to wait and someone would get to me, only they didn't."

"This is a busy place, Miz Millet," Archer said. "A lot of people wait."

"They shouldn't have to. Not all of them—not if they've got important information like I do."

"Come and take a seat," Archer said, dragging another folding chair forward. "How did you know I was on this case?"

"These questions are all a waste of time."

From the corner of an eye, Fisher saw her sit down and cross her legs. Nice legs. Nice body. Little, but definitely worth more than a look. Some sensations began to fade, all but the intense and growing feeling that he should prepare to

"We
flushi
there
The
along
way t
things
had n
"Yo
Detec
about
She
had ki
to me
mind
place
I can'
be rigl
Gray
featur
and w
really
He h
of his
straigl
quietly
Marley
ions to
She
athleti

defend himself. Why did the anticipation stimulate rather than put him on guard?

"I heard someone say your name. Several times. And I could figure out they were talking about the women who are missing—" She paused. "I went to the ladies' room on the main floor and then just started walking along corridors. When I didn't find you up there, I came downstairs and here you are."

"This has been a bitch of a day," Archer said.

"I agree," Marley Millet said. "I'm pooped out."

Fisher smiled to himself.

"I came to talk to you about Liza Soaper and Amber Lee." She wound her hands tightly together. "I don't suppose you've found them yet, have you?"

4

This was the right place and the right man, Marley thought. Archer's body had tensed, and he leaned toward her. His face was a study in reluctant curiosity. Curiosity, she understood. Why reluctant, she didn't know.

"How are you connected to them?" he said of Liza and Amber.

Archer was the one she'd come looking for, but . . . she looked sideways at the man seated in a chair . . . this one had the power, a special power. A gripping, a tightening around her midsection disoriented her. Who was he and why was he here?

Arche
know I
attempt
"Yes,
but not
The
Marley
with h
skimm
had be
had bla
and ca
be, but
ance th
plished
him to
each o
If you
Ther
Marl
"Det
Fisher
her. H
manag
"I th
ately
you're
"Ign
to be
not an

His thoughts were all about her. And he was trying to figure out if she was . . . dangerous?

Shocked by feeling his thoughts touch her mind, she began to cut off the connection.

Better to know potential enemies, she heard him think. His efforts were undisciplined, perhaps even accidental.

Marley didn't allow the probe to deepen.

Telepathy was something she shared with her siblings, to differing degrees depending on how firmly their guards were up. Outside the family, Marley could choose to read minds. She never did so lightly. This was the first time she had been aware of a stranger making casual contact with her.

Her own shield was firmly in place. There would be no reciprocal probing. Willing exploration by two telepathists who were strangers risked a dangerous depth of intimacy.

He was looking sideways at her, watching her watching him. Speculative eyes that reminded her of whiskey. How long had he been aware that she was sizing him up?

A sharp current traveled from her neck down her spine, startling her to sit very straight. The electric sensation curved forward to her belly and buried itself where she least expected to feel any reaction at all.

A sexy connection.

Now warmth shot across her body. Fisher shifted

in his chair and the expression in his eyes made her look away.

"What did you come to tell me?" Detective Archer asked. "Do you know where Liza and Amber are?"

Marley cleared her throat. Every word had to be weighed. "Not exactly."

She felt Gray Fisher continue to watch her quietly.

"What does that mean?" Archer asked.

"I saw Liza about ten days ago, and I was with Amber this afternoon."

If she had produced an assault rifle, she doubted these two men could be more focused on her.

"Go on," Archer said.

"Well." Her fluttering hands annoyed Marley and she dropped them to her lap.

Archer inclined his head in question and jutted his chin.

"They were both . . . They couldn't get away from where they were."

She wanted to give in to the lure and look at Gray Fisher again. Instead, she studied the office. This wasn't a place where she'd like to spend a lot of time. It smelled musty, like wet laundry left to dry in a heap. Mold. And old smoke.

"Why couldn't they get away?" This time Archer tried to look relaxed in his chair. You could almost think he was relaxed, as long as you didn't look at his tight mouth and jaw.

"Someone didn't want them to leave," she told him.

"Who?"

She really was overheating, even in her white cotton dress. Long and fairly thin, it began to feel too tight across her chest. "I heard his voice." Marley didn't want to recall that dark, smooth, persuasive voice or the power it had over those women.

"You didn't see him?"

"No. He hid himself," she said with sudden inspiration. Talking about disembodied voices wouldn't help buy her either respect or action. "They both know him. When he talked, they expected to hear him speak and did what he wanted."

Skepticism hardened Archer's eyes. "And he wanted what?" he asked.

There was a full, blue plastic bowl of Tootsie Rolls on the desk. She was reminded that she still felt drained from the journey.

"He wanted them to go into a sort of locker place in one corner of the big room and stay there," she said. "It's got a big, heavy door with no handle on the inside. Each of them did what he said."

"What room would that be?"

"Like I said, the locker is in a bigger room and I think—" Too many vague references would make them suspicious.

"No, the bigger room. Where is that?" Archer said.

Of course this was difficult, and it would only get more so. She couldn't tell him about a luminous, watery funnel, a portal to another place by way of a peeling red lacquer dollhouse! "What have you found out so far?" she said, buying time.

"Not enough, but we will," Archer said.

Beside her, Gray Fisher's hands were curved into fists on his thighs. He'd given up on his notes. His presence, her response to him, alerted her to possible risk.

"Let's come at this from another direction," Archer said. "The locker? What kind of locker?"

"Like a meat locker," she said, and swallowed hard. "Revolving hooks inside."

Silence.

"It was cold in there. I saw an atmospheric phenomenon."

Gray Fisher coughed. "Meaning?"

"Condensation, I suppose. Cold air meeting warmer air and billowing like fog." She puffed at a curl beside her eye. "Oh, I don't know. I'm not scientific—not in the way you think of. Just imagine opening a freezer door and seeing clouds of white vapor rush out."

"You sound irritated," Archer said, too mildly for comfort.

"That's because she's uncomfortable," Fisher said.

Marley didn't want his interpretation of what she might or might not feel, but she kept quiet.

"Just a minute," Fisher said.

Hearing a light scratching at the door, he got up and let Winnie sidle in. She held her bone by one end and dragged it beside her as if it would be less noticeable that way.

Marley had heard the scratching, too, but she was preoccupied.

Fisher looked down on Winnie, who attempted to flatten herself to the wall beneath the row of windows. Her wrinkled face pushed up between round eyes so moist, anyone could expect tears, and she gave him a stare filled with an appeal for mercy. She raised first one front foot, then the other, as if abjectly apologetic and expecting to be told off.

"You shouldn't leave her outside," Fisher said. "Anyone could take her."

Drawing in a short, furious breath, Marley waited until the man—and he was tall, muscular, and moved with purpose—dropped back into his seat.

"Winnie wouldn't let anyone take her," she said, her voice soft and low. "Winnie is an operator and she just worked a number on you. She wanted in here, and here she is."

He shrugged and found his tatty little notebook again.

"I'm going to tell you exactly what happened," she said, breathless. "Please just let me say everything before you interrupt."

What she was about to do was reckless. "The abduction happened—"

"Which abduction?" Fisher said.

"Liza Soaper. It happened early in the morning. Of course, I didn't know who she was then. I happened to be about because I couldn't sleep and I like to walk when I think." Partly true. Mostly untrue. Marley's mind scrambled. "Liza was, er, kidnapped. I think she was lured into a car. I jumped in a cab and had the driver follow."

"What kind of car?" Archer said. "You got the license?"

She was sinking. "I'm not good at cars and I don't see well when I'm upset. I think it was a black car, a big one. I didn't think to look at the license plate."

"Great," Archer said.

"It was still dark and I was so busy trying to keep the other car in sight, I didn't notice where we were."

It's so much easier to tell the truth, Marley. That way you never have anything to explain or get embarrassed about. Great, now Mama Leandra's voice wanted to twist the knife. Her parents—on the rare occasions when she saw them—remained full of pat wisdom, and Papa Antoine usually let his adored wife do most of the talking.

"Are you reconstructing what happened?" Archer said.

Marley looked at the makeshift candy dish and swallowed rapidly. "Do you suppose I could have one of those?" She pointed. "I, er, haven't eaten enough today."

A little noise to her left annoyed Marley. "I'm glad you find me funny, Mr. Fisher."

"Call me Gray. I was thinking you don't look as if you ever eat anything much."

"Thanks."

"I didn't say you don't look great. Perfect, in fact."

Fisher cleared his throat and Marley figured it was his turn to feel awkward. Not that she didn't like the compliment.

Archer held the bowl under her nose and she managed, with great effort, to pick up only one candy.

"Have more," Archer said. "Wish I had a sandwich or something."

Looking at him, she smiled and took a handful of Tootsie Rolls.

Fisher sputtered and she looked at her hand. The bowl had been withdrawn and she was left with a fist crammed so full that some candies stuck out between her knuckles.

Marley laughed at herself. "Overkill," she said. She got up and dropped the extra candies back into the bowl. "Thank you," she said and stuffed several pieces into a pocket. This was not a time or a place for fainting. She unwrapped two candies and put them in her mouth, packing one in each cheek. Her energy was fading again.

"By the time the big car stopped, I was frantic." She shifted to the front of her chair, chewing and gulping as fast as she could. "I threw money at the cab driver and raced after Liza and whoever was with her. I was so agitated and it was so dark, I rushed behind them—being careful to stay out of sight behind, er, bushes, and managed to sneak through the same door they used to go into the building."

"What building?" Fisher said.

Damn him. "I don't know. Not the faintest idea. That's where the cops come in. They're good at that stuff. Now let me finish. I've got to get Winnie out for a run."

Neither man commented. Good, off-the-wall comments could be used to shut them up.

"As I was saying, I slipped in behind them when they weren't looking." *And?* "They got ahead of me and I thought I'd lost them. It was pretty scary in there. Just concrete walls and floor—dirty and damp. Then the locker—big locker—opened in the corner and a woman in red—I mean, black, with black fishnet hose and very high shoes—came out. She was frightened, I could see it."

"This was another woman?" Archer squinched up his eyes. "I thought you meant—"

"Liza Soaper? I did. Only I didn't know it was her then. I didn't know until I saw the picture of her on the TV today. I saw the mole above her mouth, too.

"She looked terrified and when she saw me, she reached out. But that voice came. Just like black molasses dripping into a puddle on a shiny floor."

"You have a way with words," Fisher said.

"Please just let me get through this, Mr. Fisher." She should only have put one Tootsie Roll into her mouth.

"Gray," he said shortly and bowed his head. He bowed his head but looked behind him at the same time.

Marley heard a familiar slithering sound and soon Winnie came into view. Flattened (as flattened as a solid little Boston terrier could get) to the floor, she pulled herself forward, inch by inch to join the party.

"No," Marley said, but wished she could gather up her faithful friend and hold her close. "Back you go, please, Winnie. I'm having an important conversation and you do have a tendency to distract me. Do go and sit where you were before and wait until I'm finished."

Another strangled sound came from Mr. Fisher.

"What now?" she snapped.

"Nothing. I was surprised by his level of comprehension, is all."

She narrowed her eyes. "Her. Just as I don't believe in baby talk for children, I don't like it for animals, either. Back, Winnie. Now, can we continue?"

Fisher wore jeans that rode below his waist, and a black T-shirt. The T-shirt shouldn't have to be so tight. Surely he could find one big enough for all those muscles. Men could be like that. They liked showing off what studs they were.

"Liza had a mark on her neck," Marley said and

her eyes widened. She hadn't remembered that until now. "A round, red mark right in the front. I thought it was blood, but I don't know for sure."

Fisher snickered. Complete with bone, Winnie had dragged herself beside him and rolled onto her back. She lay there with all four feet in the air, displaying her pink tummy.

Absently, Marley pulled another candy from her pocket. Her dog was a floozie, letting a strange man scratch her belly.

"Can we stay with the program?" Detective Archer said.

"Happily." She was amused at how easy it was to ward off Fisher's attempts to read her thoughts. "As soon as I got closer to Liza, the voice got more intense."

"What was he saying to her?"

Marley concentrated on the detective. "Honestly, just like I said before, I couldn't see him and I couldn't make out everything he said, except he wanted her to come to him. That was obvious. I think he was hiding in the locker."

"So, you just heard sounds really?"

"More than sounds." She frowned at Fisher. He petted the dog, but his motions were jerky. Twice he stopped to rub his hands together. Marley looked at her own hands. They remained cold. The nail beds were blue.

"And?" Fisher said.

Archer shrugged and grinned at Marley. "I told

you he keeps forgetting he's not a cop anymore."

"And?" Fisher repeated. He had an unforgettable voice himself. She didn't doubt it could be mesmerizing in the right circumstances.

"You think this guy was mesmerizing Liza?" Fisher said.

Stunned, Marley barely stopped herself from shooting to her feet. He had heard her think about a voice being mesmerizing. At least, he'd picked up that idea and twisted it a little, even if he didn't realize it. "He could have been," she said tightly. She had never encountered anything like this before.

"I've never believed in that," Archer said.

"Well, you ought to," Marley said. "There's a great deal more in this world than meets the eye." She had to stop getting goaded into careless statements.

"Liza backed into the freezer or locker or whatever it was and the door shut."

"Did you try to get her out?"

She looked back at Archer with a horrified feeling. "Yes, but I couldn't. I had to leave."

"You were frightened?" Fisher said. "More frightened than ever. That's understandable."

"No," she cried. "That's not it. She stayed in that place and she must be dead. I know she is. I felt her die."

The office door opened and Marley slumped in her chair, relieved by the interruption.

A uniformed officer entered, handed a folded piece of paper to Archer and left again.

But Archer didn't take his eyes off Marley. "What do you mean, you felt her die? You're sure she's dead, aren't you? How about Amber Lee?"

"I don't know." She swallowed. "I don't really know what's happened to either of them. If I try to explain, will you promise not to disregard everything I've told you?"

"Your report will be checked out," he said. In other words, there was no commitment.

"There wasn't a car or a cab. I made that up because I was afraid you wouldn't believe the truth."

He raised his brows, but didn't interrupt.

"I traveled there."

Still he listened without speaking, but he did look at the paper in his hands. Probably trying not to let her see his impatience.

"You see, I . . . Well, I'm psychic, but I also have out-of-body experiences. I saw each of them, Liza and Amber, when I was away from my body."

5

"Give me a minute here, please," Archer said, buying time while he decided what to say next.

He unfolded the piece of paper that had been delivered earlier.

Most medical examiners would have picked up the phone. Not Blades. He preferred using other methods so that he didn't have to answer questions until he was ready.

Archer, Blades's fax started.

Get over to the morgue in the morning. Make it 8:30. Still got a lot to do.
Preliminary:
  Shirley Cooper.
  White female.
  Age: 28.
  No water in lungs. (This means victim was dead when she was put in the water.)

"Thanks for the education, Dr. Death," Archer said under his breath. Immediately, he looked from Gray to the crazy lady fate had visited on him. They both watched him expectantly.

He returned to Blades's cryptic note:

Extensive damage could be consistent with alligator attack postmortem. Looking for further substantiation.
  Provisional cause of death:
  Crude removal of larynx.
  Extensive blood loss.
  Shock.

"Oh, my God," he said, and was tempted to reach for the Bong vodka again. The beast who murdered her had cut out her voice.

6

Finding out the name of the club where Amber had sung with her partner, Sidney, had been harder than Marley expected. The club wasn't well-known and only after making call after call had she caught up with the duo. Marley didn't expect to find out much, but she had to start somewhere and Scully's Club seemed her only choice.

"You want me to wait?" the cab driver said.

Marley looked through the car window, making up her mind. "No, thanks," she said finally and got out, paying him off quickly. It was really late and she might have been better waiting until the morning, but for Liza and Amber, every minute could count.

The entrance to Scully's at the Hotel Camille was set back from the sidewalk just off the foot of Canal Street. Marley heard live music through the closed doors.

Not far from the river and barely on the edge of the Quarter, this had to be a minor foot-in-the-door place for fledgling musicians.

Her stomach squeezed, and letting the cab go didn't seem such a good idea anymore, but she pushed on a polished brass handle and went in.

Inside the club, laughter and conversation came in bursts. Scents of beer, booze and perfume made her nose itch. The light was low, but not so low she couldn't see clearly enough.

The bar dominated the middle of a big room decked out in green-and-white stripes, heavy chintz fabrics, crops of British hunting scenes on every wall and an overstuffed Victorian atmosphere. Men turned to look at her but Marley had expected that, coming here alone at almost midnight. But she was only blocks away from home and she'd get another cab when she left.

Accompanied by a pianist, a woman played a guitar and sang the blues. Nice voice. Not remarkable, but nice and mellow. She looked and sounded melancholy. The pianist was worth listening to on his own.

Marley went to the bar and climbed on a stool. She would rather have hidden herself in one of the curtained alcoves at the far end of the room, but that would not be the way to do what she'd come for: to find out what she could about Amber Lee.

Scully's had been Amber's last gig before she disappeared. The place wasn't famous and neither were Amber and Sidney, but Marley had tracked them all down.

"This'll help you make up your mind," the bartender said with an Irish brogue. He opened a list of drinks in front of her. "Unless you already know, colleen."

She smiled at him and decided he was about her

age, but his worldly brown eyes had probably seen much more . . . of *this* world.

Marley looked at the list. "Only martinis?" She laughed. "Every kind of martini."

The bartender put his elbows on the counter and crossed his forearms. "And every kind of gin. But if you don't drink gin, try me with whatever takes your fancy."

"I'm having one of these," she said. "Kiwi and sour apple martini. That sounds good." She wanted to fit in, preferably to just about disappear.

Sitting sideways on her stool, Marley watched the singer. Someone behind her tapped her shoulder and Marley glanced around.

A blond man, maybe in his forties, smiled at her from the next stool. "Is it okay if I hit on you?" he said, and giggled at his own brilliance.

Marley smiled politely and turned back to the singer.

Another tap on the shoulder.

This time she ignored him.

The bartender slid a large martini glass filled to the brim with a pale green drink toward her. In amber-shaded light the contents of the glass reminded her of other things, like a tunnel she'd swum through, and its consistency was as if it had been mixed with light oil. Pretty in a way.

A big hand shot out from beside her to throw down a fifty. "The lady's drink is on me, Danny," the blond man said. "Take it out of that."

Marley rallied quickly and looked Danny in the eye. "I'll be running my own tab," she said, pleased that she could sound as if she did this sort of thing regularly.

"You've got it," Danny said, ignoring Blondy's money.

"What's the singer's name?" Marley asked.

Danny squinted, appeared to become distant. He looked past Marley. "That's Sidney. She got the pianist for tonight. Amber, that's her partner, she plays the keyboard—and sings, mind you. Now that girl's got the voice of an angel."

Marley turned back to stare at the singer. This was the Sidney of Amber and Sidney. Right there. It was far more than she had hoped for. She had to know where Amber lived, who her friends were, and at least *something* that would be useful in helping to find the woman. The police probably already knew the details, but they wouldn't be sharing any information with her.

After making the mistake of being direct with him that afternoon, Detective Archer had treated her kindly enough, if a virtual pat on the head and a warning not to let what she saw on television fool with her imagination were kind.

Archer had warned Marley that people who tried to get attention by pretending to know something about a crime could get into big trouble. The tingling embarrassment she had felt then made a return appearance and she hunched her shoulders.

A cloth in Danny's hands squeaked around the rim of a glass. When Marley looked at him, he was staring at her and frowning. He threw down the cloth and crossed his arms on the bar again, leaning closer to Marley. "It's late," he said. "Can you call someone to come and see you home when you're ready?"

"I'll be fine." She smiled, liking him for the concern. "I'll get a cab."

"What are you doing here?"

"Having a martini," she said. So she stuck out like a nun at a Chippendale show.

"Okay, have it your own way, then."

"Thank you, though." She smiled at him. "Does Sidney . . . Do Amber and Sidney sing here every night?"

"They used to," he said, noncommittal. "Most nights, anyway."

"When did they come back?"

"This is Sidney's first night back since . . . Amber—you've heard of Amber before?"

"I have." Nothing would be gained by pretending otherwise. "And I know she's missing, but you talk as if she's still here."

He gave her a speculative stare and moved away to serve several other customers. For the time of night there was plenty of business around.

Sidney had a face not easily forgotten. Latin features and olive skin. Dark arched brows, large, heavily-lashed brown eyes, a narrow-bridged nose, fine, high cheekbones and jaw. Her hair shone honey-colored, but Marley didn't think it was the natural color—it ought to be black. A lovely woman with a lovely figure—and something markedly aloof about her.

A different bartender asked if she wanted another drink. Marley looked at her almost untouched glass and shook her head.

"Can I talk to you?" Danny appeared at her right shoulder. He was anxious, everything about him troubled—and vigilant.

"Of course," she told him, excited in case she was finally about to learn something useful.

He led her between round, brass-topped tables to one of the alcoves where looped and fringed draperies gave an impression of privacy for the table and banquettes inside. They slid onto seats upholstered in green cabbage-rose fabric.

"Are you here about Amber?" Danny said without preamble. "You don't look like a cop, but that doesn't mean you're not one."

"I'm not one."

"But—"

"Yes, I came to see if I could find out anything about Amber."

"You're just looking for a diversion?" Danny said. "You get a kick out of other people's tragedies?"

She shook her head fiercely. "No way. I hate that kind of thing. I've got a good reason for being here. Take it or leave it."

Danny studied her awhile before he glanced away. "Okay, if you say so."

"Thanks," Marley said. "I'm amazed to see Amber's partner here. I thought she wouldn't talk to anyone."

"She won't. But she wants to get back to work. She's ambitious."

The tone of his voice was neutral, but Marley thought something other than her was making him uncomfortable or angry.

"And you don't think she should be singing again."

He shook his head. "Not as long as Amber's missing. It's not right."

"People need money to live," she pointed out.

"Yes." He shrugged. "I don't know anything about her, really, except she's private, just like Amber was. Like she *is*." He corrected himself forcefully.

"Are you two friends?" she asked, prepared for Danny to refuse an answer.

"Yes," he said.

She waited, but he didn't add any more.

"Do the police know that?"

He shrugged again.

"They're scratching for leads," she told him. "They'd want any information you've got."

"I love her," he said, looking at his hands. "She doesn't take me seriously so we're just friends. I think something happened and she took off. Could be her brother. She used to talk about him and I thought he worried her. Maybe she went to look for him."

"Don't you think the police could use your ideas?" Marley said, while he kept staring at his fingers, laced tightly together on the table. "Why are you telling me these things when you won't tell the police?"

"You're different." He pushed back on the banquette and stared at her, his lips parted. His eyes darkened and faint lines of color rose high on his cheeks. "I don't know why I'm telling you. I've been desperate. I suppose I . . . I can feel that you care about her, too. You know her, don't you?" His whole upper body lunged over the table.

"I do care," Marley said. She controlled an automatic need to move back from his face. There was nothing new about someone being drawn to her. They felt her empathy and it attracted them. People talked to her, told her personal things that would surprise her if she didn't understand why it happened.

"You didn't say who you are," he said.

She hesitated.

"I'm not dangerous," Danny said. "Anyone will vouch for me. I've been here at Scully's two years."

He could say anything, but she had no means of knowing if he was truthful. "Is Amber your girl-friend?"

"No. I told you she's a friend, but not my girlfriend."

"Why doesn't she want more?"

"I can't talk about that."

"Okay." He hadn't said a word that would help her find Amber. "Where does she live?"

"She's so private. She wouldn't forgive me if I gave away the peace she's made for herself."

"But you do know where she lives?" Marley persisted. Detective Archer had pretended not to hear the question when she asked him.

Applause broke out for Sidney and the pianist. Sidney had been sitting on a stool, but now she stood and Marley saw that she was tall.

"I do know," Danny said.

Marley cocked her head. "I thought you did, but I didn't expect you to admit it. Didn't the police ask you a lot about her?"

He looked closed, stubborn.

"They did, but you didn't tell them much." Suddenly she was uncomfortable and wished she was back in her flat. He had admitted something to her that he'd refused to tell the authorities. Was he trying to gain her trust?

How could she know if Danny had played a part in Amber's disappearance?

"Why don't you let me take you home?" he said. "Ben's covering for me. I'd feel better if I knew you were safe."

Each little hair on Marley's neck rose. Her back

prickled. "I'd like to finish my drink," she told him, with no intention of doing so.

"Of course. Take your time. You won't repeat anything I've said, will you?"

She had to lie. "No."

He walked away, only to come back with her drink before she could decide on the next step. "Why are you looking for Amber?" he said.

The only surprise was that he hadn't asked that very question before. "It's hard to explain."

"Do it anyway." His voice grew more intense and his lips scarcely moved. "Tell me what you know. You owe me that."

"I don't owe you anything." Marley expelled a breath through pursed lips. Too often she spoke too fast and before thinking enough. "I'm in a bad spot about this, too."

When he closed the fingers of his left hand around her wrist, Marley winced. She wouldn't allow herself to try pulling away. "That doesn't feel so good." She looked pointedly at his hand.

"If you know anything about what's happened to her, tell me. Now." His grip tightened.

"Loosen up, Danny," a familiar male voice said, and Danny's fingers went slack. Pain contorted his face.

Marley snatched her wrist away and turned on her seat, shifting back in the booth at the same time.

"You okay, Marley?" Gray Fisher asked, still squeezing a tendon in Danny's shoulder.

7

The longer she slept, the better. Eventually her screams would excite him, but until he was ready, he preferred silence.

Breathing, sounds of the idle, automatic push and pull of air in unsuspecting human lungs raised bubbles of hysteria in his throat.

On it went, unaware that it would soon be silenced. Before long, the human woman would begin her final, endless sleep.

The itching began.

He opened his mouth wide, inhaled long and slow, to hold back the noise that wanted to erupt. His skin grew thicker and the thickening made his body larger. He felt himself swell, felt his spine grow supple and bend forward. Already he wore the loose, hooded black robe he could adjust to cover him completely, no matter how hulking his form became.

Power flooded his bulk and he swayed, reveled in the loose, heavy swing of his limbs.

Fingernails became talons, gradually lengthening, curving, hardening to points as capable of wounding as ice picks.

Beneath the cracked and crazed hide that was replacing skin, his raw flesh stung. Beautiful pain. Agony inflamed his muscles, his nerves, but his purpose only intensified.

Until yesterday, it had been more than two years since he fed his need for fresh death. Far too long. Ah, yes, where he came from, deep beneath this earth in Embran, they fought and killed for supremacy daily. Only the strongest survived and their number were replenished by the young—those of them considered worthy of a chance to live.

But it was here, not in Embran that he wished to remain, among the luscious flesh of humans where sex with them increased his power and destroying those he no longer wanted brought him the deepest satisfaction of all.

His kind were only allowed on earth one-by-one. The Supreme Council feared losing control of the pack if they didn't keep them together. To earn passage to the surface, a man- or woman-Embran— for the only common element they shared with humans was their sex—the one who got to come had to defeat all who competed for the honor. Some, severely wounded, gave up. Many more ceased to exist.

He had won the prize thirty years earlier and lived among his beloved victims disguised as one of them—except when he needed to resume his rightful form to perform a kill.

Warnings had started to surface from below, telling him it was time to return and report what he had found out that might be useful. But he ignored the warnings. It was too soon to give up the wonder of all this.

The signs were there that he could be weakening and should return home for regeneration, but he was the strongest of them all and he would find a way to restore himself and stay where he was. How unfortunate that he was not a puppet prepared only to study the reasons for Embrans' increasing difficulty in keeping deterioration of their bodies at bay. That's what the Supreme Council wanted from him. He should find out what had happened all those years ago in Belgium, when a woman-Embran had returned below, taking with her some disease visited upon her by her ungrateful human husband.

He would get to all that—but not when he was finally enjoying himself again.

Two years ago bad luck had forced him to give up the ultimate pleasure of the kill. Before that he had savored countless delightful terminations until he had been unfortunate enough to come upon a series of seven victims who forced his temporary seclusion. Those seven had come to him willingly, as their kind did once they were promised money for their time. But all seven, each one in a row, had lied in saying they had no one who cared where they were and what they did. And so their disappearances were reported to the police by their wretched survivors and New Orleans became too dangerous a hunting ground for him.

But at last certain events had caused him to return to his natural ways and, in particular, the woman he left in the river earlier had reminded him of all he missed. He had perfected a new system to cover his tracks and that woman was only the beginning—a decoy to keep any attention away from what was really happening.

For as long as he stayed safe he would continue. Then he would retreat again, and watch the silly little humans scurry in search of what they would label a monster, while never knowing who he was and having no means of pursuing him.

How he had hugged himself with glee at the sight of the so important policeman trying to quiet the citizens of New Orleans from a television screen, even as his own fear showed in his eyes. They found the one in the river faster than he'd expected, that much he admitted.

"Who's there?"

Damn, the captive woman was waking and he hadn't completed his transformation. His head was always slow to resume its magnificent and rightful form. Quickly, he shuffled back into the shadows. His vision had changed and he saw her through a film of red. The slashes that were his pupils elongated her. This next prize was a gift from a fool who crossed him and broke his rules. But to be fair, the fool had also brought him renewed vigor.

Sounds broke from deep inside him, muffled, baying roars. He tossed his head. His mouth stretched open wider, and even more wide. A muffled snap and fiery spears darting into his brain warned him that his human jaw had dislocated. Not long now.

From his mouth, a broad, slime-coated nose and lipless jaws thrust out. They slid steadily forward and he rocked his human head, felt it fold back on itself to make way for the final, full exposure of his authentic self.

"Where are you?" *the woman moaned.* "Why am I here?"

As if he would tell her, the foolish creature. She had wanted too much, but she would get nothing. He would take everything away from her.

Slowly, he stepped toward her. She lay on a heap of cushions in a corner. The switch he flipped sent the cooling system into rapid mode. Icy mist curled upward and the woman shivered.

He needed to bite, but must contain himself. It was the bites that killed, not the scratches since only his teeth secreted poison.

Even if he'd been unable to see at all, he would still have known the instant when she saw him. Her breathing stopped, for a long time, before it started again, wheezing, high-pitched, punctuated with choking shrieks.

Don't die before I can kill you, *he thought.*

I hate it when one of you dies from shock. I want to taste warm blood in my mouth. I want your heart to beat until the final strike.

"Oh, my God," *she whined.*

Pale now, her eyes wide and staring, her mouth

an ugly, stretched hole, she scarcely looked like the same woman who had come to him.

He tossed his head and bayed. And he parted the robe, let it fall.

Her scream convulsed her. Back and forth she scrambled, dragging hair from her face to search for escape. Then she was on her feet but staggering on the soft pillows. She pushed herself as far from him as she could, shoved into the wall as if she could make it open and swallow her.

She might be swallowed if the idea appealed to him, but if he ate her whole she was too large not to disrupt his digestion. He would only have to regurgitate her.

A button he pushed flooded pulsing pink light over him, and her. He knew that she would see his eyes as gouges filled with blood and his mouth, a cavern lined with great, slathering, needle-tipped teeth.

He hooked his talons beneath the neck of her dress and opened bloody gashes that stretched the length of her body by the time he had torn off her clothes.

Too bad she was too terrified to attempt to cover herself. He savored the futile efforts of a victim who clung to conventions that would never have meaning to her again.

"Don't," *she whispered, and that surprised him.* "You're a man. I know you are. I've already made sure someone knows where to find you and what to look for."

She lied.

Welts and scarlet scratches violated her white breasts, her belly and thighs.

At last his own trembling began. Sexual demand sprang in his loins. He swelled, and lunged, took hold of her legs and yanked her feet from the ground. She crashed down like a disjointed doll, struck her head and shoulders on the hard floor.

His one regret was that the hide that sheathed him dulled feeling and when he fanned his claws over her breasts, he could only imagine the texture of that flesh.

No matter.

Wild, stronger than he had expected, the woman struck out at him, tried to push her nails into his eyes.

A fine idea.

Two talons returned the favor, only he didn't miss. He pushed through her eye sockets until he felt sinew tear and small bones break inside her head.

Damn.

Dead.

He should have held back but she was dead and much too soon. He shrieked and rocked over her, picked her up as he could have a child, and shook her broken body.

For a few moments he clutched her against him and sobbing sounds of misery tore from him.

He cradled her with exquisite gentleness.

8

Gray increased the pressure on Danny Summit's shoulder and stared into Marley's shocked eyes. He couldn't look away. The bunching muscles in his back had less to do with his flexed arm than what he was thinking about; he wanted to touch her, just touch—for a start.

He hadn't been surprised to see her here.

But he should have been—he should have been amazed.

"Hey, man," Danny Summit said, squirming. "You're killing me here. I need that arm."

Gray released his hold on the other man, who muttered under his breath, gingerly opening and closing his fingers. He stared from Gray to Marley, managing to convey confusion, suspicion—and physical pain—at the same time.

Too bad.

"Are you okay?" Gray repeated to Marley. The way she looked at him suggested he'd grown horns—or worse.

"Yes, I am, thank you."

"That's great, then." His attention was split between Marley, who visibly shrank away, and Sidney's voice from behind him. "You got a problem, Danny?" he asked.

"Yeah, I reckon I do. There's something going on here. You two know each other."

Gray raised his brows. "Why would that be a problem? I came to meet up with Marley. She's a friend." He looked into her very green eyes, willing her not to call him a liar.

Freckles showed plainly over her nose. Such white skin, but he guessed that went with the red hair. He hadn't known many redheads.

"You're late," Marley said.

She narrowed her eyes slightly and he figured he'd probably have to pay for her cooperation. An interesting thought. What could he have that she wanted? Must be something.

"I shouldn't have touched you," Danny said to Marley. "I don't usually lose control like that. Sorry."

"What's with you?" Gray said to Danny before Marley could respond. He took off his jacket and slung it over a shoulder. Unless you stood in front of icy blasts from air-conditioning vents, the place was tight with wet heat.

Danny started to walk away, but he stopped. "She won't tell me why she's asking questions about Amber," he said, nodding at Marley. "You understand what that means to me. You know what Amber means to me. She hasn't come back. I haven't even had a call from her. I don't know what to do next."

Gray didn't know Danny was involved with Amber, or he hadn't until now.

"You could start by coming clean with the

police," Marley said, then she wouldn't meet Gray's eyes.

"I'm not having them poking around in her things," Danny said to Gray. "And it's none of their damn business how I feel about her."

"Danny," Gray said. "How long have you known Amber? You know what I mean—personally?"

"Why would that matter to you?" Danny bristled. "I should be the one asking you questions. Two of the people you were supposedly writing an article about have disappeared. Liza Soaper and Amber were doing just fine till you showed up."

"Coincidence," Gray said, knowing that in the other man's place, he'd be coming to some of the same conclusions. "I've written about a lot of people."

Then he noticed Marley's face. *Stunned.* She clutched the edge of the table.

Damn, if Danny hadn't opened his mouth she still wouldn't know about his connection to Liza and Amber. It hadn't been mentioned in front of her at Nat Archer's office. She didn't have to say a word for him to know she was connecting dots and drawing an ugly picture of him. At least she wasn't linking him to Pipes Dupuis, or to the Cooper woman's death—yet.

Danny sat on the end of the banquette across from Marley. He closed his eyes and rubbed a hand back and forth over his mouth.

Gray met Marley's eyes. She had already collected herself and shut away whatever she felt.

"Do either of you know anything?" Danny said. "If you do, for God's sake tell me. I don't know where to go for help."

"Did Amber live with you?" Marley said.

Gray watched Danny's reaction.

"That's it," he said, getting up again. "I know when I'm being taken for a ride. You two have got your own agendas and they're not about helping Amber or me. The only people I'll be talking to are the police. And don't think I won't tell them to take a long look at the two of you."

Just what I need. "That's up to you," Gray said. "But don't forget I like Amber. She's got a lot of guts and she hasn't had it easy. I've got no reason to wish her any harm. If you point the cops in my direction you could make yourself feel better, but you'll only be taking their time away from the case."

"I gotta go," Danny said. He shook his head slowly all the way back to the bar.

"You know Liza and Amber?" Marley asked softly.

Gray puffed up his cheeks and studied his shoes.

"You do, don't you? You've been writing a story about them. And now they're missing. When I showed up, Detective Archer must have been questioning you about it."

"Congratulations," he said. "You don't waste any

time getting your wild guesses together. If Nat had brought me in for questioning, we wouldn't have been lounging in his office when you arrived." Not entirely true, but Nat hadn't seen any reason to hold him, either.

Marley Millet still wore the white cotton dress she'd had on earlier, but with a short pink sweater that tied beneath the breasts and a filmy, multicolored scarf around her neck. Everything about her appealed to him and he didn't like the idea of her being alone in Scully's at almost one in the morning. There weren't many sober patrons around.

The glass of green-something Marley picked up shook slightly on the way to her lips. She barely touched the liquor, but continued to hold the glass in both hands.

"I know where you live," he told her, and almost bit his tongue when he saw what she thought of that announcement. "You gave your name at the station and you said you lived on Royal. I put it together with J. Clive Millet. The antique people. I worked in the Quarter a long time—I probably know just about every business around."

"You followed me here?" she said.

"No. I didn't know you'd be here. I came for the same reason as you, to see if I could get a lead on Amber. This is the last place I know she was seen. I don't expect her to walk through those doors, but I keep hoping."

Marley raised her chin, but abruptly her eyes lost focus on him. She seemed . . . distant, as if she was listening for something. Or *to* something.

Gray looked around, but didn't see anything different. When he glanced back at Marley, she had rested her chin on her hands and closed her eyes. Tingling crept up his spine, and he got that sensation of heat in his lungs and belly again. There was fear in this woman, and urgency. She needed and wanted to do something but couldn't, not without help.

The flicker of a memory shoved into his mind. He didn't allow himself to go there to that place where a small boy was tormented for being "different." The boy had made the mistake of knowing when bad things were going to happen, and trying to warn the other children. He had been that boy.

No, that was a long time ago. Whatever he'd thought he knew was dumb kid stuff.

Marley was so still, he could almost imagine she wasn't breathing. Under the low lights in the room, her hair glowed a deep, shocking red. Her brows were fine and feathered and even her lashes were dark red. She fascinated him. He'd never considered himself a masochist, but he must be if he was excited by Marley of the laser tongue who walked into a precinct house and announced she could travel without her body!

She was concentrating on him again and he almost said, "welcome back." This time sanity prevailed. "You look really nice," he said. *Sanity?* With a grin, he added, "You do, but I'm also trying to soften you up. It would be good if you could like me a bit. I'm a decent guy, honestly. Just a journalist trying to make a living and having problems right now."

Her stare never left his face.

The same sensation he'd had in his fingers yesterday afternoon slipped into his head. The very tips of his fingers were still affected. Numbing cold.

"Tell him he should go home."

Who said that? He frowned. Not Marley, but he heard it.

"If he knows what's good for him, he'll leave now."

A man's voice.

Was he losing it?

"Marley, did you say something?"

She shook her head and looked past him toward Sidney, who was making moves to start another set. "You should go home," Marley said. "Excuse me."

Shoot, had he heard someone giving her instructions just now?

Gray pushed his shoulders back and watched her through narrowed eyes. She disturbed him, yet he didn't want to leave her. Could someone really choose to leave their body and go "traveling"? That he would even ask himself the question worried him.

"If you know what's good for you, you'll leave," Marley told Gray.

Gray held his breath. She sounded like a soft echo of the male voice.

Marley couldn't concentrate. Her attention was split. Uncle Pascal had never, ever communicated the way he was doing now. He had located her mind—just found it and started talking and telling her what he wanted her to do. And he'd come because he had sensed danger, sensed her alone out here and with a man she knew little about. Did it mean her uncle could find and transmit to any mind—at will? Had he simply never chosen to do so before tonight? That was incredible. She considered herself a strong talent, but her own telepathic abilities were mostly short range and by mutual invitation.

Marley wondered what Gray would think if he knew she and her uncle were talking about him—in a manner of speaking.

"Who is he?" Uncle Pascal asked. *"Do you know anything about him?"*

Marley responded in thought: *"Not really. He's a journalist who used to be a policeman. I'm not sure what to think, but he could be okay. How did you find me?"*

"All you need to know is that I can."

Gray sat opposite her and reached for her hands. She was too surprised to pull away in time.

"I . . . I'm not sure, but I think I'm feeling something weird," he said. "Did you hear a voice? I mean . . . someone talking without being here? Are you cold?"

"Uncle, he's picking something up from us." The last thing she would have expected was for Gray to mention being cold.

"He can't be."

"Can you hear what he's saying?" Marley asked.

"No. I'm aware of a man with you and what you feel about him. You feel threatened."

She didn't want to discuss that. *"He's a sensitive. I don't think he even knows it yet, but he could be a problem eventually."*

"Get home to me. Has something happened, something you haven't told me about? I think you've traveled recently."

Marley worked hard to close her uncle out. She must think unobserved for a while. *"I'll talk to you tomorrow."*

"Marley, do not shut me out. I must be in contact and know you're safe."

He could find and enter her mind, but not see where she was. That was something. *"Be patient,"* she told her uncle. *"This man is hearing parts of our communication. Not much—or I don't think so—but he's getting caught up in the open channels between us. We should stop now."*

"Marley—"

With an effort that left her weaker, she shuttered

Uncle Pascal from her. What he'd just done was unheard of, at least in reputable psi circles. He had simply found her telepathically. She didn't like it and from now on, she would make it as hard as she could for him. Safety was one thing. Fear of being spied on was another. But he would always make his presence known, wouldn't he? That was one of the family's rules of honor. They didn't just sneak in and out of each other's heads.

How had Uncle Pascal known she was in the middle of something bizarre?

"You look so serious, Marley."

"Could have been just a fluke this time," she said carelessly, still feeling his hands holding hers.

"What?" Gray said.

"Um. You asked me if I'm feeling cold?" She couldn't risk involving him in her world. His fingers were icy. Apparently he was too cold to know her hands were also deeply chilled. "Are you sick?" She didn't know what else to say and looked at the way he held on to her, at his big, well-used hands and the way they covered hers.

"I'm not sick," he said.

He was a man who would be noticed wherever he went. Marley decided she would certainly notice him and felt uncomfortable with the idea. She stood up, pulling away from him as she did so. "I have to talk to someone," she said. Rather than starting another set, Sidney was getting ready to leave.

"Sidney?" Gray said. "You want to talk to her before she leaves."

Marley didn't respond. She didn't have to, but was it an easy assumption that she would try to talk to Sidney before she left. Or had Gray picked up on her intentions again?

Hurriedly, she left him and walked the length of the club.

Sidney was much taller than Marley, who had to look up at her.

"Hi," she said. "I'm Marley Millet. Could we talk for a few minutes?"

"I don't think so," Sidney told her in a slightly nasal, purely upper-crust New Orleans accent. "Maybe another time."

"It's about Amber," Marley said. "And you, of course."

That earned her a more interested look down Sidney's elegant nose. She took the card Marley offered, but barely glanced at it.

"You're with Gray Fisher," the woman said.

"You know Gray?"

One shoulder rose, causing the front of a black dress to gape.

Sidney laughed low in her throat. Her lashes fluttered. "I suppose he's decided I'm good enough for his little story now."

"That's not what I wanted to ask—"

"You were always good enough for a story, Sidney," Gray said, joining Marley and cutting off

96

whatever she had been going to say next. "You're in my lineup. Or I hope you'll agree to be."

Sidney watched him through narrowed eyelids. "Would I have been in your lineup if you hadn't lost two of your preferred interviews already?"

"If that's what you believe, I won't try to change your mind. Let's forget we had this discussion."

"I will not, Gray Fisher," Sidney said, all but purring. "I'd be honored to talk to you, but not tonight. My family worries if I'm out too late."

"When, then?"

"I hoped we could talk," Marley managed to get in. "Could I call you?"

Sidney smiled at her, but spoke to Gray. "Give me your number and I'll get in touch with you."

He was taking a card from the inside pocket of his jacket when Marley saw her brother, Sykes. Or rather, more-or-less saw him.

Nearby, one ankle crossed over the other, his weight braced against a post, stood all more than six and a half feet of Sykes Millet. His black hair curled to his collar and his brilliant blue eyes laughed at her. The smile that curved his lips would be a killer to any other woman looking at him.

No other woman looked at him tonight because only Marley would be able to see him. And she could see straight through him to the wall behind.

9

"Marley! Wait!" Gray caught up with her when she reached the curb in front of the Hotel Camille. "Marley—"

"I can't talk to you anymore."

"Never again?" he asked.

She glanced at him, but didn't crack a smile. "Most likely."

Gray prepared for battle.

"Sidney won't call you," he told her.

"Do you really think she'll call *you?*" she asked tightly, scanning the street in both directions.

"Yeah, I do. She's still ambitious enough to want publicity. You saw that. Amber was the talent. Hey, you don't live so far from here. We can walk."

Marley stepped off the sidewalk. "I'll get a cab," she said, searching up and down the street again then back at the hotel entrance.

The Camille wasn't the kind of place that kept twenty-four-hour doormen around. No help would come from there.

The street was silent and empty.

To the west, even the neon flare from Harrah's Casino looked subdued against the hazy sky.

The first chill of early morning slithered off the Mississippi, barely shifting the odors of old buildings, old beer, or the scent of flowers in hanging baskets.

"You don't need a cab," he said. "I'll walk with you and you'll be fine."

A ship's horn bleated from the river and Marley jumped. Standing in the street with him on the sidewalk, she seemed even smaller. "I'll be fine?" she said, only it wasn't a question really.

He threw up his hands. "Oh, for God's sake. Do you really think I'm some sort of perverted killer?"

"I don't know what you are," she said.

No, of course she didn't. He pulled out his wallet and searched through it. "I may have a cab number in here somewhere," he said. Why fight her logical arguments? In her position he wouldn't want him to walk her home, either.

Mentally, she had moved away from him again. He felt it without looking at her, but when he did glance up, he knew he was right.

Green, gold and pink, Scully's neon sign pulsed over Marley's shuttered features.

"Marley?" he said, deliberately quiet.

Her face moved in his direction, but not her eyes, or not immediately. "Doesn't look as if I'm going to get a cab," she said finally.

He took another look through his wallet.

"We can probably be home before I get a ride," she said, but she didn't sound convinced. "Let's go. If you're sure you don't mind."

"Are *you* sure?" There wasn't much he liked about this. She behaved as if she were acting under pressure. "We could go back inside and find a phone book. Hell, someone in the club will know who to call."

Again she looked away and thought about it. "That would be silly. You know I've had . . . It's been hard today. I don't go around telling people about myself, not the stuff they'll only laugh at."

She didn't need more grief, not after what she'd taken from Nat earlier. "Okay, then." He grinned and offered her an arm. "I didn't laugh when you said you saw things . . . or people, was it? When you aren't in your body you see them?"

"Thanks," she said, "but you're laughing now."

She started walking.

"No, I'm not," Gray said, catching up and falling into step beside her. "I'd like to know more about . . . more about it all." What did bother him was hearing voices, or feeling things he shouldn't feel.

"There's nothing more to know," she said.

She was probably right and it might be kinder to his health to think so. Anyway, he knew better than to press her again on the subject and they went in silence to the corner of Iberville Street and made a left. His shoes rang on the sidewalk. The soles of her shoes must be soft.

"Tell me how you got to know Liza and Amber," Marley said. "Why did you choose them? Detective Archer said you were a good cop. Or he more or less said that. So why be a journalist at all?"

Gray wasn't sure what to say, or if he ought to

tell her anything at all. But it couldn't hurt to see if talking about himself a bit would put her at ease.

"My old man was a cop," he said, unsure why he started there. Then he knew. "So I wanted to do what he did. He was . . . is a good guy." Talking about his father was easy.

Illness had shrunk Gus Fisher from the big, strong man he'd been into a memory of himself. Sometimes Gray thought of his dad as two people, the one who slew a boy's lions and seemed invincible, the other still wise and funny, but who had reversed roles with his son. Gray was his father's rock now, or he was when Gus would allow him to be.

"I like to hear people talk about their families," Marley said.

Gray gathered himself. "You work with yours, don't you?"

She laughed. "Yes."

When she didn't go on, Gray let it go. "Gus didn't really want me on the force. I thought he did, and he pretended that's the way it was, so we fooled each other for years. He was proud to have me there. When I made my first moves up through the ranks, he was about ready to pop, he was so pumped. It didn't matter to him that he was what he called a plain cop and always would be. That was good with him."

"You love him a lot," she said and he heard her soften.

"I thought I was a cop for life, but I only got more frustrated because I wanted something else. Long story short, with my dad's blessing—and I knew he'd give it—I took time off to see if I could make it as a writer."

She was quiet once more and her pace slackened. They walked slowly through the heavy night. As they got farther from the river, nothing moved but the two of them. Gray didn't remember the city being so quiet at this time of the morning. But then, he didn't hang out in this area anymore.

"Whew," Marley said. "It's so muggy."

His turn to laugh. "That's new?"

"No," she said, shaking her head and smiling up at him. "I've never liked the real heat even though I was born here." Her smile faded very slowly.

She'd gone away from him again. And his spine began to tingle as it had several times in the hours since he met her.

He almost laughed at himself. Even journalists had libidos. Marley Millet had his doing contortions, not that he knew why. She was good to look at in a kind of breakable way, but that wasn't it. The lady appealed to his need for challenge. He wanted to know her and know about her.

Come on, Gray. You think she's got something to do with this case.

"You were going to tell me about Liza and Amber," she said.

And so she persisted—because, like him, she

wanted something. They wanted things from each other.

"Writing about jazz singers in New Orleans is a natural," he said. "It's not a new idea, but maybe it is the way I'm doing it. I'm not going after people who are institutions already. It's the strugglers who interest me—mostly the women. Women always came, but not in the numbers there are now. What is it that makes them want to make it badly enough to come here? This can be a dangerous place for a woman more or less on her own."

"From where I'm looking, it *is* a dangerous place," Marley said. "Liza and Amber know it is, too."

Gray figured he'd walked into that.

Marley would not have gone two steps with Gray Fisher, alone, if Sykes hadn't threatened her with a fate worse than death if she didn't.

"How," he had asked, *"are you going to find out if the guy's a threat without giving him a chance to jump you? Trust me and do it."*

She hadn't laughed, or not on the outside . . .

While she listened to Gray, Sykes loped along on the journalist's other side. Now that he had Marley's attention, Sykes had dimmed himself. When she saw his face, it was almost clear, but the rest of him blended into the background and appeared as a figure made of transparent shadows.

And Sykes had never had any trouble making himself heard and understood whenever he felt like it. Unlike Uncle Pascal, they all knew Sykes was a scary-when-he-didn't-smile, scarier-when-he-did-smile, outrageously powerful paranormal talent.

"What do you make of Danny Summit?" Gray asked. "I didn't know he was so involved with Amber till tonight."

"I don't know anything about him," Marley said. "Maybe he's just what he seems to be, worried about his girlfriend."

"Girlfriend?" Gray snorted. "Neither of them said a word about it to me."

"Until tonight," Marley said.

"And they live together."

"Seems that way," Marley agreed. "I don't think he meant to tell us that. Earlier he told me he loved her, but she wasn't his girlfriend. Go figure."

Sykes nodded and took mincing steps as if he had to struggle not to outpace Marley and Gray. That wasn't as true when it came to Gray, who was almost as tall and long-legged as Sykes.

"Don't do anything to make me laugh," Marley communicated with him. *"You don't need to walk at all, do you?"*

"You are such a killjoy," he responded. *"It's boring to float. Too easy."*

To Gray, Marley said, "You still didn't say how you chose Liza and Amber."

"I didn't, really. A drummer at Blues Heaven mentioned Liza and Liza introduced me to Amber

104

Lee. They were both right for what I wanted. What I still want."

"Which is?" The more she could get out of him, the better.

Sykes leaned forward and touched the tips of a thumb and forefinger together.

"Glad you approve." She let him know she didn't appreciate his interference.

"Sarcasm never suited you," Sykes said.

"The story's about the network here, the jazz network, and what it takes to break in," Gray said. "I'm not interested in anyone with connections. Not anyone who already knew people who would help them out when they got here. All Liza's got is her voice—and she's easy to look at."

"This is where you tell him all men are the same," Sykes said. *"We only care how sexy a woman is."*

"All he said was, she's easy to look at."

"Code for sexy," Sykes said. In a single long stride, he bounded forward and turned to walk backward in front of Gray. *"Do you know he's sensitive?"* he asked Marley. *"He's just waking up to it. Don't know why, unless it's something to do with you. Yeah, could be. He's trying to pretend he doesn't notice anything really different."*

"I do know about him," Marley said. *"Be careful he doesn't intercept you talking to me. Keep your guard up. I think he heard Uncle Pascal."*

Sykes snapped his fingers soundlessly and

danced in front of them to music only he heard. *"Baby, baby,"* he sang in his husky tenor. *"My guard is always up, up, up. I'm always ready. Bring it on."*

"I'm glad we're having this opportunity to talk," Gray said.

Marley did her best to shut out Sykes's image. "Really?"

"I was serious when I said I want to know more about your . . . what do you call that?"

Her instinct was to leave him flailing around, searching and finding ever more foolish terms for the powers she had. "You don't have to call it anything," she said, taking some pity. After all, he hadn't jumped her yet. "You don't have to think about it at all."

"Didn't mean to offend you."

"You didn't." But he might very soon.

"So tell me," he said. "You saw Liza and Amber somewhere since they went missing?"

"Does anyone even know how long they've been missing? Who told the police about it first?"

He laughed.

Marley risked glancing at Sykes, who made an owlish face.

"How useful you are," she told him.

"Anytime, sis."

"Why are you laughing at me?" Marley asked Gray.

He held up his palms. "I'm not. No, no, never. It

106

was the way you turned me from questioner to questionee. You do that all the time. You have a thing about being in charge, don't you?"

Marley stood still to consider that. "Yes. Now I think about it, I do like being in charge." She glanced at Sykes. "That could be because I've had to deal with a lot of domineering people in my life. I don't put up with that stuff anymore."

That got her a wide, eerily white-in-the-night grin.

"Good," Gray said. "I'm sick of wishy-washy women."

She wondered which wishy-washy women he was talking about.

"At the club you told me you were really cold?" Marley asked, suddenly remembering.

"I was," Gray said. "I'm not anymore."

He looked sideways at her and her tummy tightened. She swallowed. The Millets had a few problems when it came to sex. Potential problems. Dating was fine, but the Mentor's family honor—or rules—insisted any sexual partner had to know the dangers ahead of time.

The Mentor was a mysterious person—or thing—they had all been taught to respect as the family oracle. Marley had never seen the Mentor and mostly didn't know what she thought about him—or it—but she wasn't about to be the first to mention doubts about the Revered One.

Marley shook back her hair. Wow, Gray Fisher

had her racing in dangerous directions. She didn't even know him and didn't intend to . . . but she might.

That cold green drink she had left at Scully's would taste really good about now. A past experience with telling a man what it meant to get really close to a Millet's powers, and the curse they supposedly carried, hadn't encouraged her to try it again.

"You okay?" Gray asked.

She wasn't. This man had a force field all of his own. He was incredibly sexy.

"Now what?" Sykes said. *"Holy—Marley, you're lusting after this guy."*

"Shut up," she told him. *"You don't know what you're talking about."*

"I can feel you reacting to him." He studied Gray. *"He's not my type, but I guess if I was a lonely little woman I could get turned on."*

"Sykes! Stop it!"

He sniggered and she noticed Gray was giving her an odd look. "Can I see you again?" he asked abruptly. "Maybe tomorrow evening when we've both got our acts together."

"No," she said.

"Okay."

He walked on and she caught up this time.

"You don't know anything about me, but what I've told you," he said. "I'm going to give you my card and I'd appreciate it if you'd do some legwork to find out what my reputation is. I'm pretty boring so it won't take long."

She doubted if he was boring at all—ever.

"He's not," Sykes said. *"He's complicated and I think he could be dangerous. But I don't think he's a threat to you."*

"You're pushing it," Marley said. *"And you're breaking the rules. I didn't invite you to read me."*

"Uncle Pascal called me in. We wanted you found, physically and mentally. He can't do that, but I can."

She crossed her arms. *"Aha. You guided Uncle Pascal to me. That explains everything. I couldn't figure out how he managed to find me."*

"He was very worried about you."

"So you helped him invade my mind? You're not supposed to do that."

"It's Gray I'm reading now," Sykes told her. *"Be careful here. We need to know what his game is."*

"Maybe he doesn't have a game. Is your guard strong enough?"

"To keep Gray out? What do you think? Watch your own."

"Are you sure you won't see me tomorrow?" Gray asked. He ducked his face closer to hers and light from a window glinted in his eyes. "I'm okay, really I am. We need each other."

"Why?"

"You and I are mixed up in the same thing and

it's nothing good. We may need each other," he said.

Marley wanted to trust him.

She did need someone's help, badly, but she couldn't fool herself that she was not strongly attracted to Gray for other reasons, as well.

"I think I should go to Detective Archer and tell him what Danny said," she told him, feeling shaky. "The police ought to know Danny and Amber are involved—and that they probably live together. The police said they were having difficulty finding a lot of information on Amber or Liza, didn't they? Danny said he hasn't told them anything."

Gray cleared his throat. "He did say that, but I've got to think Archer knows more than he's going to share with anyone he doesn't think needs to know. Would you do me a favor? You could do it because I believed what you said and Nat Archer didn't. Don't go to Archer about anything for a bit. Come to me. Tell me if you remember something else."

Looking straight at Sykes, she thought about that.

"Think he's crooked and trying to get any information you may have before you give it to the police?" Sykes asked.

"You're reading my mind," she told him neutrally.

"Nah, just a lucky guess."

"I know roughly where Danny lives," Gray said. "What can he say if I just stop by to say hello?"

"Get lost, I should think," she said. "He spelled

out that he doesn't want interference. He wants Amber back, period."

Gray inclined his head. He watched her too intently for comfort, Marley decided. Her breath shortened. "The detective won't like it if you get between him and his investigation," she said.

"Maybe he won't. But he laughed at you, remember. Maybe that's why you could be on my side."

"I don't know. I'll have to think about it."

They reached Royal Street and Marley tried to pick up the pace, but Gray continued to measure his strides. After a few seconds he said, "I don't want to get there too quickly."

"Why?"

He sighed. "You just don't mince words. Because I want to keep you with me as long as possible," he said.

She looked at him sharply.

He looked back and she could have sworn he was as surprised by what he'd said as she was.

"Because we haven't decided anything," he added, but she wasn't sure she believed the excuse.

"There isn't anything to decide," she said. "I don't make rash decisions." *Of course not, only most of the time.*

"This is it," he said.

They were in front of J. Clive Millet, Antiques. Beside the left-hand shop window a wrought-iron gate, with a griffon at its center, led to the Court of

Angels at the back of the shop. Marley would rather Gray didn't know exactly how to reach the family's homes.

She had the keys to the shop and decided to use them. If she had to, raising the alarm wouldn't be hard once she opened the front door. Not that any of that mattered, since Sykes was with her.

"We didn't meet under good circumstances," Gray said. "I wish we had."

"Why?"

"Damn!" He looked skyward. "Sorry. But can't you say anything but 'why'? It's annoying."

"I can say other things," she told him.

He put his hands lightly on her shoulders. "Can I come by and take you for dinner tomorrow? Around seven?"

"Sykes?"

Sykes didn't answer and she looked around, but couldn't find him. "Damn," she said sharply.

Gray rubbed his palms up and down her arms and laughed. "You, too, huh? At a loss for useful words? Just say yes."

"I'd rather think about it."

"Yes, of course you would. You do that and call me."

"Okay," she said, anxious to get away.

Sykes had left her in her hour—her moment of need.

"Good night, Gray."

"Night," he said. "How will you phone me?"

She frowned.

"You don't know my number. It doesn't really matter. I'll call you."

Marley turned to unlock the shop door. She felt shivery and not only because she was responding to a very sexual thrill. Real fear climbed her spine. He could follow her into the shop and there would be nothing she could do about it if Sykes had really chosen to take himself off.

"Good night, Marley," Gray said. "Tomorrow?"

She turned back for a moment. "Maybe."

He nodded and faced the street to step off the sidewalk. His hands were deep in his pockets. Every move he made flowed. He had a powerful grace, like a big cat.

The instant before she looked away, Gray glanced at her over his shoulder.

That look wasn't soft or humorous anymore. Just for a flicker of time he stared, and Marley went into the shop and slammed the door. She shot home the locks.

It was the light, it had to be. But then, it had been the light the first time she saw hardness in those eyes that looked black, not whiskey-colored anymore. The light had turned his face into a facsimile of a black-and-white photograph. What the living face amazingly concealed, a negative image revealed: a thin, white scar passed through Gray's mouth, sliced upward beside his nose and across his cheek.

10

Marley didn't want to wake up.

Between night and dawn, sleep and the drifting time, Marley's old companions waited: the Ushers.

They had come for her. They wanted her to travel again.

Should she resist—or give in and go where they took her?

They were there again, beckoning.

In her dream-state, Marley felt herself drawn back to something that had happened to her more than two weeks earlier. She saw her feet aimlessly wandering along a sidewalk as they had that day. The colored layers of her skirt floated, pointed hems curling about her ankles and flashes of gold—from the sandals she wore—gleaming through gauze.

A woman called out, "Marley Millet?"

Marley didn't recognized the voice, but it was kind.

"Marley Millet, you came! I've been expecting you. This way, my friend, follow me." A welcome in every word. "I've waited for you and now you're here. You're going to help me do something that must be done. Come and see what I have for you."

"Yes," the Ushers whispered to Marley when she

hesitated, whispered in sounds like soft smiles. "Come on, Marley."

An alley and an archway opened before her and once through the arch, she entered a small shop. She twirled around and felt her skirts fly wide, then wind tight. Glass cases filled with toys. Dolls. All around her beautiful, wide-eyed dolls, their ringlets shining, dressed in silks and satins.

Teddy bears and stuffed horses, foxes, lambs, piglets, kittens and puppies, an elephant, an ostrich, a giraffe, a parrot—they lined two rows of shelves, one above the other, all around the shop.

Marley turned and turned.

A baby buggy of palest cane stood there, and there a cart with woolen chickens inside, and there three penguins with nodding heads. They must be on springs—those heads.

Wooden blocks, a jack-in-the-box, bags of jacks and decks of cards, marbles, bubble mix, balloons, soldier sentries in their fort, fairy wands, scarlet capes, tiny cars and trucks and trains stood everywhere in piles, on hooks, in open drawers.

"My name is Belle," the woman said. "Take this. It's not big, but it's heavy, so be careful not to break it."

Marley stretched out her arms and Belle placed there a small, wooden house lacquered a brilliant red, with the silhouettes of the people inside showing through closed blinds at the windows.

"Do not tell anyone you've got this," said Belle.

"If you do, others will try to take it from you. Don't let them. Protect the house from friends and enemies. Whatever it takes, keep it until I can return for it. Keep it and use it well."

Almost afraid to do so, Marley looked at Belle. She was slim, quite tall, and shapely in a gray leotard, tights to her calves, and a glossy skirt the same color that reached her knees. Brushed straight from her face, Belle's black hair, knotted at the nape of her neck, glistened, just as her dark eyes glistened. An exotic creature captured in a place where she didn't belong.

"You're a dancer," Marley said.

"Oh, yes. Thank you for noticing." She pointed the toes on one of her bare feet and traced on the floor. Lines formed in the dust there, shapes. "The house will be your way, but you will need courage. You have courage. Use it."

"What do I have to do?"

"Go there."

"Where?"

"You'll find it if you follow," Belle said. "I know there is a force for evil that needs the little house to complete his plans. We won't allow it, you and I."

Marley leaned the house against her. "Why me?" she said.

"Because you're like me." The woman smiled and appeared younger and even more beautiful. "You're a traveler, too."

"Can you tell me more about—"

"The beast has come home. You must stop the killing."

Marley woke up. Twisted in her sheets, she flung out her arms and tried to breathe slowly. Parts of the dream replayed, vivid, full color and too real.

That woman's last words echoed: *"The beast has come home. You must stop the killing."*

It was a dream, not reality. Once she calmed down it would all fade.

A rough, wet tongue, Winnie's, made rapid swipes over Marley's face. A solid dog on your chest, even a not very large dog, could make it even harder to breath—and it hurt.

"Off," Marley panted, rolling to her side and grabbing anxious Winnie against her at the same time. "I'm all right, Win. Relax."

It wasn't all a dream—or nightmare, but an echo of something Marley had already experienced. It brought back the day when that woman she'd never seen before really had given her the red house. What had been different was what she had heard said this time.

And the house was on her workbench to prove everything.

Marley kicked her feet and legs free of the sheets and scooted to sit on the edge of the bed. A cotton nightie stuck to her clammy skin.

She had been on Dumain Street, walking back

117

from delivering a package for Uncle Pascal and wishing her two sisters would call from London. Dawdling along, she heard someone call her name.

A shop bell had jangled and she'd noticed the tall woman beckoning her toward an alley. Unafraid, Marley had allowed herself to be led.

Since that puzzling day, Marley had returned to Dumain Street several times to search for the shop. There was no alley, archway or toy shop to be found. And there was certainly no elegant, barefoot woman dressed for ballet practice and calling herself Belle.

Marley gritted her teeth and got up to open her goody cupboard. Like traveling, intense dreams and nightmares made her hungry.

In Marley's sleep just a little earlier, that woman had told her to stop the killing.

Did it mean she should go back through the tunnel now, and quickly?

At least she had to get to the workroom and find out if the portal was open.

Snacking would have to wait. Marley fished out a manageably sized chew for Winnie before slamming the cupboard door. Winnie's favorite big plastic bone would be a liability when Marley was trying to move quietly. She pushed her feet into flip-flops, grabbed up her robe and pulled it on while she hurried from the flat, scooping up her keys as she went. Winnie gamboled along behind, her snorting made louder by the rawhide between her teeth.

Marley wasn't sure of the time, but the sky had lightened past early dawn and she could see minuscule droplets of moisture whirling in the beam from an outside wall lamp. This would be another hot and humid day. The beat of music from a radio, or a band in a loft somewhere, pulsed under her skin.

Sykes would dance down the steps, but he was more sure-footed than Marley. More than once she had slipped on the painted metal treads when they were damp. She was satisfied with letting the music take an edge off the fear that propelled her.

When she reached the courtyard, she raised her chin to see what lights showed in the upper-floor flats. Nothing above the shop, where Uncle Pascal lived, and nothing in Willow's place, or in Sykes's, to the right of her own. Not that Sykes was known for using lights much.

None of the lights in Sykes's most often empty flat had been visible after Gray left and Marley ran to get home. For all she knew, Sykes had gone elsewhere after he had made himself completely invisible to her.

She hurried on, acknowledging the silent angels as she went. They held a mystery she still hoped would become clear to her. Since she'd been a small child, this courtyard had been her favorite place.

Inside the shop, Marley quickly turned off the alarm system.

All of the Millets' senses were highly developed, but even in the world of paranormal powers, conventional science had its uses.

Utilizing the ambient glow from highly polished surfaces, she dodged quickly between stock displays on the floor and, clinging to the banister, dashed up the flights of stairs to her workshop.

She unlocked the door, let herself and Winnie inside, and bolted them in.

Stacked high all around, her projects obscured any immediate view of the workbench, but looking in that direction, she could see flickering, like green flame, reflected on the ceiling in that direction.

As always, what she did next was her choice. But she wouldn't discount Belle's plea yet, just in case.

Winnie cried behind her.

"Quiet," Marley hissed. "Not another sound or Uncle Pascal could wake up." Wake up, come to find her and make it very difficult to continue what she'd started.

She went to stand in front of the bench and stared at the chinoiserie house. Whatever happened, she would not disclose that it had sinister connections.

No wavering tunnel extended from the roof or one of its walls. No urgent whispers begged her to enter. But the leaping glow, a fiery dance of green tongues, turned the ceiling above into a wild

120

reflection. The lightest touch of her left hand on the peeling roof caught at her skin like warm gum.

With each step backward, a funnel, blue, turquoise, whirled to life, pulled bigger and bigger as if it were moldable liquid spun from the very tips of Marley's fingers.

A bump against her legs caused Marley to glance down. Winnie looked back, her chew still gripped in her teeth. Marley scooped the dog up with her free arm and sat in the old leather chair with her.

Finally the Ushers came, but not to whisper. They babbled, squabbled, their sounds rising and falling, angry and frightened by turns.

They were arguing.

Marley closed her eyes to concentrate and her limbs became heavy. She couldn't raise her eyelids again.

"We know we should help her to go, but we don't want to this time. It's too dangerous."

She understood what the Ushers were talking about. For the first time they were worried about urging her to travel.

Growing warmer, and even more relaxed, Marley sank back against her chair.

"She mustn't go. Stop her," an Usher said.

A collective, indrawn gasp shocked Marley. She sat very still and listened. The sibilant sounds were there, but in a muttering, fearful chorus. She heard, *"He's here,"* and looked around, expecting to see someone looming over her.

"It's dangerous," one voice, timid but determined said.

Marley closed her eyes and swallowed hard—and she saw a face, a man of indeterminate years, striking to look at with dark blue eyes and dark hair streaked with gray to his collar.

"Who are you?" she asked aloud.

He appeared to study her closely and then he said, in a clear, deep voice, *"Yes. Belle chose well. I argued it should be a man, but she laughed at me."* His smile transformed him and his eyes shone. *"Trust your companions to guide and guard you. You do this for the family. There is a lot to do, so be strong."*

Marley tried to respond, but he had gone again.

She had felt good in that man's company. He was familiar, but she wasn't completely sure why, except that he reminded her of Sykes, at least a little.

"I'm ready," she said aloud and firmly.

This time separation happened so quickly she felt herself tear from her body, and once free, she floated at the entrance to the funnel.

The irritated mutters softened to encouragement and she felt herself loosen. Into the opening she swam, and every thought faded, but for what she must do. *"Stop the killing."* And whatever she did was for the family. She had believed her strange visitor.

Once more, like the aperture of a camera lens, a space opened into another spectrum.

Disorienting sound met her, hammered at her ears, her temples, her whole face. She felt the thump of noises colliding with her body and breaking apart into screams.

Someone cried. A man. The screams were a man's, too.

What was this place?

Rather than the dirty room she had seen before, a sleeping woman lay, naked and facedown, atop a heap of vivid silk pillows. The pillows cast their own startling light against absolute darkness.

Marley looked around in search of any clue to where she was. There was nothing.

The male cry of anguish sounded again and Marley threw up her hands as if they could shut out the howl. Instead her wrists scraped a cold, spined thing. Red eyes, the black pupils like those of a giant feline, blinked once, then disappeared. All sound retreated and cold calm descended.

Terrified, feverish in her haste to get away, Marley reached to wake up the woman. She would take her away from this place, back to safety.

An abrupt current buoyed Marley and she floated. She couldn't go without the woman.

This time the heartbeat she heard was her own, the pounding of blood, her own. She wanted to shout that she couldn't leave yet, not without the other one.

"Come! Please wake up and come!"

Marley's throat closed with the last word she

uttered. Panic forced her to fight against the tide that took her farther away.

Her thrashing arms and legs met sluggish resistance. When she struggled against the tide, it only grew stronger, carried her away—back through whirling blue-green matter to the waiting portal.

11

"This had better be good," Gray said. He slid to face Nat in a booth at Ambrose's, a bar and diner across from Café du Monde on Decatur Street.

"I got you coffee," Nat said.

"And I got three hours of sleep last night. Maybe less."

Nat had called before six and the summons to Ambrose's didn't fall into the friendly invitation category. Nat sounded pissed.

"Drink," Nat said. "You aren't the only one around here who's sleep deprived."

The coffee tasted burned, or old and reheated, but it was strong and that mattered to Gray. The tone of Nat's voice on the phone had been irritating enough—and interesting enough to get Gray from his home in Faubourg Marigny to the appointed place in half an hour. The city wasn't awake yet. Pigeons still snoozed on statues in Jackson Square. The pickings from sidewalk diners weren't worth pooping for yet.

"Tell me what you've got and let me get back to

bed," Gray said. He hung over the table, hands clasped between his knees, head bowed.

Nat tapped the rim of Gray's mug with a fork. "Shut up and drink some more coffee."

The detective's plate overflowed with a muffuletta big enough to roof a round shack. Olive salad and cheese spilled from inside and Nat carefully stuffed every scrap back into the sandwich. He picked it up in both hands and took a big bite.

With a mouthful of bitter coffee not wanting to go down his throat, Gray watched his buddy chew slowly and swallow.

"Hey, Ambrose," Gray called to the establishment's owner, who sat on a stool beside a pocked, wooden bar and took all food orders. "I'll have what he's got." He pointed at Nat's plate.

That got him a grunt, but the food would arrive quickly and be good.

"Bucky Fist's on his way," Nat said. "He had a short night, too."

Gray took a swallow from Nat's water glass. "Damn," he said. "It's warm."

"You hear what I said about Bucky coming?"

"Yeah. So I'll bite. Do you and your partner hang out in here every morning, or does Bucky have news?"

Nat paused with what was left of the muffuletta halfway to his mouth. "Maybe he's got something interesting to tell us."

"You don't know?"

"Where were you late last night?" Nat asked. He'd laced his own coffee with cream and tipped down half the mug. "Don't tell me you were interviewing another singer."

Evidently the Bucky Fist tack was a diversion. Gray left it alone. "I wasn't interviewing anyone," he said. He took Nat's lead and dumped cream in his coffee. "How come this place makes the best food and the worst coffee?" he said, not expecting a sensible answer.

He got one. "Ambrose makes money on booze, not coffee. Order a Bloody Mary and you'll go to heaven."

"Why am I here?" Gray said, hoping the screwing around with "niceties" was over.

"I already said. Where were you late last night?"

"When did that get to be your business?"

Nat rescued several fallen olives and put them in his mouth. "When you came into my office with some bullshit story about looking for a woman we already knew was missing. That and other things."

He could shut up and wait, let Nat get at this when he was ready or try to hurry things. Hurrying wouldn't work. Gray got down more coffee.

"You were at Scully's," Nat said. "Down at the Hotel Camille."

"If you know, why ask me?"

"Why do you think? To see if you'd own up to it on your own."

Gray hated cat-and-mouse conversations. And he

126

wasn't thrilled with Nat's manner. "How do you know where I was last night? I wasn't followed."

Nat's eyebrows arched and he set down his fork. "You don't know that."

"I sure as hell do," Gray told him. "I was at Scully's, but I wasn't followed there."

"Maybe you were followed when you left."

"Not then, either," Gray said. "The streets were empty. You could have heard a gnat swallow. You know I'd know."

Begrudgingly, Nat nodded. Gray had been a good cop, a good detective—and more than one said, a loss to NOPD. They used to say he had a sixth sense. . . .

Screwing up his eyes, Gray swung from the booth and bought thinking time by wandering to the bar to check on his food.

Ambrose could be sixty or ninety. His white hair curled in a tight skull cap and his face shone dark and deeply lined. Gray had come here for years and Ambrose, sitting on the same stool every time, didn't seem to change.

"You kin carry your own plate, then," Ambrose said, flashing a gold front tooth. "You in such a a'mighty hurry t'eat."

The food arrived from the kitchen as Gray got to the bar. "I'll do that," he told Ambrose. "Thanks."

"Good to see you back on the beat," Ambrose said. "Don't be a stranger no more."

Gray didn't set him straight. "Thanks,

Ambrose." Loaded plate in hand, he made his way back to the booth, passing a few early customers and a few really late all-nighters on the way. The late ones had the fixed stares and disconnected hand-eye coordination of the past-drunk, legally comatose brigade.

He wondered how long Nat would take to get to the point and whether his ex-colleague was waiting for his partner before dropping some bombshell. If he had to guess, Fist either wouldn't show, or didn't have much to drop.

Nat waited until Gray's mouth was full to say, "That nutty little redhead was with you at Scully's, right?"

Two could play games. Gray kept his face in neutral and chewed. He pointed at his mouth to indicate he couldn't talk yet and considered his response.

After a swig from his mug, he said, "I don't know any nutty redheads."

That brought Nat's battered notebook from the pocket of his shirt. He slid a stubby pencil from the wire spiral and flipped a page over. "Marley Millet," he said, looking down as if Gray would believe his ex-colleague would forget a name that fast. The kind of name that belonged to the kind of owner it had.

"Nice woman," Gray commented.

"You were at Scully's with her last night. The two of you talked to Danny Summit, the bartender."

The picture got clearer for Gray. "How is Danny doing this morning?" Somehow he hadn't expected Danny to follow through with his threat to call the cops.

Nat straightened against the back of the banquette. He indicated to a waitress that he wanted more coffee and Gray sat silent until the woman had come and gone.

This wasn't going to work the way Nat wanted, which was for Gray to start saying things Nat might not already know.

The sound of cutlery on thick china didn't bother Gray. Nor did Nat's steady stare.

"You were there with her and Danny," Nat said. "Now I want to know what you talked about."

Gray smiled. "How do I know you know I was there? With Marley?"

"You already said you were there. And she's Marley now, huh?"

"Yes."

"Shit." Nat threw the notebook on the table. "You could make this easy."

"For whom?"

"Okay." In a forceful move, Nat leaned hard across the table. "One way or the other you'll tell me what you've found out."

"Because you don't know anything?" Gray said. "If that's right, you're off your game. I don't know exactly how you found out where I was last night—although I can guess—but you're on a fishing trip. Tell me what you're trying to find out and I'll see if I can help."

"Did you call Marley at the shop where she works and make a date? That would have been after you left my office."

"No, I didn't. I'll tell you this much and you ought to feel like an ass. Sidney, the woman Amber Lee sings with—I found out she showed up at Scully's last night. I went there looking for information. Marley was already there. We talked and Danny Summit was there, too. That's it."

"Then you left with Marley?"

"I left right after she did."

"You didn't walk her home?"

"Yes." Why deny it? "She couldn't get a cab so I went with her."

"And?"

"Nothing. Not a thing." He wouldn't voluntarily share that he hoped to see her again.

"Do you know some of the stuff they say about her family—and her?"

"I can imagine."

"Witches, wizards, voodoo," Nat said, but he smiled a little.

"That's crap," Gray said. "Maybe Marley thinks she sees things. And knows what's going to happen before it happens." Kind of like he was starting to do.

"And she says she leaves her body and goes other places—that's what she told us," Nat said.

Gray said, "Hmm." She believed what she'd told them with enough conviction to pretty much convince Gray.

"Pretty crazy in my book. And they've all got red hair," Nat pointed out.

"So what? Red hair runs in families."

"From what I'm told, *every* member of the family has red hair. They only marry redheads."

Gray spent a few moments on his food.

"A call came in a couple of hours ago," Nat said. He pulled an already knotted tie from beneath his jacket on the seat and slipped the noose over his head.

Gray said nothing while he watched the man fasten the top button of his shirt, put up the collar, arrange his tie and smooth the collar down again.

"So who called?" Gray decided to throw Nat a couple of bones just to help his day. "And what did they want?"

"What did Danny Summit say to you?" Nat asked.

Gray yawned and shook his head. "If there's nothing else, I'm going back to bed. I'm betting you know just about every detail about the missing women's lives, who their families or whatever are and a bunch of other details. That's all more than I know. I'll have to catch up."

"Why do you need to know anything? You can sit back and wait for us to sort this out."

"I could do that, but you know and I know that

there's something obvious about these women. I spoke to two of them and was about to talk to Pipes—I'm not counting the dead woman. I never heard of her. Wouldn't you want to do what you could to help solve this . . . if you were me?"

Nat frowned. "I—This isn't about me. Gray, I want you to back off. Just tell me you'll do that. Otherwise I'll have to look for a way to . . ." He let the threat trail off.

"Something's happened," Gray said. "Did someone else go missing?"

"You're messing with my case," Nat told him.

Denying it would be pointless and an obvious lie. "I'm going through some harmless motions."

"This Sidney. What did she talk to you about?"

"Not a damn thing, Nat. She said she had to get home."

Nat didn't look convinced. "So you backed right off and didn't push her? That doesn't sound like you."

"It isn't. I asked if we could talk later and she said she'd think about it. At least, that was the impression she gave."

Massaging his temples, Nat stared into Gray's eyes.

Bucky Fist arrived and clapped Nat on the shoulder. "Hey, my man," he said. Young, not more than thirty or thirty-one, stocky with a good-humored grin that showed square teeth with a big gap in the middle, Bucky wore a baseball cap turned back to front. Sandy hair showed at his sideburns and nape.

"This is Gray Fisher," Nat said.

Gray had met the man before, but he said, "Bucky," and offered his hand.

Bucky pumped his fingers in a punishing grip and sat beside Nat.

"Just heard Shirley Cooper was a maid, not a singer," he said. "She was last seen leaving work at a club. I don't know why the boyfriend didn't tell us that right off. He may not be involved but I've told him not to leave town."

Nat grunted.

"Not a singer, huh?" Gray said. "Are we relieved?" He was. So far he hadn't interviewed maids for any article.

"Ask me in a week if we still don't have someone in custody," Nat said. "The dead woman worked in a club. She could have been killed by someone who mistook her for a singer."

Gray grunted.

"So what d'you think?" Bucky asked, looking from Gray to Nat. "I guess it could be true. But the kid could also be making the whole thing up."

"What kid?" Gray said.

"I haven't told him about that yet," Nat said.

Bucky nodded. "A kid called down at the big house for Nat. A boy. I talked to him. He said he'd been told to let us know they didn't like you interfering at Scully's, Gray. The kid sounded scared."

"Any idea who 'they' are?" Gray asked. This was coming from nowhere.

"Nope. He didn't say it straight out, but he could be in danger. Someone doesn't want you poking around in this case."

That didn't make Gray feel bad. "I'm getting under their skin so I must be doing something right. Are you sure it was a kid who called?"

"He more or less said you could get him hurt if you don't quit meddling in this case," Nat said. "He said he's called Alan and he's Amber Lee's boy. We checked. Amber may have a son, but no one seems to know where we'd find him."

Gray thought he saw a trap, or at least got a whiff of one. Amber hadn't mentioned a kid to him and he thought she would have. But he hadn't finished interviewing her yet.

His cell hummed in his pocket and he leaned away to work it out of a jeans pocket.

Any way he looked at it, Danny was behind contacting Nat and trying to pull Gray away from the case.

"Who's that?" Nat said.

While the phone buzzed a second time, Gray stared at his old friend. "Do I ask you about your telephone calls?"

Nat shrugged. "Always worth a try. I could catch you off guard."

Gray didn't recognize the incoming number. When he clicked on and answered, the line went dead.

12

"Marley," Sykes hissed into her ear. "Pretend you're with us, will you?"

With Winnie on her lap and still in her nightie and robe with a work smock over the top, she sat in one of Uncle Pascal's green suede wing chairs. Sykes crouched beside her, wickedly handsome as ever in a white poet's shirt, dark jeans and with his feet bare. "Yeah," she muttered, but her mind wandered just the same.

Uncle Pascal had convened this meeting of all Millets present in New Orleans. Ten a.m. sharp. Marley was there in body, but whichever way her thoughts strayed, they found their way to Gray Fisher, Amber Lee and Liza Soaper.

And why hadn't she, Marley, been able to stay and rescue the woman she had seen earlier that morning? A new twist occurred to her; there could be a limit on how long she could be away from her body.

This time the decision to terminate the trip had been made for her.

Frantic to reach the woman again, as soon as Marley had reentered her body, she attempted to travel back through the funnel. With her energy sapped, she had been powerless and the tunnel disappeared. She could not summon it up again.

"A discussion about the Mentor is overdue,"

Uncle Pascal said. "You've all lulled me into thinking I didn't need to remind you. I was wrong."

Marley looked hard at Sykes, who rolled his eyes, then at Willow who sank deeper into another of Uncle's green chairs and wouldn't meet anyone's glance. She wore a green Mean 'n Green Maids T-shirt—standard issue to all those who worked for her maid service—over white crop pants. Her white tennis shoes had thick green soles and green laces.

"Before we get into reminders about our family pledges," Uncle said, "I must tell you how disappointed you've made me, Marley. I don't know everything you got up to last night, but I will. Sykes will help me make sure of that."

Marley met Sykes's blue eyes again and sent him a secret message. *"Talk to me before you talk to him."*

Sykes turned on his impassive face and just as she thought he would ignore her, she got the response. *"Don't forget the Tally Book. Be thinking about what you'll do to repay me for keeping my mouth shut."* The Tally Book was imaginary, a childhood threat they had against each other.

"What have you already told him?"

"Nothing important," Sykes said.

A corner of Willow's mouth hooked upward, but flattened out quickly. Not quickly enough for Marley to have missed it. Who knew how powerful Willow might or might not be? She adhered so tightly to her story about not believing the Millets were different from any other family that she had almost convinced the rest of them she was nothing more—or less—than human. To various degrees, the Millets were in contact with several other psychic families. These people were also "normal" according to Willow.

Marley was almost sure her younger sister was picking up at least hints of the channels opening and closing between Marley and Sykes. If so, little Willow was a good deal more than human, even though it wouldn't be possible for her to actually intercept conversation unless invited.

The biggest puzzle for Willow's relatives was the reason for her apparent determination not to accept who and what she was—or probably was. There had been a relationship with Benedict Fortune, the eldest son of one of those families with whom they shared similarities and it had ended badly. Marley had never been quite sure why, and Willow wouldn't discuss Ben. There was no doubt that she and Ben had appeared very much in love.

From the closed expression on Willow's face, nothing was about to change her attitude soon.

Today had dawned with the promise of heat, and that promise had been kept. The overhead fans in Uncle's clubby quarters above the shop did little more than move hot air around. Tired, desperate to be on her way, Marley had groaned when Uncle

Pascal's summons arrived. For her it had come while she was in her workroom and barely conscious after her unceremonious reentry from her travels.

Sometimes Uncle Pascal's dark moods were immovable. This morning his frown was formidable and he kept sinking into long silences.

His shaved head shone. Marley knew the family story about how he had cut off his mahogany red curls. At that time he told his brother Antoine—her father—that he chose to have "no hair color at all if it means you're going to stick me with your offspring and the care of this impossible family." That had been when the final decision about Sykes had been made; a dark-haired male could not be entrusted with the Millets' fate, not when he might well bring disaster on the family.

Sykes, so the story went, had laughed too much when he insisted he didn't care that he was being cast out of his family position. He had said he wouldn't have anything to do with such responsibilities anyway. Sykes, still a teenager at the time, had announced that he would spend his life honing skills none of the rest of them could hope to share. He'd been right. In addition to being an impressive psychic power, he sculpted figures from lumps of stone and rarely finished a piece without more than one buyer demanding to be the owner.

But although they made light of their parents' decision to leave New Orleans (and Papa's rightful place as head of the family) and search for answers about the family curse, Marley, Sykes and their sisters doubted just how hard Antoine and Leandra Millet were looking—and they were quietly saddened by the willing defection of the older Millets.

"Willow," Uncle Pascal said, "you will have to put in more work improving yourself. It's time you got over this silly *business* nonsense. You know you have special gifts and ignoring them won't make them go away. It will make them sag a bit. Think of them as flabby and unreliable. A quick-minded, quick-moving, fit young thing like you shouldn't want to be associated with anything *flabby and unreliable.*" His voice didn't rise, but he emphasized each word.

"I don't know what you're talking about," Willow said. "No, I don't know at all and don't want to."

"Then you can sit there and I'll tell you."

Willow's beeper went off. She unhooked it from her waist and took a look. "Time's up," she said. "I've got a business to run."

"Business?" Uncle Pascal echoed ominously.

Willow got up, yawned and stretched, then let her arms fall heavily. "You're all an embarrassment with your gifts and powers garbage. I don't know why you hauled me in here to watch you play games. G'bye."

"Willow," Uncle Pascal said, and the warning was implicit.

She smiled and stood on tiptoe to kiss his chin. Her hair, currently the reddest in the clan, bounced.

"Let her go," Sykes said although Willow had already opened the door to the flat.

The door closed again and Uncle Pascal threw up his hands. "She's living a lie. Eventually something will happen and she'll have to face up to what she really is. What a terrible shock that could be."

"I know," Marley said. "When I'm not feeling wobbly I worry about her." She let her eyes close and knew it was useless to hope Uncle Pascal and Sykes hadn't noticed what she'd just said.

"Wobbly?" Uncle said on cue. "Yes, yes, of course that's how you feel and it's because you've strayed from the Mentor. You must correct yourself at once."

Marley sighed at the imperious tone of voice. Whether Uncle Pascal liked it or not, he had possessed the qualities needed to head the family after what was now referred to as Papa's "abdication."

In addition to having a strong mind, Uncle Pascal lifted weights and it showed. Even in the green robe—he favored green a good deal—he wore over workout gear, his muscles were impressive.

All the Millets were good-looking, or so Marley had been told often enough, and her uncle was no exception. Anyone who didn't know he dealt in obscure objets d'art would never associate him with anything other than a very physical occupation.

"I've heard from Antoine and Leandra," he said abruptly. The grim set of his mouth warned that he had not learned anything that pleased him. "Apparently Alex and Riley are enjoying their stay in London."

Sykes stood. "What does that mean?"

"Just what I said. My brother and his wife—your parents whom you only see if you follow them around the world—are having a charming visit with your sisters."

Marley got to her feet, as well, tipping Winnie to the floor, but quickly sat again. She was light-headed.

"Look at you," Uncle Pascal said to her. "You're worn out. You've been experimenting with something again and it's against the rules unless you make sure I'm informed."

That was only partly true. She had a right to use her powers without telling anyone, Uncle Pascal included, unless she was certain she needed help. As long as Marley thought she could manage alone, she would do so.

"The Mentor means for us to rely on one another," Uncle Pascal said.

"Am I the only one who's been wondering about the Mentor lately?" Sykes said. "Seems a long time since anyone has pointed out that we're no closer to finding out if there ever was an actual Mentor."

"The Millet family Mentor is a fact," Uncle Pascal said flatly. "What we don't know is whether the term refers only to the code of honor we live by, or if there was once a being the family referred to by that name."

"And our parents have contacted you to say they're still no closer to finding out the truth?" Sykes said. "You didn't have to bring us here to say that."

Uncle paused and they listened to the ticking of a rare French industrial clock in the form of a fishing boat. Uncle Pascal spared a smile for the shimmering gilt piece before he responded. "Eighteen-eighty," he said of the clock. He made a habit of stating details of the treasures that filled his flat. "You're right, Sykes. I have more on my mind but I choose to start with just how little progress your parents have made."

"Are we surprised?" Sykes said. Apparently he didn't care how disrespectful he was. "I've got a thought for you. What if this Mentor of ours still *is?* What if he or she—or it—is still lurking around the planet and the parents do dig it up one day? That would be by accident, of course, but it might happen."

"I hope it does exist," Marley said. She needed chocolate. "I've got questions that need answers and so do you."

"So do I," Uncle Pascal added. "When I agreed to take over the reins for Antoine, I didn't expect it

142

to be for twenty years! He was supposed to come back with answers and help figure out where we go from here. Someone has to carry on after my generation."

"Yes," Marley said, looking pointedly at Sykes. "We've got to get over our hang-ups. This old tale about a curse is crazy. A dark-haired male Millet can't take his place as head of the family? Good grief, we still say head of the family, as if we were in the middle ages."

"Our problem was around then, too," Uncle Pascal said. "Do you question your powers, Marley?"

She wrinkled her nose. "Of course not."

"That's what I thought. So why question the curse unless you have some proof? It's dangerous."

"Let's move on," Marley said. "Someone has to run the business. Let's talk in twenty-first-century terms. And since the Millets remain stuck on a male heir, and you don't want to keep doing the job, Uncle, then either Papa should come back or Sykes must take over."

"Your father can't return to his former position," Uncle Pascal said, his mouth pursed. "Once he stepped down that was it for him. I'm a sort of stand-in till we come up with the next in line."

"You may be standing-in till your legs fall off, then," Sykes said with a smirk. "As Marley points out, according to the curse, a dark-haired Millet running things means disaster, and we wouldn't want that."

"Only if you marry." This time Uncle Pascal did shout. "Which you show no signs of doing."

Winnie made sounds like a crying piglet and Marley whispered, "Hush."

"We don't know what I may do one day," Sykes said. "You can't take the risk of trying to leave things with me."

Marley was grateful that her brother didn't grin when he said that. He often announced that his parents' dysfunctional marriage was a warning and he intended to stay single.

"Have you met someone?" Uncle asked.

"I meet lots of people," Sykes said. "And I could meet a woman I want to . . . It could happen that I find a woman I really like one day."

Marley had been holding her breath, hoping Sykes would say the *B* word. She should have known better. "Someone to bond with," she prompted, energized by her own daring.

Sykes gave her a withering look. "If I ever feel the slightest hint of a bonding, *you* will be the last to know." He spread his broad artist's hands and looked at the ceiling. "*Bonding.* Now we're really heading into the weeds with all this. It isn't as if I live like a monk, and I've yet to feel shivers up my spine."

What he meant was that as long as there was no bonding between him and a woman, a casual relationship worked just fine for him. "Is there someone now?" Marley asked. She made big eyes at Sykes.

He shook his head as if weary and didn't answer.

Uncle Pascal lost interest in the exchange and paced again. "I want to spend more time training," he said. "And collecting. I'm sick of sending someone else after rare finds when I've hunted them down. It annoys me more all the time. I want to be free to travel the world myself."

"We can't solve that here and now," Sykes said. "Did you want to talk about something else?"

Marley felt sorry for their uncle, but she saw Sykes's point of view. Why would he want to give up total freedom to watch over the Millet fortune—whatever that consisted of these days.

"The code," Uncle Pascal said, his chin jutting fiercely. "It's simple enough, but I'm not sure how careful everyone's being about the most important rules. First—Only use your powers for good."

Marley nodded and saw Sykes do the same.

"Second—Never invade another family member's mind without an invitation," Uncle continued. "If you begin to intercept accidentally, leave."

She didn't remind him he'd come close to doing that last night. True, he had made a tentative approach at first and waited for her to acknowledge him, but finding her like that, remotely, had been over the top, even if he had been worried about her. But she took some comfort in knowing he'd had to go to Sykes for help and he wouldn't make a habit of that.

"Three—Don't act alone if you could be in danger."

That was the rule he wanted to skewer her with. She didn't look at him.

"Marley?" Uncle said. "What have you been up to? Why were you with someone who frightened you last night?"

"He didn't," she told him promptly. In fact, Gray had terrified her. She would never forget the shock of seeing those pale marks on his face and remembering at once the man she'd seen in the unknown place.

"Isn't there another rule about telling each other the truth?"

Marley ignored Sykes's interference.

Uncle Pascal stopped in front of her and peered down. "I know what I felt and it was fear. Explain yourself."

For the good of a serious cause she would not betray the trust Belle had placed in her. "I don't get out enough," she said. "Last night I went to find some good jazz and ran into someone I know."

"That's a stretch," Sykes signaled.

"It takes a stretcher to know a stretcher," she told him.

"But you weren't comfortable," Uncle Pascal said. His tone eased and he became the concerned surrogate dad he'd been to her for years. "You know I worry about all of you, especially you girls. This hulk can take care of himself." He gave Sykes's shoulder a glancing punch.

"What is going on with you?" Sykes asked Marley. *"You were edgy with your friend Gray. You're into him, though."*

"You're imagining things. I can handle it."

"Would you ask me to come if you needed to?"

She glanced at him and felt Uncle Pascal grow edgy.

"Later," Sykes said. *"Uncle's feeling left out."*

"Marley?" Uncle Pascal was still waiting for her answer.

"I am dealing with something unusual," she admitted. Truth between them was their accepted strength as a family. "I want to continue on alone, but I promise I'll ask for help if I have to."

Uncle Pascal turned to Sykes. "You were there. What did you think?"

"I wasn't there long," Sykes said, his blue eyes guileless. "Marley knows she shouldn't take stupid risks."

Marley's brother looked at her and she caught her breath. She had forgotten the man she'd seen right before she traveled, completely forgotten him. And now she had only the faintest recollection of his brief appearance. She tried to recall the sound of his voice but couldn't. But had he been like an older version of Sykes?

"Are you being careful, Marley?" Uncle Pascal asked.

She nodded vaguely. Who was the man and why had he been there?

A jarring ring intervened. Uncle Pascal had one of the first dial telephones, a 1919 version he liked to call "a useless invention." He did laugh at himself over that.

"Who?" he said into the mouthpiece. "Do I know you?"

Marley accepted Winnie onto her lap again. Sykes swayed, a sure sign he was anxious to be off.

Uncle Pascal grunted into the phone and signaled to Marley. "For you," he said.

This time she hauled her dog under one arm and went to take the instrument. "Hi."

"You called?"

She knew Gray's voice. And she had called him while she'd still been groggy and flaked out in her workroom, but she'd hung up before he could answer. When she punched in his number she had actually wanted to ask him to come at once so she could tell him what had just happened. She barely stopped herself from reaching out to him for help. Her reason unnerved her; she had a hunch he was an okay guy. Just thinking the word *hunch* gave her chills. The Millets didn't have hunches, they had clear insights. Nothing was clear about Mr. Disappearing Scar Face.

"You called me," Gray said, prompting her.

"That was a mistake."

"Too late," he said and didn't sound as if he were joking. "Your sister said you were upstairs with some of your family members. She said I could wait for you down here in the shop."

13

Gray heard Marley coming before he saw her, or rather he heard her dog snuffling, and its nails clicking on old oak stair treads.

Marley's slim feet and ankles, and her knees appeared, then the rest of her followed rapidly. She wore a paint-daubed blue denim smock buttoned to the neck. Other clothes bunched underneath. One look at her face and he was glad the sister who let him in had locked the door behind her again. He would rather not be interrupted at the moment.

"How did you get in here?" Marley asked. "We're not open."

"A gorgeous redhead let me in," he said.

She bared her teeth and muttered, *"Willow,"* in a threatening tone. "She's never careful enough."

Gray wanted to move on. "Have you been to bed?" he said. "You don't look good."

She didn't even smile at his gaffe. "Yeah, I know. Not that it's any of your business."

"True," he said, jerking his head back as if she'd struck him. "You're in a great mood, too."

Marley gave him an uncomfortably direct look. She came closer, then closer. Without another word, she came within kissing range although he was damn certain that wasn't on her mind.

Bucking the urge to ask what she was staring at, Gray held still. While she peered at him, he took advantage of getting up close with her.

When it came to women, he considered himself an animal-magnetism type. Plenty of all the good female stuff appealed to him—long legs, big eyes, soft mouths of the lips-to-lips touchable kind. This woman bedeviled him. The big, green eyes sucked him in and he'd really like the full mouth to suck him in. He'd seen her legs and, considering her lack of height, they were long and meant to be looked at. Marley had very nice breasts and yesterday he'd seen that she had curvy hips, but she was small.

What did you call it when a female made a man want to be careful with her, and have hot, sweaty sex with her at the same time? Unhinged was the word that came to mind.

His heart was pounding and he had an inconvenient stirring. Inconvenient and intoxicating. He was grateful her interest was in his face, not in his lower regions—although the rogue side of him wanted to see her reaction.

The examination had gone on too long for his health. "What?" he said and could not believe it when his voice cracked. "Why are you looking at me like that?"

Marley just about leaped back a step, and another. "I want you out of here," she said, turning red. "Go on. Leave. I don't know what you're up to, but I don't like it. Out."

He barely managed to keep his hands from his face to check for lumps, bumps or missing bits. "You were really staring. Come on. Have pity on a man and let me in on the secret."

"There isn't one." She drew herself up, but rather than make her look fierce, she seemed embarrassed. "I'll see you out."

Instead he sat on a chair with a square seat, arms that joined at one corner, and no back unless you sat sideways against one of the arms. Damned uncomfortable it was, too, but he was making a point.

"That's a valuable chair," she said. "You're not supposed to touch things like that . . . not like *that*."

"I can't imagine wanting to get anywhere near it," he said, getting up. "It looks like a mistake and it's damned uncomfortable."

She puffed and said, "It's a sword chair for a gentleman wearing a sword. Not that you care. This isn't the best time."

"You bet it's not," he told her. "Our mutual friend Detective Archer hauled me out of bed before six this morning and you know I hadn't been there long enough."

Apparently the "don't touch" rules didn't apply to the dog. Wagging her tail, and her entire body with it, Winnie wiggled to jump onto one of those fainting couches. This one was covered with some faded gold brocade Gray wouldn't want draped over a birdcage—not that he had a bird. He looked pointedly at the dog. Marley smiled indulgently at her pet.

"I thought you'd like to know what Nat Archer had to tell me?" Gray said.

As if only just waking up, Marley blinked rapidly, started to stretch but changed her mind when the smock rose higher on her thighs. She gave him a panicky look. "Not here," she said, glancing up the stairs. "I'll call you later, okay?"

"And hang up like you did the first time? We need each other. Get used to it." He checked out the frilled pink material poking from the hem of her smock. "Did you come right down from bed? I didn't mean to wake you up."

"You've got to leave," Marley said.

"There's nothing about me that's going to upset anyone," he said.

Her hair looked wild . . . and appealing. And her sleepy, half-lidded green eyes were pure, sexy come-on, not that she could mean to send him that kind of impression, not given the way she was talking to him.

"Seriously," he continued. "I think you're telling the truth. You know something useful about what's going on in this town and I want to help you follow it up."

"You want to pick my brains," she said shortly. "I don't know if I should trust you at all and you can't blame me for thinking that."

He thought for a moment. "No, I can't. But what other choices do you have, unless you're planning to forget these desperate women you supposedly saw? *Missing* women. Don't you feel responsible?"

Whatever she thought about his question didn't make her happy. She bit into her bottom lip, then said, "I can get someone down here to help me anytime I want to," and the way she said it sounded believable. "Come with me. But remember what I've just told you. Someone will come if I need them."

From that he was to take it that if he put a foot wrong with her, all hell would break loose? He started toward her. "Should I bring your dog?"

"Don't touch Winnie," she said, her eyes narrowed. "She'll do her own thing."

Sure enough, the instant Marley turned to walk back upstairs, Winnie followed, bustling past Gray and eventually leading the way for Marley, as well.

On the third-floor landing, a small recess held a door with stained-glass panels. Marley used an old-fashioned key on the lock then pushed the door open. "Come in," she said without looking back at him. "Please don't touch anything. My projects are

153

piece and washed it down with whatever was in a glass on the table.

"Mmm," she mumbled, part of another praline already in her mouth. She put her shooting chair in reverse again, gave him the box of pralines and returned to the cupboard. More rustling followed.

"Here you are." She exchanged boxes with him and resumed her seat. "Those are chocolate-covered coffee beans and they pack a wallop. They'll keep your eyes open for a week."

Gray doubted that, but smiled at her and chomped some of the beans. Maybe she was right—he did begin to feel a slight buzz. Or was that from the headiness of being alone with Marley Millet? He had difficulty not staring at her—especially at her legs, which were even more displayed now that she was sitting.

He studied a bean between finger and thumb. "We've both got the same addiction, y'know," he said, waiving at the box of chocolates. "It's all about caffeine."

"There are different ways to get it," she said, smiling, turning her expression into pure charm. "Chocolate is queen. Don't argue, just take it from me. Now, what did the detective say?"

His plan had been to say just enough about the meeting at Ambrose's to get her talking about what she thought she knew. "Why don't we try to stay focused," he said.

"Meaning?"

"Tell me more about what you actually . . . saw."

She sighed and rested her head against the back of the chair. "I already told you. Liza and Amber. In a place I can't locate."

She chewed her bottom lip again and this time it suggested she had more on her mind than she was saying and it worried her.

"Shirley Cooper wasn't a singer," he said. "She worked as a maid at a club."

"So she probably has nothing to do with Liza and Amber," she said.

He wanted to be sure of that, but wasn't, not entirely. "She could." It would make him feel less of a suspect if the three were connected. Damn, he didn't want to think about the other two being dead.

"Do they have any suspects in Shirley's killing?"

He shrugged. "Sounds like her boyfriend has been told not to leave town, but that doesn't mean much."

She reached for the glass again. When she drank, her sleeve slipped up her forearm. Glaring red welts showed on the inside of her wrist.

"Those are nasty," he said.

Marley looked blank.

He turned over the hand that rested on her thigh. More wide scrapes disappeared beneath her cuff.

"What?" She seemed confused.

He was confused. "How did you do this?" Where he touched her, his fingers throbbed faintly.

157

"Don't you know you've scratched yourself badly?" he said. Gently, he ran his hand along her arm. Last night he'd put his hands on hers to show her he was cold. As soon as he did it he wondered why he felt compelled to touch her, and why he didn't pull back right then. Instead of letting go, he had held tighter and felt tingling, but nothing like what he experienced now.

The sensation quickly became intense, close to pain, like the heavy pulse of arousal when he was close to a climax.

"These must hurt you," he said, and the huskiness in his voice was obvious, even to him.

The color of Marley's eyes changed through shades of green, growing darker. He leaned closer, and he thought she moved nearer to him.

"They're nothing," she said, pulling away. She tugged her sleeves down, but her face had turned pale.

Gray took a deep, calming breath. "Did you clean them?" he asked.

As quickly as she'd paled, Marley's face glowed red. He recalled that redheads blushed easily. She didn't answer him and she probably wished he would forget what he had seen.

Could someone have deliberately hurt her? Women often denied abuse. He'd seen enough of that as a cop.

In one corner, a deep stone sink stood on metal legs. "Why don't we wash those?" he said.

Marley sat quite still. "They're all right. I don't think the skin's broken."

He hopped to his feet and found the clean handkerchief he carried out of habit. There was only cold water. Sticking his head under the faucet sounded like a good idea, but he doubted Marley would be impressed. He soaked the cloth and returned to her. When she didn't move, he took hold of her right wrist and dabbed the wounds.

No blood came off on the cloth. He repeated the process with the other wrist with the same result— no blood. Through his thin linen handkerchief he could feel the swollen welts.

"Thank you," she said when he finally finished. "I'd forgot. I slipped in the courtyard."

Gray didn't believe her and he wanted a closer look at her arms. She wasn't going to let that happen. He didn't recall seeing the same type of marks before.

The dog whined and Marley patted her lap. Winnie jumped up. A grown man shouldn't envy a dog, but Gray just might. Having Marley stroke him all over could be heaven.

He got an instant, erotic reflex.

"I'm considering trying to do remote drawing," she said quietly. "They use it a lot in law enforcement."

He wanted to know who "they" were, but kept his mouth shut, hoping she'd continue. No one he knew had ever used a psychic on a case—with or

159

without remote drawing. That didn't mean it hadn't happened.

The faraway expression on Marley's features seemed to mean she'd as good as forgotten he was there.

Since last night his hands had warmed up, but the quivering he still felt along his tendons wasn't normal. A prickling sensation, a shooting thrill, hit hard enough to wind him. Objects around him grew fuzzy at the edges. He wondered if he could be ill, but no, this wasn't any illness, or not the kind most people thought of.

She was aware of him again, piercingly intent on his face. What was she thinking? He couldn't unlock his gaze from hers. She stared inside him— or he felt she could? Did she know what he was thinking? An impulse to make his mind a blank didn't work. Instead he got a vivid image of her holding up her arms, untouched arms. In his mind, she screamed and drew them back. There were the marks again.

He had no idea why he would imagine that.

"Talk to me more about Detective Archer," she said. "You were going to."

All he sensed now was that she wanted to change the subject.

"I think it was all about warning me off," Gray said. "He knew I was at Scully's last night. With you."

She blinked slowly, like someone as tired as she

obviously was. "Does that mean Danny called him? I didn't believe him when he said he would."

"I'm not sure. But someone did," he said.

"Who?"

Nat hadn't told him to keep quiet, but then discretion was taken for granted. But if he wanted something from her, he'd have to gain her confidence. Shared information could help.

"I hope you won't say anything about this. It was a child who called. A boy who said the people he was with would make him suffer if I didn't back off asking questions about . . . this case."

Her study of him lasted seconds too long. "About Amber," she said. "That's what you almost said. Does the boy belong to Amber? Does she have a son? Was it him?"

She was telling him, not asking him. He was certain she already knew Amber had a kid. "Ask Nat," he told her, and she nodded as if he had agreed with her "guesses."

"I've got to go back there," she said.

"Explain what you're talking about."

Marley looked past him and he swiveled around. The crowded workbench was the only thing between him and a wall.

"I have to be alone."

"So you can try to see what you said you saw before?" he asked. "I don't get any of it."

"No." Her eyes widened and he could have sworn she was listening closely for something.

"I've never looked for them before. They come to me when they want to."

"Who?" He wanted to go with her wherever she was going, and to hear what she heard.

Flickering overhead drew his attention to the ceiling. Green, glowing streaks wavered there. Blue mixed with the green and he couldn't look away.

His cell phone vibrated in one of his pockets. Vaguely, he wondered how long ago that had started.

"Answer your phone," Marley said.

"How—" Instinctively he knew it was best not to ask her how she knew his phone was vibrating. He pulled it out and answered. "Yes." The readout showed the Caged Bird, a jazz club he liked a lot.

Bernie Bois answered and his message was short, and sweet to Gray's ears. "Thanks," he said. "I'll be around later."

Marley gathered her hair at the nape of her neck. "You feel good," she said to him. "It's making you smile."

"Remember Pipes Dupuis?" he asked.

She frowned. "Oh, of course. She's the other missing singer."

"Not anymore," he told her. "She sings at the Caged Bird and she just showed up there."

14

Just as with Scully's, Marley didn't recall seeing the Caged Bird before. She didn't care much for either place.

In the center of the club there was an oversize gilded cage suspended five or so feet from the floor by a thick pole threaded, top to bottom, through its middle. Marley could only think of one purpose for the contraption.

"This is a guy place," she said. "Women dance in there."

"What makes you think that?" Gray asked.

She stood on tiptoe to get a slightly better look at the cage, then took in the rest of the Caged Bird. A fresh thought amused her. "You mean men pole-dance in that thing, and that one over there?" The gilded showcase had a twin on the far side of a circular bar in the middle of a room resembling a large padded cell. Padded with quilted parrots, their once brilliant colors faded by dust and years.

"Men?" Gray screwed up his eyes to peer at her as if she was manic.

"Might be cool," she said. "I've never seen pole dancing so I'm curious."

"You want to see men pole dancing?"

She let it go. "If you thumped the wall, you'd choke on the dust," Marley said, pinching her nose. "And it stinks of beer."

"That is the aroma of a fine drinking and jazz establishment, ma'am." Gray arched his brows and grinned. "This is a great old club. And I like it here, so watch it."

Marley was more intent on watching him, on watching his face to be precise. She had studied it from every angle since he showed up at the shop. There was no sign of a scar that she could find.

In her workroom she had come close to telling him about her most recent journey. The interruption from this place was a good thing since she wasn't sure who to trust yet.

She had a hunch that he was one of the white hats, the man a woman could trust. Not finding an evil-looking white scar running from cheek to jowl and bisecting his mouth on the way didn't hurt her new faith in hunches.

"There's no one here," she told him.

"So there isn't," he said.

"Why are we here then?" Her heart gave a big thump. "It feels creepy. This kind of place doesn't open in the middle of the day."

"Baby, in N'awlins you can find this kind of club open any time of day."

"Baby?" He had to be kidding. "Are you playing some game with me, or just passing the time?"

He slid his hands into his pockets. "I didn't invite you to come, Marley. Like you say, the place is empty, but I'm patient so I'll wait for the guy who said Pipes Dupuis was here."

Gray had not invited her, but he did wait while she went back to her flat and dressed. His tone stung. "I'm not here because I can't live without your company," she said shortly. "Just like you, I need leads and I'm hoping to get some here." She stopped herself from voicing the panicky way in which she felt time running out.

"Okay," he said. His smile softened her annoyance. "Sorry."

Hot as it was, she'd put on a black T-shirt with tight, long sleeves. She didn't want him grilling her about the frightening marks on her wrists again. He'd noticed them before she had.

"Aren't you hot in that shirt?" he said.

Marley gritted her teeth. One more time, her thoughts and what he said appeared related.

"Black wasn't the best choice," she admitted of the shirt.

"It suits you."

That was not anything she expected him to say, but it brought a flush of pleasure. She swallowed and made a visual journey to the ceiling with the nearest brass pole.

He hummed.

Marley felt him studying her. He made her aware of her body. And aware that Gray enjoyed what he saw.

"Listen," she said. "Every minute that passes

makes me more scared for Liza and Amber. I really want Pipes to show here. She could know something useful."

"I hope she does," Gray said. Muscles in his jaw tensed. "I'm thinking Bernie, the manager, contacted the police to tell them she's alive and kicking. Maybe they already came and picked her up. They'll have questions for her."

"If she knows something it could make all the difference," she said. "For both of us."

He gave her a speculative look.

"The front doors of this place are wide-open," Marley said. "But the lights aren't really on, are they? Or is it always gloomy like this?"

Gray raised a brow. "You don't like a lot of light, remember?"

"In my own space," she told him. She caught hold of his arm. "Are you taking any of this seriously? I thought all you wanted was to find Liza and Amber, but—"

"You can't know how badly I want that," he said, cutting her off. "But it isn't all I want."

The corners of his eyes crinkled. A flinch? Or a wince? Then he smiled faintly and she wasn't sure, but he had a lot on his mind and he wasn't in a hurry to share it with her.

"I get it," she said, although she didn't really. "This is supposed to be a one-way street. I put myself on the line and tell you whatever I can. You give me nothing in return. Forget it. I've got problems of my own to solve."

"I don't want you to put yourself on the line." The smile was gone as if it had never touched his lips. "We're both on edge. If Pipes isn't here, she's probably with the police. We'll give her a few more minutes, then move on. Either we'll take another shot at comparing what I know and what you think you do, or we won't. I'm game but it's up to you."

"What you know and what I *think* I know?"

He put a hand over hers on his arm. "I didn't mean it that way."

Marley caught a breath. His eyes really were the color of whiskey and right now all they were seeing was her. Gray's lips parted. He pulled air in slowly through his nose and kept on looking at her.

"I had a dream early this morning so I traveled back." The words tumbled out. "It was about something that happened to me a couple of weeks ago. I got a message in a dream. I didn't want to travel to that place where I saw Liza and Amber again. I had to. That's what the message was about."

"Do you always believe dreams?"

"No." She couldn't help being defensive. "But this was different."

"So you did whatever you say you do and went—wherever." His fingers curled around hers, crushing them together. He pressed them against his arm.

"I went," she agreed.

A current flowed between them, from hand to hand, and from his arm to her hand. Not a tremor. An exchange of energy.

"What did you see?" he asked very quietly.

"A woman lying on her face." Without knowing why, she wanted him to believe her. "She was on top of a lot of silk pillows."

"Was it in that other place again? With the cold storage room."

He startled her. "Cold storage room? I don't know for sure if that's what I saw the other times. There was a room with cold fog."

His features were hard, completely stark, except for his eyes. Gray's eyes were vividly alive and filled with questions.

"Couldn't that have been a cold storage room?" he asked. "A place for keeping things . . . cold?"

She shivered involuntarily. "I didn't see it this time."

"You mean you went to a different place and saw a woman? Was it Amber or Liza?"

"It seemed . . . I think I went to the same place and it looked different. Or maybe the light was different. I don't know who she was—she was sleeping."

Gray's grip tightened. "You're sure she was sleeping?"

Marley wasn't sure, couldn't be. "I hope she was."

He looked away. "Did your arms get hurt while you were . . . traveling?"

For an instant she was back there, her skin connecting to that foul, spined thing.

"What is it?" Gray said.

"Stop it," she said and startled herself by giving him a push. He stood fast, but she staggered. "I don't like it here. And I don't want to talk to you anymore."

"You're not going to have a choice," he said, his voice even and firm. "We're going to be together. I feel it."

Flight was her first impulse. Her second was to put a little distance between them and hold her ground. "You sound strange," she told him. "Do you know that?"

"Nothing strange about me," he said, the easy smile tipping up his mouth again. "Although I could be a bit punchy."

Intuition made her almost certain Gray was either a psychic, or becoming one. And if he was turning into a psychic she thought it was happening because he was around her. Similar cases were documented, but she hadn't encountered one before.

Another overhead light came on, this one behind a small dais where empty mike stands, an upright piano and two high stools kept company.

A door opened in a parrot-padded wall and a woman came through with a tall man behind her.

"Is this them?" Marley whispered.

When Gray didn't answer, she glanced at him and realized he hadn't moved, or turned toward the light. He still stared at her as if he would find the answer to anything that bugged him if he only studied her long enough.

"Gray Fisher!" the tall, thin man hollered. The thick walls muffled his voice. "Here we are."

"No kidding," Marley murmured.

"Careful what you say." Gray had snapped to life and he gave her a warning nod. "Pipes is a jumpy one."

I'm getting to be jumpy myself. "Gotcha," she said. "You can rely on me."

"Hey, Bernie," Gray said. "Is that you, Pipes?"

The woman said something but Marley didn't hear what.

"We were just attendin' to some business in the office," Bernie said. "I want this songbird of ours back at work. When she isn't here, we don't do so well."

Blonde and nicely made, Pipes hung her head and the shiny, straight hair fell forward to conceal her face.

Bernie chuckled. "She's still a shy one," he said. His accent was Cajun, softly rounded on the edges and impossible not to like. "Best voice in N'awlins, this one." He said this to Marley.

"I hope I get to hear you sing," Marley said to Pipes.

"Uh-huh." Shaking her hair back, Pipes set her head on one side and looked out from long bangs. "The show's not till nine."

A pretty, dark-eyed woman, she had an emptiness about her. Marley wondered if she could be high on something—which wouldn't be so unusual.

"Good to see you," Gray said. "You haven't forgotten we've got a date for an interview, have you?"

Pipes shook her head.

"You were reported missing," he persisted. "How did that happen?"

She drew up her shoulders. "They don't listen. The band. I said I was goin' to be gone awhile. Went to visit the folks a few days."

"Are you in the band?" Marley asked Bernie politely.

"Nah," he said. "I'm the manager around here."

"Has someone let the police know you're okay?" Gray asked.

Pipes's eyes got bigger. "I don't know."

In other words, she hadn't done it herself.

"How come you didn't call them as soon as you saw yourself on the news?" Gray said.

"I don't watch the news," Pipes said. "Bernie said they thought I was gone."

"I'll give the police a call for you," Gray said.

"Why?" Pipes said. "I'm back now."

"There are people out looking for you," Gray

said. He gave Marley an uncomfortably long sideways look—like he was trying to send her a message.

"Pipes took her little girl to stay with her folks,"
Bernie said. "She didn't know about the murder
case till I told her."

Marley heard the conversation, but there were
more important things to deal with. She was getting a not very subtle battering at her mind.
Someone was trying to make contact. It had to be
Gray.

Effortlessly, she turned back his probing signals,
but before she disengaged completely, she touched
an image that held her. An image in his mind. It
belonged to him because he was the one seeing
bright colors and, for a brief moment, black hair
flowing over silk pillows.

Marley cut herself off from him. The only place
he could have gotten such a picture was from her
and she didn't like what that could mean. Only a
rogue telepathic power on the hunt would break in
and poach an experience that didn't belong to him.
Unless he was invited, or wandered in by accident.

Or unless he was shown the way.

"Marley?" Gray said.

"Yes." She frowned at him.

There could be circumstances when one psychic
actually allowed another to enter their private
world. The circumstances weren't anything
Marley was ready for. When the joining happened

between a male and a female subject, it was usually a sign of potent sexual desire.

"I don't know why you left Erin with your folks," Bernie said to Pipes. "You know she's always welcome here. She's no trouble. You're goin' to miss her and you don't sing as good as you can when you're sad."

The unspoken exchange between Marley and Gray hadn't interrupted the conversation, Marley realized. The other two hadn't noticed anything.

"I surely will miss her," Pipes said. "But a room behind a club is no place for a little girl to be for hours and hours." She sounded as if she had rehearsed the last line.

"What's her name?" Marley asked.

Pipes looked at her a while before she said, "She's Erin Dupuis. She's five and smart as can be. Erin knows how to do as she's told. You learn early when you have to. Good thing, too, bein' there's times when it's easier to just go along. You know what I mean?"

"Yes." Did she?

Gray cleared his throat. "Was it you who reported Pipes missing?" he asked Bernie.

"Yes," Bernie said, snickering. "But Pipes is here now and I have never been more relieved to see anyone."

Straightening her shoulders, Pipes gave a big smile. "Erin needs to be with the folks for a bit." She carried on as if she hadn't heard Gray and

Bernie talking. "I don't have time to teach her some things. Like eatin' the way she ought to, and speakin' right. Growin' up like a lady—stuff like that. She'll learn quick."

"Gray here wants to talk to you," Bernie Bois said. "You all sit and I'll bring a pitcher of somethin'."

Pipes went straight for a table and slipped into a bamboo chair.

"Is she okay?" Gray said once the woman was out of hearing.

Bernie shrugged. "Pipes is Pipes. Who knows how okay she is, but she sure can sing. Who's your lady here? You afraid to introduce her in case I steal her from you?"

Marley smiled at that and stuck out a hand. "Marley Millet."

He shook and held her hand. "Like the antiques people? On Royal?"

"That's us." She didn't get out so much. The idea that people who lived in this town knew her family always came as a surprise.

"That explains the hair," he said. "My-oh-my, that is *red*. Never saw redder hair than that. Is it true you all have it—red hair?"

Marley cleared her throat. "Not quite all." Bless Sykes for his black mane.

"And you are all cursed, right?"

Bernie slapped his thighs and laughed. He laughed till tears trickled from his squeezed-up eyes and ran down his bunched cheeks.

Bernie didn't stop laughing until he finally noticed he was making a lot of noise in an otherwise silent room.

He shut his mouth over all that hilarity a good deal too late for Marley's liking. She didn't have a single idea where this man would get secret information about her family, but she hated it.

"Just kidding," Bernie said. He coughed into a fist. "Lighten up, all of you. I made a little joke. You know how it is with me, Gray. Folks in the Quarter think I run all the gossip around so they tell me crazy stuff sometimes."

"Right," Gray said.

He glanced at Marley and her stomach turned. Bernie was protesting too much and too long and Gray knew it.

"Anyway," Bernie said, chuckling in little bursts. "What difference would a little curse make among friends?"

15

The approach of raised voices broke the tension. A man's loud voice and quieter responses from a woman.

"It's Danny," Marley said, so grateful for the diversion she swallowed big gulps of air.

"I was expecting Nat Archer," Gray told her. "Stay cool."

As if she wasn't already working on that.

Sidney, the female singer from Scully's, was with Danny and he wasn't making any secret about how mad he was at her. She glided ahead into the bar and he strode to keep up with her.

"It's a lousy idea, I'm tellin' you," he shouted. "And it's wrong. Why are you in such a goddamn hurry to move on? You think Amber's dead, don't you?"

"No," Sidney said clearly.

Danny grabbed and swung her to face him. "Liar," he said. "Off with the old and on with the new. That's the kind of friend you are. She'll not thank you for it when she comes back."

"Ah, hell," Gray muttered. "Angry people never make any sense. I need cool heads."

"Uh-huh," Marley said. "And loose tongues."

Gray snorted. "You come up with the damnedest things."

"I'm right, aren't I?"

He put an arm around her shoulders. "Yes, you are."

Marley turned rigid. He was warm against her side and his hand cupping her shoulder held her there—unless she decided to duck away, which would make her feel foolish. They must look like a couple. She thought about that and suddenly had to stop herself from threading her own arm behind his waist.

"Relax," he whispered.

"I am relaxed."

Gray shifted
have a son nam

"She never m
would have if h
thing. Hi, Pipes
Gray.

With her arms
bowed her head

"Hi, Pipes," Si
"Yeah," Pipes

"You said she
wants to see you
"Doesn't look lik
"Why don't yo
off," Sidney told
for my stuff you
I wish you hadn't

"It's not stoppi
ness," Danny said

"You did call m
you wanted to tall

Pipes nodded ar
the table.

"I got a pitche
announced in a b
you. Holy mama,
along with the we

Glasses clinked.
by the stems, a big
the other hand he

"Sure you are."

"What are you two doing here?" Danny said. He came toward them, his hands curled into fists. "What the fuck are you doin' here?"

"Watch your mouth," Gray said. "We were here first, remember?"

"Did you call them, Bernie?" Danny said. "You did, didn't you? You've got a big mouth, my man. Biggest mouth in town and it needs filling up." He raised a large hand as if he intended to do just that.

"Hey, hey," Gray said. "Simmer down."

"You listen to me," Danny said. "I've been stuck in a room with two cops for hours. They asked me questions that aren't any of their business. I'm goddamn sick of not knowing what's happened to Amber, and goddamn sick of being treated like I'm the reason she's gone. And I'm pissed off with you two because I think it's all your fault."

Gray tightened his hold on Marley's shoulder. He rubbed her upper arm and felt a jolt. Touching her was electric. Under other circumstances, he'd laugh. "That makes a lot of sense, Danny. Listen to yourself run off at the mouth."

Danny came a threatening step closer. "You asked a lot of questions last night. Just like the cops. You used to be a cop, Fisher. And her—" he pointed at Marley "—her family's a bunch of psychics. Or maybe that should be psychos. You're not the only one who can dig around in other people's business. The Millets are a strange lot.

Why are they m
like to know."

Marley set l
Intimidation tact
blustering. "Run

"Talk to me," (
to you because y

"You told them

"You should l
pointed out. "A1
Pipes?"

"How the hel
"Sidney's the on
the cops."

"She called m
here."

Gray looked at
in about Amber'

Nobody said a
Finally Danny
son."

"Really?" Gray
know, Sidney."

Sidney didn't s
don't know wha

Marley was st
gant features. Th
wore looked ex
She was effort
cold.

"What do you have in mind, Pipes?" Sidney said. She sat at the table with the other woman.

Bernie filled glasses, but only Danny reached for one.

"Amber's gone," Pipes said. "You don't have anyone to sing with and you don't like singing alone so we should get together."

A crack made Marley jump. Bernie had come close to dropping his jug on the table. "What d'you mean? You sing alone, Pipes. We're not payin' for two singers."

"Amber's coming back, I tell you," Danny said.

"I want to sing with Sidney." Pipes still didn't raise her head. "It's sad about Amber. I'll sing with Sidney. That's the best thing."

"People like you are solo acts," Bernie said.

"Tell him, Pipes," Sidney said.

"What?" the other singer said, looking up.

Sidney spread her hands. "About us. About what we're going to do."

"We'll sing at Scully's," Pipes said. "I'll go get my things."

"You can't." Bernie looked at each of them.

"That's a great idea," Danny said. His shoulders dropped to normal height and he grinned. He was hearing the plan for the first time. "Welcome to Scully's," he told Pipes.

"So much for wanting to look after Amber's interests," Gray said under his breath. "Doesn't look upset anymore, does he?"

"Nope," Marley agreed.

"Hoo mama," Bernie said. "I gotta stop this. Pipes, when Amber comes back, she's gonna want her job. If she comes back."

Marley closed her eyes.

"Don't talk like that," Pipes said. "You don't know. She could—"

"This is horrible," Sidney said calmly. "What an awful thing to say. Come on, Pipes, let's go."

Gray stirred beside Marley. "Pipes and I have an appointment," he said. "I'll walk her over later. First she'll have to let NOPD know they can stop looking for her."

"They're turning this town upside down," Bernie said, pausing in the midst of chewing a strip off a thumbnail. "Everyone I know—in the club scene—they're all getting questioned. It's been a couple of years since that string of women went missing and never showed up, but this is bringing that back full force. This wouldn't be the first time a serial killer went quiet for a period of time, then started up again. Folks are scared."

"They ought to be less scared once it's put out that Pipes is back," Marley said, hoping for a little reason.

"Yeah," Danny said, and guffawed. "Now there's only two women missing and one dead. That should make 'em feel better."

He didn't, she realized, look too steady on his

feet. Bartenders who did a lot of drinking had more than the usual problems.

"Why don't they find Amber?" Danny said loudly. "You tell me that."

"I know they're looking for her," Gray said. "This is a different case than the Shirley Cooper one. This time we've got a body."

Danny snorted. "One body and you can't be sure it's connected to Amber and Liza."

Gray felt Marley shudder.

Sidney clasped one of Pipes's hands and pulled the woman to her feet. "What were you saying about getting kicked out of your place?"

"I—" Pipes had her head up finally. Her eyes filled with tears. "That's right."

"That's what I thought," Sidney said. "You're staying with me. I live in my folks' house. There's loads of room."

"They might not like—"

"I told them and they're glad," Sidney said. "We need to rehearse if we're singing tonight."

Marley didn't like Sidney. What she was doing felt disloyal to her missing partner.

"Pipes," Bernie said, but kept his voice level. "At least come back and tell the boys in the band what you're doing."

She shook her head. "It'd make me cry."

"So why are you going at all?"

"I need a change."

"Sidney," Gray said. "Do you have any ideas

where we could look for Liza and Amber? Has Amber talked about somewhere she likes to go—to get away?"

"No."

Sidney started to walk away. "You can talk to Pipes and me about the article at the same time," she said, turning back toward Gray. "Danny'll let you know our schedule at Scully's."

Bernie poured himself a brimming margarita and sat down. "Thought we were saved when Pipes walked in. Shows what I know."

"Plenty more where she came from," Danny said. Either he wanted bad feelings, or he really was drunk.

"Time to go," Gray said to Marley. He checked his watch. "I'd see you back, but I've got to get on."

"You're going to see Nat Archer," Marley told him quietly, not that anyone else was interested in what they might be saying. "I'm coming, too."

"Why would you want to do that?"

"I'm only going to back you up about Pipes being around again."

"I don't need backing up."

Of course he didn't, but she had decided to stick to him regardless. "Between us we won't forget anything the detective will want to know," she said.

She wanted to be with him, period.

Marley liked being with him—too much.

Leaving a dejected Bernie gazing into his margarita, Gray put a hand at the small of Marley's back and guided her behind Danny and the two other women.

"Thanks for nothing, Pipes," Bernie said behind them.

Pipes didn't answer. Marley gave the man a sympathetic smile.

Outside the front doors, clammy heat hit them in the face.

"Whooee," Gray said. "Too bad we don't have time for a swim."

She was getting used to his unexpected remarks. "It would be if I could swim," she said. Her mouth remained open. The female Millets couldn't swim. They didn't know why, but they couldn't. But one of their unwritten rules was that they never let anyone else know.

Gray didn't say anything. Thank goodness he was preoccupied. She hoped he would forget Bernie's inconvenient suggestion about a curse.

Danny hailed a cab, although Marley couldn't imagine why when Scully's was so close—unless he didn't trust himself to walk. She opened her mouth to say as much to Gray.

"Probably because he's feeling his liquor," Gray said.

Marley squinted against the sun to look up at him. "Yes," she said. He didn't show any sign of knowing his ideas weren't his own.

"Why is it call[...]
shouldn't have as[...]

"How do you k[...]

"You mentioned[...]

"Really? It's fi[...]
them."

He looked at he[...]

She nodded. "S[...]
ones, pretty ones,[...]
ible." Her little sm[...]
try getting a rise o[...]

"Good," he sai[...]
guardian angels."

"I'll take as man[...]

He nodded, fresh[...]

He'd done some[...]
Internet and disco[...]
the really odd thin[...]
usually containin[...]
cryptic innuend[...]
couldn't get back[...]
tried to print sor[...]
seemed like a sel[...]
what looked like S[...]
indecipherable.

"Well." She gave[...]
be going. Good luc[...]

"I thought you wa[...]

She spread her ha[...]
want me tagging al[...]

"Bye," Sidney called when she was getting into the taxi. "Talk to you soon, Gray."

Pipes waited to follow Sidney into the backseat and Danny lowered himself into the front with the driver.

Traffic jostled, horns honked, and pedestrians passed on the sidewalk. A guitarist sat on a box at the corner and played, his instrument case open in front of him for tips.

"It's all so normal," Marley said to Gray. "Look around. It's like there's nothing wrong with the world."

He gave her a long look. "Strange, huh?"

She nodded.

Pipes bent to get into the cab. Her shiny blond hair did its pretty, slipping forward thing.

Two red, swollen welts marred the back of her white neck.

16

"There they go," Gray said. "Shucks. And they barely said goodbye. I'm wounded."

"You could *try* to sound hurt." Marley gave a nervous little laugh. "Weird, though," she said. She looked different, distracted.

The cab carrying Danny and his newly formed singing duo had cut a left at the end of the block.

Standing there in the sunshine, gold hoops

glinting in her ears
her hair and skin
seemed to him.

"You'll want to
said.

It took an insta
meant. "Nat Arch
said she was going
"Yeah. I need to k
something I find c
too? Or shall we v

He didn't much
needed to be as lo
was great on her ar
he appreciated the
showed off her le;
thighs would feel :
all the way aroun
would make swe
handfuls.

Shoot, he had lo
Marley dug in h
"Wow, I thought I
She didn't sounc
would bet she wa:
and searching for
If she had any i
already done on th
"The key to my
the air. "Difficult t

With an awkward, bouncy step, she backed away.

"Okay," he said slowly. Her act wasn't convincing. Marley didn't want to be with him anymore, and she was in a hurry. That was obvious, but not why.

"Thanks for letting me come here with you," she said, wiggling her fingers at him.

A few more feet separated them. She was hiding something, but he didn't think it would help to press her.

"It's nice to have company," he said and felt lame. "Better than walking alone. Hey, I'm going right past your place anyway."

She flushed, that lovely bright blush he was getting to like a lot. "You go on. I'm already out so I'm going to do a few things first. Better than breaking away from work again later."

Marley, he decided, was perfect to look at. And she'd be perfect in bed.

He actually sucked in his gut. When was the last time he had thought about sleeping with a woman and felt as if someone had punched him? He couldn't remember.

"Bye then," she said.

He grinned. "Bye then, Marley. We've still got a date for tonight, remember?"

She all but danced in place. "We do? Oh, yes, we do. See you then. Bye."

"Bye."

Marley jogged away and ducked down a side street.

Gray's attention switched at once to a police cruiser heading his way. It swerved to a stop at the curb beside him.

"What are you doin' here?" Nat Archer said through the open front-passenger window of the car. He threw open the door and got out.

"You tell me first," Gray said. He didn't like it that he hadn't been able to hang on to Marley longer.

"According to you I was keeping you out of bed earlier. When you left, you said that's where you were heading—bed."

"I changed my mind. Is that a new crime?"

"Only if you make it into something I don't like," Nat said. He wasn't known to be argumentative, but no one would know that here and now.

Bucky Fist climbed from the other side of the car and crossed his arms on top. He wore dark sunglasses. "Hey there, Gray. I bet you think we're followin' you around."

He did. "Why would you do a thing like that? I'm boring. You making any progress with the case?"

"Nope. Nothin's movin', not one damn thing. Except the phones. Those phones are ringin' off the hooks. Lemon's ready to quit if somethin' doesn't happen soon."

Gray wrinkled his nose and thought about it. "What would make you happy? More bodies?"

"Don't goad me," Nat said.

"Me?" Gray feigned shock.

"Where's your lady friend?" Nat said, catching Gray unprepared.

"Who would that be?"

"Don't get cute with me. You know who I mean. Your new psychic *amour*. Is she still inside?" Nat indicated the Caged Bird.

They hadn't seen Marley on the sidewalk. That was something positive.

"How the hell do you know who I've been with or where I've been? Or where to find me?"

A slow smile spread over Nat's memorable face. "You got a short memory? I've got my ways—you found that out earlier."

Bucky came around the car and onto the sidewalk. He hitched his wrinkled suit jacket across his chest and did up a button. He wore a shoulder holster and it bulged.

"You go on in and make sure nobody leaves," Nat said to his partner. "I'll be right there."

Like the good command-taker he was, Bucky walked into the club, his pant legs flapping. Gray noticed he kept on his sunglasses. Maybe he used them to look inscrutable.

When they were alone Nat said, "Now you can answer the question—what were you doing in this club?"

"Visiting old friends," Nat said.

"When did Pipes Dupuis get to be an old friend of yours?"

He ruckled his brow. "Who told you she was there?"

"Anonymous tip."

"Ah, of course. So how about letting me in on who you've got following me around." The idea irked Gray. When he'd been with the department his ability to lose tails was legendary. "I must be losing my touch."

"I doubt it," Nat said, suddenly really interested in the sky. "Now and then a real talent comes my way, that's all. I want you with me. Let's get inside."

He ought to tell the man Pipes had already left with Sidney and Danny. "Would it be okay if I wait out here?"

Nat hesitated.

"It's a stuffy place and I'm tired," he said. "I don't want to drift off on you."

"Yeah," Nat said. "It wouldn't look good, you asleep on a barroom table. Leave this sidewalk before I get back and I'll have you picked up so fast you'll think it's yesterday."

"Nice," Gray said. "I'm not leaving."

Nat shrugged his big shoulders inside a gray seersucker jacket. He strode across the sidewalk and into the club.

Gray rested his arms on top of the police vehicle,

just the way Bucky had. Too bad he didn't have a pair of cool shades. He grinned and let his eyes close. Damn, he was tired.

A tap on his shoulder sent a shock down his spine. He maintained his casual position and looked over his shoulder.

"Hi," the man who stood there said. "Gray Fisher?"

Giving out his name or any other personal information to strangers was at about the bottom of Gray's list.

"I'm looking for Marley Millet," the man said. "I was told she might be with you."

"She's not."

"Is that never, or not anymore?"

"It's 'I'm on my own right now,' which you can see, and I don't like people who sneak up on me. Are you a friend of Nat Archer's?" As a tail, this guy would have a hard time. He would be difficult *not* to see.

"Never heard of him," he said.

Tall, dark and handsome was a cliché, but it described the dark-haired, blue-eyed man Gray was looking at.

"Where do you live?" the other man asked.

"I didn't tell you my name when you asked. What makes you think you'll get my address?"

"Worth a try."

Gray rolled to lean his back on the car. He crossed his arms. "Who are you?"

"Sykes Millet."

Not one response came to mind.

"Marley's brother. Her only brother," the guy said.

Gray straightened up and slowly extended a hand. "Gray Fisher."

"Yes, I know." Sykes Millet shook Gray's hand.

"Uh-huh. You already said so. Marley left."

Sykes smiled very faintly. "Mmm. I'm very fond of my sister."

Gray wasn't slow. "It must be nice to have siblings you get along with." He was being warned off—or at least told his intentions had better be honorable.

"You don't have any family?"

"Just my dad." As far as he knew, and it was none of Millet's business.

"Are you married?"

Shit. "No. Never did get around to that. You?"

Sykes laughed and Greek gods came to Gray's mind. Now he was getting fanciful. He had better watch himself if he kept on hanging around with the mystical Marley.

"I take it that's a no," Gray said.

"You take it right," Sykes said. "I watch out for Marley."

Gray didn't doubt it if this "call" was typical for Sykes. "That's a good thing."

"You used to be a cop."

"I'm starting to think everyone either was or is

a cop. You've been doing a little investigating yourself."

"That's a yes?" Sykes said.

With a sigh, Gray said, "Yes."

"Now you're a writer."

"Yes."

"I don't get too deeply into my siblings' affairs," Sykes said.

Unfortunately I'm not having an affair with Marley. The car was heating up against Gray's back. He stayed put. "I'm a big believer in respecting personal boundaries," he said.

"I agree, unless safety is involved."

"You're suggesting I could be a threat to Marley?" Gray said. "Get that right out of your mind. I'm a pussycat."

Sykes grinned. "That would be a really big cat, Gray. But I'll trust you till you give me a reason not to."

"You've got four sisters," Gray said. The other man would assume Marley had shared family details, which she hadn't. "How does that feel?"

"Crowded sometimes," Sykes told him. "Very female and emotional. I like it. I like them."

Sykes didn't look like Marley. There wasn't a hint of red in the man's hair that Gray could see. But the manner reminded him of Marley. Self-assured and with a quick mouth, but someone you wanted to know better.

"Marley always knows she can call on me,"

Sykes said. "We make sure we look out for one another—all of us."

"Nice," Gray said.

"I thought you'd like to know that." Sykes smiled broadly. "If you see her before I do, give her my love."

Gray nodded.

"Hey, Fisher!" Nat strode from the Caged Bird. "Why didn't you tell me?"

With his hands in his pockets, Gray dodged a kid on a skateboard and walked to meet Nat.

"You are one meddlin' son of a gun," Nat said. "You knew Pipes wasn't in there anymore. Why didn't you say so up front?"

"You didn't ask."

"Does obstruction ring a bell with you?" Nat said.

"It might if it was relevant. You've been on my case since I walked into your office yesterday. I'm one of the good guys, Nat."

Nat passed a hand over his face. "This one is getting to me," he said in a low voice. "I've got people on my case in every direction. They think things are moving fast so I should sew it all up fast. I hate dealing with politicians."

Gray didn't have to ask who Nat was talking about. In New Orleans there were plenty of folks looking out for their elected positions and with women dropping out of sight, or showing up as alligator bait, public pressure would be running high.

"Bucky's bringing Bernie out," Nat said. "He's got a big mouth, but he doesn't say anythin' unless it's to his benefit."

"That pretty much sums up Bernie," Gray said. He was aware of Sykes behind him, but didn't want to introduce him to Nat.

Bucky Fist arrived with a sullen-looking Bernie in tow.

"You can't just haul me in like this," Bernie said. "I haven't done anything."

"We're gonna make sure of a few things," Bucky said.

"Like what?"

"If your dancing permit's in order," Bucky said, grinning.

Bernie shook his head heavily from side to side. "You are shitting me."

"Would we do that?" Nat asked.

"There *ain't* no dancing at the Bird," Bernie said. "Except for invitational and I don't need no permit for that. I don't need no more permits at all. I got permits comin' out my ears."

"Invitational dancing?" Nat asked.

"The cages are open," Bernie said with a shrug. "Anyone feels like climbing in there and strutting their stuff, they can consider themselves invited."

"Get in." Nat opened the back door of the cruiser and let Bucky deal with settling their guest.

"Dancing permit?" Gray said.

"Bernie thinks he's got a right to know everything and share nothing," Nat said. He narrowed his eyes at Gray. "Maybe he isn't the only one."

Nat hopped into the car beside Bucky and they drove off.

"Sorry about that," Gray said, turning toward Sykes Millet.

There was no sign of him.

Gray looked up and down the sidewalk. A man like Sykes shouldn't be hard to spot—if he was around. Gray hadn't seen him move from the spot where he'd left him.

"He didn't just disappear," Gray muttered.

17

By the time he saw the last of Nat and Bucky's vehicle, Gray was pumping his legs along North Peters Street and breaking a sweat.

The sweat had as much to do with praying that he could catch up with Marley before she got into trouble as with running hard on a muggy day.

He must be losing his touch. When she had announced she had "places to go and people to see"—more or less—she might as well have admitted she was going after Sidney and Pipes—only he hadn't immediately put the two things together. Allowing himself to be sidetracked by Nat hadn't helped.

And how did he know if he'd really met Marley's brother? She hadn't mentioned him other than in passing and never said what his name was. Sykes Millet sounded like a made-up name to Gray. The man had been built like a strong, lean athlete and a little woman like Marley would be no match for him if he decided to grab her.

Hell, where was his head? Even Bernie Bois had talked about all of the Millets being redheads. Gray had met one of Marley's sisters already and the woman's hair had been an amazing coppery-red.

The man who called himself her brother had dark hair. He had also been in a hurry to take off the moment Gray's back was turned—a cop was in sight. A lot of people could tell a cop when they saw one.

Marley could be irritating with her overgrown *attitude,* but she wouldn't be the first small woman to pretend she could look after herself no matter the circumstances. If so-called Sykes had a mean streak and was on his way to use it on Marley, she would be no match for him.

Pedestrians crammed each sidewalk and the narrow streets were clotted with cars, trucks, bikes and motorbikes; anything wheeled that would move. People yelled, and laughed—and jay-walked. And the street bands played, confident of their right to gum up progress as long as they kept toes tapping.

Damn. Depending on how fast she could move, he might have no chance of catching up with her.

He didn't want her following Danny and the two women into Scully's. Until he was sure Danny wasn't involved in whatever had happened to Liza and Amber, he didn't trust him.

He hardly knew this woman, but he cared about her. That almost stopped him in his tracks. *Keep moving and quit thinking.* He did care about her. There was something different about her, and not just her psychic talents—which he was less and less inclined to doubt. Marley didn't spend a lot of time thinking about herself—that was different. She cared about other people and it showed.

Gray cut through an alley. Marley had deliberately tried to throw him off by making it look as if she had headed into the Warehouse District rather than toward Scully's. He was betting she didn't go far off the track before doubling back and making directly for the other club.

The traffic was slow. He ended his sprint at Canal Street.

A fresh spurt of honking turned him around. At the entrance to Chartres Street, someone in a bumblebee suit pushed a double-decker cart loaded with hats of every shape, color and size into the intersection.

At any other time, Gray would laugh. Not now. He was too strung out. He didn't have any options left but to head straight for Scully's.

He stopped a block short and mingled with the strolling tourists. Ahead, the neon club sign flashed, its colors anemic in the daylight. A cab stood at the curb outside the Hotel Camille, alive now that guests came and went through the revolving front doors.

Not a single red-haired woman, tall, short or in between, could he pick out in the crowds.

Scully's didn't serve food in the daytime so only a few hardy drinkers straggled in. There wasn't any music until the evening. Danny said the reason was that any daytime tourists in search of a meal headed for Bourbon Street. The regulars were all he got.

He had to go in, Gray decided. And he'd think of something to say by the time he got there.

At the curb, waiting for an open-topped tour bus to pass, he had an interrupted view of the door at Scully's. Riders' heads got in the way, then breaks came and he glimpsed his target through grubby windows.

Not so grubby that he didn't see the sun catch on the polished brass door handle when two women left Scully's. One tall, dark haired and dressed in beige, the other shorter with long, blond hair.

He readied himself to erupt across the street as soon as the bus was out of his way. To his right sat another taxi, just idling away, its filthy noxious exhaust trembling in the heat.

The women across the street got into a black BMW that surged away, threading through impossibly small spaces and skimming the sidewalk when necessary.

Why such a hurry? he wondered.

Gray dithered an instant, deciding whether to try following.

Most likely an instant too long. He decided to go after the women and waved in the wing mirror of the cab closest to him.

A small woman nabbed it before he could reach the handle. Intent on securing the ride, she didn't look in his direction, but she wore a black T-shirt and shorts. Even if a stray red curl or two at the back of Marley's neck, beneath the wide brim of a veiled, black hat hadn't given her away, the flash of her long trailing leg would have.

Up ahead the BMW made a right turn followed by Marley's cab.

Gray felt doom bearing down on him. He was going to lose Marley and he didn't want to think about the potential outcome of that.

A bicycle messenger ran down the steps from a military model shop. "Hey," Gray said, hopping in front of the lanky, blond kid. "Can I borrow your bike?"

"Do I look stupid?" the kid said.

Gray grabbed the handlebars of the messenger's rusted-out bike. "I've got to get somewhere. I'm desperate."

"I gotta get back to base or I'm toast."

Whipping out some bills, Gray flapped them in

the blond boy's face. "Would this buy the bike?" It was three times what the heap of rust was worth.

The kid was moving a wad of gum from one cheek to the other and closing his fingers on the money when Gray leaped on the bicycle. As he rode away, he grabbed the messenger's black baseball cap.

"What's that?" the kid hollered. "Now you gotta get extra with the deal."

"Why not," Gray shouted without turning back. "Don't we all expect a little *lagniappe* with our deals? I gave you extra, didn't I?"

He pedaled away with the sound of disbelieving laughter in his ears.

The BMW, with Marley's cab on its tail, made a loop and headed away from the French Quarter. Gray pulled the baseball cap down over his eyes and pedaled like hell, making sure he didn't get too close, or a traffic light too many behind. He soon saw their route led back through the warehouse and business areas toward the Garden District.

Bikes were good things in tight spots. Somewhere in the back of the garage at the Creole cottage he shared with Gus in the Faubourg Marigny there was a bicycle. He'd check it out and keep it handy.

The Garden District came up fast, partly because of the speed the BMW managed to make by keeping up its weaving path between all vehicular comers.

Greek Revival, Romanesque and Italianate mansions glowed in the sunlight along streets lined with old oaks and sycamores.

Between elaborate columns, closed shutters helped trap cool air inside the high-ceilinged rooms they hid.

Here there were fewer cars. Gray hung back and hoped that Marley wasn't looking.

His next thought was gratitude that he had slowed down. The cab swerved to the side of the road and stopped as if it had encountered a spike strip.

Under most circumstances, Gray would have ridden past, but that would be pushing his luck. He rode onto the sidewalk, leaned the bike against a hedge and crouched down as if he was having problems with a chain.

The black car had pulled into the driveway of a vast pink mansion with intricate wrought-iron railings along its flower-laden galleries and central double doors at the top of a tall flight of white stone steps. The house stood atop mounded lawns so green they didn't look quite real and pristine pathways snaked through the grounds. Just visible at the back of the property was a white pavilion surrounded by flower beds. As Gus would say, this house wasn't bought with green stamps.

Marley got out of the cab and paid it off. Gray could make a few guesses at the next move she intended to make and any of the possibilities could mean trouble.

She stood behind the trunk of a large tree and peered around to look across the street. He understood why she needed to cover her hair, but where had she come up with the huge black straw affair? She might as well be in a raincoat with the collar turned up!

Sidney ran up the front steps of the mansion and paused, looked back to watch Pipes's slow climb. Gray saw Sidney's impatient head motion. Then he saw Marley prepare to leave her cover.

One of the front doors of the house called Bord De L'Eau opened and the women went inside.

Gray sprang. He caught Marley in the middle of the street, hauled her from her feet and carried her, kicking, back to the sidewalk.

"What do you think you're doing?" she hissed when he plunked her down behind the tree she'd recently left. "Where did you come from? You followed me, Gray Fisher."

"You're right. And I'm going to keep on following you as long as you seem to have a death wish."

18

"You are so out of line," Marley told Gray. "Get out of my way."

His expression went from inscrutable to steely determined and he muscled her against the tree. "When I can trust you not to try something bloody stupid—like showing up at that house over there without an invitation—I'll let you go wherever you want to."

"Trust me?" Her voice rose to a squeak. She cleared her throat. "You are out of your mind. It doesn't matter what you do or don't trust me to do. I'm none of your business."

"You've become my business," he said and she could tell he was deadly serious. "When you announced you'd seen two women the cops kind of think I could have knocked off, your life and mine got wound up together. Live with it."

"How did you get here?" she asked him. At least she knew where to find Sidney so she could come back again once Gray lost interest. She looked at him. He didn't show any sign of losing interest.

"What do you think you're going to do?" he said.

"What I'm not doing is giving you chapter and verse on my movements. Before or after I make them."

A woman pushing a baby buggy approached. Beside her, holding the buggy handle, a toddler boy with a tattered red cape tied around his neck trotted along. The boy chattered while the woman murmured responses.

"If you don't get out of my way," Marley said through her teeth, "I'll make a scene."

"In front of a couple of kids and their nanny?" Gray said. "Into scaring women and children, are you? Very nice."

"Ooh," she said under her breath.

Gray held her hand again, too tightly for her to get free, and said, "Hi," to the passing trio.

"Nice," Marley said when they were gone.

"That wasn't hard, was it?" Gray commented. He smiled down at her and felt too close for comfort.

"We can't just stand here like this," Marley said.

His eyelids lowered a fraction. Gray Fisher looked from her eyes to her mouth and she knew what she was seeing. All of his thoughts weren't about missing singers.

Marley wasn't breathing so well herself. She straightened. "Have it your way. I won't go to the house. Okay?"

"Great. I'll get you back to the Quarter."

Marley thought about Sykes and immediately wished she hadn't.

"It's nice the way your brother looks out for you," Gray said.

Gray had taken to all but parroting her thoughts and this could get annoying.

And the vision of Sykes, be it ever so vague, grinning at her over a nearby hedge set Marley's teeth on edge. *Stop creeping up on me,* she warned him.

I didn't creep.

Go, she told him. *Have you already forgotten the talk we had about the Mentor? That was only this morning.*

"Until I see there really is a Mentor, I plan to rearrange the little house rules. You might need me around, so be polite."

"I don't need you."

"We need each other," Gray said. "Can you accept that and stop trying to run away?"

She glared at him.

"Where did you get the hat?" he said, screwing up his face to stare at her. "It's horrendous."

"I like it," she told him.

"I don't," said Sykes. *"And I'm here because you thought about me. Don't argue."*

Marley ignored this. "I got it from a street vendor," she told Gray.

"You followed me here," she said to him. "And I don't like that idea."

"I'm not thrilled about it myself," he said. "But you followed Sidney and Pipes and that made me nervous."

"If someone inside that house recognizes us out here, it could be unfortunate," Gray said.

"Listen to the man," Sykes said, turning on a faint echo effect in Marley's mind. *"He's got good instincts."*

"You can do one thing for me," Marley told him. *"Take a good look at his face and tell me if you see anything weird. Like a scar."*

Sykes approached Gray and got so close Marley couldn't see where one man's face ended and the other began.

She rolled her eyes.

"Not a thing," Sykes said, gliding back to the other side of the hedge. *"Good-looking guy. I thought you were into the ugly, deep kind."*

"Go away now." It was hard to show Sykes any gratitude when he inevitably managed to get in a dig with whatever he did.

"I'm not going without you," Gray said. "Get down by the hedge. We'll be out of sight there."

She gave him a withering look. "I'm not groveling on the sidewalk for anyone."

Unceremoniously, he grabbed her hand and yanked her behind him to a disgusting-looking old bike. He knelt beside the thing, pulling her with him.

Gray whipped off her hat and replaced it with a baseball cap he picked up from the ground. When she tried to tear it off, he stopped her.

"I'm exchanging one way of hiding that gorgeous hair of yours for another," Gray said. "Big black hats with veils get noticed. Baseball caps don't. Help me out here. I've got your best interests at heart."

"I like this guy," Sykes let her know. *"He's masterful and that's what you need. You're too bossy for most men."*

"You are so out of line."

"So's Gray—I heard you tell him that. What's your connection to him?"

"None of your business."

208

"There's trouble, isn't there? Do you need my help or—"

"I don't need your help," she said and hoped she wasn't being rash. *"Would I interfere in your . . . love life?"* Now she'd done it.

"Love life, huh," Sykes said. *"Now you've got all of my interest. I'm sure you'd try to meddle in my love life if you could figure out how."*

"Turn off the echo, you're giving me a headache. Let's get back to rules before Gray notices I'm not present—to him. In future you can't come interfering unless I say, 'Please come here, Sykes.'"

"That takes too long."

"Seconds is all," Marley said. *"Okay. Sykes, come! If I say that, you come."*

"Yes, ma'am. Just like Winnie."

"I don't speak to Winnie like that."

"Your brother seems like a nice guy," Gray said. "He came by to check up on who you were hanging around with."

She clenched her fists and frowned at the bike. Gray had witnessed the episode that just took place with Sykes? This was horrendous.

"He showed up outside the Caged Bird right after you left," Gray said. "He doesn't look like you."

"Oh." Marley was so relieved she almost sat on the ground to calm down. "I wonder . . . I must have mentioned where I was going before I left

Court of Angels. Sykes was there." She wasn't a good liar.

"I see." He bopped up to peer over the hedge and she squeezed her eyes shut. If he saw Sykes hanging out nearby there would be more than a few questions. She'd never seen Sykes get violent and didn't want to think what he might resort to if the need arose.

"I don't think we've been seen," Gray said.

Marley shook herself. Of course he wouldn't see Sykes in his invisible mode. She only saw her brother like that because she was conditioned to do so.

"Listen to me," Gray said. "Closely. I want us to work together."

He was tough. Every line of his hard face, every solid contour inside his jeans and T-shirt, suggested he was a man other men might regret bumping into if he was in an aggressive mood.

Gray would know how to use his fists. She looked back at him. His gaze never wavered and she didn't have to resort to reading his mind to know he was willing her to do whatever he asked.

"Sykes?" she signaled tentatively. Would he keep his word and not interfere unless she asked him to?

He didn't respond.

"You're very close to your brother, aren't you?" Gray said.

Marley jumped. "Yes," she said shortly. She

needed a chance to analyze exactly what Gray was picking up from her. Without a doubt, he didn't know what was happening. Like any new psychic talent, he needed molding and training if he was to gain all the strength he might have.

What was she thinking? He was nothing to do with her—even if he was keeping her kneeling on the sidewalk.

"I'm going to see if I can get into that house and talk to Sidney and Pipes," she said, expecting argument. "I've got to."

"You won't be doing that." He sounded so calm, Marley blinked. He turned all grave. "I'm the one who's going in. I've got an excuse, you haven't."

She started to argue, but shut her mouth instead.

"My job brought me here," he said. "Believe it or not, I do have a job and I'm so behind on my deadline I'm starting to get calls from my editor. I don't sound like I'm making excuses for going in there because I'm not. Now, I'm making sense, aren't I?" he said.

Marley was glad he didn't look smug. "Yes," she told him grudgingly. "But I need to get closer to Sidney and Pipes. I've got a good reason for wanting that. Pipes knows something about what happened to the others. I'm sure of it."

"You can't be sure."

"I can." Men could be so hard-headed. "She's got big welts . . ."

"Yes?" He brought his face closer to hers.

211

"Damn." Marley closed her eyes. "Don't ask me a bunch of questions because I won't answer unless and until I want to. Pipes has a couple of marks on the back of her neck just like these." She held out her wrists.

"So that's why you suddenly didn't want to go to Nat's office and you had to take off in a hurry." Gray whistled soundlessly. "I figured you were chasing Sidney and Pipes. And those marks have got something to do with what happened when you traveled this last time? Something to do with what you saw?"

"I don't want to talk about that now." She really did have to think about how much to share with him. "But you understand why I'm the one who should go in now, don't you?"

He thought about it. "Sure, but it's not going to happen."

"Watch me," she said and started to get up.

Gray grabbed her arm and she landed on her bottom on the sidewalk. "I hate pushy people," she told him.

"I'm not pushy. You're impossible. You need saving from yourself. When you have a good cover for going to see Sidney, I'll be the first to back you up. Do it now and you'll blow everything."

She rubbed her face. He made too much sense.

"Stay here," Gray said. "If I'm not back in an hour, ride the bike back to the Quarter and get Nat Archer."

"An *hour?*"

He left her there and she tucked herself as close to the hedge as she could get. She wished her watch at least had a second hand so she could watch *something* happening.

19

The morgue wasn't Nat Archer's favorite afternoon destination, but he'd been there often enough to take the scents and sounds in stride. He knew when to shove a bottle of wintergreen under his nose—for all the good it did—and how to neutralize the hollow noise of casket-size metal shelves sliding out and thumping shut. The shelves closed faster than they opened. Without resistance, dead weights slid easily.

Under glaring white lights, Dr. Blades sat at a stainless-steel table attached to the walls in a corner, and wrote on loose papers inside a folder. The man's hollow cheeks held shadows the size and shade of big, ripe avocados. Nat got a fleeting image of nicking one of Blades's veins to see green fluid oozing out.

Geez, Archer. He could tell this case had already gotten to him, but he hadn't realized how badly.

"Archer," Blades said without looking up. "Glad you could finally join me."

Nat was ten minutes late. "Good to see you, Doc," he lied. "You said I should get right over here."

"*Right* over here," Blades said.

"And here I am," Nat said, refusing to be goaded into an apology for something as trivial as ten minutes in a busy day.

With surprising speed, Blades unfolded his long, thin body and drew himself up to what had to be about seven feet. "I want you to see something," he said, and scuffed toward the bank of steel drawers. "Did you close the door when you came in?"

"Yeah," Nat said. "Did you want it left open?"

That got him a faintly evil glance from ice-blue eyes. "No."

"Oh. I thought maybe you wanted to air the place out a bit. I can open it if you like."

Blades gave a humorless chuckle and pulled on a handle. The drawer slid out easily enough, which was always the case with small victims. The shape inside a white bag with an encircling zipper was no more than five feet, by Nat's estimation. Maybe an inch more, but this was a diminutive corpse.

Without ceremony, Blades parted the zipper and revealed a woman's body, or what was left of it. Shirley Cooper's remains weren't pretty.

Pity was never enough. Nat looked down with respect, and the cleansing surge of anger he needed to stay focused.

He frowned and shook his head. "Damn, I'd like to know exactly how this happened. What d'you want me to see?"

Blades sighed and rotated narrow shoulders. "No

water in the lungs. She was dead before she went in the water."

"You let me know that yesterday." Nat looked at the other man and wondered if he'd dealt with one DB too many and was starting to slip.

"I know what I told you. I also told you about the neck. That happened prior to all the other wounds. Who knows if there was a gator attack on the body?"

Nat bent closer. Looking like a tracheotomy incision, a dark hole shone with a gelatinous sheen. He stood abruptly and put a hand in front of his face. "It smells different." Even more overwhelming if that was possible.

"Yes, and that's interesting." Blades snorted. "But whoever did this is an amateur. They don't know the voice is complex. Takes more to cut it out, or whatever the fool thought he was doing, than punching a plug out of the larynx."

"Yes." Trying to be patient, Nat submitted to the anatomy lesson and decided to allow Blades his moments of drama. "I wonder why." His eyes watered.

"Making a point about picking on singers, I should think," Blades said. He pointed at the wound in the corpse's neck. "That would mess up a singer, but some reconstruction wouldn't have been off the table here. She would have been able to communicate."

Nat stared at him. Of course, he probably didn't

know. "Shirley Cooper was a maid at a club, not a singer," Nat said.

"Huh." The hairless places where Blades's eyebrows should be rose in a ripple of wrinkles. "Well, that's easily worked out. The killer wanted to pretend he wasn't just killing singers, but then he couldn't resist leaving his trademark."

"We've never seen this mark before that I know of," Nat pointed out.

"You will when the women who actually are singers turn up," Blades said, so coldly matter-of-fact that Nat was reminded why he didn't like this man, not at all.

"Is that everything?" he asked, unimpressed by the macabre little show. "I need to get on."

"You're going to need all the help you can get with this case," Blades told him. "Look at the wounds all over the body."

"Hard to miss them." There was hardly any clear skin between gouges and welts.

"Some are from teeth, but not all of them."

"What about the others?"

"Claws." Blades shrugged. "The different odor is in the bite marks."

"Are they what she died of? Is there a wound I can't see?"

"I've got a tentative diagnosis."

Nat watched Blades's face.

Muscles jerked in the man's jaw. "Yeah." He

shoved his hands in the pockets of his white coat. "She was frightened to death."

"You serious?"

"Have you ever known me not to be? She was dead before most of the wounds were made. Definitely before the poke in the neck."

Shit, if Blades had said Shirley Cooper died of shortness of breath Nat wouldn't feel any more hopeless.

Nat exercised his aching jaw. "Did you get good tissue samples? There must have been plenty under her nails and even in those wounds."

"Matter," Blades said. He crossed his arms and faced Nat. "There was matter, is matter. All over the place."

"What do you mean by that?"

"What I say. Not tissue, but matter. Unidentifiable stuff."

A slow thud started in the region of Nat's left temple. He massaged the spot. "I'm not following you."

"We thought a gator had attacked the body. The wounds are consistent with that—maybe. Nothing else we can think of is. Every piece of trace evidence we've removed probably can't be typed. I'm getting that from experts in the field. Very preliminary, but you can take it to the bank. We don't think whoever, or whatever did this has DNA—not that fits with any DNA we know of."

20

Standing at the top of the steps to the front doors of the house called Bord De L'Eau, Gray understood how a wolf ought to feel silhouetted against the moon. Any hunter with good aim could pick him off.

He deliberately avoided checking out the spot where he'd parted from Marley. If she left, she left; he couldn't control her.

Gray smiled. He didn't imagine anyone would have an easy time trying to make Marley do what she didn't want to do.

If he had not seen the two women and their driver go into the pink Italianate mansion, he would wonder if anyone was at home. The bell had echoed inside the house, but so far he hadn't heard as much as a footfall in response.

He approached the door again, and it opened wide.

An elderly man, using a shiny black cane, turned brilliantly dark eyes to Gray's face. "You're not going away, are you?" he said. Thick white hair waved away from his unlined face. The skin was so fine and pale, a net of blue veins showed over his forehead and temples.

"Are you?" the man repeated, his voice strong and deep. "You're going to stay until someone talks to you. I'm talking to you, have talked to you. Now you can go."

Gray found his composure, and his voice, in that order. "Good afternoon, sir," he said. "I'm Gray Fisher. I'm a journalist, and I'm working with Sidney and with Pipes Dupuis. They said they would be here." He was stretching things a bit, but why not? Too bad he didn't know Sidney's last name.

"What would you want with her?" the man said. "Oh, come in, come in. For all I know you've got a photographer hiding in the bushes. Might as well get you inside."

Gray stepped into a soaring, green-and-white marble hall that rose to a leaded-glass dome three exposed stories up. Staircases with intricate balustrades curved from either side to meet at a central landing on the second floor and from there more stairs and balustrades climbed in circles, revealing much more white stone, many marble busts, heavily carved doors, and an atmosphere of overpowering wealth.

"Could I talk to someone who lives here?" Gray asked the butler, or whatever he was. "Preferably Sidney and Pipes."

"I live here," the man said. "I am Bolivar Fournier. This is my house. Sidney Fournier is my granddaughter. I suppose this is something to do with her singing thing."

"Yes," Gray said.

Fournier snuffled. "Very well. We'd better see what we can do about you, then."

"Grandfather?" The man who came from behind one of the staircases looked a lot like Sidney. "Who's this?" He gave Gray a direct stare, but seemed friendly enough.

"He's here to see your sister about writing something," Bolivar Fournier said. "Gray Fisher, he said. He's going to make that silly girl more inappropriate than she already is. Writing what people want to read about people like us."

"Eric Fournier," the younger man said, shooting out a hand and shaking Gray's firmly.

"They're all looking for ways to criticize us, you know," Bolivar continued. "We're too rich for them. They want what we've got. I told you no good would come of this singing thing of Sidney's. Attracts the wrong kind of attention."

"Sorry," Eric said to Gray, shrugging. "Let's go in here and I'll give Sidney a call to come down."

They went as a threesome into a surprisingly comfortable room furnished with antiques, but the kind that appeared touchable and touched. Gray sat on a faded purple chair with wooden arms while Eric picked up a telephone and pressed a button. "Someone's here for you," he said after a few moments.

"Pipes, too," Gray said clearly.

Eric didn't look thrilled. "Bring Pipes with you. It's about an interview, I think. We're in the nook."

Their "nook" was bigger than two or three of the

rooms together at the Marigny cottage Gray shared with his dad.

The grandfather made his way, cane giving dull thumps, to a chair that matched Gray's and sat down slowly.

Silence closed in and Gray took it he wouldn't be offered any other niceties.

From time to time Bolivar gave a dry cough. His chin slowly settled on his chest and he snored lightly.

Eric shoved his hands into the pockets of fine, gray silk slacks and propped himself against a gilt table. He looked off into the distance.

Sidney put her head around the door and did an inventory of those present before stepping across the threshold. Pipes entered immediately behind her, choosing where she put her feet so as to expose as little of herself as possible.

"I hoped we could make some headway," Gray said, expecting Sidney to ask why he was following her and invading her home without an invitation. "Could you spare me half an hour or so? My editor is complaining about how long I'm taking on this story." He looked significantly from Bolivar to Eric. Neither of them showed any sign of leaving.

"I forgot all about this," Sidney said, her eyes wide. "I'm so sorry." She checked her watch and made a face.

"Nothing to be sorry about," Gray said carefully.

"Yes, there is. I told you to come and now I've messed everything up. Pipes and I are going to sing together for the first time tonight. If we don't practice, we'll be terrible."

Gray weighed his response.

"I'll call you later, if you like," Sidney said. "Would that work for you?"

She was lying for her brother and grandfather's benefit. He didn't have the faintest idea why. "Sure," he said.

Pipes hovered. There was no other way to describe the way she rocked from one foot to the other, looking up from a narrow gap in her long, pale blond hair. Her hands moved incessantly.

"Why don't you sit down, Pipes?"

Eric Fournier, talking to Pipes and reaching out to take her by the arm, surprised Gray. The man sounded entirely different now, engaged, animated—wholly focused on the singer.

She nodded and he ushered her gently to a window seat overlooking the grounds in front of the house.

Gray wanted, more strongly than he could believe, to look through that window. He wanted to know if Marley was still out there. He looked at his own watch and figured he had about twenty minutes before she could be racing away on the bike to get Nat Archer. That couldn't be allowed to happen.

"I'm glad you've got Pipes staying with you,"

Gray said, feeling his way. "The way things are in New Orleans, it's not a good idea for a woman to be all alone."

"What does he mean, Eric?" Bolivar said. He seemed completely awake again. "What things?"

Eric winced. His attention kept returning to Pipes. "Nothing, Grandfather. Gray sounds a bit old-fashioned." He laughed. "Women aren't sheltered the way they used to be."

"The way they should be," Bolivar snapped. "What's wrong? Something's dangerous, isn't it? You're hiding it from me. Is Sidney in danger? We should have stopped her from going to that club."

"No," Sidney said quickly. "There's nothing wrong with me. But men are always old-fashioned about the women in their own families. I understand that."

"You're not in her family," Bolivar said, pointing at Gray.

Sidney's expression showed she had already realized her mistake. "Of course not. I was talking about you, Grandfather."

Pipes got up and approached Sidney. The two locked gazes and Sidney nodded.

Without warning, Gray felt heat building inside him. And hairs rose at the back of his neck. He glanced around, but nothing was different. Pipes had gone back to shifting her weight rhythmically.

Eric went to the two women and draped an arm

over Pipes's shoulders. "You two run along and get your practice done." He looked down on Pipes with unshuttered absorption.

Taking her into this house hadn't been a complete act of charity as far as Sidney's brother was concerned.

"I'd love to listen," Eric said quietly, his nostrils flaring.

"No," Sidney said promptly. "We'll call you, Gray." She whirled toward the door and all but ran from the room with Pipes behind her.

For an instant Gray was disoriented. For the first time ever, at least since he'd been an eight-year-old expecting to die at a man's hand, his vision faded until he barely saw the scene around him. Darkness filled his mind and in that darkness, Marley ran, arms outstretched. She sobbed. He wanted to sit down, but didn't dare draw that kind of attention.

Marley needed him. His lungs tightened and felt on fire.

Ten more minutes had gone by, Gray saw from a mantel clock. He managed a man-to-man chuckle. "Women. Unpredictable," he said. "I'm sorry for interrupting your day."

"We're glad you did, aren't we, Grandfather?" Eric said.

The older man snuffled some more, but didn't comment.

"He's tired," Eric said as if the older man wasn't

224

there. "The men in this family don't have an easy time of it."

Gray made a polite noise and took a couple of steps toward the hall.

"Look," Eric said. "We worry about Sidney being out in the Quarter at night. We do our best to protect her. It's a bad idea for her to be singing in clubs, but we're afraid she'll . . . Sidney's not stable. She's had episodes in the past when we tried to stop her doing what she wanted. Not her fault. The weakness is there."

There wasn't a sensible answer that Gray could think of.

"Our mother's the same," Eric said. He raised his eyes to indicate upper regions of the house. "Very hard on my father. He's devoted to Mother. Spends most of the time with her. She won't even come down for a meal anymore and she never goes out."

"Sad," Gray said. Why would this man tell him all this?

Eric Fournier was staring at Gray.

"I should go," Gray said.

"Please take this the way it's meant," Eric said. "I love my sister very much. Growing up we were like twins. But she isn't the same."

"Why are you telling me this?" There was no way to avoid asking the question.

"Because you think you want to interview her for an article. You said so and she obviously knows about it. It's a bad idea and I'm asking you to drop it."

Gray wavered between his need to leave, now, and letting Eric Fournier talk as much as he would. The chance that the man would say something really useful made it almost impossible to stay objective.

"I wouldn't be so worried if those other women weren't gone," Eric said. He glanced at Gray sharply. "I don't think there's anyone in the city who isn't worried about what's going on. Unless it's Sidney. One of those women was her partner, but Sidney won't discuss any of it. I don't get it. It's frustrating."

"It must be." Gray hoped he sounded polite but casual.

"Look." Eric walked him to the front door. "To be honest, my father and grandfather aren't well. I don't want them worried more than they already are."

"Mmm."

"It doesn't matter what I say, does it?" Eric said. "You're onto a story. It's getting better all the time—from your point of view—and you're going to write it."

"Something like that."

"Do me one favor if you can. Remember that Sidney has too much imagination. She lives in her own world most of the time. She makes things up about herself and everyone around her. If she says something outrageous, ignore it."

Curiosity overcame Gray's hurry for an instant. "For instance?"

"Anything." There was frustration and desperation in that one word. "One of the ways she tries to put herself in the center of attention is to make wild confessions to things she had nothing to do with. Just use your discretion, will you, please?"

Eric opened the front door. In the sharp light from outside there was no missing the signs of strain in the man's face.

"I always do." Gray raised a hand, hesitated, then put firm pressure on Eric's upper arm. "I'm not anyone you have to worry about. Thanks for letting me take up your time."

The door closed behind him without any response from Eric Fournier.

Gray jogged down the steps and along a brick pathway beside the driveway. The wide gates still stood open.

He got outside and scanned the area ahead.

"Oh, Marley," he muttered to himself. She'd gone. He imagined her pedaling the bike—too big for her and the typical no-brakes messenger variety—into the heavy French Quarter traffic.

He'd better call a cab, then call Nat.

He reached the tree where Marley had hidden herself and made the left turn along the tall hedge.

Marley sat on the sidewalk, her arms wrapped around her legs and displaying scratched-up knees to advantage.

The bike lay on the sidewalk and from Gray's angle, the front wheel looked suspiciously bent. He noticed his borrowed baseball cap crumpled under the frame.

Marley's head was bowed and her hair shone fiery red in the sunlight. Where it parted, the nape of her neck showed pale and vulnerable.

The pain that hit his gut, radiating through his pelvis to his groin, all but collapsed him. He saw her as if she were at the end of a tunnel through which a beam shone like a spotlight, making her the only figure on a blank canvas.

Slowly, bending slightly to guard the pain, he walked toward her.

She must have heard him. "Gray?" Marley looked up and her eyes glittered as if she'd been crying. She held her arms out to him. "I wrecked the bike and it's almost time. I was coming in to get you."

Gray didn't laugh, although he knew she was being outrageously brave to even think of storming the Fournier house. "Never mind," he said, sinking to kneel beside her. "Are you okay?"

She slid her hands around his neck and he couldn't look away from her green eyes. He got lost in those eyes. "I'm not okay," she said, sounding breathless. "It's . . . Are *you* okay? There's no . . . Are you in pain anywhere?" Her voice faded to nothing.

He nodded and pulled her hard against him. The

next stab into his belly took his breath away, but he didn't want it to stop.

"Oh, Gray. I never thought about this happening. I didn't expect it. We'll have to talk. No, we mustn't talk. Leave me now. Don't ask any questions, just go and forget about me."

Gray swung to sit down and lifted her effortlessly onto his lap. Dark and light colors—red, green, purple, orange, a rim of silver—spun and he couldn't tell if it was really out there or just in his mind. He didn't care.

She pushed her fingers into his hair and he kissed her.

Their gasps mingled. Their mouths explored, testing one angle and another, their teeth nibbling at each other's lips, their tongues reaching to steal away sensation.

Gray's whole body ached.

He covered her breast and cried out. She was like fire and ice and he felt as if their naked bodies were layered together. Sweat broke out along his spine.

"Don't stop," he whispered. "Never stop."

A voice faintly penetrated his mind: "Get a room," followed by a chuckle. While he pulsed and grew closer to a climax, Gray raised his head to see a boy of about fifteen.

The kid stood there, moving gum from one side of his mouth to the other and grinning. "I'm savin' you from yourself, man," he said. "You can thank me later." And he took off, laughing loudly.

21

Marley looked through the cab window, but didn't see anything but a passing blur. The episode with Gray on the sidewalk meant that even if she never saw him again, she was forever changed.

She couldn't talk to Uncle Pascal about this.

Although she must have been told about it, Willow would only pretend she had never heard of the Bonding. The relationship she had with Benedict Fortune ended abruptly and Marley's assumption had been that they simply hadn't Bonded. Although Benedict had left New Orleans immediately after the two separated and relationships between the two families had become strained . . . One day she would try to ask Willow what had happened.

Marley absolutely would not discuss Bonding with Sykes.

She growled inwardly. Where were her other sisters when she needed them? She was sure one of them had gotten at least a hint of the amazing experience Marley had just had.

In accordance with tradition, on her twelfth birthday—and to her awful embarrassment—her mother told her about the Bonding, or what it meant to find the perfect partner.

Marley sneaked a glance across the backseat of

the cab at Gray, but started to feel pink and looked away again.

When a Millet met a suitable partner, their physical reactions to each other were exquisitely heightened. And the first time they made love was a test involving pain before explosive consummation.

She sank lower in the seat. She refused to let herself consider it all deeply, not now.

One thing she couldn't ignore was that although the Millets were not casual, they were eager lovers. She already knew that when they fell for someone only to discover the ultimate chemistry wasn't there, the disappointment was crushing.

She did question if exactly the same circumstances applied to male Millets as to female.

The sensations she'd had just looking at Gray coming toward her on that sidewalk, then touching him and having him touch her—their kiss—didn't point to disappointment in any department.

She shivered.

Gray had paranormal powers, she was certain of that now. There had been too many episodes of mind-meeting to ignore. What did it mean? Should she help him develop his potential? Would he want that? Would he even accept there was anything "abnormal" about him, as Willow would say?

"It's going to be okay," Gray said. "Relax. I got a bit carried away back there, is all. Probably because I was tense, then I was relieved to see you were there and okay."

He didn't get it that the connection he felt to her was unusual when they'd only known each other for such a short time? She kept her distance, leaning against the door.

"You don't understand," she told him.

"I understand we're attracted to each other." He snorted. "That's a bit weak, isn't it? In the short time I've known you, you've taken me from thinking you're interesting and sexy, to needing you so badly, I hurt."

"That's a bit weak, too," she said. "You didn't just hurt, did you? You were in real pain." She should not have said that to him and she wouldn't admit to feeling sensations too wild and raw for her to have contained them if there hadn't been an interruption.

"Why don't you want me to know what you felt?" he said.

Marley didn't trust herself to say anything.

"I want you," he said. In his need he looked haunted. "I've got to know if we're—Are we going to do something about this?"

You're the one who will have the control. "Let's slow down. We're only together because we've got a common problem." *You'll have to be sure you want me enough to accept everything that goes with me.*

"Yeah," he said, trying to hold her hand. "Much

more than a problem and we both know what that is."

He had taken his first shot of the vaunted Millet Sexual Compatibility Potential Assessment like a man. She smiled very faintly. Anything less from him would have been a surprise. He was virile, incredibly strong and currently distracted from what should be his main purpose. Whether they liked it or not, they were tied into a crime wave.

"You haven't told me what went on inside that house," she said.

"It can wait."

"No, it can't. Time is something we don't have, Gray. Do you have any idea how helpless it feels not to be able to find Liza and Amber when I've seen both of them? It feels as if I'm treading very deep water and I can't move. It's desperate!"

"I know, I know. We're doing the best we can."

He ran a forefinger along the side of her hand where it rested on the seat. They both sucked in a sharp breath.

"We can't get into our feelings now," Marley said. "Why are we going to the Faubourg Marigny?"

"I live there. And work there."

She stiffened. "No, Gray. I know what you're thinking and this isn't the time." There might never be a time for them, but he couldn't even guess the energy it would cost him to make love to her—if he was what she suspected him to be: her predestined Bond Partner. If she tried to explain the danger she could be to him, he wouldn't believe her.

Neither of them were ready.

"Relax," he said and she could see muscles jerking in his cheek. "If it's okay with you I need to check in on my father before we do anything else. He isn't in great shape."

"I'm sorry," she said. Until now she hadn't thought about his family or even where he might live. "You live with your dad?"

"My dad lives in part of the house. He's in a wheelchair. He can get out into the sunroom at the back, but that's about it. He's quite a guy. Never complains. I've never heard him say, 'why me?' even once."

She didn't need to remark on seeing how much Gray loved his father. "What's wrong with him?" she asked. "If it's okay for me to ask?"

"It's complicated. His bones are deteriorating. It started ten years ago. We thought he'd just live with it and do fine, but he's in a wheelchair now." He sucked in a corner of his mouth. "I think seeing him looking so much smaller is the hardest, and what an effort it is for him to do even the little things."

"You'll want to be with him on your own," she said. "Why don't I carry straight on once you get out at your place?"

"I'd like you to meet Gus."

Marley took in a breath. "Okay." She couldn't refuse to see his sick father.

You should be putting distance between the two of you as fast as you can. She hadn't asked for any of this to happen. But it wasn't as simple as running away now that the connection had been made, even if only in its beginning stages.

By last night she had almost convinced herself that Gray couldn't have been the man she saw on the second journey, the one when she had encountered Amber. But why did he appear to have a facial scar outside the shop when she could see no trace of it now?

She didn't have the luxury of blaming her mind for playing tricks. . . .

"I think we should—"

"Here we are," Gray said. He hopped out of the cab and ran around to her side.

Once she was on the sidewalk, he paid off the taxi driver and turned her toward a classic Creole cottage. Faced with red brick, shutters beside the door and windows were dark green. Arched dormer windows in the roof flanked a single chimney. Although the front of the house was flush with the sidewalk, overflowing window boxes and hanging baskets softened the facade. These cottages usually had a garden at the back.

"This is so pretty," she said. "I've always liked these cottages. This is one of the later ones, isn't it?"

"We've done a lot of work on it," Gray said. He looked the place over. "The second story was added, and the sunroom. I grew up here. It was a great place for that. Come on in."

They found Gus Fisher in the sunroom Gray had mentioned, leaning forward in his wheelchair to water plants along a windowsill. He turned as soon as they stepped down from a small kitchen onto the red tiled floor in a glass-enclosed area where pots lined most surfaces.

"Hey, what do we have here?" he said to Gray with a huge grin on his too-thin face. "Who have you dared to bring me? I'm tough, you know, ma'am, don't take to strangers easily."

Gray laughed and so did his father.

Marley looked from one to the other, searching for family likenesses. She didn't find any. Gus's hair was still more sandy than gray and he had nothing of Gray's dark blond elegance. From the set of the man's frame, Gus must have been a big man before the flesh fell away, but Marley visualized him more as a workhorse than a racehorse. His big-knuckled hands dwarfed a long-spouted green plastic watering can.

"This is Marley, Dad," Gray said. "A friend of mine."

Gus's bushy brows shot up. He had bright blue eyes. "Hats off to your taste, son. She's a pretty thing."

Gray shrugged and grinned at her. He seemed

perfectly comfortable with Gus's forthright approach.

"You're a surprise," Gus said. "I thought your species had died out."

Confused, Marley smiled politely.

"A woman my son brings home. Never happened before."

"Quit blabbing," Gray said. "I've got secrets I want to keep, like you, you old coot. You think I'd risk letting you meet just anyone?"

"Nope," Gus said. His smile had disappeared. "Nope, I don't reckon I think that at all."

He gave Marley a look that lasted long enough to make her uncomfortable.

"Everything okay with you?" Gray asked his dad hurriedly.

"You bet." He frowned at his son. "What's on your mind? Can you talk about it in front of Marley, or do we get her some earplugs?"

Marley put a hand over her mouth to hide a grin.

"She doesn't need earplugs."

"I'm part of the problem," she said, surprising herself. "I mean—"

"You mean you're part of the problem," Gus cut in. "I already figured that out. But I'm betting Gray's just as much involved. He's got a way of falling in the middle of things. Gray, where are your manners? Get Marley settled."

"Yessir," Gray said, smiling at Marley.

Her heart made an unaccustomed flip.

"You can have the rocker with the patchwork quilt, or the rocker with the sunflower quilt. Take your pick."

Marley took the patchwork.

"What time is it?" Gus said.

"Four already," Gray said, looking at his watch. "This day has gone by fast."

"They tend to when you're having fun," Gus said, his expression innocent. "I'll take a little whiskey. It's early, but what the hell."

"You've got it." Gray poured from a bottle on a wheeled cart with a floral tablecloth draped over it. "Same for you, Marley?"

She saw the wisp of a smile on his lips and almost called his bluff. "I'll pass, thank you. I'm a cheap drunk so I avoid strong stuff most of the time."

"Let me know when you feel like letting your resolve sag," Gray said.

She ignored that and said, "Do I see iced tea?"

"Sure do," Gray said and filled two tall glasses.

"You were late last night," Gus said to Gray. "Or this morning. Then you were gone before I got up. You any farther forward with this thing?"

Gray raised one eyebrow.

"Don't play cute with me," Gus said. "I've still got friends in the right places and even if I didn't, I can put the pieces together from what information they've put out to the public. We'd better be praying the one body is the only one. Gator attack, huh? How does that fit in with murder?"

"Damned if I know," Gray said.

Gus coughed. "That woman, Pipes, showed up again so the others could, too."

Marley wound her hands together tightly. She avoided meeting eyes.

"But you don't think so, Marley," Gus said. "You think there are at least two more dead women."

"If they aren't dead now I think they're going to be." She closed her mouth, shocked that she'd just made such an announcement.

"Gus is one of those cops who get you talking without you even knowing what's happening," Gray said. "And he's got the kind of intuition you're born with. He knows this town and he respects elements some of us try to pretend don't exist."

What exactly did all that mean?

Gus looked at her intently. Despite the deep vertical lines in his face, his stooped back and the way his check shirt and khaki pants hung against bony limbs, life sparked in his face and a quick smile. He watched her quizzically.

"Are you waiting for me to say something?" she asked at last.

"Only if you want to," Gus said. "Some of us carry secrets with us. Secrets or suspicions or even knowledge—mostly about people or a person— that we'd like to share with someone else. First we have to decide when we've found the right one to trust with our mysterious stuff. Then there's another decision—whether it's a good idea to share even if you have found the right person. Truth can hurt. It can be more than someone's ready to deal with."

Marley glanced at Gray. He took a deep breath and brought Marley her glass of tea. "Gus doesn't always want an answer," he said, meeting her eyes.

Their fingers touched against the glass.

Marley inhaled sharply. The skin on her face tightened and grew cold. She barely stopped herself from reaching her face up toward him.

Gray smiled a little and brushed her cheek with the back of a finger.

Then they both stopped breathing.

"My God," he murmured.

Marley's heart beat double time, and where he had touched her, the skin pulsed.

"This is all about the big story, isn't it?" Gus said. "Those women are some of the ones you're writing about, Gray."

"Yes. I need to get on with writing about them, too."

"Did you talk to Nat Archer yet? He's bound to find out you knew them."

Gus and Nat were mutual fans.

"Yes," Gray said. "I went to him first." He explained how yesterday had unfolded, but stopped short of talking about anything from the previous evening onward.

"How come you were there?" Gus said to Marley. "At Nat's."

Marley closed her eyes. She didn't know what to say. Uncle Pascal insisted that honesty trumped everything else unless it could hurt someone. Then he encouraged them to trust their instincts.

Gray hadn't brought her to his home, to his father, casually. He wanted to see them together and that had to be because he valued Gus's insights.

She turned to Gray, who shrugged faintly. He was tossing the decision on answering Gus back to her.

"My family . . ." Where did she start with her story and how did she make it short? "We're not like some people." She shrugged.

Gus laughed. "I didn't want to say it right off, but as soon as I heard your name I figured who you were. I know about your family. Paranormal powers, every one of you. Or so the story goes. And I'm looking at the red hair. That is really red."

"I like it," Gray said sharply.

Gus laughed again. "I think my boy likes you a lot, Marley. He's already defending you. I think your hair is real pretty. Never saw anything quite like it before. You could say it doesn't look like any color a person would be born with, but I guess you must have been."

"It is natural," she said, chuckling. "You should see my sister, Willow. Now that's amazing hair."

"I'll look forward to that," Gus said. "You haven't told me why you were at Nat Archer's office."

She did tell him. Sometimes rushing, sometimes halting, Marley made her way through the story of her travels to the cold room, and she waited for Gus to become dismissive, or to be politely disbelieving.

"Your family has been through a lot," he said. "It's never easy when you don't fit into any mold. You lucked out again, Gray—this one could be a keeper."

Marley wanted to ask him why he'd think that, but knew better.

"Things are moving even while they don't seem to be," Gus said. "You two are tryin' to make things go faster than they're meant to. While you're doing your thing, the cops are busy, and the rest of them. Wouldn't be surprised if our old friend Dr. Death is having a hand in something."

Gray's laugh was more a bark. "Nat says I'm going to call Blades that one day." He didn't seem surprised by anything Gus said.

"You already did, remember?"

"Nat meant I could get careless enough to do it again." He turned to Marley. "Blades is the chief medical examiner. Not a man with a big sense of humor."

"Doesn't sound like he's got such a funny job," Marley said. She was edgy and growing edgier.

There was a subtle change in the atmosphere. Elements moved, grew agitated.

She needed to be somewhere else.

The sensation disoriented her and confused her at the same time. She felt exposed.

"Almost forgot," Gus said suddenly. "That back gate keeps banging. I think it's unlatched."

Gray nodded and went outside without a word.

The instant they were alone, Gus said, "I meant it when I said he never brought anyone home before. He's been through a lot, had things happen to him that would damage most people for good."

Marley swallowed. "We only met yesterday—"

"So I'm imagining there's something strong going on with you two already?"

"No."

"I didn't think so. I can't do anything about any of it, but trust my instincts. They've usually been good. If it looks like you're going somewhere together, make sure you mean it. Otherwise back off. He won't push it if he isn't serious."

"I understand." She thought she did, but wished she didn't feel a little sick with apprehension.

"Good," Gus said. "He's coming back. Good-looking boy . . . man."

"He'd be mad if he heard you say that, but yes, he is."

"Gate's shut," Gray said when he stepped back into the room.

"Don't get bent out of shape with Nat for doing

his job," Gus said. "He doesn't think you had anything to do with the disappearances, but until he's got someone else to focus on, you're it."

"He's not amusing me," Gray said.

"I don't suppose you liked it when he didn't take Marley seriously, either," Gus said. "Don't forget who his girlfriend is. He's taken a lot of flack for that."

"Glinda the good witch?" Gray said.

Gus shook his head. "Is he still calling Wazoo that Oz stuff? She'd hate it if she knew."

"She probably does," Gray said. "She seems to know most things."

Gus turned to Marley. "Nat Archer's girlfriend, Wazoo, is . . . well, she's different and Nat thinks the world of her, so why should one more woman with psychic talents be so hard for him to believe?"

Marley didn't know how to respond.

Gray stared at him. "Yeah. Why?"

"I think he probably does believe Marley, but if he intends to try to use her, he's decided to keep it quiet until he can do it without the department getting wind of it."

"Use her?" Gray said. His frown was ominous. "The hell he'll use her. It's too dangerous."

Marley cleared her throat. "That will be for me to decide," she told him. "I don't do anything if I don't want to."

"I want you to stay out of it," Gray said.

He didn't even show signs of chagrin, Marley noted. Amazing. "I appreciate your concern. Now I have to get home. It's been nice to meet you, Mr. Fisher."

"Call me Gus. Will you come back, please? You don't have to bring him."

Gray shook his head at his father. "Come on, Marley. I'll see you home."

She decided not to refuse.

A clear rush of awareness warned her that a family member was asking to make contact. She opened reception. *"Who is it?"*

"Uncle Pascal."

This wasn't going to work, having Sykes lead Uncle Pascal to her. *"You and Sykes are in my black book. Now, please leave. I'm in the middle of something."*

"This is short. There's a policeman looking for you. Detective Nat Archer. Says he needs you fast."

22

Gray insisted on going with Marley to see Nat.

Willow waited for their cab a block from the precinct house. Her lime-green accents were impossible to miss. She stood on a corner drinking from a green plastic bottle, apparently oblivious to the thick veil of mugginess that had settled on the city.

At her feet with a familiar disgruntled glower on

her face, sat Winnie. Her favorite, Great-Dane-size plastic bone propped her mouth wide-open.

A beer truck backed up in front of the precinct and the driver took advantage of the pause to sing along louder with KWOZ.

"I guess the dog's your boss," Gray said.

"Yep." Willow had called when they were leaving Gus to say Winnie had been searching for Marley all day and was going into a decline. If "decline" meant a dog looked sleek, shiny-eyed, well-fed and pissed, then Winnie could be in one.

"Your sister's different from you," Gray said.

Marley hoped he was only referring to Willow's glaring green-and-white uniform, but suspected it could be something else.

"What's she angry about?" he continued.

She looked at him sharply. He must have picked up an undercurrent when he met Willow in the shop. "Maybe I'll explain one day. Let's get out here."

They left the cab and hurried the last few yards. Rather than leap with joy at the sight of Marley, Winnie turned her back, thumping Willow's shin with one end of the massive plastic bone in the process.

"Winnie," Marley said, running to greet the spoiled little beast. "Don't you love being with Auntie Willow anymore?"

Marley scratched her dog's head. Immediately, Winnie all but threw herself into Willow's arms, snuffling and managing to sound as if she was sobbing. She didn't let go of her bone.

"Hey, sis," Willow said, grinning. "This dog is what you made her."

"She's what you've helped her become," Marley said, giving Willow a poke in her ribs. "We've ruined her perfectly. Thanks for bringing her to me."

Willow stood and looked up at Gray. Marley was short, but Willow was shorter, and Gray's face was a very long way up for her. She studied him speculatively, took a step or two back and gave him a slow once-over. "Mmm," was all she said.

"Are you going right back to the shop?" Marley said, taking hold of Winnie's leash. She was anxious for Willow to leave.

"One of my people called in sick," Willow said. "I've had to take her jobs all day. I've still got an apartment to do on Clay. We only work in the Quarter," she informed Gray.

"What do you do?"

"I own a maid service," Willow said. "Mean 'n Green. D'you live in the Quarter?"

Marley wanted to shake her sister. Willow never missed an opportunity to look for business.

"Marigny. My dad would really like you and we've been looking for someone. We'd send a cab for you."

Marley ground her back teeth.

Willow crossed one green-and-white hightop

sneaker over the other and deep thought furrowed her brow.

"Of course, you don't go out of the Quarter," Gray said, "I understand."

"You're so busy," Marley said, imagining Gus sparring with Willow—and some of the things Willow might decide to share. "You wouldn't be able to do the job yourself."

"I wouldn't trust anyone else to do it," Willow said, and her eyes twinkled. "Yes, I'll fit you in somehow, Gray. We provide our own supplies and transportation. We can also run errands, do the grocery shopping, and we do clean windows. We do minor repairs, too. Gardening. Organizing. Mean 'n Green will consider any task." She whipped a fold-over card from the pocket of her shirt and gave it to him. "Talk to you soon. Bye."

She swung away and swung back. Her expression blanked. For seconds she stared at Gray and Marley saw her swallow. "Bye," she said, more quietly, and rested a hand on his arm. "I'm glad we've met."

"I like her," Gray said while they watched Willow dodge between pedestrians on the sidewalk.

"Me, too."

"You didn't get a call about Nat wanting to see you," Gray said. "How did you know?"

She didn't meet his eyes. "I thought we were finished with the third-degree." She had also hoped that since he hadn't mentioned it before, he hadn't noticed.

"I was waiting to see if you'd tell me the truth."

Marley started toward the precinct. "I don't owe you anything. I heard the detective was looking for me. You don't need to go with me, but if you do you'll find out I'm telling the truth. Nat's got something to tell me."

"Ouch!"

"What?" Marley stopped. "What's the matter?"

"Your dog slammed her weapon into my ankle."

She wouldn't allow herself to laugh. "Winnie is very protective of me. She doesn't like it when someone gives me a hard time."

"Hard time? Me?" He widened his eyes. "I couldn't give you a hard time if I tried."

She walked past black, wrought-iron gates and up to the precinct house. Once inside she stopped and turned a sweet smile on Gray. "I'd rather go straight down to Nat's office without passing the front desk barracudas. Can we do that?"

"Sure." He held her elbow and guided her toward a door.

"No dogs," a voice boomed at them.

Gray looked over his shoulder. "This one's evidence," he said and pushed Marley through the door ahead of him.

No one chased after them.

Downstairs, he knocked on Nat's door and pushed it open without waiting to be asked. When

Nat saw them, his feet slid from the desk and thudded on the floor. "Your uncle said he didn't know where you were. He tracked you down pretty fast."

"We've got cell phones," Marley said, knowing how snide she sounded and making sure she didn't catch Gray's look. "I don't know what we did without them."

"Yeah," Nat said.

He took a mouthful from a paper cup. "For you?" he said, holding the cup up to Gray.

"No, thanks."

"You?" Nat said to Marley. "It's vodka. Good stuff. Bong." He pulled out a tall, elegant bottle from a drawer in his desk.

She didn't think cops drank on the job, except in mystery novels. "Not for me, thank you."

"You don't know what you're missing. Had a nice day?"

Marley took a moment to respond. "Great. Thanks."

"You, Gray?"

"Memorable," Gray said.

A silent pause followed. Nat took several sips of vodka and hummed. Then he set down his paper cup, but kept on humming.

"You wanted to see me," Marley said.

"I did—do. Nice dog. There's something about Boston terriers. Glad you brought her back. C'mere, puppy."

Winnie considered, but not for long. She trotted to Nat and rolled on her back.

"Slut," Marley muttered.

Nat scratched the dog's belly. He made the mistake of trying to take hold of one end of her bone, but let go when she snarled.

"What's up?" Gray said.

"I had a command appearance with Blades."

"Yeah?"

"Shirley Cooper died hard."

Gray cleared his throat and Marley didn't miss his significant glance in her direction.

"You don't have to edit material for my tender ears," she said.

"How's the case looking?" Gray said. "Anyone interesting on the radar so far?"

"Apart from you, you mean?" Nat said. One side of his mouth flickered up. "We've got some interesting clues."

"Did Blades come up with something you can work with?"

"Loads of it," Nat said.

"If you want a swab from me, say the word," Gray said.

Nat nodded. "Marley, you really thought you saw Liza Soaper and Amber Lee after they went missing?"

The room was too hot. She shifted in her seat. "Yes."

"This kind of thing has happened to you before?"

"Yes."

"Couple of times with search and rescue?"

"Yes." Let him work out whatever he wanted.

"Get to the point," Gray said.

Winnie gnawed loudly.

"I don't recall askin' you to be here," Nat said to Gray. "I know you've made yourself responsible for Ms. Millet's comfort, but I'll make sure she gets home when we're through here."

Gray turned to her. "I won't stay if you don't want me to," he said.

"I want you here."

"Well, I don't," Nat said. "And this is my turf, friend."

"Is she under suspicion of something?" All expression had left Gray's features.

"Smart-ass," Nat said. "Stay if you want to, but keep your mouth shut."

Nat punched at his phone and ordered a pot of coffee. Then he turned to Marley and said, "I like to get coffee at the little place next door. Do you want some? Or would you rather have something else, Marley?"

"Coffee would be fine." She didn't really want anything.

"I've still got a bag of Tootsie Rolls," Nat said, looking smug that he'd remembered her reaction to the candy yesterday.

Marley's mouth watered instantly. "If it's not too much trouble." She didn't figure it would be like giving him a hold over her because she ate his candy.

Gray took out his cell phone and called directory enquiries. He asked for the number of Aunt Sally's in the French Market. While Nat and Marley stared at him, he got through to the shop and asked if they could deliver a large box of mixed pralines.

"You don't have to do that," Marley said to Gray.

"One-upmanship," Nat muttered. He tipped Tootsie Rolls into his blue plastic bowl and held it in front of her. She couldn't believe it when she heard Gray talk the French Market candy store into making an emergency run to the station in the name of promoting law and order.

"Sheesh," Nat said when Gray slipped his phone away and sat there, smirking. "The chief better not hear you did that."

"He doesn't pay my salary anymore," Gray said.

This time Marley controlled herself and put only one candy in her mouth. She closed her eyes and savored the warm flow of sweet energy.

"You tracked down a kidnapped boy," Nat said.

She smiled. "I was so lucky."

"You don't like anyone to know you've been involved in their rescue."

"*You've* been poking around in my business," Marley said.

"There are others incidents I could mention."

"I love Tootsie Rolls."

"More than pralines?" Gray said.

"Mmm, no. I don't like anything better than pralines."

"Nothing?"

She looked at him. His gaze didn't as much as flicker. Her own most sensitive little muscles contracted hard enough to make her shift in the chair.

"How difficult is it for you to make the kind of contact we're talking about?" Nat asked.

"The kind of contact?" Marley gave him a slightly puzzled look. "What does that mean to you?"

He shrugged. In another of his vividly white shirts, his tie loose and with long, muscular legs stretched out in front of him, he was noteworthy, Marley decided.

"We've got a situation on our hands," he said. "People are starting to get panicky. They want something, anything, so they can think we're getting somewhere."

"Only you're not, even with the *loads* of evidence Blades found."

"Thank you, Gray," Nat said. "No, we're not. I can't say too much, but this is a fucking—sorry. This could get out of hand if we can't get a break. That's why I'm coming to you, Marley. When you don't have anything, you might as well try anything, even if it's really far-fetched stuff."

She kept a straight face. "That bad, huh?"

Even Nat's dark skin turned a ruddier shade. "I didn't mean it like that."

"Sure you did," Gray said. "How come all the evidence you've got isn't helping?"

"You don't . . . You can't even guess what we're faced with. It's no joke, Gray. Marley, if you could give us some help, we'd be grateful."

"And the pay's great," Gray said.

She frowned at him. Her shirt stuck to the metal chair and the seat dug into the backs of her knees. "What can I do?" she asked.

"Take one of your trips and find Liza and Amber."

She gaped, then collected herself. "Just like that?"

"Would something that belongs to them help you?" Nat asked. "I read that's the way it can work. It wasn't easy but I managed to shoehorn a couple of things out of Danny Summit, and Liza Soaper's landlady came up with a scarf. Says she wants it back to keep it for Liza."

Marley wasn't finding this so funny anymore. She had used personal objects to make contacts, but only when she had no alternative.

"You're not fooling anyone," Gray said. "Something's changed and if I had to guess, I'd say it's a recent change. It might help Marley. Why not share the news?"

"Because I don't have to," Nat said.

"Then maybe Marley doesn't have to put herself on the line for you, either."

Winnie gave a sudden, protracted moan and rolled from side to side.

"She doesn't like conflict," Marley said, standing up. "I need to go somewhere calm until she settles down."

Gray got up and joined her. Again, she didn't feel like telling him she'd go alone.

"Would you think about what I've asked you?" Nat said. "I could call you in an hour. We really are against the wire on this one."

"I'll get back to you," Marley said. "Please don't call in an hour. I doubt if I'll be able to answer the phone."

23

Pearl Brite left Alexander's by the side door into an alley. She liked singing to the afternoon crowd because the club manager said she kept a steady clientele showing up to hear her. But she wanted to move up. She wanted to be a headliner in one of the big clubs.

This was the dead time in New Orleans. Apart from the tourist shops, much of the city's retail had closed up and although it was getting darker, the lights in the Quarter didn't show up enough to work their magic.

She had been paid by check. Although she told Lenny she needed the cash, he said they couldn't spare the change. That was a lie. He knew the banks were closed and figured he had a chance of floating what little she earned at least until tomorrow. Lenny was so tight with money she had to ask for hers every week, and he made her wait around until she was almost too embarrassed to stay at all.

It was past the point when she could ride her bike home before complete darkness fell, but she didn't have the price of a cab. Her dad had a deal that she was always to call if she wasn't sure she'd be safe on the trip home. He would get out his old Ford truck and drive to pick her up, peering over the steering wheel because even with glasses he didn't see so well. They lived in Marigny, close to Kenner. She wanted her own place, but didn't have the heart to leave her father completely on his own.

With the helmet her dad insisted she wore, Pearl walked toward the far end of the alley where she locked her bike in a rack pushed back in the covered entry to a mostly unused warehouse. The place kept the bikes out of easy sight and so far she'd been lucky enough not to have it stolen. A small, dark-colored van just about blocked the exit to the street, but she figured she could get past.

Mist started to turn into rain. She tipped up her face and smiled. Rain made the ride slower, but she didn't mind—unless it got really dark.

The van's engine turned over and the vehicle moved toward her, but very slowly. Pearl waved and pointed toward the warehouse. The driver gave his horn a light tap and waved at her out of his window. He stopped on the other side of the entrance.

Pearl kept going, anxious to get started toward home. A hot bath and whatever her dad had made for dinner was a friendly beacon to head for.

She broke into a run, not wanting to keep the van driver waiting.

Her dad would be mad when she turned up after dark, but she could always talk him around.

Traffic on the cross street passed with a steady hum, the headlights starting to shine on wet pavement.

Pearl glanced at the van when she veered left to get her bike, but she couldn't see the driver through the windshield. Just the same, she waved again and mouthed, "Thank you for waiting."

The building doors, almost always shut, were wide-open. Usually Pearl didn't like that because she couldn't see very far into the gloom. This evening a light shone just inside. Just as well since someone had shoved the bike rack inside, complete with her bike.

She checked over her shoulder, expecting to see the van drive on, but it stayed where it was.

Her stomach tightened and sweat popped out along her hairline. This was no place for people who scared easily. She'd get going and take the main streets rather than the smaller, more deserted ones that were her shortcut.

Although the warehouse wasn't huge, it was big enough and it didn't make sense that it was completely empty. Empty with the doors open, a light on and heavy shadows blanketing all but the area closest to Pearl.

As usual, the padlock key had hidden itself among the small things in the bottom of her bag. She felt around but finally held the zip wide-open and peered inside.

The light went out.

The purse slipped through her fingers.

Pearl turned toward the doors, just in time to see them swing shut. Blackness saturated everything.

She dropped to her knees, searching for her bag—and heard a sound, like breaths passing in and out through an off-key harmonica.

Two fiery red gashes bobbled toward her.

24

Fine rain fell steadily in gathering gloom by the time Gray and Marley left the precinct house. "I want to come with you," Gray said.

With Winnie's chew under her arm like a military baton, Marley hurried along the wet street. She was visibly preoccupied.

"Marley, say something."

She squinted up at him, her expression very intense. "This is life or death," she said. "I've got to get back to the Court of Angels."

"Someone must have had a sense of humor when they called it that," Gray said.

"Meaning?"

Once again he should have kept his thoughts to himself. "Nothing. Just an odd name for a place is all."

She gave him a long look. "Odd because you don't think it fits the kind of people who live there? Angels are interesting. You should read about them."

This time he kept his mouth shut.

The dog panted.

Gray scooped her up and barely suppressed a grin. He'd found the way to slow Marley down. In fact, she skidded to a halt and frowned. "She doesn't like being picked up by other people."

Winnie settled her wet nose into the skin where his T-shirt met his shoulder and sighed.

Despite the satisfaction he got out of the pup's defection from her mistress, Gray knew when he was on dangerous ground. "She's tired," he said seriously, stroking the dog's damp, seal-like coat while she snuggled closer. "She missed you all day and then she got hauled all over the place. And she probably doesn't like being in Nat's dungeon office."

Marley's tongue was in her cheek and her eyes narrowed. "Hold the leash then," she said and stuffed it into his hand.

For an instant their fingers met and seemed joined by fire.

Marley bowed her head and muttered what sounded like, "Really inconvenient." He could have misheard.

"I'll take her from you at the shop," she said. "But you don't have to carry her and come with me if you don't want to. We'll be just fine."

"Nope."

"What do you mean, nope?" She was motoring again.

"You're not going on your own."

"Do you know how you sound? You can't tell me what to do." Her voice rose a notch. "You hardly know me."

"Doesn't feel like that, though, does it?"

"Oh, dear," she said. "So many problems."

She broke into a jog and he lengthened his stride. "I'll help any way I can," Gray said. "I hope you're not going to try what Nat wants. Solving this case is his job, not yours."

"You don't know anything about . . ." She didn't finish.

"Explain it, then, whatever it is."

She scuttled in her hurry to make conversation impossible.

"I'm not just going away," Gray said. "You can run, but I can run faster."

"Chauvinistic drivel."

"I've got your dog and she likes me. Run away and she's mine."

"Don't be ridiculous."

"You're magnificent when you're mad."

"Get some original lines." Marley looked both ways and crossed Royal with Gray right at her side. Headlights slicked across rain-soaked road. "This is serious. I don't know why you can't understand that I need to be alone so I can think and make decisions."

"That's exactly what I'm afraid of. I know a softy when I meet one. You're a softy, Marley. You're going to do anything to try to get those women back."

Once again, she stopped running. "Of course I will," she said, hands on hips, pointed chin raised. "What kind of person wouldn't go to any lengths to help someone else get back to safety?"

"Would you like to take down names?"

She threw up her hands and caught Winnie's chew just in time. "I've never based my decisions on the way other people behave."

"I just bet you haven't. You're special, Marley."

Their eyes met. "Really special," he told her. "Are we going to have some time together—just the two of us?"

The shop was a few yards ahead. "Can we talk about that later?" Marley said.

"Whatever you say." But he would rather know now. "We're supposed to have dinner tonight."

"First things first. Something's happening. I've got to hurry. Give me Winnie and I'll call you later."

He held the dog against him. He was liking the feeling of her in his arms. "What does *something's happening* mean?" Whatever it was, it made him nervous.

She bounced on the soles of her feet. "Only . . . nothing. I just meant there's a lot going on."

"No, you didn't. Do you think there's a new development? Are you getting vibes or whatever?"

"When you face up to your own vibes you won't find them so funny." Her teeth came together sharply.

"More mysteries?" he said, but he did get feelings. The only true surprise about this conversation was that Marley seemed to know what he did or didn't feel.

She didn't enlighten him.

"What's worrying me is that you could do something that's dangerous."

"I'm not your responsibility."

"I think you're getting to be my responsibility— I like it that way." He didn't see any way to step back and make this a leisurely game of "getting to know you." In fact, he wasn't even going to try pussyfooting around. "You're not *getting* to be my responsibility. You *are* my responsibility. So give it up. Hey, just say the word and I'll be your responsibility, too."

"You already are," she said. Her blush furious. "Please give me Winnie," she said quietly.

"I promise I'll call you. If not tonight, then tomorrow."

Gray reached for her, but let his arm drop to his side again. "One woman is dead. You heard Nat. She died hard and I'm not standing by and risking your life. I won't do it, Marley, I mean it."

"How can you stop me?"

"I'll go to your family and tell them what's going on."

She laughed, but her heart wasn't in it. "We're a tight family. We stick together."

"Good. Tell me how you go about this out-of-body stuff."

"What?" She gave him an amazed stare. "Are you out of your mind? I can't explain something to you when I wouldn't know how to explain it to anyone else."

"You leave your body and go somewhere else."

Marley looked right and left, grabbed his elbow and towed him into the shop. She closed the door resolutely behind them, but the bell jangled on.

"Hello," someone called from deeper in the shop. "Can we help you?"

"It's Marley, Uncle."

"Good, good, I've been looking for you." A man came into view. Husky in a toned, muscular manner, he was handsome with definite signs of the same genes as Marley. He shaved his head, but his brows were auburn and his eyes a glowing green. He wore a green jacket over an open-necked shirt and green plaid cravat.

"Who are you?" the man asked, frowning, his attention ricocheting between Gray and Marley.

"Gray Fisher," Gray said, smiling, keeping a firm hold on Winnie and offering his hand. "Marley's one of a kind. I don't blame you for being suspicious of any man she brings home. Ouch!"

Marley had, very surreptitiously, stepped on his toe. Apparently he'd said something wrong.

His jaws tightened, but Gray kept on smiling. "You are, sir?"

"Pascal Millet." He shook Gray's hand. "Marley's uncle and guardian."

Oh, yes, and there was ice in those words. "You've done a great job raising her as an honorable person, sir."

"How would you know? Marley, who is this guy? He's trying to impress me and we both know what that means. You and I need to talk."

"Gray is my friend, Uncle," Marley said.

Gray nodded and tried not to look too smug.

Another man entered the shop from upstairs. This one also exuded health, but he didn't have Pascal's elegance. The newcomer wore sweatpants and a muscle shirt. Blond tips scattered his hair and complemented sharply defined, male-model features.

"Pascal," he said. "I could hear you two floors

up. You have to consider your blood pressure. Let me make you an energy drink."

"Anthony," Pascal said, indicating the man. "My trainer."

"Good idea, Anthony," Marley said. "Please look after Uncle Pascal's nerves. Gray and I are going up to my workroom. He's interested in the restorations I do."

"Is he really?" Pascal said, his voice entirely too soft.

"Sit, sit, at once," Anthony told him, pulling a chair over.

Marley and Gray left the two of them. They arrived at her workroom and she unlocked the door.

"Any reason why you keep that locked all the time?" Gray asked. It seemed odd to him.

She didn't answer. He walked into the workroom behind her and she locked them in.

"I don't like to be interrupted when I'm working," Marley said abruptly. "What I do calls for concentration."

He nodded. How did you argue with that?

"You're going to wait a few minutes, then leave," Marley said. "Thanks for bringing me back."

He sat on the same stool he'd used before and Winnie crawled higher on his neck.

Watching her dog, Marley frowned. "I don't understand what she's up to."

"She likes me. Some women do."

"I like you," Marley said. "I've got a bunch of questions about you, but I do like you."

"More than like me, maybe?"

"Don't push it."

"D'you have any more of those chocolate-covered coffee beans?"

"You're stalling," Marley said, but she went to her big, cavernous cupboard and delved inside. Then she spun around. "We left without the fresh pralines from Aunt Sally's. Will they eat them down there?"

She looked so stricken, he laughed. "If they do, I'll get you some more."

"Oh." More crumple and shove followed and she emerged with the coffee beans and a bag of broken chocolate pieces. She gave him the beans. "Take those with you," she said.

He put the box on the floor and started eating.

Marley sat down in her leather chair and leaned forward. "Did you notice anything about Pipes Dupuis when you saw her this morning?"

He frowned.

Marley pushed up the long sleeves of the black T-shirt she must have roasted in all day and rotated her arms to show the angry-looking welts on her wrists. "Pipes has some of these on the back of her neck. I told you that before you went into the house."

"Damn, there was too much going on." He

stood up, furious with himself, but still clinging to Winnie. "I forgot. Why didn't you explain to Nat?"

"He doesn't believe in me. If he wasn't desperate, he wouldn't have asked me to help." Her tight smile worried Gray. "People should know better than to doubt just because they've never seen something. If they can't touch and smell, they pooh-pooh. Skeptics are always so righteous —until they start feeling foolish because they're proved wrong."

That was what he'd been afraid she'd say. "Don't blame Nat. His job is to look for proof. If he doesn't have evidence to show, the people he works with, and for, don't want to know. It's all about proving things in a court of law."

"But he's against the wall so he asked me for help."

"Because he's too good a cop not to go after anything that could help."

Marley wagged her head. "I guess."

"How do we get to Pipes Dupuis? She knows something."

"She surely does," Marley said. "But I don't think she wants to talk about it."

"Why wouldn't she if she's scared?"

"I don't know." She thought about it. "And I could be mistaken about what those scratches are. Either way, she has to want to talk to us about it."

"Nat needs to know."

"Does he? If I tell him about Pipes having those marks, I'll have to talk about the ones I've got. I don't want to talk about more details until I'm ready."

"Why, if you say you want to help? You already told him the main stuff about you."

"I've been laughed at before. And it wouldn't help because they'll ignore whatever I say. You said they work on proof so I'll get them proof, *then* I'll tell them more if I think it'll help."

Without intending to, she had confirmed his fears. She intended to go searching for a killer—again. And if she could sustain the visible wounds she already had, was it so unreasonable for him to be scared sick for her life?

He thought about the corpse of Shirley Cooper.

Winnie squealed. He had squeezed her too tightly.

"Don't worry," Marley said, sounding softer than he'd heard her before. "I know what I'm doing."

A glance at her face didn't reassure him. "You want to believe that," he said. "I wish I could." She wasn't convincing herself and he knew he was right to be skeptical.

The dog wiggled and he set her down.

And he gathered himself to come up with more persuasive arguments for Marley.

She wasn't looking at him. Or listening to him. He frowned, watching her face change. All expression smoothed away and her eyes didn't appear to see anything. He wasn't sure she even remembered he was there.

Her hands rose, fingers extended, and Marley stood up. The focus in her eyes completely dulled. How small and shaky she seemed.

Marley had not started what was happening. Of course he could be wrong, but he thought she would have preferred to wait for him to leave first.

Gray wanted to take her in his arms, to shake her and plead for her to let go of whatever had started to lead her away.

Faintly, he heard a hum and inside the hum, a rustling. The rustling had patterns and he strained to understand what they might mean.

Marley stood in front of her workbench. Her hands came together, the fingertips steepled, and she touched the elaborate roof of an old red dollhouse on the bench. Chinese-looking and like nothing he'd seen before. Three stories with silhouettes of people behind shaded windows and set in what was left of a garden surrounded by a stone wall. It had a corner door, like a shop, with a window on either side. What looked like baked goods were heaped there.

He glanced quickly at the dog who stood beside Marley's chair, absolutely still, watching and waiting.

Backward Marley moved, making motions as if pulling against the little house, or pulling something from it. He stared. The gap between the house and Marley widened, but there was nothing connecting her to it that he could see.

She sat in her chair again, her feet flat on the floor, her hands on the arms. And Winnie curled herself over Marley's feet, and closed her eyes.

Gray cast about, afraid to move, afraid not to move. "Marley," he said quietly. "Marley?"

Her eyelids slid shut, but her face became rigid. As if she was wide-awake and tense inside a sleeping body. Gray saw her breathing grow shallow and rapid.

He bent over her. She hardly breathed at all. Automatically he lifted her into his arms. Sharp currents ran through his body.

"You must not interfere."

Gray looked over his shoulder. In the multicolored haze suspended over the house, a wraithlike series of shapes coalesced into a dim face. He screwed up his eyes, strained to see. Gray-streaked dark hair. Sharp features, he thought.

The pattern of a voice rose out of that rustling, clear and demanding. It came from the direction of the workbench and the hovering face.

Gray held Marley tighter, gritted his teeth at the battering of sensation passing to him from Marley.

He sat down with her on his lap and stared ahead. Like the still-sleeping dog, he waited. Gray waited because he felt he must. At least Marley kept breathing faintly, but she was limp. He was afraid, but not for himself. He wanted to know more about whatever was happening around him.

The rustle continued.

His attention rose to the ceiling above the house. The colors there glowed, green, blue, pink.

They throbbed and he heard the sounds take shape again.

"She will live or she will die. She is uniquely gifted. You must only wait and be glad for your own emergence. Be ready to seize your own talents."

This time the words definitely came from the ethereal being.

25

Marley's flesh quivered.

She had closed her eyes, but now she opened them and barely held back a scream. Hurtling through spaces too fast to grasp any one image, light and texture changed as she passed.

Vibrations buffeted her.

She spun around and around, then rotated head over heels.

Through an empty, dark-paneled room in an instant.

Into a pale chamber echoing with the Ushers' voices. *We had to take you. We could not wait. You have failed each time. They need your help.*

"What do you want me to do? Where are Liza

and Amber?" Each word felt thrust back into her throat where it faded away.

A corridor grew narrower as she shot toward an open door. Then she burst through.

Sunlight shone on a woman's face, a woman with dark hair—and a blindfold. Marley could tell it was Liza Soaper.

Marley started to call out to her. Too late. In a crushing collision, she passed inside Liza's seated body. This time there was no doubt what had happened. Marley was in a tight, clamoring place where she stared out at blackness, then down, past a narrow gap, at a stone floor. She looked left as far as she could, then right. Nearby was a wooden furniture leg. A table leg? Baseboards beneath cabinets. A white enamel door.

Marley was seeing through Liza's eyes, out of a small opening at the bottom of the blindfold.

She must find out where this was. Until she did she couldn't change anything.

"Why are you doing this to me?"

Startled by the loud voice, its vibration, Marley blinked. Liza had spoken.

"You were getting above yourself," a man said in an unremarkable voice. "You're very sexy, but you know that."

Marley felt fear emanating from Liza.

"Please let me go."

The man laughed. "So you can turn me in to the police? Now, Liza, you know better than that."

273

"I thought I was coming here to talk about my career," Liza said. "I haven't been here long enough to be missed yet. If I go now I'll be quiet and no one will ever know a thing about this."

The man sniggered. "You'll get out of here how and when I decide. But you're here to talk about your career. You've hit that glass ceiling, baby. Time to get out of the way and make room for people with more talent."

Marley felt Liza's confusion. And she had her own questions that didn't produce sensible answers. If Liza had only been missing a short time like she'd just said, then . . .

Time and events had changed.

Panic set in. Marley understood. For some reason she had gone back in time to the beginning of all this, when Liza first disappeared. This had happened just after her abduction.

Liza jerked to her feet. She struggled. "Get your hands off me. Don't touch me like that."

Helpless, Marley tossed with Liza's emotions. The sliver of vision beneath the blindfold moved, twisted. Liza scuffed forward. Still the floor was white, but Marley watched the tiles pass until Liza stopped again and a door opened. They moved into a room where brown paper packages were tied shut with string and pressed tightly together on a bottom shelf.

Another door opened and while Liza gave muffled shrieks, Marley fought against closing her eyes while a steep wooden staircase tumbled away beneath them.

"I'm good, y'know," the man almost purred. "No woman ever complained about being with me. They all want more when I'm finished. You're lucky."

Liza's scream pounded Marley's brain. She wanted to scream herself, to find a way to drag Liza away.

Very little light showed now. Liza was on her back, writhing from side to side, trying to escape.

"You'll only hurt yourself," the man said, intense excitement in his voice. "But struggle. I like it when they fight me."

Marley heard Liza cry out and tried to shut out the noise.

A thud, followed by more and increasingly hard and rapid impacts made Marley's mind feel dull. She was helpless and trapped inside the mind of a desperate woman.

As precipitously as her joining with Liza had begun, it ceased.

Revolving slowly, moving away from a scene she couldn't see clearly and didn't want to see at all, she felt herself begin to swim. There was the funnel, its opening facing her. She was so tired. Even lifting her arms was too much.

"Wrong, wrong, wrong," came the Ushers' cries. *"She went the wrong way."*

She couldn't concentrate on what they might mean.

"She wasn't supposed to go back."

Marley moved weakly, like an exhausted swimmer treading water.

"We must get her to the right place or it will be too late. She can't stay much longer."

A sound like a tornado, a freight-train roar, buffeted Marley. She felt consciousness slip.

Once more she spun and projected forward at a pace that shook her through and through. She looked, but couldn't see anything but darkness. The sound turned into a screech like brakes fighting to take hold.

She landed on a hard floor against something hard. She touched it, but pipes and other pieces of metal were all she felt.

A wheel. Marley ran her hand over the tire and over a frame to a seat. A bicycle in a rack. Small items pressed into the underside of her thigh. She pulled out hard things; most she couldn't identify, but there was a little pair of scissors, a round piece of rubber, a lipstick, a key.

Through utter darkness came a familiar sight, two glowing scarlet eyes with the quality of fire. She kept absolutely still.

Coughing. The thing coughed and wheezed to catch its breath.

Marley lost sight of the eyes as it must have turned away.

A breeze filled with a foul stench passed across her face.

Then the eyes were over her, burning down. This thing was aware of her presence, but she didn't feel it had power over her. Closer it moved and made a slashing downward motion with those eyes. She threw up a hand and moaned inwardly. Searing heat jabbed her palm and dragged its way for several inches. She heard the sleeve of her T-shirt tear.

The coughing began again and the eyes were obscured.

Seconds later a door opened and an elongated neon sign on a nearby building flashed from top to bottom. A picture of an animal, or a bird. Marley wasn't sure. Turquoise and yellow reflections slipped into the place where she was, across a dirty floor. An empty place, but for a figure crumpled in a dark heap.

Marley tried to reach the person, only to see him or her dragged over the floor.

The door closed again.

From outside came a low rumble, an engine turning over. Then the crunch of wheels on gravel.

"Now!" the Ushers gibbered with excitement. *"Go now before it's too late."*

Marley saw the funnel again and reached for it —but unconsciousness claimed her.

26

Gray felt Marley move, or he felt something move inside her. "Marley?" He shook her. "Open your eyes. Look at me."

The electrical force that bound them whenever they touched had faded to almost nothing since he'd felt her leave him, but it was back. Not as strong, it was true, but stronger than it had been.

She stirred and made a faint sound.

He struggled with his automatic instinct to call for help, but he had heard the warnings. Under normal circumstances, he would have attempted to bring Marley around, but there was nothing normal about any of this.

There was nothing normal about his hearing voices rising out of patterns deep inside a rustling sound.

Or seeing a ghostly form assemble to speak to him.

"Marley?" He put his cheek near her mouth and nose and smiled when her breath lightly touched his skin.

Winnie lay on his feet and from her sleeping weight, she ought to be a much bigger dog.

What had happened to him? In a short space of time he had gone from worrying about not being able to find two women he had interviewed, to being embroiled in a murder case, discovering he had paranormal powers and getting involved with a woman he couldn't stay away from even though her touch all but hurt him.

Her eyelids opened a fraction.

"Marley?" He didn't want to stay away from her. He was addicted to searing encounters with her, dammit. "Marley, honey?"

She blinked, then seemed to drift back into sleep.

Paranormal powers? Stable, feet-on-the-ground men like him didn't abruptly start thinking they were witches or whatever. Warlocks? Psychics? He was green when it came to all things you couldn't see, touch, smell, possibly hear and always identify. This woman had played with his mind.

He had heard those whispering, implacable voices ordering him around. Heard them and done exactly what they told him to do.

They put people who heard voices in padded rooms.

Maybe not that exactly, not anymore, but there were medications and nasty hospitals, that much he knew.

"What are you doing?"

Marley's question disoriented him. He stared down into her very green eyes.

She crossed her arms, if lethargically and in slow motion. "I asked you a question." One forefinger rose to point directly into his face. "Where do you get off manhandling me?"

A lesser man would remind her that she didn't seem to be trying to get away from him.

"How do you feel?" he asked her.

She took a long breath through her nose. "How would you feel? I'm tired. I've worked hard."

The dog rolled off his feet and stood up. Tottering, she sniffed the air and yawned.

"What do you mean by, you worked hard? Where did you go?"

"'Scuse me," Marley said and yawned wider than her dog. "I gotta get something."

"Tell me what you want. I'll get it for you."

"I'm not an invalid." But even when he helped her to her feet and stood up himself, she gave him a blank look and sat down again, hard. "Just tired," she said.

She looked past him toward her big cupboard and attempted to get up again. "Anything chocolate," she said. "In the cupboard."

The bag of broken chocolate pieces was just inside. He took out a piece and handed it to her. Chewing it rapidly, she reached for the bag as she demolished what she had.

A thump turned him around. Winnie was in possession of her Great Dane bone and chomped on it with gusto, her teeth sliding from time to time with a sound that made him wince.

"I think Winnie has some sort of experience when you leave her like that. She sleeps, or passes out. It's not normal."

"Of course it's normal. Dogs are closer to the other world. Winnie's in touch with these things. She's trying to guard me."

Marley pulled the candy bag from his fingers and kept munching. "Where are your coffee beans?" she mumbled.

"That dollhouse had something to do with you leaving or traveling out of your body or whatever you call it," he said.

Her eyes turned up toward him. A secretiveness veiled that look. She might be stuffing sweets, but she was too thin and pale.

"Now what?" he said.

Marley's hands stilled in her lap, collapsing the crackling bag in her fingers.

"I saw colors on the ceiling over your workbench," he told her, then wished he hadn't. "Probably some sort of trick of the light." Wishful thinking. He couldn't bring himself to tell her about the ghost.

There couldn't have been a ghost. There were no ghosts. "Those colors," he muttered. "Trick of the light."

"No," she said quietly. Her engrossed study whetted his appetite for some enlightenment.

"Why 'no'?" he said. "What else could it have been?"

"You mentioned it, I didn't. Very few people would see those colors. You're a latent sensitive and you're just awakening."

Maybe he didn't want to be a sensitive of any kind. "Was what I saw a signal of some kind?"

"They were part of a summons to me. Calling me to enter . . . to follow instructions. My help . . . was needed . . . is needed."

She blanched totally. Not a speck of pink showed in her cheeks and her mouth was the same color as the rest of her skin. Her hair was shockingly red against the pallor.

Marley erupted to her feet.

She walked into his arms and clutched his shoulders. The spark in her eyes let him know they shared an intense awareness. Her mouth worked and she looked away.

"Tell me," he said and slid a hand behind her neck. "You're wiped out. Let me do what you think you have to do." So far he hadn't grilled her about what had happened while she'd been away, but he doubted he could wait much longer.

"Nat," she said. "We need him now."

His stomach turned. "Are you seeing something I can't see?"

"I already did that. The exhaustion saps my strength and my memory, but it's all coming back. Terrible things have happened. I think I'm too late."

Gray used his cell phone to call Nat who picked up on the first ring. "Archer," he snapped.

"I think we've got something," Gray said. "Marley has." He stopped short of mentioning that she had left her body again.

"Where are you?"

He covered the speaker. "He wants to know where to meet us."

Her eyes were wild. "Not here. You won't talk about this shop or this place, will you, Gray?"

"No," he said without hesitation. "What you share with me won't go anywhere else. Tell me what to say."

"Meet us in the Quarter. We're going to walk, I don't know where. It's all I can think of. I don't think I'm looking for a big place or a popular place. It's a bar or club, I think. We could get together outside Fat Catz on Bourbon Street and fan out from there to search."

"Fat Catz on Bourbon," Gray said into his phone, and listened to Nat's response. "He wants to know if he can bring officers with him."

"No," she said sharply. But then she rubbed her face and thought. "Can they come without looking like a cop convention?"

Nat heard her and said, "No problem. They don't have to be where I can see them for me to communicate."

Gray told Marley.

"Okay then. Tell him, I think . . . Tell him we've got to find someone, only I don't know who it is."

Gray winced and passed the message along.

"Let's go," Marley said. "Now."

Gray bent to pick up Winnie and took a belt across the nose from her bone. Tears stung his eyes, but he stiffened his chin and led the way from the workroom.

In the shop, immobile as if frozen in the moment when Gray and Marley left him, Pascal Millet sat on the chair Anthony had provided. The trainer, his face expressionless, stood guard at his boss's shoulder.

The one change was the presence of Willow, who was uncharacteristically quiet although she smiled at Gray.

"We're going out for a . . . for a meal." Marley stumbled over her words. "Be back later."

She hovered in front of her uncle who studied her with both eyebrows raised. He gave Gray several glances.

Marley shook her head and Pascal frowned at her. "Don't make me regret the trust I place in you," he told her.

"You say that a lot these days," she said.

He glared at Gray. "I'm trusting you, too. Not because I think I ought to but because—" A puzzled frown replaced the glare. "You should go with her."

"Shall I take Winnie?" Willow asked. When Marley agreed and thanked her, she approached Gray, who put the dog in her arms.

Willow peered up into his face. She cleared her throat and frowned and the instant before she lowered her eyes, he saw a film of tears.

She disconcerted him utterly. This reaction, for

the second time, felt more personal than it should. There was no reason for Willow to behave as if he upset her.

"Bless you, sis," Marley said, squeezing Willow's shoulders. "If it gets late I'll leave her with you tonight."

"Leave her with me anyway. She keeps me company."

Gray and Marley made their parting remarks and left the shop. They headed directly for Bourbon Street.

"Can you tell me anything?" Gray said. "You're worried, aren't you?"

"Yes. Scared sick would be closer. Something weird happened."

He wondered how weird something would have to be for Marley to call it that.

"I saw Liza." She paused, squeezing her eyes shut. "It was so horrible, and it wasn't now, it was right after she went missing. I went back in time. That's never happened before. She . . . she . . . she got hurt badly and I couldn't stop it."

"But you've got an idea where she is now?"

"No. It was what happened after I left Liza that could help. I've got to find a place, a building."

She ran along beside him and slipped her hand into his. He gritted his teeth before he smiled and felt the world lighten. Marley was letting him know she trusted him, and maybe even that she'd like to be closer to him.

Oh, yes, fate smiled on him. He wanted her more with every passing second. He wanted her, out-of-body experiences, whispering voices, colored lights, ghosts, weird family, pigheaded dog and all.

What he felt for her was new and irresistible to him.

And that was as deeply as he wanted to look at it right now.

The good-time seekers were out in force. Tourists sipping daiquiris from white plastic cups laughed and fell against each other. Nearby a guy leaned from a balcony swinging rows of bright beads over the heads below. He spied a buxom wench and sent a, "Hey gorgeous, want some bling?" in her direction.

The woman raised her cup to him and he jiggled the beads. He winked at her and made motions as if he had something on his chest that needed drawing attention to.

Seconds of laughter later the man got what he wanted when the object of his "affections" handed off her daiquiri and hauled her thin white tank top above her breasts. She added a little shimmy to set twin peaks wiggling and was rewarded with at least two dollars' worth of bright, flaking plastic beads.

"Some things never change," Marley said, unmoved.

Gray laughed. "This is the stuff a lot of them come here for."

A guy dropped his pants and shrieks went up when part of his prize landed on him like a perfectly thrown fairground hoop ringing its target.

Gray didn't think he liked Marley snickering at something crude like that. "He could get arrested for that," he said.

"Double standard," Marley responded and laughed—a sound he was glad to hear coming from her.

They reached Fat Catz and didn't even get to slow down. Nat whipped out of the shadows, placed himself between them and linked arms. He thrust all three of them forward.

"Next right," he said and aimed them into a tiny entry road at the back of some shops. "Now talk to me, Marley."

She gave a big puff. "A gravel alley. An empty building with a bike rack inside. A bike in the rack. Stuff scattered on the floor. A woman's stuff, like lipstick."

When she fell silent, both Gray and Nat shifted from foot to foot, waiting.

"There's a neon sign you can see through the doors—when they're open."

"Huh." Nat continued to wait.

"It could be an animal or a bird. I wasn't sure. Not a girl or a martini glass with a swizzle stick or anything like that."

"I see."

"The neon was mostly turquoise and yellow and

the sign lighted up at the top first then moved down until it was all on. Then it went off for a second. Then it started again."

"Yes," Nat said. "Okay. And this was where?"

"If I knew that we wouldn't need you," Marley said, her voice growing higher. "You get paid to solve these things. All those people you've got will have some ideas about where that sign is and they'll solve it. They'll find the place."

"From a gravel alley, an empty building with a bike rack inside, and a flashing neon sign that could be an animal or a bird? You want to make a guess about how many neon signs there are in the Quarter?"

"Forget it," she said and spun away from them. "I'll do it myself."

Gray had her elbow in his grasp before she went five feet. "We'll do it together and Nat will help. Be reasonable. It's going to take just the right little memory jog to give us a real lead."

"I'm not playing silly games with people who sneer at me." She shot a look at Nat. "If you're doing so well on your own, why do you need me anyway? You don't believe anything I tell you."

Gray thought Nat looked like a man in the company of a woman who puzzled him. But then, he was.

"Okay, everybody, calm down," Nat said. "I need to put out some information and instructions."

While they waited, Marley surprised Gray by putting her arms around his waist and resting her face on his chest. "I've got to wake up," she said in a shaky voice. "I usually have time to get strong again."

He didn't answer, just let her talk while he tried not to let her know how his body reacted to the feel of her layered against him. He surrounded her shoulders and bent down to put his chin on top of her head.

"I think it's too late, but I can't give up until I'm sure," Marley said.

"Did you see someone, Marley? Someone else?"

She rubbed his back. "Yes."

"Do you know who it is?"

"No. It was too dark. I don't even know if it was a live or a dead person."

They stood under a light and Marley leaned away a little. She turned her hand palm-up and his heart thundered.

"We're going to an emergency room," he said. "My God, Marley. The wound needs stitching."

"It looks worse than it is," she said, and pulled together a tear in her sleeve.

"Show me that." Nat took hold of her wrist before she could hide her hand. "When did you get this?"

She shook her head.

"Tell me!"

"I don't know exactly, but it was this evening at that building."

"Who did it to you?"

"I don't know."

"What did they use?"

She hesitated. "A spine on their skin—or hide," she said. "As far as I could tell."

"Uh-huh." Nat didn't sound convinced. "My guys are spreading out. They'll keep checking in. If what you describe exists in this city, we'll find it."

"I want to be there when they go in," Marley said.

"Any particular reason?"

"Because I care. If I'm right, someone suffered there. I don't want anyone walking all over it like it's a park."

Nat put his hands in his pockets. "My people are very careful."

"I want to be there before they go in."

"Okay. If they find it, you will be. Now I want you to come with me."

Marley frowned at Gray.

"I'll stay with you," he said. "Nat's a good guy."

"I want to go home and sleep," she said, never taking her gaze from his.

With me? Sometimes his basic urges carried him away. "Can't this wait?" he said to Nat. "Marley's had a long day."

"No, it can't. Unless you insist on my getting an order from a judge, Marley, I'd like our people to run DNA from that wound."

27

A steady, warm drizzle fell. Rain and a murky damp had taken turns for hours to make the night as difficult as possible.

"We're going in circles," Gray said.

"Uh-huh." Marley hardly had the energy to keep walking. "We are. That's kind of the point. Eventually I'll see something I didn't notice before. I need coffee."

Without breaking his stride, Gray landed a hand on the back of her neck and pushed her through the door of a corner café with empty booths along both of its windows.

Marley slid onto a split, green plastic seat and shook her head. She was glad she couldn't see what the humidity had done to her hair.

"Look at those curls," Gray said. "You could audition for Orphan Annie."

She scowled at him. "Thanks, I needed that."

His smile made her laugh.

"You're bad, you know that?" she told him. "Do you think they have toasted cheese sandwiches here?"

"You don't want chocolate syrup on chocolate cake?"

"That's dessert."

A waitress brought coffee and nixed the toasted cheese. They could have pizza by the slice.

"Do you have anything else?" Marley asked. "Oatmeal? Grits? Corn pudding?"

"Nope. We'll nuke the pizza for you, though."

"Six pieces, then," Marley said.

The woman rolled her eyes and left.

"You're going to eat six pieces of pizza?" Gray said.

"I'll share."

"We're avoiding the issue, Marley. This isn't going anywhere, this hopeless search. You don't want to hear this, but go back to the beginning and think it through. Second by second, move by move."

He was right, she didn't want to hear it. "Coffee first."

"Nat's still out there, too," he said. "He'll keep going and so will his people."

"Nat believes me," Marley said, surprising herself. "I'm not sure when I knew it, but it's true. He doesn't think I'm making any of this up."

Gray settled his spread fingers on the table and looked at her.

She inclined her head in question.

"You're not making it up," Gray said.

Marley formed another comment, but stifled it. Instead, she watched Gray. Slowly, his expression became distant, as if he was moving away and withdrawing into himself.

The waitress set plates in front of them, then slid a platter of pizza slices into the middle of the table. "That's more than six," Marley said.

"We got extra," the waitress said with a one-sided smile that shifted with her gum. Her eyes crinkled when she looked at them. "Nice. You make a nice couple. Even if you could use a bunch more good meals. Get plenty of bacon fat in your greens. Gumbo puts meat on your bones. Rice. Beans. A couple a muffulettas for your mornin' snack." She looked Marley over. "You got the best hair, though. If I don't have a perm, I got bleached pumpwater. Yeah, you got the best hair, kid."

She left and Marley scooped up a piece of pepperoni and olive pizza with plenty of pesto. She took a big bite and munched. "Heaven," she said. "Eat, eat."

Gray continued to look at his hands on the table. He turned his gaze slowly up to Marley's face and her tummy flipped. Those whiskey eyes had darkened and his heavy lashes cast deep shadows.

"Talk," he said. "Tell me everything."

She breathed in deeply and started again, not touching what she'd witnessed while she'd been joined with Liza because it couldn't have any bearing on what had happened in that empty building.

Gray leaned across the table, watching her mouth with every word she spoke.

"Stop," he said. "Go back and tell me that last bit again."

She followed his instructions.

"Where was the bicycle helmet?" he said.

called to the waitress, putting the money on the table.

"It's a snake," he said as they hit the sidewalk. "A yellow snake and there's a turquoise border with green leaves inside."

"A quiet area. Away from the center of things," Marley said while they ran. "We don't know where we're going."

"I think we do. That's the Gold Snake—a hole in the wall. It's near a club called Alexander's."

He pulled out his cell phone and dialed. "Nat. Meet us at the back of Alexander's. I'm sure you know where it is. Let's get there."

Gray grabbed a cab that showed it was off duty and the driver agreed to take them where they needed to go because it was on his way home.

They got out in front of a small club called Alexander's and Nat walked to meet them. Marley couldn't see any other cops, but presumed there were some around.

"There's a warehouse out back. It opens onto an alley, but goes all the way to the street behind. The warehouse is locked."

"Unlock it," Gray said, holding Marley's hand and striding past the side of the club.

"You know I can't do that without a warrant," Nat said, keeping up. "We can wake up a judge for that if you're sure this is the place, Marley."

She caught sight of the illuminated sign on the other side of the wall to her right. "That's it," she said breathlessly. She broke into a run and they reached the entrance to the warehouse. "Can't we just get in there? We could say we found it open."

"That would be nice and convenient," Nat said, but with laughter in his voice. "Cops are pretty stupid. They fall for stuff like that all the time."

Marley felt mortified and said, "Sorry," in a small voice.

Gray let go of Marley and used his sleeve to try the handles on the double doors. He turned his back on Nat, produced a credit card and in seconds the doors swung open.

"Well, would you look at that?" Nat said. "Some people watch too much television."

Several uniformed cops materialized from the darkness. They hesitated as if waiting for instructions.

"I want to go in there," Marley said and walked through the open doors.

Someone pushed a powerful flashlight into her right hand and she shone it around. She broke out in a sweat, but walked forward, moving the beam from side to side, pierced the darkness all the way to the walls.

"Empty," one of the cops said.

"We already knew that." Nat sounded tetchy.

"Where's the bike rack?" Marley said. She started to move rapidly around the space. "And the bike? They're gone. But they were here. I swear they were."

Nat used his own flashlight to look more closely at the concrete floor. "Do you remember where it was—the rack?"

"No. It was dark and I only found it because I felt it."

"Could you have been by the wall, ma'am?" one of the officers said. "There're pipes in places. And brackets. They could feel like a rack of some kind if you were nervous."

"I was nervous," Marley snapped. "Who wouldn't be? But I felt a bike rack. And the wheel of a bike. Its seat. It was pushed into the rack."

"There's no sign of any of it now," Gray said quietly.

"They were here," Marley said stubbornly. "They've been taken away."

"They'll have to look for evidence of that," Gray said.

"It's late," Nat said, joining them. "I vote I have my people come back in the morning and look at things in the daylight. I'll have someone run each of you home."

"If you still believed I was telling the truth you wouldn't leave this place without taking it apart," Marley said.

"I . . . I want to believe you," Nat said. "In a way I do, but you can't deny that the things you said were here aren't."

"I don't understand it," she told Gray. "Honestly,

I saw someone on the ground. I didn't have a chance to get close."

Gray held her arm and Marley sucked in a sharp breath. If this went on with him, she'd have to discuss what it would mean if they . . . well, if they made love.

Still holding on to her, Gray went toward the door, but rather than walking outside, he pulled the right-hand door away from the wall.

"We could wait in here until morning if that's what Nat wants," she said.

"Nat's going to want a bunch of things," Gray said. "Look at this."

He stooped to pick something up and when he straightened, Marley trained the flashlight on what he held.

One shiny pink bicycle helmet.

"This should help," Gray said. "Must be the brand. We'll need to follow up on dealers who carry them. Come and see this, Nat."

On the back at the very bottom in black script were the words *Pearl Brite* in the symbol of a lightning flash.

28

Four in the morning when temperatures pretended they were cool. It was the coolest part of the day, but it wouldn't last long before the air warmed and the myriad scents of the Quarter rose about as fast as the familiar noises of the populace getting about their business.

"How are you doing?" Gray asked.

They stood outside the gate into the Court of Angels. "If I told you the first word that comes to mind, I wouldn't sound polite," she said. "Every one of my muscles aches. I don't feel I could walk another step. But my mind is doing jumping jacks. I wanted to keep going and at least do *something*."

"I know," Gray said. Most of all he didn't want to leave Marley when he doubted he could think of anything else but her. He sure as hell wouldn't be able to write and he needed to get back to a proposal he was working up for a piece on oil rig workers in the gulf. He didn't want to think about it.

"Would you feel comfortable coming in and talking?" Marley asked. "I still don't feel like I can wind down. Anyway, I don't know how you'd get back to the Faubourg Marigny at this hour."

He looked ruefully at his feet. "The options don't appeal. If you can stand me a bit longer, I'd love to come in. I'll make us some coffee."

"I'd rather pour us a brandy, unless you don't drink."

"I drink." He grinned at her. "Not Nat's Bong vodka, but a glass of brandy would be perfect."

She unlocked the gate and led him through a cool, dark alley with gray stone angels tucked into niches.

The alley opened out into what must be the Court of Angels and he saw how it got its name, even if a goodly number of gargoyles and questionable statues mixed, apparently harmoniously, with some really classy standing angels.

She put her finger to her lips. "Sykes won't be here. He's at his studio almost all the time—wherever that is. Willow and Uncle Pascal are heavy sleepers. But I don't want to tempt fate—or a third degree."

Gray followed her up green-painted metal steps, treading carefully to keep the noise down. He leaned forward and whispered to her, "I'm curious about where you live."

She put a finger to her lips again and opened the door into a small hallway. She locked the door behind her, but still tiptoed along. "The living room," she said, pointing into a dark room on the right. Next she said, "My bedroom," and another dark cavern confronted him. "There's a second bedroom like a boxroom where I have my computer and the kitchen's back here."

At last she put on a light and sent bright wash over an eclectic room where the appliances were the old, expensive kind, including an Aga cooker. A table built to fold up against a wall was lowered with three chairs pulled up to it. High above the speckled, green enamel sink two small windows reminded Gray of a pair of dark glasses. The walls were covered in unexpected red-and-white horizontal stripe paper with a shine to it.

"It looks like you," Gray said and meant it. "A little bit wacky, but nice to be around."

She gave him a sideways glance, then smiled. "That was meant to be a compliment. Thank you."

"I don't suppose too many people have sets of antique miniatures on their kitchen walls."

Marley chuckled. "You just have to be able to spot the cheap and deceptive. All the paintings of doors were done by a guy who sets up in Jackson Square once a month."

Gray laughed at himself. "Shows what I know."

"That's a little treasure," she said, pointing to a slightly splotchy mirror with a plaster Rococo frame. "It's English and very old."

He tried to look sage and Marley burst out laughing. "You'd rather have the doors. Never mind. You can leave the art appreciation to me."

She turned her back to him and found a couple of brandy bubbles into which she poured healthy measures from an unidentifiable bottle.

"I wish the guest room wasn't full of junk," she said. "I'd have taken everything off the bed if I'd known you might need it."

He stepped back to let her leave the room first. "Have you forgotten we're more or less strangers?" he said, and silently cursed himself for his drive to be disgustingly honest. "You probably wouldn't want me sacking out in your guest room."

"It would be fine," she said, her voice completely steady. "You and I aren't strangers."

He almost missed his footing. "We aren't?"

She went into the living room and put on lamps. Then she drew heavy green drapes over the front windows. "Do you feel as if we're strangers?" she said. "Or do you sort of get the sensation we've known each other forever?"

Marley plunked down on the couch and patted the seat beside her.

"Well—" He blinked several times, then frowned. "I think we must always have known each other. How can that be? You were there, I just didn't know it."

"That's because we were coming together. Slowly because that's the way these things work. But it was part of the plan."

He sat on the couch sideways so he could look at her. "How can you say things like that?"

"Because they're true. Or they're true in my reality. They don't have to be in yours."

"Did you know that the first time we met in Nat's office?"

"I started to suspect something when you were busy sorting through the edges of my mind."

He stared.

"You didn't know it, but that's what you were doing. You have paranormal powers. I don't know the extent of them, but when you met me they went into high gear. Sykes had an idea that was the case, too. But Sykes usually figures everything out first."

He took a deep drink of the brandy and it burned all the way down. That was a sensation he didn't think could be overestimated.

"Do you know why I knew that helmet was in the warehouse?" he asked. "I guess I don't have a choice about what you call *powers,* but I don't have to like them."

"You might as well like them. They're part of you. If you hadn't known about the helmet, Nat and his officers were going to walk right out of that place and relegate me to nut status again."

"You expected to find things there and they were gone. You say you didn't see the helmet so why did I know it would be there?"

Marley swirled the brandy in her glass. "Either I saw it without realizing and you picked it out for me—from me—or you've got remote sight most paranormals would kill for."

"Kill?"

"Forget I said that. If you have the power to visualize details without ever being in a location first. You're off the scale, Gray." Her voice grew breathless. "You're off just about any scale I can think of."

He took another drink and when he looked at Marley again, she was watching him. Her face had softened, but not in the comfortable way a friend looks at a friend. More in that vaguely predatory cast when the eyes darken, the nostrils flare and the tongue makes slow passes over the lips.

Gray couldn't look away from her mouth.

"It's there, isn't it?" Marley said. "The sexual thing. It's not anything gentle."

"Uh, no." But he hadn't met a woman who was quite as blunt on the subject as Marley. "I'd have said it has all the indications of turning into a tornado."

"Would you like that?"

If he were someone who blushed, he'd be red in the face. His own nostrils flared. He was so hard there wasn't a darn thing he could do about hiding it if she chose to gaze south. And his heart pounded in time to the thunder of blood in his ears.

"Are you hot?" he said. Sheesh, that sounded like a line.

"Take off your shirt, Gray."

Another goodly sip of brandy—and Marley matched him swallow for swallow—and he hauled his T-shirt over his head. This was one of those times when a man could be grateful if he'd kept himself toned and hard around the edges. He had always been fit.

"Nice," Marley said, her head tilted, her assessment unabashedly direct. "I like a little hair on a man—especially if it's dark. Your stomach looks as if you eat ground rock for breakfast."

"Thanks, I think."

"You're welcome. Feel cooler now?"

He laughed. "What do you think?"

Her smile was unexpectedly wicked. "I hope not."

She sobered and lowered her eyes. "I don't know what's come over me. I don't even sound like the Marley everyone knows."

"What does that mean?"

"I'm not sure of myself around men."

"Really?"

"Really." She bowed her head and studied her hands. "Now I'm embarrassed."

He inclined his head and waited until she looked up again. When she did, he smiled at her. "I'm not embarrassed," he said.

"Oh, boy." Marley took in a deep breath and blew it out. "Perhaps we should try to focus on something constructive. We could make a list of what we discovered tonight. I find it helps if I write things down."

"What I want right now doesn't need writing down," he said. "Do you think you can say the things you've just said then move on to another topic? It's not going to happen."

"Gray."

"What, Marley?"

"It's not fair to let you get in any deeper with me. I bring some pretty unusual baggage with me."

"Tell me about it."

"Ooh." She set down her glass and held her head in her hands. "Why does it all have to be so complicated? The Millet Bonding. There's a phase that should scare the pants off you."

He laughed until he fell against the back of the couch. "Nice line," he said when he could speak.

"If this Bonding does exist between one of us and someone who comes into our lives, there's a kind of test." She held up a hand. "Please don't interrupt. It's a stupid test because it causes some sort of shocking reaction. Pain—addictive, so I'm told, an explosion, I don't know because I've never experienced it and, frankly, I'd decided I never wanted to."

"Until me?" he asked quietly.

She closed her mouth tightly.

"Marley, love, something happens every time we touch."

She nodded.

"Has that happened with any other men you've met?"

"Never before. Once I thought it might, but I was wrong."

His stomach rolled over and his body clenched. "But there's more? If this bond is there, the results can be bizarre?"

"Not bizarre," Marley said. "Mind-blowing. And according to our lore, once experienced, it's hard not to want to repeat the process at every opportunity."

"I see."

"No, you don't."

"Are you hot?" Gray asked.

"Yes."

"Take your shirt off."

She turned bright red. He reached out to her with only his face and sucked on her lips. Marley shuddered and so did he, kept on shuddering and kept on kissing.

Putting inches between them, Marley grasped the hem of her T-shirt and pulled it over her head. The long, tight sleeves took some working off.

Her body was beautiful. Small and compact, and completely desirable. Her soft pink bra didn't quite cover her nipples and Gray was tempted to sit on his hands just to control them. He wanted to grab her.

He caught sight of the angry marks on her wrists and the palm of her hand. "I don't want to hurt those wounds," he said.

"You won't. And if you do, I'm not going to notice."

Gray leaned toward her again and this time he curled his tongue beneath one bra cup to tease the nipple from its hide-and-seek lace. Marley made a sound and leaned back on her hands, thrusting her breasts toward him.

He grasped her waist and pulled her close. All sensation melded together, a mix of pleasure and pain that made him feel drunk and very thirsty for more.

Vaguely he was aware that their timing didn't

feel so right. But the thought was gone as quickly as it came. She was fire and silk in his arms.

Pressure mounted through his body, expanded his veins and muscles and pumped power into him. He was a strong man, but with her he was iron.

"I can't wait," he said against her ear. And he kissed her deeply while she drove her hands into his hair. And from his hair she went to the bulge in his jeans. She unsnapped and unzipped the pants and forced her hands inside.

Gray moaned and heard the answering sound from Marley.

He picked her up by the hips and buried his face in her breasts. His fingers destroyed the clasp on her bra and he panted at the sight of her naked breasts. He worked his thumbs in circles, getting ever closer to her nipples until, with a growl, he used his teeth to bring sobs from her.

Walking with her, he pressed her back against the wall and let her slowly slide down until her toes touched the ground.

"I'm on fire," he told her. "Burning up."

"Yes."

With one sweep he ripped off her shorts and panties and shucked his jeans.

"I want to know what you like," he said, and slid the heel of one hand down her tummy.

Her eyes didn't leave his. With parted lips, she panted. Her pelvis met his palm and he curled his fingers into her.

"Gray." She said his name, long and low and pressed herself tightly against his hand. "That's what I like. You know. You just know." Her wince, the break of sweat on her brow, excited him even while fresh pain thudded from deep in his loins, down his thighs.

She stiffened with her release and wound her body more tightly about his.

Pounding in his groin and belly built and he gasped. The sounds from his own throat amazed him. Keening, animal cries. Tears slid from Marley's eyes.

Once more he lifted her.

This time he lowered her rapidly and filled her, locked his thighs and knees against wrenching vibrations to make a kind of unworldly love he had never, could never have imagined possible.

He couldn't see clearly. The room moved.

Pressure built. He clung to Marley and clung to the wall. Dimly he feared what he might be doing to her, but she helped him, drove herself down over him again and again.

A searing, like a white-hot spear, seemed to split him in two and then, as quickly as it had all mounted, it ebbed on the sweet, soaring tide of their climax.

Gray looked down at her, at the undulations of their slick bodies, at the mixture of pleasure and pain on her upturned face.

He didn't know how long they kept on moving

together, and against each other, or how long they stroked, skin to skin, and he would never remember all the words that tumbled out of them. But when they slumped against each other and slid to sit, leaning body to body, on the floor, he knew one absolute truth. They would be drawn together again and again and they would never as much as glance at each other without thinking about the incredible sex they could share.

29

Marley watched first gray light filter through the slatted blinds on her bedroom window. She couldn't have slept for more than an hour yet she was wide-awake and filled with a premonition that something huge was about to happen.

Lying on his stomach, his face turned toward her, Gray had her pinned to the bed with a muscular arm and a powerful leg. He was heavy, but in a way she'd like to get used to.

Ideas and impressions crowded in on Marley.

Today there would be change, major change. She shut her eyes and concentrated. It would be the case. Nat would make progress and they would start to get closer to finding Liza and Amber.

Her eyes wanted to pop open, but she squeezed the lids together tightly. A pinpoint of light became a pearly, glowing little heap. She centered her attention harder, brought her focus to the center of the light.

She looked at the ceiling. The bicycle helmet had been there all along, close to the victim, but camouflaged in the shadows. When Red Eye dragged the person across the floor, the helmet must have been caught up, then shaken loose and left behind.

Gray's ruffled hair curled at his neck and across his brow. His eyes moved beneath the lids and his lashes flickered. His cheek and jaw were dark with beard stubble. Relaxed, his face looked young and achingly appealing. Her tummy flipped. They had made love twice before exhaustion claimed both of them. The experience defied description and she wanted to feel again what they'd felt together. The Bonding had been theirs and it was a sign she must soon explain to him all its implications.

There was nothing to force him into melding his life with hers, but she would never be whole again without him—any more than he could hope to experience with anyone else what they had shared.

Across the bed, faint stripes of gold stroked them through the blinds. The sun started its ascent. Outside the bedroom, a small stone terrace with fancy iron railings overlooked gardens behind a house tucked in the middle of the block. The owners were rarely there and Marley enjoyed the privacy of her haven. She enjoyed it even more with Gray there beside her.

He mumbled in his sleep and tucked her tightly against him.

Her family would have to be dealt with and they would have questions no man should have to answer about making love to a woman.

The blinds rattled.

Marley frowned and peered at them. A breeze flowed over her and she saw Gray's hair move so she wasn't imagining what she felt.

The windows were closed and locked. The bedroom door was shut. The fan ran, but she often lamented that it didn't create any real air current.

On the ceiling a shape formed, a gold rectangle.

Marley blinked several times. The image was fuzzy and she wanted her eyes absolutely clear. There it was, not the sunny gold that lay in bands over the bed, but deep, dark, rich gold like molten ore poured into a mold.

The shape trembled, came a little closer, then receded. Part of it flapped down and she looked at the gorgeously embossed flyleaf of a book. When the tissue-thin flyleaf flipped away, blinding arcs of color beamed forth as if from deep inside an empty cavity. Then the cover settled gently back and more prisms blazed from the depths of jewels mounted in the gold surface.

Marley closed her eyes again. The image unsettled her. A field of magnetism emanated toward her, tugged at her as if to pull her from the bed.

"Marley, may I come in?"

Uncle Pascal, requesting her attention while she could still see the fantastic book, disoriented her.

"Marley, may I—"

"Yes, " she signaled. *"Tell me what's wrong."*

He didn't respond immediately and when he did she could tell he was unsettled. *"You're needed here in my flat. I have no choice but to ask you to come."*

"Can I at least have coffee and wake up?"

"We have coffee here."

"Yes."

As carefully as possible, she eased herself away from Gray and stood up. Her legs felt rubbery and her head ached. Neither discomfort surprised her. When she started to move around, a number of parts hurt. She wished she could curl up with Gray again.

She scuffled into the bathroom and took a five-minute shower. After cleaning her teeth and washing her face she looked in the mirror to see if she had erased any signs of wild lovemaking. She didn't think she had managed very well. In a drawer she found a fuzzy scrunchee and gathered her hair into a volcanic bundle atop her head.

Naked, she returned to the bedroom and rushed into a bra and panties and a yellow cotton sweatsuit.

"C'mere," Gray said from the bed. "Where d'you think you're going? We aren't finished yet."

She got just close enough to make it impossible for him to grab her. "You're right. We're not fin-

314

ished. But I've got to go over to Uncle Pascal's. I think there's a family meeting going on. As soon as it's done, I'll be back. But don't stay if you have to get on with something."

"What I have to get on with is leaving me all alone in this big bed. Cruel, cruel woman. I didn't hear the phone, anyway."

"It didn't ring." If he was going to be around her, he might as well start learning the ropes. "Uncle doesn't need a telephone if he knows where I am and he really wants to reach me."

He groaned and threw an arm over his face. "What have I gotten into?"

She bit back the temptation to tell him he was free to get out the second he wanted to. She didn't want him to so why give him ideas?

"Bye," she said.

On the way out of the flat she looked around, expecting to see Winnie curled up somewhere. Willow usually popped the dog through Marley's front door before leaving for work.

Winnie wasn't in the flat this time.

Marley covered the distance to Uncle Pascal's in minutes and tapped on his door. Rather than call her in, he opened it himself and gave her a piercing look. "I tried to stop this from happening," he said quietly. "I was overruled."

Marley patted his hand and kissed his cheek. "Don't worry. Hey, Sykes. I thought you hated early mornings."

"I do." Sykes sounded furious and Marley got edgy.

Her brother held Winnie so she flopped over his shoulder while he kept an arm across her back legs. She gave Marley an indolently satisfied glance and settled her head down again.

"How's Gray?" Willow had curled up tightly in a wicker chair shaped like a bird's nest. "He's so dear."

Again, her sister's reaction to Gray bemused Marley. "Gray's fine. Really good."

"Amazing," Willow said, shaking her head. "Time heals."

Marley was too tired and too overwhelmed to dig for explanations.

"Who is this man you have accepted?" The man who asked wore his strawberry-red hair tied in a ponytail that reached his waist. He turned to look at Marley with dark green eyes.

"Papa," she said, almost under her breath. "Papa?" She held out her arms.

"Yes," Antoine Millet said, his thin face tensed. He gave her a quick hug. "It is your papa. You have become a woman, but it seems you have forgotten your responsibilities while I've been gone."

"Oh, boy," she said. "Some things never change. I'm doing just fine with my responsibilities."

"Fornicating with unsuitable people is one of your duties?" Antoine said. "I think not."

"Antoine," Pascal said. "Marley is an exemplary girl, a joy who has helped me a great deal."

"You are talking about *my* responsibilities, Papa?" Marley said. "I haven't seen you in years. How many? Fifteen? Uncle Pascal is my mentor."

"Don't—" Antoine pointed at her "—use that word lightly. There is only one Mentor and that's why I'm here. Your mother and I are making progress tracking down the Mentor. When we find him, he will help us deal with the curse. At last we'll find a way to deal effectively with any dark-haired male Millets—without having them visit disaster on us."

Sykes made a sound that resembled a snarl and Marley wouldn't look at him.

Antoine continued as if Sykes hadn't interrupted. "The Mentor will also want to be sure all of us—including you, miss—are following the instructions he left for us."

"Sykes?" Marley attempted to make contact with her brother.

"Yo, Marley. This is bizarre, but keep your cool."

"Has Papa been told about—Does he know anything about me being involved with something that could be sticky?"

"Not the way you mean. But as you can see, he's picked up something about your love life. Uncle Pascal knew you weren't home all night, then he figured out you had someone with you when you

317

did get back. He didn't tell Papa, but he seems to know anyway. How's Gray in bed? Nuclear from the look of you—which may be what gave Papa his ideas."

"Sykes!"

"Did he have any reason to wonder what he'd got himself into?"

In other words, Sykes wanted to know if Marley had met a potential Bonding Partner. *"Later."*

"Marley's in love. Well, well, well."

"Gray's probably a powerful paranormal sensitive," she said and enjoyed watching his flaring brows rise almost to his hairline.

"I've got to get back to your mother," Papa said. "She and your two older sisters are alone in London."

Marley held her breath, waiting for someone to remind her father that he'd left most of his family alone, for most of their lives. Silence greeted Antoine Millet's announcement.

"Sykes," Antoine said. "You will make yourself more present to the family. It may be that you will be required to take up your position after all."

"I think he's lost his mind," Sykes told Marley.

"Until I let you know otherwise, we will make sure the entire family is never all in one place at the same time," Antoine said.

"For a change," Willow said, surprising everyone and bringing a grin to Marley's mouth. "I thought we'd been doing that for twenty years."

Antoine ignored her. "If something untoward should happen, we can't afford to have all of us destroyed at once."

"Well," Sykes said. "That's a conversation killer. Do you have something else you want to share with us, Pops?"

Antoine scowled, but Pascal hid a grin.

"Leandra and I believe the Mentor is manifested in a sibylline casket he has left for us. Perhaps it is inscribed on the inside, or the outside—or this object could be an urn of unimaginable value. There are many possibilities, but whatever it is may well be the source of our troubles. It could be for the possession of this priceless artifact that disaster originally befell the Millets. Our dilemma now is to decide if Sykes is the next carrier of destruction."

"Carrier?" Sykes said. "Am I a harbinger of some sort of disease?"

"Quite possibly as far as the Millets are concerned," Antoine said. "But if not, you will have to lead the family."

Marley couldn't bear to look at Uncle Pascal, who had perfected the art of fuming in silence.

"This mysterious urn or casket," Sykes said flatly. "Where did that idea come from?"

"From years of selfless searching, my boy," Antoine said. "We now know that the Mentor's revelations were stolen by a woman in Bruges and she sold it for its great value. After the theft, what is rightfully ours was recovered, but we don't know what happened to it. When its whereabouts are known there are those who will try to take it from us again—by any means."

"Twaddle," Willow said from the farthest corner she'd been able to find.

Antoine shook his head in exasperation. He scowled at her. "You need a lot of work, and you," he pointed at Pascal, "should be dealing with that. This young woman is denying her powers and no Millet is allowed such outrageous behavior."

"Perhaps you have forgotten that I am the head of the Millet family," Pascal said in a far too pleasant voice. "I will take everything you've said into consideration. Please contact me the moment you learn anything else. Meanwhile, we will start our own enquiries into this casket or whatever. Have a good trip back to London, brother."

"What is it, Marley?" Sykes asked her in secret.

"I'm not sure. I have to think." But had the vision she'd seen of a glowing golden object been no less than a precognition of the Mentor's dangerous treasure?

Antoine looked around and slowly a smile spread over his face. "Feisty lot. Wouldn't have you any other way. Sykes—straighten up. Willow—whether you like it or not, you are gifted and will soon come into your own. You won't be able to fight it."

320

To Marley's horror, Sykes, an evil smile on his handsome face, began to fade out.

Antoine snapped his fingers at his son. "I knew I shouldn't have taught you that. It's far too powerful."

"You didn't teach me," Sykes said, sounding as if he was in a wind tunnel.

Pascal cleared his throat. "Like all of your children," he said, "Sykes was born with his, er, *gifts*."

Antoine shrugged and turned to embrace his brother. "You have the better part, Pascal," he said. "Being in charge is a great thing. You certainly wouldn't want to be rattling around the world, responsible to no one at all, like I am."

Pascal grumbled under his breath.

Antoine stood before Marley, his hands behind his back and his expression foreboding. "Marley," he said and put his arms stiffly around her. "You are a puzzle to your mother and me—just as all of our children are. But we love you deeply. If you have found your Bonding and decide to do what you should and join with the man permanently, let us know."

She couldn't say a word.

"Be careful with him. Your mother and I are aware that you have awakened a wounded lion among sensitives, someone formerly suppressed by fate. Perhaps this one is completely healed and safe. I hope so."

30

When Gray's phone had rung, just after Marley left to see her uncle, the last person he had expected to hear was Sidney Fournier. They had talked briefly—she had done all the talking, or the ordering—for a few minutes, before she had lowered her voice and said she had to go.

Other than to tell him she wanted them to get together where they would definitely not be interrupted, she had refused to explain why they should meet tonight at Myrtle Wood, one of the smaller River Road plantation houses.

He thought it was pointless drama to go to such lengths, but had agreed. The possibility that he might finally get a useful lead on Liza and Amber gave him hope.

As soon as Marley left him to go to Pascal's, he had used her shower, given up on doing anything about looking like a wild-haired pirate, and tucked himself back into her bed. He hoped she would return alone, but if not, he was a big boy and he'd think of something to say—like, "I was just testing the mattress."

He snickered.

The front door opened and racing toenails sounded like an army of rats on a rampage.

The bedroom door flew open and Winnie charged in, her giant bone clenched between her teeth.

"Hey, sweetheart," Gray said to Marley. He glanced at Winnie. "Your dog's frowning."

"Probably at you," she said.

"I like your topknot."

She felt the crazy pom-pom on top of her head and turned up her palms. "Everyone should have a distinguishing feature."

Winnie jumped on a chair, and from there onto the bed. She drooled slightly around the chew.

Gray did his own frowning. "The dog's on the bed," he said.

"I've always admired an observant man," Marley said. "It's her bed, too."

"I'm waiting for you," Gray said. "We weren't finished."

"You must be a masochist."

"There's pain, and then there's pain," he told her. "I figure the more I practice pain control the better I'll get at it."

She narrowed her lovely eyes. "Just what does that mean?"

Gray could tell when he was entering deep water. "Sit right here by me." He patted the bed beside him.

Promptly, Winnie placed herself where he'd indicated and panted, working on the bone.

It wasn't easy, but Gray kept the smile on his face and patted the other side of the bed. "Come on. I want to talk."

The look she gave him suggested she thought he had something other than talk in mind.

Winnie hopped clean over him and settled in what was to have been Marley's new spot—really close to Gray.

She smiled as if she was very amused. But she also took off the yellow sweatsuit in about two rapid motions, ran, took a leap and landed on the bed beside him, kneeling so she was all sweet curves in her skimpy bra and panties.

Winnie crossed his body again, planting her feet hard on some of his unprotected parts as she went.

Gray winced and said, "Ow, ow, ow," but the dog looked smug and put herself between him and Marley.

"I've just seen my father," Marley said, and Gray thought her expression was one of the oddest he'd seen. She appeared amazed, disbelieving, a little bit sleepy and a lot cross. "First time in fifteen years."

He sat up, letting the sheet fall to his hips and making no attempt to hike it up. "Is that right? I thought I was the only fatherless child around here." Damn, his mouth never got that loose. It had to be her effect on him. "I meant motherless."

"I was talking about fathers," Marley said, inching a little closer.

He stroked her thigh and played his fingertips in the dip just beneath the leg of her panties. She jumped. But so did he.

"I met your dad," she said. "He hasn't been away, has he?"

"Nope. He's been right here in New Orleans. And whenever I needed him, he was there for me."

"That sounds nice."

"It is." He scratched Winnie between the ears. "Gus adopted me when I was eight. I was a lucky kid. I'm glad you got to visit with your dad today."

"I'm not sure I am."

He could see she wanted to ask more about his own history, but was too polite to push. He'd tell her more eventually—if he had to.

Marley flattened a hand low on his belly and stroked back and forth. She shuddered and half closed her eyes. Gray's gut turned to fire and he was a man with a body on full alert.

"What did you mean about pain control?"

He needed a tongue transplant. "I should probably have said pain management. The way to manage this wonderful pain of ours is through immersion therapy—translate that into pain management."

"Is it too much for you? Be honest, please."

He hesitated. Winnie stood up, watching first one of their faces, then the other.

"Marley, if I can't have you, why bother?" he said, watching every word, aware of how easy a pitfall would be. "There's no way I could be satisfied with less. Could I kiss you before I go crazy?"

"Just a minute," she said. "We—my family—has something called a Bonding. It's when one of us meets the right person to share . . . sex with. We tell if it's happening by the heightened senses. But it can be pretty overwhelming."

He nodded sagely. "I am so lucky. And I'm so ready to be overwhelmed with you."

She frowned as if there was more she wanted to say, but kissed him instead. She leaned over him, pushing him down and slipping her tongue between his lips.

Gray began to stroke her all over. He liked the bra and panties. They were a special kind of sexy—forbidden, maybe. When he looked sideways, it was into Winnie's shiny black eyes.

"Sweet lady," he said. "Maybe Winnie could go take a nap somewhere."

Marley laughed. "Off, Winnie. And wait."

Apparently that meant the dog did just that. She got off the bed and waited beside it. Gray could imagine her upturned face ready for the signal that she could return.

He forgot the dog.

Marley stood on the mattress. She laughed down at him and bent forward at the waist so that her breasts all but slipped from the bra. He reached up for her, but she shook her body from side to side, evading him.

"Oh, baby, come on down," he said.

"Wait." She put a foot on his stomach, balanced herself with outstretched arms and slowly moved her toes until she tangled with hair around the base of his penis. That was one thing he couldn't subdue, and didn't want to.

Marley ogled him. "Oh, my, I think I should be scared."

Then her face softened again, and Gray couldn't find any more smart quips.

She unhooked the bra and tossed it on the floor, and then she took him completely by surprise and settled a knee on either of his shoulders. Curling over, she passed her breasts across his lips and gasped each time his tongue and teeth caught a nipple.

A thumb slipped inside her panties, slid easily where he got the most response for very little effort and he felt he could go mad when she climaxed.

With her mouth, Marley drew him to the brink, all the time rubbing him and murmuring, but when he knew he couldn't hold on another second, she spun around, pulled off her panties and guided him into her.

They made love with him lying over her back and holding her breasts. Every stroke was raw bliss. He climbed to a pinnacle of aching aware-ness and just when he would have begged for mercy, he emptied himself and they rocked until they fell, spooned together and damp all over.

There was something he wanted to tell her. He parted his lips on the back of her neck where her hair rested in damp curls. "Marley?"

"Mmm?"

It was way too soon. Everything about the two of them was too fast and too soon. If he said what he'd like to, she might bolt and he couldn't bear that. "You're really something," he said.

"Only with you," she said. "Only ever with you."

He liked the sound of that. It wasn't enough, though.

His phone vibrated on the bedside table. "Ignore that," he said.

"It could be Gus looking for you."

Gray closed his eyes. There wasn't anything about the woman that he didn't like—except having her dog in bed with them.

"Okay," he said, sitting up. He had a text message. "Text message from Nat Archer," he said. "It can wait."

She rolled over, pushing hair from her eyes. "Find out what he wants. Just in case."

The message was, Call me. Trouble just got bigger.

He showed it to Marley who pushed at her pillows and sat up beside him.

Gray called Nat. "Okay, buddy. Let's have it."

"Shirley Cooper sang with a street band when she wasn't working as a maid at that club."

"Yeah?" Gray massaged his temples. "Another singer after all."

"And Pearl Brite isn't a brand name. It's the name of another missing singer. This one rode a bike to work at Alexander's."

31

Marley had worked hard all day, but always with her concentration distracted. The minutes passed, and the hours, and she felt helpless. Now she was at home in her apartment and waiting for Gray with ammunition ready.

He had told her about the call Sidney Fournier had made to him and showed every intention of keeping the appointment with her in River Road on his own.

That wasn't going to happen.

Winnie let out an excited yelp and Marley shushed her.

She heard footsteps on the metal stairs outside and went into the hall.

"I'm coming with you," Marley said the moment Gray walked through her front door. "I was the first one to ask to talk to Sidney at Scully's. Just because she's sucked in by your boyish good looks doesn't mean I'm going to roll over and play dead."

She deliberately avoided looking at Gray. If pushed she would admit that she'd tricked him into coming back to the Court of Angels on his way over to River Road. She hoped she wouldn't have to do that.

"Maybe I shouldn't have told you Sidney called," Gray said.

"You're not the secretive type."

"Aren't I?" He gave her a speculative look. "What was it you had to tell me in person?" Gray asked.

She would have to admit she'd fibbed. "Did you know Myrtle Wood is haunted?" she said. The basket of clean laundry she carried on a hip almost fell. She put it down on the floor in her living room.

"I hadn't heard that, no." He didn't look impressed. "You still haven't let me in on this secret of yours."

She bowed her head and looked up at him. And she pressed her lips together.

"Hey, hey, are you going to cry?"

She hadn't intended to, but she might try if she thought it would get her off the hook. She sniffed.

"Honey," he said. "What can I do? I can't stand to see you like this."

Marley wanted to groan. She took a deep, deep breath. "You can take me with you to Myrtle Wood and not give me a hard time about it."

He blinked. "That's it? That's why you look as if you're about to start a flood?"

"You're making fun of me."

"That's fighting dirty, Marley, and you know it. I agreed to go out there and meet Sidney. She wanted to be in a place where no one was likely to find out she'd come to me. You know what this means? She's got something really important to say. I need to be on top of my game so I don't miss anything important."

"It's always best to have more than one person listening to important things. Afterward we'll compare notes. It's a great idea. Trust me."

"What if Sidney takes one look at you and bolts?"

"I understand these things. I'll be a help to you, Gray. I'm going to be on her side."

He picked up a fat cushion from the couch, flopped down and piled the pillow on top of him. "How can you make plans like that when you don't know what she's going to say?"

"I could say I'm going to be sympathetic to whatever she says if that works better for you. We women are always getting screwed over by big, mean men. We've got to stick together."

"Big, mean men? Is that a comment on anyone you know?"

She smiled with one side of her mouth. "Nah. Just a wild guess about how Sidney may feel about males."

"What if she loves men? All men?"

Marley puffed, exasperated. "Oh, she does. Take it from me, she does. Just leave it to me to get her off her guard and talking."

"She's coming to help me," Gray said. "Why go in thinking she'll hold back?"

"Jeez," Marley said. "It's most likely you aren't moving fast enough to make her into a star with your article. So she's piling on a bit of drama to get your undivided attention."

"Couldn't she just want to help?" Gray said. "Sure, turning this into some sort of tryst may appeal to her, but that doesn't make her the enemy."

Marley held up her hands in submission. "Okay, go in thinking she's going to seduce you, all the more reason for me to be there. I've got to protect my interests."

He chuckled. "You're impossible. Okay, come, but be careful. Don't say anything to put her off."

"I'll be so good." Her demeanor turned instantly sunny. She dumped out the clean laundry and started folding. He noted how quickly she moved and how efficient she was.

She hauled out the black shorts she'd worn the day before and shook them. Then she put them on the back of a chair and smoothed them out. A bump stuck out in the bottom of a pocket and she dug around in there until she could pull out a lump of black rubber.

Marley looked at the thing from all sides and tossed it on a palm. She shook her head and made a move to set it aside.

"What is that?" Gray asked.

"I don't know. The cap off the bottom of a chair leg, maybe—or from one of those TV trays people use." She looked around the room. "I never saw it before."

"You must have. It was in your pocket."

Her mouth took a stubborn downturn. "Well, I didn't put it there."

"That's an interesting thought."

"It's just a rubber cap," she said and made a move to toss it in a wastebasket.

Gray caught the piece. "I think I'll hang on to this. You never know, I may come up with an idea about what it is."

"Which brings me to an intriguing question," she said. "You knew about the helmet, but you hadn't been in that warehouse before. Or had you?"

"You know I hadn't."

She sat cross-legged on the floor and accepted Winnie on her lap. "Gray, you're definitely psychic."

"No, I'm not. I've thought about it for hours on and off. I think I'm really in tune with you so I see some of the things you think about."

"Not bad, but not the whole story. I didn't see the helmet, Gray. I promise you, I didn't." Her attention pulled away. What was she missing? "Did you tell me I'd picked something up in that place? Before? You did, but I didn't remember."

Leaning forward, Gray absently hooked Winnie's bone from beside the couch and held it out to the dog. She raised her snubby nose and ignored him.

"You picked something up," Gray said.

"Evidently. But you knew it before I did—consciously."

He waved the chew in the air and Winnie looked sideways at him with something close to a dismissive sneer. "What if I don't want to be psychic?"

She shrugged. "I never saw anyone who was, but didn't want to be. It's got its advantages, y'know."

"Such as?"

"Finding life and death clues in criminal cases. Sometimes knowing when someone thinks you're an ass. Stuff like that."

"Charming."

"It could be that when you aren't around me anymore, you'll lose your touch."

"What does that mean?" Gray said. "When I'm not around you anymore?"

It meant that she was fishing for reassurance that she might still matter to him when all this was over. "I don't know," she lied.

"You . . ." He fell back on the couch and looked at the ceiling. "I'm not much for fooling around with feelings, Marley. I hope I'll be around you for a really long time."

She swallowed and felt silly tears. "Me, too," she said quietly. "Phew, we've dealt with that now."

Gray made a growling sound and started to reach for her.

Winnie leaped between the two of them, planted her bowed legs and snorted at Gray. Marley was grateful she hadn't actually snarled, but figured they shouldn't push it.

"Sorry," Gray told the dog. "You're a good girl to guard your mom from evil men. Have your bone." He pushed it toward her and she took it.

"There's an elephant in the room," Marley said. "I think it's getting bigger, too. We need to talk about it."

Gray nodded. "Pearl Brite? I haven't heard one darn word on her whereabouts yet. According to Nat this is one more just like Liza and Amber. Zap, she's gone."

"Nat talked to me this afternoon," Marley said. "I wish I could have been more useful, but at least we've made progress. Now he's a believer—which is good news, bad news. He wants me to keep *doing what I do* as he puts it because he's certain I'll finally get coordinates on where to find Liza and Amber."

"And maybe Pearl Brite?" Gray said. "She sounds like a nice kid. Twenty-four. Lives at home with her dad who doesn't see so well. Mother dead since Pearl was a little girl and Pearl and her dad have looked after each other. She's popular at Alexander's. Some say she's ready for bigger things."

Marley propped her chin on a fist.

"What are you thinking?" Gray said.

"It's not fair. That always sounds so stupid, but it isn't."

"No, it isn't. Did Nat tell you there definitely was no sign of any blood in that warehouse?"

She shook her head.

"That's hopeful."

"D'you think? Oh, I hope so."

"Marley, what's the deal with the red dollhouse?"

"I've been waiting for you to ask. Will you trust me to explain when I can figure out how? Some things are so much a part of me and my experience that I don't know how to talk about them. The house is my connection to wherever those women are. That's the simple explanation."

"Where did it come from?"

"It was given to me for safekeeping."

He moved fractionally closer. "By whom?"

"A woman. I don't know who she was and I can't find her again. I've tried. Please give me some room on this."

She took hold of the hand he offered and let him pull her to the seat of the couch. Sitting sideways, he looked into her face while he stroked her hair—and kissed her. He adjusted himself to get closer and closed his eyes.

"Mmm-mm," Marley said. She put her fingers on his lips. "What time are you due at Myrtle Woods?"

"Whoa." He drew back looking shell-shocked. "Darn it. I've got to go."

"We've got to go."

The day's flow of tourists had deserted the wide and winding way along River Road. Most of the once fantastic mansions were set well back, but often on modest lots cut from the vast acreage they once commanded. The visible signs of fortunes made in indigo and sugar clung to the shabby-grand houses. So did the odor of inequity.

"I haven't been out here in years," Gray said. "I like it better in the evening. You can't see the decay so clearly."

Marley said, "You're right. A bit like a faded photo in sepia tones. But it's so creepy, it's great."

"You would think that."

She didn't come back at him for the remark and he was grateful.

The devil made him ask, "Are you afraid of the dark, or ghosts, or any of that stuff?"

Marley glanced at him and, with a completely straight face, said, "Not the dark. Ghosts are okay if they aren't the mean kind. Pinching isn't my thing. And getting your ears pulled is the pits. I could do without poltergeists. Werewolves can be benevolent—but they're unpredictable. I don't think about any of those much, but I really have negative vibes about the undead."

Glad I asked. "You don't really think all that stuff's for real?"

She gave him an odd look. "Don't you?"

Gray frowned, searching for a way to change the subject. "You didn't say how your dad is. It must have been at least kind of nice to see him."

"It was. He's my dad. Same as always. Bossy. He was just fine, thank you. Gus doing okay?"

He smiled to himself. "Irascible as ever. I got in a few hours' work this afternoon and he hovered the whole time. All he wanted to talk about was you."

"Am I supposed to feel bad about that?" She gave him a puckish smile.

Gray sighed. "Gus has got a sense of humor, thank God. If you can laugh at yourself it's got to make life a lot easier—even when it's hard."

Myrtle Woods bore no marker. If you didn't have an idea where to turn in, you'd drive right by.

"I think this is it," Gray said, driving his well-used gray Volvo between the trunks of old trees. He rolled down his window and the thick, exotic scent of jasmine, magnolia and the musky bite of evening clover filled the car.

"It's a good thing I came with you," Marley said.

Gray took a moment to say, "I'm glad you came, but why is it a good thing?"

"It's deserted out here and it's going to be dark soon. I wouldn't want you here on your own."

He laughed. "You're going to protect me?"

"You'd be surprised what I can do if I have to," she said, glad she sounded braver than she felt.

"No, I wouldn't . . . Car over there. One familiar expensive black sedan. I think it's the one she was in yesterday. Do you see Sidney?"

"Nope. I hate those tinted windows. They look like they should be on mob cars."

Gray drove up and parked beside the BMW.

Marley registered that he wore a lightweight jacket. He was usually more casual. "Isn't the jacket hot?" she asked.

"Yeah."

"Take it off then. We aren't going to a garden party."

"I'll be keeping it on."

She stared at him. "Do you have a gun?"

"Yeah. I know what I'm doing. Let's go."

They didn't have far to go. Sidney fell in beside Gray before they reached the front steps of the house. She gave Marley an unfriendly look and said, "Do you mind waiting here?" to her. "Gray and I need some privacy. We can go to the gallery at the back," she added to Gray.

"We're all in this," Gray said. "Marley comes, too."

Sidney narrowed her dark eyes. "You wanted to see me at Scully's," she told Marley. "You didn't say why. I don't see why I would interest you."

"You didn't give me a chance to tell you why. I'm looking for Liza Soaper and Amber Lee." She deliberately didn't mention Pearl Brite. "I have a history with them." That wasn't a lie.

"History?" Sidney quit walking. "What kind of history?"

"Let's go out back and talk," Marley said.

"I don't like evasive people," Sidney said slowly.

"That makes three of us," Gray said. He walked up the wide front steps, wooden and rotting in places, and started off along the gallery that surrounded the house.

Marley kept up with him, and Sidney's hurrying feet in very high heels could soon be heard catching up with them.

A number of white wicker chairs lined the wall under the back windows. Two had been pulled forward, a table placed between and a bottle of white wine nestled in an ice bucket flanked by two glasses.

Marley only just stopped herself from saying, "Cozy."

Without pausing, Gray pulled up a third chair and indicated for the women to sit, which they did. He joined them and said, "Wine?"

Sidney echoed Marley's, "No, thanks." Marley crossed her legs and jiggled a toe. She didn't check out how Sidney might be looking at her.

"Let's have it," Gray said. "We don't have to worry about being overheard here." Lawns in need of mowing stretched away from the house. Coming close to the gallery without being seen would be impossible.

"I'm only going to talk to you, Gray," Sidney said. "I don't know Marley."

"Really? I thought you'd lived in New Orleans all your life."

"I have."

"But you never heard of the Millets."

Sidney sighed. "I try not to take any notice of silly gossip. I come from an old family, too, and we keep above that sort of thing."

"Silly gossip?" Marley said.

Sidney waved a white hand. "Psychic or paranormal or whatever. Rubbish. Everyone knows there's no such thing. And the red hair. Decent people would be sympathetic to something like that."

Neither Gray nor Marley responded.

"You can't help being born with hair like that. The gene must be very strong. You could always dye it, though."

Gray hummed.

Marley gave Sidney a sweet smile. "I knew the first time I saw you that you had a generous heart. Thank you." People like Sidney Fournier weren't good at recognizing sarcasm and Marley wanted to gain the woman's confidence. "You've been through a lot with Amber missing, Sidney. It must have been so hard to have people pushing you from all sides. I'll never understand why men of the law-and-order type don't have more empathy."

Sidney shook her head. She was even more beautiful in the failing light, the gold tones from the setting sun accentuating her olive skin and the fine bones in her face. "Thank you," she said. "It's been so horrible. And I haven't known where to turn."

"Why, Sidney?" Marley inched closer to the other woman. "You have family and friends."

Sidney burst into tears, shocking Marley, who got up and rubbed Sidney's shoulders. She patted her back. "Take it easy. Give yourself time. Take some deep breaths." She glanced at Gray who looked bemused.

"It's my family and friends I'm worried about," Sidney said. "I don't know what to do. I want to go to the police, but I can't. It's too dangerous."

"They said you didn't want to talk to them at all," Gray pointed out.

"I've been threatened," Sidney said through gulps. "Not openly. Oh, no, it's very subtle, but I know what it all means. If I say anything about what I think, someone will get hurt." She passed the back of a shaky hand over her mouth. "If they haven't already. I think they have, don't you?"

Marley looked at Gray who gave a slight shake of the head. "Let's not get ahead of ourselves, Sidney," he said. "Tell me what you wanted to say."

Sidney got up and paced the length of the back gallery. She stopped in front of them. "I got a call from a man who said he can prove I'm the one who knows where Amber is. He said I'd be accused of doing something to her and I'd go to jail. He said . . . he said they could convict me without a body."

She cried again. "Just ignore me. I haven't been able to tell anyone anything. It's all bottled up inside."

"The police need to know," Gray said gently.

She nodded. "For all I know you'll both go right to them and tell them about me."

"We won't," Marley said.

"If I sent them an e-mail they could trace it back to me?" Sidney said.

Marley wondered at Sidney's lack of savvy. "Yes," she said simply.

"Then I don't know. I could get a cheap cell phone to call them, then throw it away after I use it."

"You could," Gray agreed.

"I'm afraid." Sidney sat down on the very edge of a chair. "Could someone frame me for killing Amber?"

"We hope she isn't dead."

"Yes." Sidney sounded on the verge of hysteria. "But that man talked as if she was."

"Did you write down the number this guy called from?"

"I panicked. I forgot to look."

Great. "Did you recognize the voice at all?" Marley asked.

"No. But I think it's all about covering something up. I think there was . . . Amber doesn't have a son. Who would say she does? Why? Except to try stopping you from making any more enquiries, Gray."

"So who made the call to the cops and said he was Amber's boy?"

"I don't know," Sidney said. "Have they tried to find out?"

"Of course. Call came from somewhere in the city, but they couldn't trace it. So far there's no record of Amber Lee having a child. There's nothing much on her at all. Speculation is she probably left home young and she's been on the move most of the time since."

"There's something I do know." Sidney looked all around and dropped her voice. "What did Danny tell you about him and Amber?"

Marley thought about it. "At first he said she didn't really know how much she meant to him. He made it sound like it was a one-sided thing with him crazy about her and Amber joking along."

"That was a lie."

Gray drummed his fingers on a thigh.

"But he did tell me he was crazy about her," Marley said. "It wasn't until later that he let it out they were lovers and lived together."

Sidney crossed her arms tightly. "Amber did love Danny, but he was jealous. Mad, jealous. He beat someone up once just for talking to her. She and Danny had troubles for a long time. She was finally finished with him. She'd already moved out when she disappeared. He'd been following her everywhere and threatening to kill her if she didn't come back to him."

She got the stunned response she must have wanted.

"And you don't think the police should know this?" Gray asked.

"I've got to go. I'll be late for my first set."

32

"Just like that," Gray said, watching Sidney's tail-lights swing down the driveway and turn out onto River Road. "What do you make of it?"

"She didn't need the elaborate setup to give you her information," Marley said. She paused. "Or maybe she thought she did. I believe she's scared—even if I'm not completely sure why."

"I think she's *really* scared."

"Did you believe her when she talked about someone trying to frame her?"

"Why would she make it up?" He kicked up some gravel. "I'd like to know more about her relationship with Amber."

"Yes," Marley agreed. "She wants us to tell the police about Danny, doesn't she?"

"Yep. Question is, what if she's being straight with us and it would be dangerous for her to talk—to the cops? Or if it came out that she was responsible for letting information out that got to them."

"She doesn't really have information," Marley pointed out. "She's guessing. And we don't know if everything she says is true. She was suggesting Danny Summit could be a murderer."

"We've got to think. Nothing's standing still with Nat. He's got people taking New Orleans apart."

Marley laughed. "It's funny the way you talk about cops when you used to be one."

"It has its advantages," Gray said. "I can put on a couple of different hats and the appropriate brain is inside."

This time Marley sniggered. She put a hand to her face and made a snorting sound.

"That funny?" Gray said.

"It's a pretty interesting picture."

"That bottle of wine's still on the back gallery," Gray said. "Maybe that's what we need to help us think clearly."

"It's getting awfully dark out here."

"I saw citronella candles back there. I've got you for protection. You've got me for protection. And I've got a gun."

"Let's have some wine," Marley said. She hooked a hand under his arm and they returned to the back of the house.

Gray lighted two buckets of citronella with matches left for the purpose. He put one bucket on the table and opened the wine. The ice in the bucket was long melted. Sidney hadn't forgotten to bring a wine opener, and she'd left it behind with everything else she'd brought with her.

They sat, drinking white wine that tasted good even if it was tepid, and listening to frogs and crickets while fireflies winked in the tops of tall grass.

"Knock, knock, Marley."

Momentarily disoriented, she turned to Gray who looked out into the darkness.

She gave a long, long sigh. *"Sykes?"*

"Permission to enter?"

"Very funny. You're already in."

"Nope. Only on the doorstep. I'll go away if you insist."

"What are you doing here, Sykes?"

"You'll just have to let me off the hook. Uncle Pascal again. He's not himself, girl. He's jittery and it's all your fault. It doesn't help that our dear papa is passing through and asking questions."

"He doesn't have any right to ask questions. And I thought he'd already left."

"He has," Sykes said. *"But Uncle Pascal's been so uptight all day in case Papa asked more about what's going on with you, he's a wreck. So here I am to make sure no one has to rescue you."*

"And I'm great, thank you. You're kind to care."

"I came for our uncle."

"Of course," Marley said. Sykes preserved his reputation as selfish and only out for himself. It might fool most—Marley wasn't among them.

"I've got some interesting tidbits of news,"

Sykes said. *"Our papa might really be making progress digging up the Millet mysteries."*

Marley felt excited and jumpy, but had to keep a blank face. *"You have terrible timing. I want to know all about it, but I can't now—obviously."*

"You're quiet," Gray said. "But your mind is doing somersaults."

She sat very still and calmed herself. She flattened her emotions and pushed Sykes to a corner of her consciousness.

"You've known Nat Archer a long time," Marley said. "Is he someone we could talk to off the record?"

Gray was quiet for a while before he said, "I think so. He's always been a maverick—never played the rules completely straight. What d'you have in mind?"

She wasn't sure.

"Ask him to come out here," Sykes said. *"It's not far. He's in a war zone and he's an army of one being fired on from all sides. Everyone wants this case broken and they want it broken yesterday. The new disappearance could be all it takes to set off mass hysteria."*

"I haven't heard too much about those old unsolved disappearances with what's going on," Gray said. "But the Pearl Brite incident might be enough to start people making connections."

"Why—" Marley cut herself off before she could ask what made him make those comments right when he made them. It sounded as if he was answering what she'd heard Sykes tell her. "You're right," she said, trying for a breezy tone.

"We need a scrambled frequency here."

"You're talking about something that's nothing to do with you," Marley said. *"What do you know about the case? Have you been spying on me?"*

"No. And it hurts me for you to think I would. I live here, too, remember?"

Marley ignored Sykes. She couldn't make herself feel guilty for tromping on his delicate sensibilities. She almost laughed.

"So you think we should try to get Nat out here?" Gray said.

She cleared her throat. "Gray, I didn't say anything about asking Nat to come out here. You're reading my mind." *Or in this case, picking up on what I'm hearing from my brother.*

"No. You said that."

"No, I didn't," Marley told him.

"You're looking for these signs or whatever."

"It might be nice to have Nat come out where the territory feels neutral, though," Marley said. "He always seems on duty. Do you think he drinks too much?"

"You never stay on topic."

"Butt out, Sykes."

"Why? You gonna have sex under the stars?"

"Nat knows what he's doing," Gray said. "He's

349

always in control. We'd better get back to the Quarter and find him."

"No sex under the stars? Aw, shucks."

"My turn is going to come, bro. Just you wait."

"You don't need anyone's permission to call this cop yourself. Just do it."

Marley consigned herself to dealing with these two. "I'm calling him." She found her phone in her bag. "What's his number?"

"I wish you wouldn't do this," Gray said. But he took out his own phone, punched in a programmed number and handed it to Marley.

"He's got possibilities, sis. Some guys would have refused to give you the number, let alone dialed it for you."

Marley agreed, but didn't give Sykes that message. She waited, watching stars pop in a pewter sky above the black-shadowed crowns of trees.

"Nat Archer."

Marley swallowed and set out her proposition. She finished with, "I think it's time I explained a number of things I haven't wanted to talk about. I don't think I've done any harm yet, but maybe I can make a difference now."

"I'm on my way," Nat said. "Thanks, Marley."

She smiled and closed the phone.

"Why the smile?" Gray said.

"He's a nice guy."

Gray leaned toward her across the little round

table. "That's a switch. D'you have any idea how sexy you look by candlelight?"

"I'm gone," Sykes said and Marley felt his instant absence.

She widened her eyes at Gray. "I like you by candlelight, too."

He peered at his watch.

"What is it?" Marley said. "Did you forget an appointment."

"Nope. I was just figuring out how long we've got before Nat can make it out here. Long enough. Just. Sit on my lap. Please."

She tingled all over, but more in some places than others. . . .

Gray reached for her hand and guided her in front of him. She started to turn sideways, but he held her where she was.

He ran his hands slowly up beneath her white cotton skirt, parted her aching thighs and settled her where she fitted the best, squarely astride his hips.

For seconds they absorbed the physical shock of their contact. They connected with their mouths and the night turned all white heat and the rushing clamor of arousal.

351

33

This Marley Millet was a spoiler. She wouldn't bring him down; that wasn't possible. He would find and deal with her.

But there was a fitting irony in this new battle with the Millets. Marley couldn't have been pitted against him by accident. This was someone's deliberate plan to destroy him by using a descendant of the very family that had caused the long-ago woman-Embran to return to her species with a disease they had never been able to cure.

That woman-Embran who married a Millet in Belgium had been blamed for dire threats to the safety of that family. It was after her return to the Lower Place that the Embrans first encountered bodily decay. They had learned how to renew themselves through the contents of their own unhatched eggs, but the results were temporary, a mere hundred or so years' reprieve, and they wanted their immortality back.

He had been allowed to come to the surface of the earth after others of his kind had visited but failed to find an antidote to the plague. Now he knew what he could not have before—discovering what the Millets had used on the Embrans could take many visits, especially when there were so many luscious diversions to enjoy in the meantime.

He wanted to hiss, to aim his face at the black

sky that was his friend and rattle his jaws until he drowned out every other night sound and left the human vermin in this city too terrified to leave the perceived safety of their homes.

Yet they had no safe defense over an enemy they did not know and who could strike wherever he pleased.

The Millet woman had barged in where she had no right to be. The deepest most disturbing question was, how had she obtained information she shouldn't have? What had led her to find him? Who?

He dragged himself over a thick layer of gravel at the bottom of the tunnel only he had ever used. Fleeing that warehouse, he had injured himself. The woman's fault again. She had interfered. Harm was not supposed to happen to one such as he and there would be retribution for this inconvenience.

Many times he had come through this tunnel to pursue his pleasures. Tonight, for the first time ever, he knew the kind of fear only anger could produce. He had been betrayed by someone who should be too afraid to cross him, and when he discovered the identity of his betrayer, he would grind their bones to dust.

If he had to, he would cut a path of death across New Orleans, searching for his enemies. Afterward he would have to withdraw to Embran, deep in the earth, perhaps for longer than these little people could fathom. And when all those who could get in his way were gone or forgotten here, he would fight all comers in Embran for the right to come back and reclaim the fruits he had earned.

There would be those in the Lower Place who would blame him, try to have him demoted for failing to find a cure for their eventual decay, but he had his cover ready. Alone, he had developed a means of staving off total disintegration of the Embran form for short periods—long enough to get one of them home if the need became dire.

He had already tested his prototype and pre-pared a small stash.

He resented his need for air. Breathing slowed him down. Next time he came back to this part of his reality with its toothsome fleshly prizes, he must increase his efforts not to need any of the ele-ments the weaklings used.

But he wasn't ready to leave yet, oh, no. First he must finish with the fools who thought they could stop him, but even that had to wait until he knew if the unthinkable had happened and the one object he must have had been stolen.

The way was too long. Once he had been able to rush to the small but perfect white pavilion, some-times every few weeks when the hunting was exceptional. He had taken his victims there to enjoy. Some years had passed since then and his precious antidote was losing its power to sustain him.

He reached the steps at the end of the tunnel, worked his way upward and outside. The pavilion stood before him and he turned his head from side to side to bring the walls into clear focus. Here, too, there were signs of aging. Moss clung, and the surfaces had darkened. None of it would do.

Heaving, he fought for calm. If he could hang on a few more days he would be finished with what must be done before he returned to his source of renewal and strength—to Embran.

Just a few more days.

He pulled himself up, stair by stair, to the door of his sanctum and strained to clamp onto a recessed handle. With renewed vigor, he used the small onyx key that was the only means of entry.

The door closed behind him automatically. In the center of a single room draped with diaphanous, many-colored silks and lined with gilded divans, an enameled cabinet stood on a carved table.

He allowed himself a sneer of glee. Shuffling, reaching, trembling in his haste, he touched the chest and tapped the jade and mother-of-pearl inlay. A beautiful thing fit to contain his most precious possession.

The other end of the onyx key slipped easily into a lock that released double doors. They swung open.

On a black velvet bed inside, an image shimmered, a memory of what should have been there.

He recoiled.

As he had desperately feared, the red dollhouse that was his only escape to his own world was no longer in its place.

He stared at the wavering, transparent represen-tation of his very being—and his salvation—and slid soundlessly to the floor. There was only one course of action now. He would set about repos-sessing his property—by whatever means neces-sary.

From the folds of his robe, he brought out the tiny scrap of black cotton that had clung to one of his claws when he had struck out at Marley Millet. Holding the fabric to his brow, he crawled onto a divan and opened his inner eye.

He concentrated, searching for the channel that would take him to her.

34

"Barefoot in the park," Marley said. She smiled up at Gray although she could scarcely see his face in the darkness.

Hand-in-hand they walked in the damp grass behind the house at Myrtle Wood. Here and there a bird flew up, startling Marley.

She and Gray had left their shoes on the gallery. Nat should arrive shortly and they intended to be as collected as possible when they saw him.

"The grass feels good," Gray said. "And so do you."

She heard the smile in his voice. "It feels as if we're stealing time."

"We are. But we deserve it. I could be wrong, but my gut tells me we're about to go into high gear. Mad gear. Does a scuffle in a cupboard mean anything to you? Could be a cupboard, a pantry or who knows what. And a lot of flailing down some stairs. Or am I starting to make up some of what I think I see?"

Marley pulled him to face her. "It means something, Gray."

"I was afraid you'd say that."

"Remember yesterday, when I said I saw Liza before I was in the warehouse? There was a cupboard where Liza was—a big one like a storeroom. We went through it and down wooden stairs before the man . . ."

"Before the man what?"

She wanted to shut that out. And she wanted to think about how the transference was happening between her and Gray—and if there was some way they could make these connections work for them.

"Marley?"

"He attacked Liza."

"You saw this?"

She opened her mouth to breathe. "I was inside Liza. My mind was inside hers. I saw through her eyes, or what she could see at the bottom of a blindfold."

"Oh, my God."

"We need to hurry or Nat will get here and we'll be wandering around the lawn," Marley said, walking faster.

"Did he—"

"Please. Don't push. It can't be changed now. Do you hear an engine?" She paused to listen. "A great big engine. Who can that be?"

Gray followed her up the steps to the gallery. "It can be Nat Archer in his black Corvette. His baby. Let's keep going. If it's someone else, I don't want him walking up on us while we're sitting."

"Why?"

He carried on toward the side of the house and Marley followed. "Let's just say I'm into making sure I've got every advantage available. Between being looked up at and looked down on, there's no contest about where the advantage is."

"Hmm," she said, and speeded her steps to keep up with him. Evidently she would always be at an extreme disadvantage.

"Sure enough," Gray said when they got to the front. "One flashy black money sink. He loves that car."

"We all have things that are important to us. I think for a lot of men, a car takes the place of a wife or children. In a very general way."

"Nat loves a woman a hell of a lot more than he loves that car," Gray said. "I hope you meet Wazoo one day. She's something. Doesn't come to New

Orleans often. And before you start with the questions, I don't know why they haven't taken things farther. Nat's a city cop, Wazoo's a country witch. I guess they're having problems working out the logistics."

Marley laughed and clung to his sleeve. "Country *witch?*"

"I'm serious," he said. "Now you get serious. And never mention Wazoo to Nat unless he does first. Which won't happen. Maybe if you know him four or five years, you'll meet her."

She chortled. "I want to."

Nat had bent down and his head and upper body were invisible from the back of his car. When he emerged, he carried several paper sacks.

"Hey," Gray called.

Nat searched for Gray and Marley and nodded when he saw where they were. "Shall I come up there?"

"Why not? Unless you've got a better idea."

"No one around?" Nat asked.

"Not a soul."

"It won't get better than that."

Nat jogged up the steps and fell in with Gray and Marley as they started toward the back of the house again.

They got to the table and chairs, where the citronella flames threw long tongues of shadow and light. Gray waved Nat to the chair Sidney had used then sat down with Marley beside him.

"What's in the bags?" Marley asked. She had never mastered patience.

"Things I want to show you," Nat said. He slid forward on the seat of his chair and laced his fingers behind his neck. "Your turn first. You called me, remember?"

"We should probably have come in to you," Gray said. "Now we're all here, I don't know why we didn't do that."

"Because we need neutral ground where we've got a chance at clear heads and no interruptions," Nat said.

Marley decided she liked the way Nat thought. "And this is a haunted place," she said. "That can be helpful." She brought her lips carefully together. *What would make her admit to something they couldn't possibly understand?*

"If you say so." At least Nat didn't laugh at her.

"I just meant the place has that reputation and it's kind of . . . well, you know. It's a thoughtful place."

"Yeah," Gray said. "There's a little wine left if you want it, Nat."

Nat declined and made no comments about why they might be out here drinking wine together.

"I'm going to tell you things you'll have every right to question," Marley said. "A lot of it is beyond understanding when you don't have any background in paranormal events and the way they can happen with some subjects. Will you hear me out? Then we've got to talk about a suggestion that was made to us tonight."

"I like to listen with my eyes closed," Nat said, doing just that. "I'm wide-awake in here."

Marley tried to start at the beginning. When she talked about a portal, she didn't mention the Chinoiserie house and when she glanced at Gray he showed no change of expression. *"You understand why I've got to keep that back,"* she thought.

"Yes."

Startled, she looked at him again and found him watching her with the same kind of shocked awareness she felt.

"I've never communicated this way with anyone outside my family before, Gray."

"What does it mean? Tell me—" He frowned and she felt the channel close.

He held her hand and she didn't immediately realize he'd done so with Nat there. They both looked at the detective whose eyes were still shut. They kept their tingling fingers together.

"Then, after I left your office the last time, I was so confused about what to do. I went home and Gray went with me."

She brought Nat up to date, all but Sidney's not very subtle suggestions.

"So you came out here this evening because Sidney Fournier asked you to?" Nat said. He slitted his eyes and this time he did give the wine bottle and glasses a long look.

Marley said, "She didn't expect me to be here," and giggled when Gray pinched her fingers.

"Gray always did like someone reliable watching his back." Nat's teeth were very white when he smiled. "He's got good taste in that department and I'm sure you could make mincemeat of any bad guys or women."

She bowed her head. "So, now you think I'm completely crazy," she said. "And it probably doesn't matter what Sidney had to say because you don't believe a word from me."

"I believe every word from you," Nat said.

Gray's grip on her hand tightened.

"You do?" Marley said.

"I don't know what happened in that warehouse yet. Not for sure. But something did and you saw it. I've got to believe the rest. What do you say, Gray?"

"I'm a believer."

"Sidney told us Amber had already left Danny before she disappeared," Marley said. "She said their relationship was already over."

Nat opened his eyes and sat up. He only gave their joined hands passing notice. "No shit. No kidding, that is."

She shook her head. "That's what she told us."

He started to get up. "I'll have her brought in. Danny, too."

"You think that's for the best?" Gray said.

"No." Nat settled back in his chair. "Knee-jerk.

362

But I'll have Danny watched starting now. He looked me in the eye and lied. You'd have thought the church bells were already warming up for those two."

"He needs to get his story straight," Marley said. "At first he tried to pretend Amber didn't return his feelings. Then he let it out that they were close."

"And now there's another take," Nat said. He made a call and gave succinct orders. "I take it Sidney had some story about why she wouldn't talk to us—to the police?"

"She said she was afraid." Gray paraphrased Sidney's conversation.

"I was going to tell you we're pretty sure Amber doesn't have a kid," Nat said.

"Figures," Gray said. "How much longer will it be before you can get some preliminary DNA results back on Shirley Cooper?"

Nat hesitated. He cleared his throat. "Shouldn't be too much longer."

"Damn, I wish they were faster. It could change everything about the case."

"Will you look at these for me, Marley?" Nat said, not responding to Gray's last comment. "I know I can't expect too much, but it's what I was talking to you about in my office. The things that belonged to Liza, Amber and Shirley."

Marley came close to telling him again that she'd never worked with objects like this. Nat was lumping all paranormal gifts together and coming up with something resembling the type of stuff they put on TV series about psychics.

"I don't think it's a good idea," Gray said when Nat put a silk scarf on the table, and a pair of gloves. "Marley doesn't do party tricks."

She was grateful to him, but sorry for Nat, who was doing his best to be open.

"I know that," Nat said. "But it does happen that touching something belonging to someone can bring about an impression of that person, doesn't it? It can be helpful in locating them." He looked with hope at Marley.

"I've heard it can, yes."

Nat didn't miss her noncommittal response. "You don't think there's anything in it?"

"I don't know." She had to be honest.

They fell silent. Critters in the grass and nearby shrubs tuned up like they were getting ready for a rock concert.

Nat reached into one of the bags and retrieved some sort of hat made of draped and embossed mauve satin. "I won't say who this belongs to, but will you hold it?"

She rubbed the spot between her brows. The start of a headache threatened to make this a hard night. "Yes." Marley took the turban from him.

"I don't like this," Gray said.

"Say something unexpected," Nat retorted.

"Please be quiet," Marley said. "Both of you."

Marley tried to sit comfortably. She began to

shiver. A breeze gained strength and her flimsy white dress frothed around her calves.

The soft, satiny turban slipped between her fingers. Where the fabric was embossed, the texture felt rougher. Marley looked at the shimmer on the satin, at the shadowy lines where the folds settled. She let her eyelids lower and went into neutral. With her mind wide-open, she invited any response to come in.

Time passed and she felt peaceful. She also felt nothing unusual and saw no inkling of a portal, and heard no whisper from an Usher.

"You know better than to try putting on shows."

Sykes was back. She deliberately ignored him.

"If you're short of money, maybe I can help you out."

"What does that mean?" She felt snappy.

"I leave you to your own devices and you get into the entertainment business? When do you pass the hat?"

"I'm not even answering you."

A change in shadows along the balcony railings carried Marley's attention in that direction. Flickering in and out, she saw the suggestion of her brother, wearing black tonight and looking vaguely demonic.

"Watch out for Gray," Marley said.

"Oh, yes, little sister. I'm watching. He won't get in on anything from me, but you better

watch yourself. When you're in lust with some-
one your judgment could get clouded."

"That's it," Marley said. *"You can report back*
to Uncle Pascal that I'm cool. Thanks. Bye."

He sat on the balcony railing with an arm
around a slender column.

Marley set the turban on the table. "Nothing
from this, Nat. I tried, but I don't feel anything.
I'm sorry."

"How about this?" He gave her the gloves. They
were black, crocheted and fingerless.

"I like them," Marley said, trying unsuccess-
fully to see the pattern. "They look old."

"They probably are. Feel anything?"

She didn't. Going from one item to another she
grew tired and irritable.

"Give it up," Gray said.

Nat's phone rang. "Archer," he answered.
"When? You know her?"

Marley quit breathing.

"Friend Danny has a new lady love," Nat said,
slipping the phone away. "They were pretty
cozy when they went into Danny's place a few
minutes ago and Danny didn't seem to be
looking upset over anything. That's probably
unimportant. The guys are just looking for
something to report."

Marley didn't say anything and Gray got up. He
walked to the railing and stood there looking out
over the dark grounds. He also stood right in front

of Sykes, whom Marley could see grinning at her. Gray's hand rested on top of Sykes's on the column, a fact Sykes obviously found humorous.

"We've got to wonder if we should be worrying about any woman being alone with Danny," Gray said. "I always liked the guy, but that doesn't mean anything."

"Surely doesn't," Nat said. "But we can't do anything unless there's a complaint. Other than keep an eye on Danny."

Sykes looked into Gray's face as if he was looking for something.

Watching her brother unnerved Marley.

"Thanks for coming, Sykes. I'd appreciate it if you'd bug out now. I'll make contact if I need you," she said.

"Is that a promise?"

"Yes."

"Okay. He's good-looking." He ought to know when he was an inch from Gray's face. *"He could be interesting to sculpt. What does he look like with his clothes off?"*

"Good night, Sykes."

"Night. See you soon."

"The only other thing I brought is this," Nat said and produced Pearl Brite's cycling helmet.

"I don't want to do that," Marley said. She stood abruptly. "No, I don't want to touch it."

"Why not?"

"There's violence there. I . . . I don't want to."

"Then the helmet is exactly what you need to hold, Marley," Nat said. "You've got strong feelings about it. That's good."

"Quit pushing her," Gray snapped. "Not tonight. Let her think about it tonight."

"Pearl Brite may not have long enough for anyone to take their time thinking about whether they want to help her or not."

"That's rotten," Marley said sharply. "You know I want to help. You *don't* know what I feel, but it's not good. I don't understand what's going on and I have to think. Please put the helmet away. I'll deal with it first thing in the morning."

Visibly reluctant, Nat returned the helmet to its paper bag.

"Why don't we all go back to town and do whatever we feel we have to do," Nat said. "I'm glad I came out. It's peaceful here. And it helps for us to spend time together off the record."

Gray said, "Yes," but Marley heard him as though through a closed window.

Her palms sweated and the still-visible welts there burned.

"Pipes has marks like these on her neck," Marley said quietly, holding out her hands.

"What?" Nat spun around. "Are you sure?"

"Yes," Gray said. "But we didn't want to tell you too soon. She's already the skittish type and we thought it best not to frighten her off altogether just in case she's got useful information. Chances are that if we leave her alone, she'll come to us eventually—if she's got something to share."

"Damn it," Nat said. "You keep throwing these direct connections at me then telling me I can't use them. I need to get to that woman and talk to her on her own."

"The only way you can do that is by telling her about Marley's experiences," Gray said. "Do that and you could blow everything wide-open. We'd probably end up no closer to a solution if Pipes clams up."

"You have gone too far, bitch."

Marley jumped so hard her neck hurt. She looked from Nat to Gray, who showed no sign of having heard a grating male voice speak to her.

"Now I have seen you clearly. You are imprinted on my senses and I will find you. And you will tell me who betrayed me by telling you what you have no right to know. Anyone in my way will be removed.

"You're going to tell me who and what you are. I will find out everything about you. I have never failed to get what I want. When I am finished, you will never get in my way again."

35

"Gray?"

Nat sounded uneasy.

"What?" Gray said.

"Something's wrong," Nat said under his breath.

Then Gray realized what the other man was talking about. Marley's hands hung at her sides and she stared toward the house. Her face wasn't so much rigid, as lifeless—except for her staring eyes.

Gray took a step toward her and felt an invisible force pushing him back.

"Do you think you should touch her?" Nat said. "What's the matter with her?"

"I don't know," Gray said. "Marley?" he added quietly. He wanted to get her away from what he felt stirring around them.

Something deeply evil.

"She can't hear us," Nat said. "They don't have a handbook on this one. Not that I've seen. Did you ever see her do this before?"

Gray was past his usual level of caution. "Not exactly." A current buffeted him and he was surprised he didn't stagger.

"Something like it, though?"

Gray ran a hand over his hair. "She's seeing something we can't see. Let her go." It would be better for him to be alone with her.

Marley walked directly toward a door that opened on a room barely visible through large windows. She paused, then took another step.

"She'll walk right into the glass," Nat said, talking about the panes in the upper half of the door. Gray broke from the restraint and shot forward to grab her.

The door swung open of its own volition and Marley walked inside.

"Holy shit!" Nat said. "I didn't see what I just saw."

"We both did," Gray said, following Marley.

"You can't just walk into other people's houses," Nat said.

"We're being let in. Invited in, if you like. But you can stay here if you feel better about it."

He went after Marley with light, rapid steps and realized he was behaving as if he were dealing with a sleepwalker.

Lamps on bentwood tables glowed, beads swinging gently from the shades. They hadn't been turned on a moment ago. The room was typical of its period and purpose. Widely spaced rattan furniture covered with cool-colored cotton fabrics grouped for conversation beneath wooden fans on heated days. Large, faded floral rugs on gleaming old wood floors.

Gray felt Nat enter the house behind him and signaled for him to stay put. For himself, Gray allowed Marley to get farther ahead. He could reach her fast enough, but he didn't want to risk intruding into whatever she was involved with in that other world of hers. Instinct warned him of the danger he could cause by breaking her concentration.

He wished he could hear her speaking to him in his mind as he had before and narrowed his eyes, willing her to talk to him.

Nothing.

Soft and muddled, a familiar sound came to him, a sound with a beat at its center, a cadence. He stood still and waited, straining to hear any discernable words that might separate themselves from the whispery jabber.

Marley entered a hallway leading toward the front of the house and Gray went after her. He glanced back at Nat and shook his head once. Nat raised his hands to indicate he would wait where he was.

"Dangerous, very dangerous." The words snapped clearly from the otherwise meaningless vibrations. Many sibilant voices seemed to argue, and he felt he was supposed to be included. *"This one is a neophyte. Whatever happened to him as a child stunted his paranormal development."*

A slow, heavy beat started in Gray's head. He knew they were talking about him. What he didn't know was how much truth there was in the suggestion they made that he had started life as a paranormal talent, but that his progress had been arrested.

Or perhaps he did know and chose not to look too closely at a past no human should have endured—particularly as a child.

"He's all we've got if the Embran attacks her." There was a bustling quality about the voices, a determination to press ahead with whatever they decided was best.

He had never heard them use the word *Embran* before.

"He could separate Marley's consciousness from her body forever."

"Or give her a chance to return just when all seems lost. He has power if he can learn to use it."

He wanted to yell for someone to teach him—quickly.

"You follow her," a voice said sharply. This time a different voice and a familiar one.

"It is not my way to interfere directly. That is not in our rules. But this Embran threatens her life. He threatens many lives."

Gray felt shadows move. A man, tall, with long, graying hair but a young and vibrant face materialized, but without substance. His image was clear for a moment, then foggy. His dark clothing was from another era and Gray wasn't sure when it might have been.

"Who is the Embran?" he asked. "Or what?"

"If you need to know, you will know. You, Gray. You follow Marley. Be there. Do nothing unless you're told. The Embran wants Marley, but we

don't know his intentions for tonight. When the time comes you will have to make sure her body is kept warm. Stay back."

Another whisperer broke in irritably. *"Remember he can only see what happens on his own aware side. What goes on beyond the veil will be invisible to him."*

"Hush," the man told this one and muttering gradually faded away.

"You, Gray. Pay attention. I don't think the Embran is aware of you. Your powers are not developed enough, but neither are you the weak stuff of his chosen prey. And you are not a Millet, which is to your advantage." He gave a humorless laugh. *"But one day I believe you will have to fight him—unless you choose to abandon Marley—and you will have only your instincts to follow. Be ready."*

Silence rushed in where the voice had been. The shadow form was gone, and Gray felt like shouting for the man to come back. "I'll never leave her," he said.

Ahead of him, Marley turned right, into a room illuminated by a few bulbs in an old chandelier. She walked to the center of the room where the only furniture was one pale couch.

Gray hung back, tucked himself just out of sight, but made sure he could get to her rapidly. He heard music. Lightly and from a distance. The tune was familiar, but old and remembered from another place. Gray didn't know what it was or anything about it except it made the hair on the back of his neck prickle.

He dug finger and thumb into the corners of his eyes and concentrated.

36

Marley didn't feel alone.

Screens made of thin wood with green, watered silk stretched over them hung from ceiling tracks and fitted into corresponding grooves in the floor. And familiar music played gently, coming from overhead.

This place felt warm and soft, enticing. She closed her eyes tightly and opened them again. A simple dark blue chair looked inviting and she sat down.

Instantly, pressure on the top of her head and her shoulders stiffened every muscle. Her back hurt. She tried to get up, but her legs wouldn't hold her weight.

The screens rattled.

"Comfortable, are we?" a grating voice from the other side of the screens asked.

Marley drew back in the chair.

"You're not comfortable? What a pity."

The laugh that followed sent a pain through her head.

"I don't believe you know me and I intend to

make sure you never do. You are an interloper and I think I know why. Soon I shall be certain. Through interference from my enemies, you have strayed to a place that holds only danger for you. But we can make this so very simple. Who sent you?"

She couldn't make her mouth work.

"Who sent you?" he repeated louder. "How did you know where to come when I first marked you? How did you find me in the warehouse? You will never succeed in destroying me or others like me."

"I don't know," she got out. "I don't know anything about you."

"You have intruded where you have no business being. You couldn't have done that without a guide. Who is your guide and what did they tell you?"

"Nothing."

A great, growling noise sent a shudder through Marley.

Without warning, a spotlight shone on the screens. Behind them, starkly silhouetted, she saw a standing figure, arms spread wide, a loose robe hanging. Wide sleeves fell from the shoulders. But it was all a dark shape without features.

"I can crush you," he said. "There is no way out for you unless I say so. I won't allow you to leave until you answer all my questions. Where is my chinoiserie house?"

Marley felt icy cold. "What?" She had no idea

what she should or shouldn't say, or how long she would have control over her mind. She felt the power of the other one.

"My chinoiserie house. You've got it, haven't you? Who gave it to you? What did they tell you about it and about me?"

Belle had told Marley to guard the house, to make sure no one took it from her, and to follow where it led her. And to stop the killing. But the woman had not told her how she was supposed to accomplish all this.

With the help of the Ushers, she had followed where the house seemed to want her to go, but apart from Shirley Cooper, who was already dead and had never appeared to Marley, there was no proof of other deaths connected to any of this.

Women were missing. More of them now. And she had heard Nat and Gray speculate about a connection to the string of women who had disappeared some years ago. She locked her knees to control the shaking.

"Answer me." The man's voice thundered, then cracked and seemed to slide away.

Marley saw him turn his head, and the way his hood draped.

But she drew back in horror at the sight of the man's profile, the thick, wide jaw, nostrils that jutted, much too big to be normal. One hand rose and pointed in her direction. "Who gave you my house?"

Not a hand, a claw.

"No one." She steadied her voice.

"Man or woman?"

"No one."

"What were you told?"

"Nothing."

"I want to tear you apart, do you understand?"

Marley closed her mouth tightly and held her jaw rigid. She would not show fear.

"This is your last warning. You are not here by accident. I can bring you back whenever I please. I have been following your mind pattern. At first I only knew there was something familiar about you although I could not believe my own deductions. I didn't want to. To me you are the most hated of creatures, you and your clan. Tell me where to find the house."

"I don't have any house." She concentrated on her story. "I live in an apartment."

For an instant he was silent. Then he said, "Oh, you think you're clever. I have my ways to make you scream. I can make you beg. I can make you as nothing, but only after you deal with horror you cannot even imagine. Tell me what I need to know."

"You're mad," she said. "I don't believe anything you say and I don't care what you say. I am more powerful than you." She was not weak. Hers was a honed talent, a dramatic skill, set of skills.

"What?" he thundered. "You are no stronger than

the others who have gone before you. Give me what's mine."

Give you what you consider yours so you don't need to keep me alive anymore?

The thought shook her afresh. Could each of the missing women have had something he wanted? Once they gave it to him, had they been discarded?

She had to be strong, for them and for herself—and for the people who loved her.

"Why should I try to help you?" she said.

"Because I've told you to."

"Why should I believe anything you say? I don't think you know anything that would interest me. And I don't believe you can hurt me or anyone else. Get away. Go back to whatever hole you crawled from. I've imagined you and now I'm casting you out of my mind. Go away. You aren't real."

Marley summoned her strength and pushed to her feet. "I have to leave now. Enjoy your fairy tales."

"Fairy tales? You impudent puppet. You will give up to me whoever it is who pulls your strings. And you will give me my house."

"I don't have your house and I'll give you nothing. You don't exist."

The screens smashed open and darkness flooded the whole space. All Marley could see were the red eyes she had come to dread. They drew closer, and closer, their uneven progress evidence that their owner limped badly.

He was in front of her, hovering so close that fear paralyzed Marley. Light-headed, she took a deep breath and coughed. An odor surged over her, so strong, so fetid, she swallowed waves of sickness.

"I will be back for you," he said. "I can't stay longer now—it's time for me to leave. When I return and find you, my possession had better be with you."

Marley tried to cover her face against the foul stench.

An arm shot out and fingers scraped the side of her head, tangled with her hair and tore painfully, this way and that.

She panted and gulped down sobs.

They were not fingers, but talons. She felt them scratch her scalp.

"You don't believe what I tell you, hmm?" he said. "Perhaps I can persuade you with a little gift. I hope you are clever with your needle, Marley Millet." He made a croaking sound as if amused, or pleased. "You see, I know who you are. I know your family. They have been a curse to us, but that will end."

Claws on the free hand poked at her mouth, pried her lips apart, and she felt cloth shoved inside her cheek.

He pushed her and she fell backward, this time onto a couch. She slid sideways and lay with her face turned into a pillow.

Shivering, her muscles in spasms, she grew

colder and colder until at last she dared to open her eyes a little. Beneath her, the couch was covered with light-colored material, pale yellow with beige leaves. Marley pulled up her feet.

She was alone.

There was no blue chair and no silk-covered screens.

The music still played, never growing any louder. And the whispering she would have welcomed while she was alone with the creature rushed in around her.

"You must find a way to help me," she said to the Ushers. "If I must turn to the ultimate form of neutralization, I will."

The Mentor demanded that paranormal martial arts be used only when one's life was in jeopardy. The Millets must never be unfair.

But if she chose to use what she could, she would have to engage that creature physically. How badly would he wound her before she prevailed?

Her mouth felt thick and she remembered the cloth that thing had put there. She pulled it out, sickened at the thought of what it might be.

Under the weak light of several bulbs in an overhead chandelier she saw a piece of black cotton and knew what it was. She held the piece of her T-shirt that had been torn from her sleeve the night she saw Pearl Brite disappear from the warehouse.

Marley clenched the fabric in her fist. The Millet

rules of chivalry even in the face of great provocation were starting to annoy her.

Growing from a confluence of shifting specks of white light, a form took shape. Marley blinked; she turned her head aside and tried to bring the apparition into focus.

Her skin stretched tight over her scalp, freshening the pain from that creature's talons.

Either what she saw was a brilliantly golden book encrusted with gems or she could be looking at the top of a box. She had seen this once before, in her flat with Gray beside her. Her father had mentioned a small casket. Marley screwed up her eyes. She thought she was seeing a book and as she decided she was right, the front cover fell heavily open, revealing a yellowing parchment title page on which there were a few words: The Mentor: Triumph Through Honor.

"You only need remember our code," a man said. He sounded so reassuring, she smiled.

37

Tonight he had finally found her for himself. With the aid of the scrap from her clothing, he had summoned enough of the old power to seek out the pattern of Marley Millet's aura. No two patterns were absolutely alike, although it was possible for him to make a mistake.

When he was fully strong, he never misread an

aura, but in times of increasing weakness such as he suffered now, his eyesight deteriorated when he was transformed.

Now, too drained to stay and deal with her further, he had returned to his own place again, and to the young whelp who was his supposed helper. Soon he would discover if his horrible notion about his enemy's identity was correct. If he was right about who had betrayed him to the Millet woman, the way forward was more dangerous than he could have imagined.

Only willpower kept him dragging his body forward while the young man scurried at his heels, gabbling in his fear. It would be easier to go alone and do what must be done, but this one must be there, too.

"Are we going to be found out?" the terrified whelp said, panting. He tried to laugh. "Can you save us?"

The questions didn't deserve answers and he tossed his head in disgust.

"I'm sorry," the younger one babbled. "Sometimes I forget you can always keep us safe."

The Embran marveled that this weakling could be the product of his own being. Completely human in appearance, it was true—and without the power to transform himself into Embran form—yet he had come to being through the joining of Embran and human. It had been wise to hide this failure's true partnership. "Shut up, you sniveling fool. Stay with me, and we'll discover if you failed in the only important task I ever gave you to do."

"I don't know what you mean. I have never failed you."

"We shall see." He must regain the chinoiserie house. How long had it been gone? Where was it now? Was it safe? He choked on his own misgivings.

With each dragging step his torment grew. The red house was his access to the renewing chambers of the Lower Place, Safehold as some citizens called Embran, where he had begun his existence centuries ago. Weeks back he had been warned that it was time to return, but unfinished business here had tempted him to gamble on how long he could put off going for the infusion that brought him back to his full might.

He had obviously waited too far beyond his own limitations and an enemy had used his rare lapse in judgment to attempt to eliminate him.

Who was it? Did he know? Had he already unearthed the identity? The possibility that his suspicions were correct made it almost impossible for him to go on.

He paused to take a package from his robes. From inside the string-tied brown paper he removed a handful of dust and tiny bones. These he crammed into his mouth while he closed his eyes and waited for even the meager flush of strength the compound could bring. Eating the crushed shell and the bones of the dead Embran young inside had become his panacea for weakness. In the Lower Place, live young were used, but they could not be kept fresh on a journey to the Earth's surface.

A minute passed. And another. Nothing.

He couldn't wait any longer.

Slowly, he stumbled down the stairs that led to the basement and his possible answer. Soon he would find out if his worst fear was a fact. If so he had to work fast, and do whatever he must to save himself.

He heard his companion's hoarse breathing and took a small pleasure from this one's fear.

The cold of the basement helped calm the throbbing in his thickened skin. Ignoring everything but making it to the ice vault in the farthest corner, he wrenched open the door and fell to all fours. Crawling, he made his way deep into the vaporous compartment. He didn't bother to look up at the swinging hooks—his tools to cause ultimate fear.

When he reached the first of the long row of white caskets, he started to count.

Grunting, he pulled himself forward. Ten, eleven, twelve, thirteen . . . there it was. Fourteen.

With draining effort he hauled himself to his feet, tore off a hasp and raised the lid.

Empty. His human wife's body was gone. "How can this be?" he shrieked, turning on his companion. *"Where is she? Your only duty has been to look after all of these."* He indicated the lined-up iced caskets.

This was his way of making sure no one ever had proof that so many missing women were not only dead, but connected to him. Here, they would never be found and he was safe—unless some fool betrayed him!

"She must be there," the other one said. *"I check the cooling systems regularly."*

"You have not checked regularly enough." He had come himself until every move he made became a decision. How long ago could that have been? Six months, seven—while the Lower Place had kept demanding his return? Then came the final desperate order and still he had ignored it— he had been so sure he could make it back at the very final moment. *"When was the last time you opened this to make sure of the body's condition?"*

A blank expression met him and rapidly turned to horror.

"You have not been checking the body," he whispered.

He leaned over and scrabbled to pick up a folded piece of paper on the bottom of the casket. Once unfolded, the paper revealed familiar flamboyant handwriting:

So now you know, husband. Did you forget the truth about me? I could always choose when I wanted to use my body. You should have made sure I was in my human form when you tried to kill me, old fool. I could not die if I wasn't there.

I have taken my body with me this time. After all, at last I can dance whenever and for whomever I please. You can't stop me now. So you are welcome to sleep where you intended me to sleep forever. After all, you will need to keep as cold as possible—for as long as possible.

But in the end you will give up and be gone forever.

Your flesh will rot from your bones first—can you smell it decaying already? Then your organs will slough away. Your foul carcass will trap you long past the moment when you beg for death.

Your loving wife celebrates your hell,
Belle

He screamed. Such a short time ago his frailty had forced him to leave that plantation house on River Road, and to leave Marley, who must know where Belle was. Belle knew too much, could make too much trouble. She could not be allowed to exist, but his only connection to her now was through Marley Millet.

If only he was as he should be, he could have made her take him to the chinoiserie house.

387

He must find a way back to her and force her to help him return to the Safehold in the Lower Place. Better yet, he would bring her to him here and get the information he needed. Dealing with Belle could wait.

Slumped against the casket, he renewed his personal promise: a woman who displayed herself in lewd dance while men watched had not deserved to live, not if she had the honor of being his wife. Belle's days were numbered.

But it was the jazz singers who were his ongoing mission. Even he protected his own and one of his own had suffered through the arrogance of one of those singers. Somehow he would hang on until he had the revenge he had promised himself.

He smiled. There he was making progress. Fear soaked the city. With each singer's disappearance, others had become too afraid and given up. The most annoying were gone or ruined. Dealing with them had become an unexpected thrill beyond compare.

His hide contracted painfully over his flesh and he stifled a howl.

When he was renewed and returned with the use of a powerful young human body, he would be showered with the female attention he deserved, and this time he would be single-minded in his purpose—apart from allowing himself some small diversions to boost his powers. When he came back to this great city it would be to finish

*his work for the Embran and eliminate the rest
of the Millets from the face of the earth.*

*He struck his pathetic offspring who had let
him down. "Worthless," he told him. "You could
not even make sure your mother was dead."*

38

Gray reached Marley and bent over her. He
found a pulse in her neck. With his heart pounding, he turned her onto her back.

Relief was short-lived. She looked bloodless
and her flesh felt so cold it was hard. Her fisted
hands pressed into her chest.

"Nat," he yelled, struggling out of his jacket. "I
need the blanket from your kit. And anything else
warm."

In seconds Nat skidded into the room. He
looked from Gray to Marley and pulled his T-shirt
over his head. He tossed it at Gray and ran out.

Gray pulled his own shirt over Marley's head,
drew Nat's on top and wrapped his jacket over
everything. Marley's eyelids flickered. She
looked at him, but her eyes rolled to one side.

"Don't you die on me," he said, shaking her. "I
won't let you die. Don't try it." He grabbed and
held her against him, sat on the edge of the
couch and chafed her back hard. He pulled the
T-shirts down as far as they would go which,
given her size, was knee-level. Wrapped against

his naked chest she sent a deep chill all the way to his heart.

"Hey, hey," he murmured. To warm her hands he forced her fists beneath his arms. "Stay awake. Nat's gone for a blanket. I'll get you thawed out and you'll feel better."

Her lips moved, but she didn't speak.

Nat pounded in and skidded to a halt beside Gray and Marley. He threw down an old plaid blanket, then snapped open the silver sheet from his kit. The thing wanted to float rather than be wrapped around her.

"Rub her arms and legs," Gray said, and they worked, side-by-side, pulling first one, then another limb free of the cocoon they had wrapped her in.

She began to shake, a steady, rhythmic shuddering from head to foot. Her eyes were wide-open now.

"You're going to be okay," Nat said. "We'd better call 911."

"No." Marley croaked out the word. "I can't do that. Don't try to make me."

Gray could feel her panic. "Okay, okay. Calm down."

"I won't go," Marley said.

"You don't have to," Gray said. He had been warned to take care of her himself and he wouldn't fail.

Nat kept rubbing an arm. "Let's get her home,

390

then," he said. "She'd be better off in bed. It wouldn't take too long to get her there."

Marley shook her head, no. She pulled away and sat on the couch with her hands clasped between her knees. "I can't go there." She hung her head forward.

"Just let us get you home," Gray said. He massaged her shoulders and held her face in his hands. "Being in your own bed will feel good, Marley."

"No," she said through chattering teeth. "I've got things to do. I can't go home."

She extended one fist and unfurled the fingers. A scrap of torn black fabric lay bunched in her palm.

Nat moved closer to look. "Is it from someone's clothing?"

"Mine. In the warehouse . . . that thing, the creature tore my sleeve and he must have kept this. Tonight . . . here, he gave it back. He was letting me know he's the one who took Pearl Brite."

"He was letting you know he can find you, too," Gray murmured.

Nat opened the space blanket bag and held it out. "Drop that in here," he said.

Marley did as he asked and turned her face into Gray's shoulder.

He met Nat's eyes and the other man made a motion with his head, offering to leave. Gray nodded.

"I'd better get back," Nat said. "But I need to know where you'll be."

"We can't stay here," Gray said. Marley still seemed as cold as ever.

"My family would try to stop me," she said and Gray knew what she meant. "Only because they love me and want to look after me," she added quickly.

"I'll take you to my place," he told her. He wanted time alone with her to go over not just the case, but what was happening to him. While he had waited for her outside this room—after the voices had faded, he had felt and visualized things he must understand and he needed to talk to Marley about them. "Gus will get the wrong idea when he sees you, but why not give him that pleasure?"

Nat laughed, but Marley's expression remained dull.

"Is it okay to go to Gus and my place, Marley?" Gray said.

She nodded and put her mouth near his ear. "I'm afraid. I don't want to be, but I am."

Rather than answer, he picked her up and carried her to the front door where Nat let them all out.

The night had turned heavy with the promise of another storm. A thick layer of tight warmth pressed in and the air was still. Gray hurried to put Marley in his car and as soon as the door was shut he walked around, passing Nat on the way.

"This isn't my first time with this kind of stuff," Nat said, looking straight into Gray's face. "Do you understand what I mean?"

"I think so." He didn't want to be the first to reveal that he put a lot of credence in areas not readily accepted by all.

"Before I met Wazoo, I thought it was all bunk. It's not. There's a lot we can't see or touch, but it's there. I feel we're close to breaking this case."

"I don't disagree. But I have to look out for Marley. She's very vulnerable."

"I know," Nat said. He gave a lopsided smile. "Now you know what it feels like to . . . Ah, hell. What it feels like to love someone with a side you can only guess at."

"Maybe." He wasn't giving everything away.

"They get so deep under your skin, you can't dig them out."

"So why aren't you doing something about being with Wazoo all the time?" Gray felt Nat had opened the door to the question.

"What makes you think I'm not trying?" Nat said and got into his Corvette. He waited until Gray left the property with Marley.

When she opened her eyes, Marley stared into complete darkness for a moment. Lightning pierced windows and slashed across a room where she lay on a bed covered with a mound of blankets.

She lay very still, afraid to move even her head.

Then she heard breathing.

The covers were pulled tight across her. Someone was lying beside her on top of the blankets.

Dull pain throbbed from her temples to meet over her eyes. The side of her head felt raw.

The face of a young, beautiful black woman hovered inches above her and Marley barely stopped herself from crying out. High, rounded cheekbones, liquid-black eyes with an Asian slant, full lips parted a little to show perfect teeth, and brows that winged away. Hair pulled smoothly back and fastened at the crown and the most perfect skin completed a stunning woman who looked at Marley with a desperate plea in her eyes.

Marley couldn't speak.

Thunder rolled, quite close, and wherever she was, the building shook. Within moments lightning struck again. She should be hot under all the many covers, Marley thought, yet she was so cold.

"Tell me what you want," Marley said at last, forcing the words past a dry tongue and lips. "How can I help you?"

"Help me, please."

"I want to." Panic overwhelmed Marley. Of course, this was the cottage in Faubourg Marigny where Gray and his father lived. How could this vision come to her like this? She was always called by the Ushers and guided where she was to go, the way she was drawn through the portal that appeared in the red dollhouse.

"I don't have much longer," the woman said. *"He told me. He said you should come with me. He sent me for you."*

"Who are you?" Marley felt mortally sick. The perpetrator of the wave of disappearances and killings, that's who this one spoke of. Now he wanted Marley. Why hadn't he taken her at the warehouse, or earlier, at Myrtle Wood?

Drops fell on her face.

The woman faded.

Marley wiped at her cheeks, wiped away tears shed by the other.

"Pearl Brite," Gray said beside her.

Stunned, she shook her head. "You saw her, too," Marley whispered, trying to turn toward him. "How?"

"I don't know, but I did. And I've seen her pictures. Nat showed me." He lifted the blankets and climbed into the bed beside Marley, took her in his arms and held her tightly. "Do we need help from someone with greater . . . with more of whatever we need to deal with this?"

She sighed and pressed her face against his neck. "Each of us—those of us with parapsychological gifts, must carry our own burdens. That's a law we live by. I was given a task to perform and I must do it. There are people in my family who are stronger than I am, but this isn't their task to deal with and in trying to protect me, they could do something I couldn't bear. They could seal off any chance I have to get to the ones who need me."

"You mean you must try to save Liza and Amber, and now Pearl, on your own?"

"Yes."

"But I've heard and seen things, Marley. Just as you said, I have powers, too, and they're getting stronger. There were voices that came out of a whispering mass that told me I must protect you. They said I must be prepared to fight for you. And I am. I'll do anything to keep you safe."

She heard the slow, hard beat of her heart. "The Bonding," she said. "I had forgotten all its parts."

"Explain."

"We are bonded, you and I. By a physical, sexual dynamic that was preordained. You have felt the pain and the strangeness and so have I. We will never touch without total awareness of each other. There is more, but I'm too tired now. Because we have a Bonding, we are responsible for each other. The Ushers must have sensed what has occurred between us."

"Ushers—"

"The voices you heard. They are my guides. To a degree, my protectors, although they tend to panic when they worry about me."

"I know how they feel," Gray said. "Tell me more about this Bonding."

The thought intimidated her. "In time, Gray. I have an unusual heritage, more unusual than you've guessed."

"I doubt it, sweet cakes."

"Sweet cakes?" The words exploded from her. "I've never been called—"

"Well, you have now. And I never called anyone that before, so you're special." He sounded smug. "What the hell do we do next? I'd better bring Nat up to speed."

"He can't help," Marley said. "It will be up to me."

"Who is the other one?" Gray asked. "The man on his own?"

She let her eyes close. "What man?"

"The one I saw. Tall with long hair that's turning gray. His face is young."

Marley held her breath. "Where?"

"In your workroom. Then at Myrtle Wood. He said he was your mentor."

"Mentor?"

"I think . . . I think he's a ghost."

He held her tighter. Her eyes were wide-open now and she stared at his dark shape. "Are you sure?"

"How would I know? I never saw a ghost—"

"No. Are you sure he said he was the Mentor?"

For an instant he was quiet, then he said, "Yes, that's it. The Mentor. He told me . . . he warned me to be watchful for you."

Gray had seen the Mentor, talked to the Mentor. There couldn't be any doubt of his existence—it was all true. And Gray was Bonded to her.

"Are you okay?" he said.

"I will be. I'll know when it's time to go for Pearl. The Ushers will agitate." She looked at the gleam of his eyes and wrestled with the notion that he could well develop a mirror image of her skills. How would he deal with that? Or not deal with it? "I need to eat first."

Gray leaped from the bed and said, "I hope to hell there's chocolate in this place."

39

"Two things," Nat said in Gray's ear and much too loudly for Gray's liking this morning. "The woman with Danny Summit last night was Sidney Fournier. She must have gone right from digging the dirt on him with you to his bed. How about that?"

Gray looked at his phone and turned down the volume.

Marley sat in the corner of Gus's comfortable chintz couch, eating her way through a box of chocolates and not seeming to take any notice of Gray's conversation. But Gus's thin face showed the animation it always did when he sniffed police business. His eyes were bright as he pretended to look anywhere but at Gray.

"Why would she do that?" he said. "Scratch the question. Just seems strange after she tried to blow the whistle on him. At least, I think that's what she was doing. She seemed scared of him."

"She left his place after four this morning. Does that sound like she's scared of him?"

"Maybe she was trying to get more information from him," Gray said. He wanted to get in the shower and think. "It doesn't have to mean she was sleeping with him."

He caught a motion from Gus, who sent him a frown and nodded at Marley. So the old man had decided she was something special and her ears shouldn't be subjected to less than pure comments.

Marley didn't miss a beat between chocolates.

Smiling at Gus, he said, "Say again, Nat."

"I said they kissed at the door—for a long time. And a car was waiting for her—the one that takes her everywhere."

"Are you going to question her?"

"Not yet."

"Good," Gray said. "You'll stand to get more if you give her longer to show what she's up to."

"Glad you approve."

Gray smiled. "I'll catch you later."

"Sure," Nat said. "You might like to know there's an unmarked car across the street. It'll be there as long as Marley is."

Gray opened his mouth to protest but Nat hung up.

"Well, hell," he muttered.

"What?" Marley said.

"He didn't say anything," Gus told her. "He's always been a mumbler. Every teacher-parent conference I had to listen to how he was so hard to understand."

Marley enjoyed that little piece of fiction far too much. "I'll leave you two to entertain each other," Gray said. "Try to find something more interesting to talk about than me."

"You gonna turn your human-interest article into a crime piece?" Gus said.

"What?" Gray ran a hand behind his neck and stared at his dad.

"That editor of yours called late yesterday. Seems you're behind on your deadline," Gus said with a grin. "I told him he'd better back off or you'll sell the hottest story ever to come out of New Orleans to the highest bidder."

"Gus!"

His dad laughed outright and his entire body quaked. "Gotcha. He said he understood, but could you get him at least something in a couple of days?"

"Damn, you think you're funny," Gray said, smiling despite himself. "A couple of days," he repeated under his breath.

Gray heard the front door open.

He grabbed his gun from the waist of his jeans and trained it on the doorway to the hall.

"You got a way of overreacting, son," Gus said.

Gray sent him a warning glance.

"Hey, Gus," a female voice called. "Okay if I come in?"

"Sure thing," Gus said loudly.

The chocolate box slid off Marley's lap and hit

the carpet. Candy rolled onto the rug. She turned sharply, just in time to see Willow Millet, with a green-and-white-striped motorcycle helmet on her head and Winnie in her arms, walk into the room. The helmet dripped water and the shoulders of her bright green jacket were dark with rain.

"Marley," Willow said. "What are you doing here at eight in the morning? Where have you been? Poor Winnie's really upset with you."

"She's with Gray," Gus announced. "He brought her here last night, but she's no trouble. All she eats is chocolates."

"I don't get this," Marley said, scooping a heap of those chocolates back into the box. "Winnie, come here, girl."

Winnie leaped from Willow's arms, bypassed Marley without giving her a glance and sat at Gus's feet, staring into his face with her bone sticking out like a yellowing handlebar mustache.

Gus patted his lap and made coochie-coo noises. The little horror of a canine dropped her chew to jump up on the man's lap and curl herself in a ball, apparently instantly asleep.

He had, Gray realized, lost any control over what was going on in his own house—and maybe his own life.

"I gave Willow a spare set of keys so she can get in real early if we aren't up," Gus said. "She's going to take over for us here."

"That'll be interesting for you," Marley said to Gray.

He shook his head. "You and Willow already met, Dad?"

"You gave me her card," Gus said. "I called her yesterday and she came right on over. She does everything."

"Including windows." Willow smiled. She took off the helmet and held it under her arm. "I talked to Fabio and he'll be expecting a shopping list from me. So you two need to write down everything you can think of. He's fast so if he gets the list this afternoon, you'll get your shopping by morning. Christa has a good-size space in her schedule next week and she'll be here to go through all your cupboards and closets to get things ready for donation."

"You can see why I hired her," Gus said. "Finally we'll get some order around here."

"I'm sorry I had to bring Winnie," Willow said. "She's been on her own too much lately. But she loves a ride in the scooter trailer. She pokes her nose through that hole next to the window zipper."

Gray watched Marley with interest. She had a mixture of sad and mad on her face. Her sister was goading her and that annoyed Marley, but she didn't want her dog to lavish attention on anyone but her.

"I'll make sure she's got an even bigger bone than that one," Gus said, oblivious to the atmosphere. "Put that on the shopping list, Gray. A bag of food just in case and some chews. And we can put a bed over in the corner for her, too."

"Is there anything else you plan to arrange while I'm not around?" Gray said.

"Just a gardener to keep things tidy," Gus said. "Willow sees to that, too."

"Oh, yes," Willow said. "You're going to love our Potted Ladies. They'll make you want to just stare out the window all day."

Gray knew when he was beaten. He also knew he was tired—and worried. Now he was overwhelmed to boot. And he didn't dare move too far from Marley in case something happened to send her back to the creature. He had not, Gray realized, seen anything of the thing Marley so feared. Very soon he would press her for more information on this Bonding, too, just to get more hints about what he could expect in the way of changes—like perhaps he might start levitating at inconvenient moments, or doing the chameleon and changing colors to match his background.

Darn, he was so edgy he was going into his flip mode and it wasn't appropriate now.

Gus looked so cheerful, Gray didn't have the heart to rain on his parade by criticizing his decision to hire a small army. His dad had needed more to occupy his mind for a long time and this Willow was interesting. He wondered what her particular psi talents were and had no doubt she did have them. The whole Millet family had always been said to be "woo-woo" and he believed it.

Willow approached him. "I'll do a good job for you and your dad," she said. "If you think of something you need done and I don't come up with it on my own, just let me know." She lowered her voice. "I really like your dad. Looks like Marley does, too."

"He's always had a way with women," Gray said, smiling. "It must be satisfying to charm females the way he does—not that he often sees any."

"I'm taking Winnie to the kitchen," Gus said. "I want her to learn her way around. That okay, Marley?"

"Of course." But she didn't look thrilled.

Gus manipulated his wheelchair like a man who had had a lot of practice and left the room. Watching him, Gray was unexpectedly relieved. Gus needed company and diversion and, thanks in part to insurance and a quiet lifestyle, there was plenty of money to cover as much help as they wanted to hire.

"Willow," Marley said. "You should not have brought Winnie."

"Gus wanted me to." Willow sounded defensive. "He's enjoying himself. Surely you can share your dog for a little. I seriously brought her because I didn't know where you were and couldn't leave her alone again. But Gus had said he misses having a dog, but he figures it would be too much work for Gray since Gus might have a problem with feeding and cleaning up after a dog outside."

Marley sat with one of Gus's lap pads draped around the shoulders of her white cotton dress. She looked a little forlorn—and anxious. Gray had been sitting on the edge of a table and he straightened up, concentrating on every hint of change in her expression.

"I might as well tell you I've got a problem," Marley told her sister. "It's nothing I can't handle, but there's a lot at stake. You could really help me by keeping the others off my case. There's too much riding on what I do."

"Okay," Willow said slowly, looking at Gray, then back at Marley. "Is there something you're telling me without telling me?"

"I don't know why you'd say that," Marley said.

"I'm your sister," Willow said. "Is there . . . Has there been a Bonding?"

"Willow." Marley frowned at her.

"I know about these things even if I don't believe in them," Willow said. "There's something different. You don't seem the same anymore."

"You're imagining things."

Willow wrinkled her nose. She approached Gray and stood too close for comfort, staring at him with her disconcerting green concentration. "Are you the one?"

"Willow!" Marley exploded. "Please. You're not

interested in . . . Well, you're not. So why ask embarrassing questions now?"

"What happened to you?" Willow said to Gray as if Marley hadn't spoken at all. "A lot of sadness. And fear. Someone hurt you, didn't they?"

Gray looked to Marley for help, but from her shocked expression, he wouldn't be getting any from her, or not soon.

Willow touched his face lightly.

He felt himself grow detached from the room and blinked to focus.

"Who were they?" Willow asked. "Your parents?"

"No!"

"I don't mean Gus. He would never hurt you. But the ones who came before them. Were they people who took you in, but didn't like you?"

He felt an urge to escape. This was another of the "gifted" Millets, all right.

Suddenly, Willow held Gray's arm. "You were abandoned. Left outside a church when you were a small boy."

"That's irrelevant," Gray said. "It happened a very long time ago and in the end I got Gus. I got the best part."

"They did things to you—"

"Please stop."

Willow didn't seem to hear him. "They wounded you. Always in places that didn't show on the outside."

Gray's mind shifted quickly. He felt his built-in

protection waver and got an impression of lying on a kitchen table. He put the back of his arm over his eyes.

"Could it be that he had powers and they were suppressed?" Marley asked. "Did it happen back then?"

"I think so," Willow said. "Gray, the young man and the woman held you down while the other man cut you."

Gray felt numb. He could see the yellowing ceiling in that kitchen. He should be able to, he'd stared up at it a number of times while he tried not to scream. But in the end he had always screamed.

"It hurts so much," Willow moaned. She covered her face and rocked in place.

"Not anymore," Gray said.

"They sat on your legs and tied your arms together behind your back. The woman said . . . she wanted you castrated."

Gray's eyes rose to meet Marley's. She looked as if she might faint.

"The men said, no, and they cut you inside your mouth. Long slivers of flesh cut out and thrown away. And you bled so much. They left you there and you rolled off the table and just bled such a long time."

Willow traced lines on his face. "I can feel where they did it. Why?"

"Cruelty and true evil don't need reasons," Gus said. He had rolled his wheelchair into the room unnoticed and approached Gray. "They went too far that night and someone heard. They called it in and my partner and I went. Both of those men are dead. They died in prison—after they found out all about pain. I don't know about the woman."

"But why?" Marley said. "There has to be a reason."

"You want to tell 'em," Gus said.

Gray shook his head.

"They had a whole bunch of foster children. That's how they lived. When they were arrested they said Gray was strange, that he wasn't like other children. They said he was dangerous—an eight-year-old boy, mind you. They said he *did* things. Made things move around. Made the other children cry. They said—" Gus paused. "They said he wasn't a human, but some sort of mutant."

"Are we done?" Gray said.

Marley got close to him, put her arms around his neck and kissed him. "It explains a lot. I wonder if you got born to people who didn't understand. Perhaps something happened to your birth mother. It's unusual for one of us to be abandoned. I don't think I ever heard of that happening."

"We'll never know," he said. "I don't want to."

"But you don't mind that your powers are coming back?"

"Not as long as I have you. I want them back."

Willow hadn't moved away. She stood close, studying them.

"And you needn't bother to keep pretending the specialness of the Millet family is nothing to do with you," Marley said to her. "So you detect the hurts of others? And you see the terrible events they've suffered. What else, I wonder?"

"I don't know what came over me."

"You came over you," Marley said. "And what you just showed could be used for good. You can pick out perpetrators, can't you?"

Willow crossed one lime-green-and-white sneaker over the other. "I don't know about that. I've got a business to run. I just wanted to help you and Gray because . . . well, because you've Bonded."

Gray narrowed his eyes at her. "How do you know that?"

"Everyone in the family will know because we have a connection at times that affects all of us. A Bonding affects us all since it's the enlarging of our circle to include fresh blood. It hasn't happened for a long time so it's a very good thing."

"They cut him in a lot of places," Gus said. "On the bottoms of his feet so he couldn't try to go for help—"

"Leave it there, *please.*" Gray's nerves jumped. Gus was fixated on this now, but there were many things better left unsaid.

"I'll always hate what they did to you, Gray, but I'm glad I was the one who went out on the call. At the hospital they cleaned up inside his mouth and they had to do some grafts, but he's okay."

"Of course he is," Marley said, and caught Willow's eye. Willow had not only been able to see the scars when Marley couldn't, in full daylight, she had known she was seeing some sort of reflection from old wounds that weren't visible on the outside, on his face.

Marley didn't intend to let her sister hide away all her lights again.

This time it was her phone that rang and she backed away from the others a little to talk.

"Marley, is that you?" a woman said for the second time. "Answer me."

"Who are you?" Marley asked cautiously.

"It's Sidney, of course. I need to see you right now."

40

The moment Marley had hung up from talking to Sidney Fournier, the Ushers started rustling and arguing across her mind. *"Don't let Gray hear you. He's more aware all the time. You talked to him when I wasn't there—I can't believe that,"* she had told them.

But they couldn't keep quiet. Their whispers followed her from the cottage, into Gray's car and kept coming in little bursts while they drove toward J. Clive Millet and the Court of Angels.

"You okay?" Gray asked. He braked the Volvo for an accordionist who played and sang his way across the street despite the rain and occasional rumbles of thunder.

"He needs to get in out of this storm," Marley said. Lightning ripped the hot sky, but the musician played on.

"Marley, are you okay?" Gray said again.

"Great," she said. "You don't have to worry about a thing. The shop is my turf and it's the best place for me to meet Sidney alone." The whispering rose again and she frowned fiercely. *"Stop it now. All of you. We'll talk when I'm alone."*

"Are you angry about something?" Gray said.

She looked at him. "No. Why?"

"I thought you were talking to yourself. Why can't I be there with you when Sidney comes?"

"She won't open up if you are. She felt some sort of understanding coming from me and she's decided to trust me. I think she'll tell me about last night."

Gray had told her exactly what Nat said on the phone and she was ready to listen closely to Sidney when she came—which wouldn't be for three hours—something Marley hadn't told Gray when she agreed to have him drop her at the shop. Sidney had said she wanted to meet Marley right away, then changed her mind and asked to come later.

Marley had a feeling. Not just any ordinary feeling, but a strong compulsion to spend time alone with the red chinoiserie house. Each time she touched it, she held her breath, expecting the Ushers to tune up and for the portal to appear. But she did not have to enter that portal until she made the decision she wanted to and this morning she wouldn't go anywhere until she answered some of her own questions.

Gray had seen the Mentor. They had talked. Family loyalty pushed her toward telling Uncle Pascal and the others, but she had to be sure Gray hadn't imagined—or misunderstood—the whole thing.

Just the idea that the mystery they had always lived with might actually be solved made her jumpy with excitement. What would it mean to them all if the Mentor became an active part of their lives?

"Sidney wouldn't have to know I was there," Gray said.

"You don't give up, do you?" she said. "I'd know if you were there even if I couldn't see you."

He slammed a fist on the wheel and Marley jumped. And like a naughty boy, he grinned at her. "Got your attention. *You'd* know I was around—I really like that. But Sidney isn't you and if she has ESP I think you'd know."

She glowered at him.

"Wouldn't you?" He looked a little less full of himself.

Marley crossed her arms and let him suffer until

she felt sorry for him. Then she said, "Yes, I would. You're developing like a racehorse with the finish line in sight. Pretty soon you'll pick out the real thing from the wannabes yourself. And don't start swaggering around every fortune-teller and tarot reader's pad accusing them of fraud because most of them are genuine."

"You're kidding. Fringed tablecloths and chintzy psychedelic wall hangings? Bead curtains? It's all a rip-off."

"It's not," Marley said. "And you're making me angry."

"Ooh, I'm so scared," he said in a high voice.

Marley glanced at his big, capable hands, narrowed her eyes, but couldn't stop the corners of her mouth from twitching. She constricted her concentration to one of his knuckles and stared.

"Ouch!" Gray shook his hand in the air and put the knuckle between his lips."

"What's the matter?" Marley asked.

"Ouch," he repeated. "Something stung me."

She sank into her seat. "Sorry." And she was. She had supposedly grown out of childish tricks years ago.

Gray glanced at her, but she didn't meet his eyes. "Did you do that to me?" he said.

She shrugged.

"You did. That was mean."

"It was. I'm sorry, but you made fun of me. It was only a little pinch, anyway."

Gray smiled and shook his head. "I forgive you. But I'm going to be careful to tiptoe around you in future."

"No you won't. You'll forget and do it again." She tipped up her nose. "But I don't care. I'll rise above it next time."

"I'm coming with you," Gray said.

"No, you're not. Nat's waiting for you." Nat had called Gray back just as they were leaving the cottage.

"Let him wait."

Marley turned in her seat and rested her face on his shoulder. "There are a lot of things I need to tell you, but they'll have to come out slow."

"I'm trying to cope with that, but you've got to promise me something right now."

Winnie yawned in the backseat. She lay with all four feet in the air and didn't as much as flicker her eyelids when they went over a bump or made a sudden stop.

"Pay attention," Gray said. "Please—note how polite I'm being—*please* don't leave your body while I'm gone."

She bowed her head so he couldn't see her smile.

"Will you listen to me?" he said. "I'm asking a woman not to leave her body. This is what you've reduced me to. Say it. You won't leave your body while I'm away."

She didn't intend to, but what if something

unexpected came up and she had to make a snap decision?

"No promise from you means Gray's not going anywhere. I'll stick to you, lady."

Marley breathed in loudly through her nose. "Okay, I promise."

"Let me see your hands," he said and when she showed them, he said, "Now say it again."

"Why?"

"You might have had your fingers crossed."

She burst out laughing. "Well, I didn't. But to repeat, I promise to remain in my body at least until I see the whites of your eyes again. Now stop here. If Pascal's in the shop and sees the car he'll want you to come in."

Gray frowned. "Why would he?"

"Because Sister Willow has a big mouth and a cell phone—and Uncle will want to start the interrogation."

"Interrogation?" He pulled up to the curb on Royal Street while Marley chastised her own loose tongue.

"Later," she said, and hopped out. "Stay where you are. No need for both of us to get sodden."

"When you see Willow, tell her I think that's some rig she's got," Gray said. "The green-and-white scooter with the little trailer on the back. Pretty hard to miss."

"That's the idea."

She hauled Winnie out and set her down on the

sidewalk where water ran in mini-eddies. "Poor baby," Marley said. "Stuffed into that nasty old trailer." Winnie whined and danced to keep her feet as dry as possible.

Marley bent down and looked toward Gray, who turned in the driver's seat. "See you," she said. "Be careful."

"See you," he echoed. "I care about you."

She couldn't move for an instant. They stared at each other, unsmiling.

"Go," Gray said. "You're getting soaked."

She slammed the door and ran with Winnie to the shop and inside the front door.

He did care about her, Gray thought, turning off the windshield wipers and making the car a private place to consider what had just happened. No declarations of love, no kisses, but when he told her he cared he might as well have told her he loved her. He did. For the first and only time in his life he knew how it felt to love a woman.

The car had already been at the curb longer than was allowed. He turned the wipers on again and looked in the wing mirror before starting to pull away.

Straight ahead, a woman in wet jeans and a sweatshirt darted toward J. Clive Millet Antiques. In front of one window, she stopped and peered through the glass. She put a hand above her eyes to shield them.

She took a few steps toward the door, then backed away. Quickly, she turned and he thought she would run away, but she skidded to a halt and returned, to look through the other window this time.

"Well, hell," Gray said under his breath. He turned off the car and got out. There would be a ticket, but so what?

Unfortunately he didn't get close enough to grab Pipes Dupuis before she saw him and started really running. She flung her arms out and cannoned off people she passed. This woman wasn't a natural runner.

He caught up with her just after she turned onto Conti Street. A truck passed, sending up a rooster tail of water that soaked them both from head to foot and he took advantage of her confusion to push her through an open gate leading to a passageway behind a hotel.

"Let me go," she said, hardly able to get the words out. "Please. I've got to go."

"You wanted to go into Millet's Antiques. Why?"

"I was just looking in the window." She panted and shook.

Gray didn't like making her more frightened than she already was. "Calm down, Pipes. I'm not going to hurt you. I'll help you if I can. Tell me what I can do."

She leaned to see around him, then looked

behind her. "You just go out the way we came in," she said. "I'll go around the back of the hotel and find another way."

"You're hiding," he said.

Her blond hair hung in wet, dark strands. Looking into her eyes was painful. She was desperate.

"Has someone threatened you?"

Tears slipped from the corners of her eyes and down her cheeks, mixing with the rainwater there. "I can't say," she whispered. "If you don't let me go it might be very bad for me."

He took a risk Marley probably wouldn't like. "How did you get those marks on the back of your neck?"

If possible, she turned paler. She wrapped a hand around her neck. "I don't know what you mean."

"Yes, you do."

"No." She shook her head hard.

He wasn't getting anywhere with the direct approach. "Are you still living with Sidney?"

No response.

"Sidney's coming to Millet's soon, did you know that?"

Still no response.

"Were you trying to talk to Marley before Sidney got there?"

Pipes shook her head hard. "I . . . I need . . ." She made a choking noise. "You mustn't try to follow me or do anything at all about seeing me. Don't tell anyone. If you do—" She tried to push past him.

"If I do?" He caught her by the shoulder and moved her hair aside. Two long red marks marred the white skin at the back of her neck.

"Let me go!"

He stood aside at once. "You need help," he told her.

"We need to live," Pipes said, racing away, her arms flapping.

Marley closed and locked the door to her workroom behind her and hurried to the bench.

Fate had smiled on her and Uncle Pascal had been tied up with a customer when she and Winnie passed through the shop and went upstairs. But he had made signals that were supposed to make her stay down there and wait until he was free.

She had smiled and jogged up the stairs. She didn't want the interrogation to begin and she had a lot to do.

Any talk of the Mentor must wait for Gray to agree. The story was his.

"Lie down," she told Winnie, who jumped on the recliner and did a lot of sighing.

With the lights over the workbench fully on, the red house looked garish and out of place. Marley deliberately rested both hands on the roof with its curly corners. Her tummy made a nasty flip. She held still while her breathing speeded. She realized she was waiting and expecting the

Ushers and the formation of a funnel with a tacky texture that stuck to her hands.

Nothing happened.

She pulled on her magnifying goggles and settled them above her eyes, ready for when they were needed.

With the naked eye she could see how crazed and chipped the paint had become, but in a fine, close way typical of an old piece. At some time, she thought the dollhouse had been refinished—probably more than once. She could see the suggestion of a flake beneath another flake. It was set on a base about four inches thick and painted green.

Here and there artificial bushes remained although she could see the places where others had been lost over the years. A low, wooden fence surrounded the garden. A border beside a pathway to the corner door was worn down to a gray stubble and more paths made a pattern across the grounds. Beds dotted with dusty flowers looked unlikely. An outbuilding could be a supposed stable. She pulled open a tiny door and found a tiny horse inside.

There was a potting shed, a teahouse, a pool and elaborate white pool house. She smiled. Any child would have loved this when all the pieces were there.

The corner door to the house troubled Marley. It didn't fit with the rest of the architecture. Set at a forty-five-degree angle to the corner of the house, with a tiled roof, a window on either side showed piles of little painted cakes—or bread rolls. Like a shop.

There was no name over the door.

With great care, she turned the house on its side. A small space showed between the bottom of the angled door and the base, and when she flipped the magnifying lenses down and used a tiny scalpel to explore the crack, she felt the whole facade of the entrance move.

Sweat popped out on her brow and she swiped at it with a forearm.

A few tiny, prying movements with the scalpel and the space around the door widened. Without warning, it popped off and Marley barely caught it before it would have fallen to the floor.

With her hands behind her back and her nose only inches from the house, she studied what was a corner of the house that matched all the others, apart from the color of lacquer. Here the wall was a washed-out terra-cotta, very faded, but absolutely level with its neighbors. The color reminded her of stucco. The door on the corner had been an addition.

She went from one side to the other, looking for any sign of another door. For the first time she realized there was no other door and the back of the house, which should open to allow a child to play with furniture inside, was secured shut.

With pressure on one side of the base where it

lay on the workbench, another gap had formed. The bottom was coming loose.

Marley made a few more delicate motions, working the scalpel between the bottom of the house and the board it stood on. Slowly, the gap widened until the green-painted base, with the grounds, separated on three sides and slowly dropped away.

She turned up the lights in her magnifying goggles, not that what she saw needed to be any clearer.

A web of tiny pipes formed a grill beneath the bottom. Marley got a finger and thumb grip on these in two places and pulled gently. They parted and came wide-open in two panels.

"A drain field?" she murmured. "Or something."

With the two parts of the grill open she looked into the open space behind them.

She was looking at a basement.

The walls inside were gray and were taller on one side than the other. In a square hole cut out in the middle, she saw the bottom of a flight of stairs descending. The stairs continued down and with the base closed would rest on the supposed floor. In one corner of the space a cubicle was walled off and there was a wide door. She pulled it open and jerked her hand back.

What looked like little caskets or ice boxes had fallen to the side of the room. Attached to an overhead pulley system, doll-like bodies in harnesses hung from hooks—like the hooks she had seen revolving behind Liza and then Amber when she traveled to the place she couldn't find. The sickening little figures also hung to the side closest to the workbench.

With her heart pounding, Marley righted the house again and set to work on the sealed back. She levered the panel open and hinges long coated with adhesive that had solidified, broke off.

There was no furniture on any of the floors inside, but off a room lined with wooden cabinets that was obviously a kitchen, was a miniature cupboard surrounded with shelves. The shelves were loaded with tiny cans and other goods, glued in place. And on a bottom shelf she saw a group of packages wrapped in brown paper and tied with string.

She also saw another door that opened from the cupboard onto the top of a flight of stairs, the same flight that ran all the way into the basement.

Marley wrapped her arms around herself. She had seen it all before. She had gone down those steps. With her eyes shut, she shuddered violently.

41

Gray didn't much like the atmosphere around Nat's office. When Gray had arrived, the chief stood in the doorway. As he left, his parting shot to Nat had been, "That's not possible. You know it, I know it, and I don't want to hear another word about it. I'm getting crawled all over and if you don't want to be broken down to patrolman, you get me the answers I need."

Chief Beauchamp had slammed the door with enough force to cause one of the mortally wounded window shades to fall down inside, then he bumped into Gray, apparently without either recognizing him or noticing he even existed.

The man's oversize face glowed an intriguing shade of sweaty purple all the way to his retreating hairline.

On the other side of Nat's door, the mood was just as grim. The grunt the detective aimed at Gray might have meant anything but the most likely interpretation was: "Fuck off and die."

Gray cleared his throat and Nat paused his pacing to aim a glare at him.

"You asked me to come, Nat."

Another glare.

Gray shrugged, used a foot to hook a chair against one wall and sat down. He crossed his arms.

"How come it's always the fools who make it to the top?" Nat said, but Gray didn't kid himself he was supposed to have an answer.

Nat pointed at Gray, then in the general direction Beauchamp had taken. "You and I know this case isn't straightforward."

Gray laughed.

"Don't," Nat said and his expression was tortured enough to wipe the smile off Gray's face. "We also know we've found out a good deal. It just doesn't want to fit together, is all."

Gray cleared his throat. "Right."

"That horse's ass is believing his own opinion of himself." He jabbed the air again, clearly referring to Beauchamp. "He thinks he's God. He thinks he can make something so, just because he says it is."

"Whoa," Gray said. "Slow down, Nat. We have found out a lot—much more than I think we had even a day ago. Don't tell me you tried to tell Beauchamp what happened at River Road."

"I didn't."

"You didn't talk about Marley and . . . you know?"

Nat sighed. "I probably should have. I'd be farther ahead—maybe."

"Now I know things are bad," Gray said. "I've got a couple of things to pass on, but you start."

Nat mumbled and went to fall into the chair behind his desk.

"I missed that," Gray said.

"Beauchamp can't think outside the box."

Gray got a sinking feeling. "What exactly did you tell him?"

"I was going to talk to you first, but he showed up here yellin' about the public. All he thinks about is the public."

"They do pay the salaries around here and they elect some, remember?"

Nat looked at Gray. "We don't have much time," he said. "That fool is going to have people crawling all over my investigation and I don't think that's going to help, do you?"

A clear, cool sheath settled over Gray. He understood where Nat was going and what that meant. And he felt the rush and crush of time sucked away. They had to run ahead of the chief and the rest of the posse he would bring in to safeguard his own position. A lot happened in this town and it could be pretty bizarre, but there were limits even here. Four women had gone—one of this second group found immediately, the other three just . . . gone. Pearl Brite was the latest and he knew the details of how not only the woman but her bike and everything to do with her had gone, too, had been leaked to the press.

And memories of the last and wider swath of disappearances that cut across the city had freshened and raised questions about connections.

In a city where voodoo was a tourist attraction, the natives were looking over their shoulders.

"They don't know we've got the helmet?" Gray said.

Nat's intelligent eyes bored into Gray's. "No."

"Good. Better to let them run around talking about alien abductions. That's the last snippet I saw on the news."

"Might as well be aliens," Nat said. "I gotta settle down. Look, I think we could have something. Pipes Dupuis. I think she's hiding some-thing."

Gray felt completely calm. It was as if he had expected Nat to talk about Pipes right out of the box. "Keep going."

"She's got a little girl. Five, I think—pretty little thing, anyway. Pipes said she took the kid to her mother because she was nervous having her here with all the business going on around singers."

"I remember." He had to be quiet and let Nat finish before spilling the encounter he'd just had with Pipes.

"If Pipes left New Orleans in the relevant period, we can't find any record of it. We were thinking she must have gone by car, but Bucky Fist says she doesn't have one. She and the girl lived in a room and they've got about nothing. Pipes doesn't date and she usually takes Erin everywhere with her. She didn't fly out of here or take a bus or train that we can find out. But Gray, more than that, we can't find any family for Pipes Dupuis."

Gray thought about that. "Including a grand-mother for Erin?"

"You've got it. Pipes came to New Orleans from New York. She was pregnant with the girl. She had the baby here—apparently in the room where they live. The landlady is the only one worrying about either of them. She helped Pipes with the baby. No insurance, no nothing, but the landlady's got a friend who came in, a midwife. They managed."

"God," Gray said with feeling. "How could that happen?"

"It probably happens every day—somewhere. We don't have time to start some sort of movement right now. Gray, there is a kid. Her name is Erin. We don't know where she is but we don't think she went to some family member of Pipes's."

"Have you tried to talk to Pipes?"

"What do you think? She's sticking to her story and says she doesn't have to tell us exactly where Erin is and she won't. She doesn't know who could be watching to see what moves she makes and she thinks her daughter might be in danger. Pipes is still staying with Sidney Fournier."

"I don't get that. Why would Erin be in danger? This joker's going after adult, female jazz singers, not little kids."

"She told me she's been threatened—Pipes, that is."

Gray stood up. "When, when did she tell you?"

"A couple of hours ago. We waited for when she was leaving Scully's. This time she said there was nothing to worry about with Erin. She's safe and will stay safe if we leave her alone—both of them alone."

"Nat, what she's really saying is she's been threatened. That means she's had contact with our guy. Didn't she give any idea who he is?"

"She doesn't know. It was dark, she says, and late."

Gray thought about it. "But someone threatened to kill Erin if Pipes said anything?"

"That's not the way I read it. Pipes was personally threatened and she decided that meant Erin needs to be protected."

"Okay," Gray said slowly. "What was Pipes threatened with and why?"

Nat threw up his hands. He got up and went to pour two cups of coffee. One of these he gave to Gray. "She won't say. All I can get out of her is that *someone* told her she was in danger and she'd better not become a problem."

"That's it?"

Nat nodded.

"Listen to this," Gray said. "I think we've got our link, but we'll have to move carefully. I think that little girl is the key we've been looking for and I think Pipes knows a lot more than she told you."

He explained to Nat, word-for-word, exactly what happened after Marley got out of the Volvo and went into J. Clive Millet, Antiques, on Royal Street.

When he finished, Nat had forgotten his coffee and stared from one wall to the next. He drummed his fingers on the desk, made to get up, but changed his mind.

"Great," he said at last. "Just great. They've got the kid. You think so, too, don't you?"

"I do now. I didn't when I came in here—I hadn't even considered it."

"Stay away from Pipes," Nat said. "She's probably being watched. We can't risk the little girl."

"I don't have any plans to dog Pipes's footsteps," Gray said.

"Good. I've got to wear glass shoes on this one. I want to watch her for a day or two and if we don't get any useful information, I'll bring her in for questioning."

"And that won't put Erin at risk?"

"She's at risk now. Take it from me, Gray, we don't dare wait long. Why do you think the mother behaved the way she did with you today?"

Gray wished he was sure of the answer to that one. "You tell me if you want me to do something and I'll do it." He decided not to lead Nat back to the obvious: Pipes was looking for someone at the antique shop and the only possible candidate was Marley.

He wanted to get back to Royal Street. What he was starting to feel now came with the spikes of cold he had come to dread. "I'll leave you to it," he said. "Thanks for bringing me up to date."

"I haven't," Nat said. "That's just the minor stuff. I want to talk to you about the best way to get Marley's cooperation."

"She is cooperating," Gray said, not missing a beat. Those shivery spikes made their way up his spine, vertebra by vertebra.

"You like her a lot," Nat said and Gray wanted to

congratulate the man for superunderstatement. "But you hardly know her."

That's what you think.

"That piece of T-shirt has changed the whole complexity of our case." Nat held up a hand. "Don't interrupt me. You don't know what I'm going to say. I'll start by telling you we don't have any final forensic results. It's too early. Well, it's not too early for the obvious stuff, but some things take too damn long for my health."

Gray rubbed his hands together. Foreboding locked his jaw and he flared his nostrils to breathe. He wanted to be with Marley.

"I'm taking you over to see Blades. He's going to stay till we can get there."

That loosened Gray's tongue. Nat's announcement sounded like some sort of death sentence. "Why? What does he want with me?"

"He doesn't want anything to do with you, but he's agreed to put up with having you there."

Gray looked at the ceiling. "Dr. Death has no sense of humor."

"Don't call him that today, please."

"I don't intend to see him today." He didn't believe he had time.

"Yes, you will, Gray." When Nat's face was expressionless—listen up. "A couple of days ago Blades told me something I didn't believe. I'm going to tell you now, but if you ever say I did, I'll find a way to make you wish you hadn't."

Gray wanted to tell Nat to keep his secrets to himself. Curiosity got the best of him. "Okay. I don't have a history of flapping lips."

"Just listen," Nat said. He talked about the corpse of Shirley Cooper and the preliminary conclusions Blades had reached about the composition of material found in wounds on the body.

No brilliant comeback came to mind for Gray. He formed one comment after another, only to discard them all as pointless. "Blades has got to be joking," he said finally.

"You know Blades," Nat said. "Does he seem like a joker to you? You ever hear him crack even a little funny, or smile, for crying out loud?"

Gray shook his head. "But it's not possible."

"Dammit, don't you do a Beauchamp on me."

"Maybe what they found had nothing to do with the perp."

"It did and does. Blades was sure before—even though he's waiting for final word from Quantico—and I don't think anyone's going to move him now."

Gray swallowed hard.

"That bit of Marley's T-shirt. Blades is sure he sees traces of the same stuff he found deep in Shirley Cooper's wounds on the fabric."

"But—"

"No, Gray. Blades says the composition of the specimen is closest to saliva. Sort of. And most of Shirley's wounds were inflicted through bites, some were scratches. Blades thinks the bites are the killer's—I don't know why. Marley's arm was scratched—or that's what I decided. But Blades is sure the owner of the teeth and claws doesn't have anything resembling DNA—not as we know it. We're looking for a killer who isn't human . . . or anything else we know of."

"You think Marley . . . She could have this poison or whatever it is."

Nat studied Gray. "Blades says he found saliva on the fabric. But Marley doesn't show signs of any bites. Also, Blades says the victim died pretty quickly after being bitten—within hours. Marley's going to be okay."

Gray scrubbed at his face. He felt sick.

"Love hurts sometimes," Nat said. "I still think it's worth having."

42

What Marley wanted most was to leave her work-room, lock the door behind her and find Gray.

"You do not run away." The Ushers started a new attack and she shook her head. *"Keep working,"* they told her.

"Do you know where this is?" Marley said to them, indicating the house. "This is why it was given to me. Because it's a replica of the place where those missing women are. Please help me find the real house, or whatever it is." She had asked them before, but got only hushed gabbling in response.

The same agitated, rising and falling sounds made her light-headed. "Hush. Answer my question." She couldn't bear the noise.

"You push and fuss," they told her. *"Work on the house and be ready to travel. Soon."*

Unwillingly, she faced the bench and selected a tool. She began the painstaking task of removing flakes of varnish and laquer from the wall facing the front gate. She had closed the back of the house again, unable to look at that cupboard and the stairs, or to remember the pounding she had felt when she was last there—and the cries she'd heard.

The flakes came away more easily than she expected and she lowered her goggles over her eyes again. Perhaps the refinishing wasn't as old as she had thought. The longer materials remained in place, the more they tended to cling, one layer to another, and be hard to remove.

This was not an item she would ever sell—in fact the sooner she could be rid of it, the better. Belle, whoever she may have been, must have recognized Marley as a sister-traveler and hoped the dollhouse would become her portal.

A small, very sharp-edged chisel wouldn't have been her usual choice for the job, but she took up the tool and began sliding it beneath the red outer coat. It lifted in remarkably large pieces and beneath each one she found more of the faded terra-cotta-colored finish that appeared to have been stippled to look like stucco.

She worked steadily for half an hour before standing back to look at her efforts. Now she knew that in addition to the added door at one corner of the building, galleries had probably been removed from an upper story. The marks where they had been could be seen now, together with the remnants of flowers painted on the walls as if hanging down—to depict the way the pretty local balconies were loaded with plants.

Surely there had been a front door. She started lifting flakes in the center front, only to have pieces of green curl away where the elevated lawns met the base of the house. Having seen the basement disguised by the mound, she knew to expect any alterations. But evidence that pillars had been removed surprised her. Why go to such lengths to disguise a dollhouse?

The basement, she realized, was not actually beneath ground level—it simply had grass-covered earth mounded against its walls. It had been hidden from the outside.

The front door began to appear in the center between places where two pillars had been.

The chatter began again. Different than she had heard before. Agitation was something she expected, but this became a rising and falling wail, anguish, and not a single discernable word except, *No,* repeated again and again.

Marley worked faster and faster, steadily revealing the walls of the dollhouse as they had once been.

She dropped the chisel. Not accidentally, but because it fell from her fingers of its own volition.

The room darkened.

Winnie gave a single muffled whine.

No lights formed on the ceiling, no sign of a funnel appeared, and the Ushers were quiet.

Marley's eyes opened wide. She couldn't blink. A deep, deep longing didn't shock her. She wanted Gray. He was her and she was him and together they were a whole with twice the power of their individuality. When she had first seen him, complete with the scars that were imprinted on his memory but not his face, he had come to her because they were destined to be together. Their Bonding had been preordained.

A wind or a strong current wrapped her body and carried her backward. She stumbled over Winnie, but couldn't react. The dog didn't cry out.

Free falling, she tried to move her arms, but they remained splayed at her sides until she settled on her back, staring upward into the darkness.

Marley had no feeling at all, other than anticipation.

She saw a small room, old-fashioned, but plush. A woman, older and plainly dressed in gray, but wearing an elaborate rose-colored tulle hat, paced, wringing her hands, but it wasn't the woman that held Marley's attention.

A little girl sat on the edge of a straight-backed chair and whereas the woman moved in shadow, the child was illuminated as if by a spotlight. Thin with blond braids and dressed in a white buttoned blouse and jeans, her sneakered feet swung inches off the floor.

She stared ahead, her blue eyes huge behind round glasses.

She stared at Marley.

The child took gulps of air through her mouth. She coughed, but never looked away from Marley. Tears ran slowly down the girl's cheeks.

Marley tried to speak to her, but couldn't.

Two small hands extended toward Marley and the little girl said, "Come and get me, please. He said if you come I can go home."

Marley reached for the girl. "Where are you?" she said, and this time had no difficulty speaking. "Tell me where to find you."

In front of the child, the face of Pearl Brite appeared. This time the woman's beautiful skin was marred by the type of welts Marley knew too well. "You'll know how to come," Pearl said. "He says you've been here before, but you must come quickly or it'll be too late."

But she didn't know how to get there. These visions had nothing to do with the house. There had been no portal. She had not left her body. There was power worked upon her, yes, but a different power.

It was that creature, she was sure of it.

"I don't know how to come to you," she said, choking on each word.

"Be ready," Pearl said, and dropped her voice to a faint whisper. "He's torturing us."

43

Gray could have closed his eyes and followed the sound of sirens to their destination. Any hope of keeping the lid on even part of the investigation was gone. Thanks to the screaming cars, their lights flashing, humanity in the streets had turned like a tide to rush, staring, after the police cars, the medic vehicles—and what most of the public wouldn't recognize as the most ominous sign of all—a large, white crime scene van with its multiple locked compartments.

He and Nat had barely arrived back at the precinct from the morgue when the call came in for Nat to get to Caged Birds on N. Peters Street, the club where Pipes Dupuis used to sing.

The meeting with Blades had frustrated both of them. He seemed to want information, but he wasn't giving any hints that might nudge them in the right direction. Nat and Gray both came away with the feeling that Blades knew more than he was telling—not that the bizarre DNA discussion hadn't been absorbing enough on its own.

Gray had tested the theory that Blades didn't have

any final reports and was probably wrong, but he only got more convinced the M.E. could be right.

Bucky Fist drove with Nat at his side. Voices barked over the radio and Nat carried on what sounded like a monologue with brief flurries of punctuation.

Sunk deep in the backseat, Gray tried to call Marley. He got her canned message—again. By now she'd be with Sidney Fournier, not an idea that gave him comfort.

A body had been found at Caged Birds.

So far there was no identification.

Bucky tucked the car into the trough formed by official vehicles ahead and cruised, one elbow resting on the window rim.

"You sure there's no ID yet?" Gray said, raising his voice over the jet stream of warm, wet wind through Bucky's window.

"If I knew—you'd know," Nat said without turning around.

"What d'you hope for?" Gray asked.

"What do you mean?"

"You want a new one or an old one?"

Nat snorted. "Nice turn of phrase. If it's Liza, Amber or Pearl I don't think I'll feel better than if it's another one. *Goddammit.* As long as they stay gone, there's hope. Maybe they're renovating that dump of a club and an accident got misreported."

"Sure," Gray said. He breathed out slowly. "We can hope." But he didn't.

In front of Caged Birds, official vehicles turned the street into a parking lot. Bucky slipped into a spot and the three of them got out.

Nat led the way into the club. Even with the doors blocked open it reeked of stale beer. Gray didn't recall a bar or club that didn't look tawdry in daylight.

Weak but definite, he smelled traces of an unforgettable odor, the one that faded slowly after Marley's encounter at River Road. The same one that hung around Shirley Cooper's body.

He deliberately looked ahead, past Nat and Bucky and the bevy of uniforms waiting for instructions.

The first face he recognized was the gouge-cheeked pale one belonging to Dr. Blades. Gray's stomach turned over. Blades was a man who considered himself too important to get down in the trenches, at least until initial dirty work was done. Since Blades had to be all of seven feet tall he'd be hard to miss in any crowd, but standing back from everyone else, staring straight ahead and completely immobile, he was as out of place in the teeming club as the Eiffel Tower would be in the middle of a school yard recess.

"That stench again," Nat said abruptly, putting his hand to his nose. "It's different from a decomposing body, but it's filthy. It was around Shirley Cooper the first time I saw her body, too."

Desperation rattled Gray. "I could still smell it

today." With every passing hour he was more convinced that Marley was marked for attack by a maniac.

Chief Beauchamp was the next unwelcome surprise. He saw Nat and approached, head slightly down like a bull coming in for a charge. "Interrupt your tanning session, did I?" he said when Nat got close enough. He showed no sign of noticing how inappropriate his comment was.

Gray saw her.

Crime scene spotlights glared on the first of the two suspended cages. Inside, her back to Gray, her wrists taped to the uppermost bars, hung a woman partially covered by strips of torn clothing.

Cameras clacked, technicians moving rapidly but precisely to get every angle of a scene worthy of a horror movie.

He recognized Bernie Bois, the club manager, his rangy body sprawled in a chair, his hands covering his face.

"Who is she?" Nat asked Beauchamp.

The older man ran a hand over his sweating head and hair. "I'll settle for who she isn't," he said. "Some guy from Scully's is being tracked down to take a look."

"Danny Summit," Nat said.

Beauchamp grunted. "The last missing female's father is being brought over, poor bastard. I'm talking about the one that went missing—supposedly—in the warehouse on—"

Gray cut him off. "It's not Pearl Brite," he said.

Beauchamp slowly looked in his direction. "Fisher? What the fuck are you doing here?"

"I thought I'd pop in for a pick-me-up."

"Funny. You heard the question." Beauchamp's face plumped up and got shinier. "Why are you here?"

"He came with me," Nat said. "He's been giving us a hand. Knows some of the singers."

"Yeah?" Beauchamp's deep-set eyes were very close to the bridge of his nose. They turned crafty. "How come?"

"I was writing about them," Gray said wearily.

"Oh, yeah. You quit the force to be a reporter."

Why bother to explain himself? "Right."

"Take a look then," Beauchamp said.

Nat and Bucky fell in with Gray when he approached the cage and the cameras were quiet.

"She's stacked," Beauchamp said in a loud voice.

Gray resisted an urge to turn back and punch the guy out. He didn't miss some snickers, but there were more muffled exclamations of disgust.

"There was no hurry to cut her down," a tech said to Nat. "The photos could be invaluable, sir."

The woman was obviously as dead as she would get. "Yeah," Nat said.

"There was a bag over her head," the same tech said. "We cut it off, so we could see . . ."

"Her face," Nat said.

"What's left of it," Gray said.

He stood close enough to the cage to touch it if he wanted to. The woman might as well be naked. She had been reduced to a crude parody of sadistic sexuality, her dress torn from her shoulders to reveal naked breasts cross-hatched with welts. Blood had dried—a long time ago—on her belly and thighs. The patterns resembled those on Shirley Cooper's body.

Slowly, Gray looked past a sizable puncture wound in her neck, and back at her face. Where her eyes should have been, two holes gaped. Her cheekbones and nose were crushed and black hair stuck to wounds in the skin.

Only the mouth, slack but untouched, was as Gray remembered it, that and a small black birthmark just above the right side of the upper lip.

Nat touched his arm. "It's—"

"Liza Soaper," Gray said. "She was special. She could belt out a foot-stomping number or sing lyrics that made you want to cry, and she was decent. I'm going to find the bastard who did that to her and—"

Bucky whistled loudly, drowning out the rest of Gray's sentence.

Nat waited until he could be heard and said, "I'll help you."

"A word?" Dr. Blades sidled near and kept on moving toward the front of the building.

Nat and Gray glanced at one another and followed quickly and quietly.

Blades left the club and walked to the opposite side of the street.

"You aren't leaving now, are you?" Nat said. "Won't you stick around until she's taken down?"

"Yes," Blades said shortly. "I don't want to talk in that zoo. I'll go back after we've spoken. She's been kept frozen."

Gray stared at the man.

"She's still fairly solid so it'll make establishing time of death more difficult," Blades continued. "That much I'll share with that fool, Beauchamp."

"What won't you share with him?" Nat bounced onto his toes.

"Did you notice the stench?" Blades asked.

"Yes," Nat and Gray said in unison.

"Shirley Cooper's body has the same odor—although it's faded a lot."

"We noticed." Gray shoved his hands into his pockets and kept his peace.

"We jumped to conclusions about this thing being some sort of alligatorlike monster," Blades said.

"But from another planet," Nat said, perfectly serious.

"From somewhere we've never been," Blades said. "I've got to get back now, but did you notice there are scratches and bites—it's the bites that drew blood. I did the sniff test, and that's also where the smell of very old rotting flesh is hanging around. Not the scratches. It's the teeth that do the real damage."

Gray swallowed.

"Okay," Nat said slowly.

"I think our particular monster may be a pretty impressive copy of something we know all about these days. Except for the obvious differences. Varanus komodoensis."

Gray shrugged and shook his head. "Doesn't mean anything to me."

"Or me," Nat said.

Blades nodded. "I don't have time for a lecture now. Take a look at what the experts say about the Komodo dragon."

44

Gray watched Nat follow Blades back across the street. Agitation pounded at his nerves. He glanced around, expecting to find onlookers staring at him.

"Hey, Gray," Nat called to him. "Aren't you coming?"

"Nah. I think I'll go catch up on a few things."

Nat raised his brows questioningly, then shrugged and carried on toward the club.

Gray hovered, thinking his way through his next steps and trying to order the sensations battering at his brain. He tried to quiet down. Marley had communicated with him before. True, they had been in the same place, but he didn't know if she might be able to reach him from just about anywhere by now. He had felt their connection getting stronger.

Royal Street was the only place he could go. He was panicking for no reason. She was the kind of woman who got immersed in her work and probably turned her phone off.

She was there.

"Remember me, Gray?" Sykes Millet seemed to appear from nowhere, just to loom up in front of Gray. "We met here once before and—"

"I remember you. Have you seen Marley recently?"

The man's face went still, except for his intensely blue eyes. They changed shades and expressions, and Gray didn't like any of what he saw there. Sykes was unsettled.

"Just answer a few questions for me," Sykes said. "No, no, don't try to interrupt. We don't have time."

Gray scrubbed at his forehead. "Ask."

"Do you know anything about a book? I think it's called *The Book of Way.* That doesn't have to be the actual title but I think it is."

"I don't know what you're talking about."

The guy turned heads. You couldn't avoid looking at him, but apart from the good looks even Gray could appreciate there was some undefinable quality about him.

"Why are you asking me?" Gray said.

Sykes didn't flinch or blink. He gave Gray a long dark blue stare, an unnerving stare. "I think you're mentioned in the book."

"What book?"

Sykes made an impatient sound. "Just call it the book of the Millets' lives. Our history—and to some degree, our future. At least, that's what I think it is. I haven't actually . . . I've only seen it, not touched it."

"So how do you know what's in it?"

Sykes took a while to say, "The pages have turned in my mind."

Gray kept on watching the other man's face.

"Willow told me to come to you. She's our sister the skeptic, but I couldn't find anyone else to ask and she said you know things if you want to share."

"I don't know," Gray said.

They were jostled by passersby trying to get a better look at Caged Birds.

Gray moved nearer to the buildings leaving the sidewalk for the gawkers, and Sykes followed him. "Did Willow say why she thought you should talk to me?"

"I read a page in *The Book of Way*. It tells of a man harmed on the inside where most can't see. He's a man sent to slay dragons."

"Slay dragons?" Gray felt the need to move, fast, only he didn't know where to go. "If you couldn't touch the book, how could you read so much?"

"I told you. The pages were turned for me. I saw them in my mind." Sykes raised his hands and they were curled into fists. "If you understand at all, let go of unbelief and tell me. I have to find the book, but that can wait. It has already waited for centuries. Now I have to find Marley."

"Dragons," Gray said softly, hearing Blades's detached Komodo Dragon announcement. "They kill with their teeth."

"You do know something," Sykes said, taking him by the shoulders. "Help me to help her."

"I can't. I have to follow where I'm led." He wasn't sure where his words came from.

Looking at the sidewalk, Gray seemed to see small sparks fire. A force field closed around him, closed him in with Sykes. "She's in danger," he said.

"You are Bonded to her?"

He raised his face and nodded. "Yes."

"When you—touch—you are energized?"

"If that's all you can call it, yes."

Sykes gave a thin smile. "And the marks Willow spoke of? On the inside?"

"They're there."

"Do you know the reason for them?" Sykes asked.

"To punish me. To teach me obedience when I was a child. I don't know anything else except that I must have had powers I was afraid to use afterward and I forced them from my mind. I've been trying to touch Marley, to bring her to me, but she doesn't answer. I'm too new at this to know what I'm doing."

"You are returning to your true self. Do you believe you are part of a world very few come to know?"

Gray said, "Yes," surprising himself with his rapid response. "Marley and I have been able to communicate . . . without speaking aloud. And I've seen things she's seen. I believe I was meant to be with her."

"Good." A pleased smile gave Sykes a piratical air of satisfaction. "Welcome."

"Thanks." It seemed the only thing to say.

"Pascal, my uncle, asked me to find her, but she's being closed off from me," Sykes said. "That should be impossible . . . unless she's a party to it."

"You mean she could be choosing to stop us from getting to her."

Sykes nodded slowly.

"Is it possible for someone else to shut her away?" Gray asked.

Sykes's jaw clenched. "Anything is possible."

"The Mentor would know," Gray said quietly.

Gasping, Sykes took a step backward. "What do you know about the Mentor?"

Gray hoped he hadn't done the wrong thing in mentioning the shadowy man. "I have seen him. He has spoken to me."

"Impossible. We don't even know if he exists."

"He exists. Not the way we do, but he's here when he wants to be."

Excitement raised Sykes's color. "You were sent to Marley," he said.

"Should I try to ask the Mentor for help?"

"It's our way to deal with our own problems. We have never asked for help."

"But he came to me." He thought better of saying he found the Millets hardheaded.

"Perhaps he'll come to you again," Sykes said, and Gray didn't miss the hopeful note. "He must have made a decision he struggled with. You are Bonded to Marley, but you are not a Millet. He showed himself to you for his own special reasons."

"To help me help Marley," Gray said. "He bent his own rules."

Sykes gave the ghost of a smile.

"You were at Royal Street?" Gray asked.

"No."

"Then we start there."

"Uncle Pascal said she isn't there."

"I think she is or that's where we'll find something to help us," Gray said. "I know she was going. I drove her there. That's where I'll start looking for her."

"Let's go, then," Sykes said and Gray was glad.

By foot was the fastest way to travel while the traffic was so snarled. They ran all the way, dodging and darting, bringing cars to a screeching halt, raising angry shouts from people who got in their path.

The trip took longer than Gray wanted it to, but anything would have been too long. Finally he turned onto Royal Street and sprinted until a hot-dog cart stopped him.

Sykes, with Gray thumping into him in the process, all but fell through the door at J. Claude Millet Antiques.

They were met by a wildly barking Winnie, who jumped up and down on the ugly gold fainting couch.

"Shh," Willow said. She and Pascal faced the two newcomers as if they'd been waiting for them.

"Anything?" Pascal said to Sykes.

"Willow was right about him," Sykes said, hooking a thumb in Gray's direction. "There's a Bonding."

Pascal Millet was a muscular, striking man who shaved his head and looked at the world with yet another pair of those extraordinary green Millet eyes. He assumed the expression of a watchful father looking over a teenage boy come to take his daughter to the prom.

"I was sure there was," Pascal said. "I felt it."

"So did I," Willow said, and when they looked at her she pushed her mouth out in an O. "I mean, I sorta thought . . ."

"You said what you meant," Sykes said. "You are in tune just as the rest of us are. About time, too. We all have our jobs to do in this family."

"Except you," Willow snapped back. "You think you can do what you like."

"That's what you think," Sykes said. "Enough squabbling, sis, we have to find Marley. Uncle, is my father back in London yet?"

Gray frowned at him, not understanding.

"Yes," Pascal said. "He went straight back."

"You and I need to talk," Sykes said. "And with him. Can we go to your flat?"

Without a word, the two of them took off.

Winnie ran back and forth to the foot of the stairs.

"What is it, girl?" Gray said. A sharp sting crossed his face, caught the corner of his eye and he winced.

Gray kept his back to Willow. Horror choked him. He concentrated and felt drawn to Marley's workroom.

Winnie squeaked at him. She jumped up and down until Gray approached her. Off she went, up the stairs, looking like a mutant greyhound jumping fences.

"Go with her," Willow said.

"Make sure your cell phone's on," Gray said.

"I won't need it."

He didn't respond. Instead he vaulted, three steps at a time, up the three flights. Already hoping his tested methods would unlock the door, he reached for the deep colors of the leaded glass and grasped the handle.

The door wasn't even closed.

Gray shot inside and shut the thing behind him, leaned on it, almost afraid to go farther into the room.

Pressure held him, pummeled him. His ear drums hurt so badly he sank to his knees.

Wet. Winnie licking his face with desperate fierceness focused him and he got to his feet. The whispering voices bombarded him, forcing themselves to find space, one over the other, vying for his attention.

"I can't understand you," he said.

The ceiling whirled with a kaleidoscope of colored lights, spun faster and faster. Gray forced himself to keep his eyes down and made his way through Marley's projects to her bench.

Curls of red lacquer littered the worktop as did pieces that seemed to be broken off the house. He picked up a piece. It was so hot he almost dropped it.

He turned it over on the bench and saw it was the door that had been at one corner. The walls came together as if it had never been there now, except that rather than red, the finish was a dark salmon color, and painted to look rough. Like stucco.

"You have to go." This was no whisper. This was a clear voice and Gray saw what he expected, the ethereal image of the one who called himself the Mentor.

"Go where?" he said. "Tell me. Quickly, please."

"Look at the house. It's there. She told me it would be."

"Marley told you?" Gray said.

"No." The man sounded impatient. *"The one who gave Marley the house for safekeeping. Belle came to me and said the house holds the key. Now get to work."*

"I can't do what Marley does." He touched the roof and raised his hand. "See, nothing happens. I don't feel anything."

"Be patient."

"I can't."

"I am Jude," the man said. *"They called me Judas because they blamed me for the evil acts of someone I should not have trusted. A woman who caused the family to be shunned and driven from their home. I married that woman.*

"They said I proved the Millet curse of the dark-haired ones—that evil befalls the family whenever a male Millet child does not have red hair. I have been patient waiting to clear my name. You will be patient finding what you want most. Continue with the house. It will give us the answer."

Gray rubbed his hands together and picked up a little chisel that felt ridiculously flimsy.

"You can't stop until we have the answer."

He slid the thinnest end of the blade beneath loose lacquer and peeled it away. More of the pinkish-brown finish appeared.

Abruptly, his face stung.

He had been slapped, hard.

She was him and he was her. One. Bonded.

The pain was hers.

They were hurting Marley.

45

With her hands tied behind her back and her ankles lashed together, Marley leaned against a wall to keep her balance.

Her cheek hurt and the corner of her left eye felt as if one of Sidney's nails had cut the skin.

The slap had come without warning. Sidney stood in front of her and brought her face down to Marley's. "Pretty pattern," she said, poking at the marks she must have made. "Ugly, freckled white skin." She tugged Marley's hair. "Ugly hair." She pulled until Marley sucked in a breath.

Sidney laughed. "You can cry, if you like."

How silly she had been to come with Sidney just because she had begged and cajoled. They had sneaked out of the Court of Angels through the alley gate and driven away—who knew where—in Sidney's BMW.

The room where she'd been taken finally had pretty furniture, old, not as old as most that Marley dealt with, but nice. "You said you needed my help, then you do this. What's your point?"

Sidney hit the other side of her face and grinned. "You've interfered. Now you need to tell me what

I have to know. I'll make points that way—those are the points that matter. I need information to pass along. How did you find out about me?"

Marley frowned. "You were Amber's singing partner. Amber's missing. I found out about you that way. When I saw you at Scully's that was the first time I saw you. I heard about you that afternoon."

"Don't pretend you're dumb. We know what you've found out."

"Then you don't need to ask the questions, do you?" Marley said, bracing for another slap.

Sidney put the tip of a high heel on Marley's sandal-shod foot and applied weight.

Tears welled in Marley's eyes and she choked with pain. She wrestled with the rope around her wrists, and she listened, longing for the whispers of the Ushers.

At first there had been a few moments when she had been left alone and that music she had heard before played. The music reminded her of the creature, but she still expected to reach help, most especially Gray. But then a sensation like slick fluid washing over her left momentary numbness in its wake. Since then she had been unable even to try to touch another mind. After that, she had not felt or seen anything beyond her immediate surroundings.

Her powers were being contained, but she had no idea how.

Was it this place that restricted her, some element there?

"Eric will be back soon," Sidney said, smiling. "He'll persuade you to help us."

Eric was Sidney's brother. He had been waiting for them in the black BMW after Sidney had managed to get into the shop and find Marley without being seen. Marley hadn't noticed Eric in the backseat until he tapped her shoulder. Less striking than Sidney, he was still good-looking and dressed like a successful businessman in a dark silk suit.

Marley hadn't liked the expression in his eyes. He looked at her with flat dislike, she thought.

Sitting in the front passenger seat, with Sidney driving and Eric behind her, she discovered she had read his feelings about her accurately.

Marley had been helpless to stop him from tying a blindfold around her eyes. The gun Sidney pointed at her, even without looking at her, made sure she didn't try any heroics.

They had brought her here before removing that blindfold.

"You've made him angry," Sidney said.

"Eric?" Marley said. "How?"

"You know who I'm talking about and it isn't Eric. You've done something stupid and now we're in danger. You've got to be stopped and he will do it."

Marley was convinced she must be very careful what she said. The agitation she caused Sidney came from her having something the other woman needed and she could only think it was the red house—yet Sidney had seen it on the workbench and shown no interest.

There could be only one explanation: Sidney had no idea that the miniature was significant.

Carefully, Marley asked, "You wanted us to believe Danny was involved."

Sidney waved a dismissive hand. "You and Gray will have mentioned that to the police by now. I did what I wanted to do. Suspicion of Danny will divert them when the time comes."

Spoken as if Sidney was certain Marley wouldn't be around to interfere.

Marley's courage wavered, but if she didn't stay strong, she would be finished. "But you don't really think Danny has anything to do with anything?"

Sidney laughed. "You made it so easy." But there were dark marks under her eyes and a tightness about her mouth. Sidney Fournier was very afraid of something.

A thought and an image came to Marley unbidden. Her mind felt clearer. She made herself weigh the wisdom of it before she said, "I want to see the little girl," Marley said. It was worth a try and she watched Sidney carefully for her reaction.

That came immediately. Sidney's face blanched and she turned away.

She spun back, the corners of her mouth drawn down. "Who do you know in this house? Who's telling you things?"

Bingo. Marley pressed on. "I'd like to see Erin, please."

Sidney's mouth worked.

"Now," Marley said.

Sidney rushed at her and pummeled her head and shoulders. "Shut up! Shut up! You don't know what you're talking about. What have you done to make . . . ? You've made people angry. I won't suffer for what you've done."

"Don't," Marley said, bowing her head to avoid the blows.

She stumbled sideways and fell, heard the door open as she hit the floor.

"What's this?" A man's deep voice asked. "What are you doing, Sidney? Oh, this poor girl, let me help you."

Marley struggled to raise her head and shoulders. The man had thin, white hair and a lined face, but gave the impression he was not as old as he seemed although he used a cane. The hand he extended was smooth.

He patted her shoulder and looked at Sidney. "Are you mad?" he said. "Is this a friend of yours you've brought here to treat like this?"

"I'm sorry," Sidney mumbled.

"Help me," he told her. He sank awkwardly to his knees and untied Marley's hands. "Give them time for the blood to flow back. My, my, what must you think of us?"

While he helped her sit up, Sidney loosened the knots at her ankles. When the rope was removed it left red marks behind to match the ones on Marley's wrists.

"She asked to see Erin," Sidney said, sullen.

"How nice," he said and to Marley, "I am Bolivar Fournier, Sidney's grandfather. Who are you, young lady?"

"Marley Millet," she told him without hesitation. Disoriented, she tried to reconcile her treatment at the hands of his granddaughter with this distinguished and charming man.

He looked at her sharply, but with kindness in his eyes. "Not Antoine Millet's daughter? Or one of them, should I say?"

"Yes."

He smiled, evidently delighted, and shook his head. "How is my old friend? I haven't seen him in many a year."

"He's well and living in London."

"Ah," Mr. Fournier said as if she had explained a great mystery. "Well, you must see the little girl. You know all about this nastiness here in New Orleans, I suppose?"

Marley swallowed. "The missing singers? Yes."

"Sidney's a singer, you know," Mr. Fournier said. "Pipes is her new partner since, well, her former partner is one of the women who disappeared. A terrible thing. We took in Pipes and her daughter because Pipes didn't feel safe living alone in the Quarter anymore. We've got plenty of room here as you can see, and we can keep the child safe."

He got to his feet, planted his cane with a sharp rap on wood and helped Marley up with surprising strength. "Marley," he said. "There is a sickness in New Orleans. So many people are afraid. I would have expected the police to solve the problem by now, but just like the last time, they seem help-less."

Marley nodded. If she asked to leave now and go home, what would happen? Chances were that the risk of disaster was too high.

Eric slipped into the room and stopped as if he needed a new battery—just inside the door.

"This is Marley Millet," Mr. Fournier said. "I knew her father. Take her to visit Pipes's little girl."

Eric nodded, backing from the room, and Marley followed on feet that tingled.

"You, too," she heard Mr. Fournier say, and Sidney caught up.

Neither brother nor sister would look at Marley. They walked into a circular, white marble entry hall. As soon as they were alone, Eric and Sidney hovered, looking at each other.

"Hi!"

Marley turned to see Pipes Dupuis running downstairs.

"We're taking Marley to meet Erin," Sidney said through lips that barely moved.

"She's downstairs. I was on my way there." Pipes's voice shook. She couldn't get any paler.

Marley glanced at Eric to find him staring at Pipes with complete absorption. What glowed in his eyes resembled possessiveness. It also spoke to lust—and perhaps frustration.

"Hey," he said. "Great. We'll come with you."

Pipes looked blank. She stood in the impressive hall with its marble busts and looked from Eric to Sidney, as if waiting for instructions.

Eric laughed into the silence and Marley's stomach turned at the sound.

"We'd best get on," Eric said, but he smiled at Pipes and touched her face lightly.

Marley's skin crawled. He was obsessed with the singer.

"This way," Pipes said and sped on behind the base of the other staircase and along a corridor. Marble gave way to dark paneling and still they kept hurrying along.

The nerves in Marley's spine jumped. She got an impression. She remembered it all because she'd been there before. Then she heard what she'd longed for, the whispers that were beloved now. Nothing she could actually make out, but the familiar excited tumbling of sibilant voices.

She kept moving, but she concentrated hard. Her inner awareness was opening wider by the instant.

Deliberately, she brought Gray's face into focus. They were Bonded. It was to him she should turn now. Together they had the promise of enormous strength.

His scars showed and she felt the impact of a blow. He was hurting and that's why she could see those hateful marks.

The vision of his face turned toward her so that she looked directly at him. Slowly the shades of gray turned to color and his brilliant eyes pleaded with her. His mouth moved.

"Gray?" She tried to reach him. He showed no sign of hearing her and no answer came.

A door lay ahead. Pipes pushed it open and Marley followed into a kitchen with Eric and Sidney.

She shrank back, head light, sweat breaking out on her neck and brow.

"Where is she?" she managed to say. "Erin?"

"You don't look well, my dear," Eric said, pulling a chair forward.

Marley slumped onto the seat. She had to, that or perhaps fall. "Where's Erin?" she mumbled, keeping her gaze on the floor, the white, tiled floor, the bottoms of cabinets, the legs of a table.

"Erin's playing," Pipes said, her voice faint.

"In the basement, I expect," Eric said and gave another barking laugh. "What is it about basements that encourages play? Let's go and find her."

Marley heard another door open and looked sideways, her eyes still downcast. Inside a room, like a cupboard, she saw string-tied brown packages piled on the bottom of a stack of shelves.

"Come on," Eric said. "I'll help you, Marley."

The last time she heard him talk in this room, she had been in Liza's mind. This must be the madman who had terrorized New Orleans.

46

Pillars had been removed from the facade and balconies. This had started as a stuccoed dollhouse, not a piece of chinoiserie.

Gray worked with the little chisel he'd found on Marley's bench. The lacquer peeled quite easily, but took some of the underlying coat of paint with it.

There had been writing on the wall in the center of the front wall, where the door must once have been. He had taken most of it off with the lacquer.

A magnifying glass hung on a hook and he used it to peer at what was left of black, fanciful words. There wasn't enough. All he made out was "Eau," which meant nothing.

He turned the piece around, but stopped when the house started to shift off its base. Carefully, he tilted it sideways and revealed what was covered by the mound of lawns that sloped up on all four sides.

A web of pipes opened to show how a base-ment—not really a basement but the lowest floor hidden with earth and grass—was reached by a staircase. In a corner, another compartment puz-zled him, until he saw little dolls wrapped like mummies and hanging from hooks.

Marley had talked about a cold room with hooks. That's where she said Liza and Amber had appeared to her.

His belly felt rigid and he stiffened, willing him-self to stay calm. Righted again, a panel at the back of the house had obviously been pried open, then put back. Gray opened it again and followed the floors up with the tips of his fingers.

The lower room was accessed from the kitchen, from a pantry off the kitchen. And to reach the kitchen you would walk behind a curved staircase and along a corridor.

A curved staircase, one of two rising up through a circular white entry hall.

"Gray?"

He dropped the chisel. Marley's voice was dis-tant but clear. He squeezed his eyelids together and concentrated. "I'm here," he said aloud. "Marley, where are you?"

Nothing.

Then, with concentrated inner will, he saw her face and the shadows of people moving around her. "Marley," he whispered. Why couldn't he talk to her with his mind as he had before?

He hammered the bench with both fists. He couldn't because he wasn't practiced enough, but they were Bonded. They were one. He must be able to go to her.

Of course he had seen this house before, a real one just like it—minus red lacquer.

"Eau," he said. "Water. L'Eau."

Knocking a picture frame over as he went, he dashed from the workroom, but was cautious going down the stairs. He didn't have time or inclination to explain where his thoughts were going and if these Millets were all so talented, they should already be on their way to finding one of their own in trouble.

The shop was empty. He looked back, expecting to see Winnie, but she hadn't followed him. She would be safe where she was.

He caught sight of Willow through the back windows. She was hauling a box to the garbage.

The shop door wasn't locked. He opened it and stepped onto the sidewalk—and walked into Pascal's trainer, Anthony, who carried loaves of French bread under one arm and a bunch of cut flowers in the other hand.

"Who died?" Anthony said.

Gray figured he looked desperate. "Nobody. Yet. I'm looking for Marley."

"She left," Anthony said, pushing open the shop door.

Gray gripped the man's brawny arm and

Anthony's expression immediately mirrored Gray's concern.

"Did you see which way she went?"

"Sure." Anthony came back from the door. "She left with a woman I don't know. In a black BMW."

"I gotta get a cab."

"Want my car?" Anthony asked, wrestling to pull keys from his pocket. "The green MGB back there. I was just dropping these off, but I don't need the car."

Gray hesitated, but only briefly. He took the keys. "Thanks. Thanks a lot, buddy."

The top of the MG was down and Gray vaulted into the driver's seat.

Sidney Fournier had left in her BMW—and Marley had gone with them. When he opened that dollhouse and recognized it for what it was, that's when he had heard Marley trying to reach him.

Bord De L'Eau, the Fourniers' home. He had never felt anything as strongly as he did the presence of Marley. She was there and she was calling for him.

47

Eric's grip on Marley's arm was not gentle. His fingers dug at her and he pulled her to her feet. "I'm tired of pretending," he said. "We've got things to do."

With Sidney, Pipes went ahead and down the

steps Marley had expected to find in the pantry. Eric hurried after them and memories made Marley sick to her stomach. Her heart thudded.

To be in this place, with him, disgusted her.

Pipes had started to cry. She drew back against a wall and covered her face.

"Don't cry, honey," Eric said. He went to her and pulled her unresponsive body into his arms. He tilted up her face and kissed her, long and deep, then released her, laughing bitterly when she slipped down to sit on the floor and sob quietly.

"What's wrong?" Marley asked. She started toward Pipes but Sidney yanked her back.

"Nothing you're not going to solve," Eric said. "Now move it—we've already taken too long."

"Make sure we do everything the way we're supposed to," Sidney said. She didn't sound confident anymore.

"I don't need your input," Eric told his sister. "We go through the locker."

Pipes cried aloud.

"Stay with me," Eric told her. "You're safe with me."

"Hah," Sidney said.

"If you weren't a jealous bitch we wouldn't be going through this," Eric said. "You had to meddle with humans. You had to want what they chase after. You wanted to be famous. Look what you've done."

Sidney glared at him.

"Aren't you human?" Marley said. It sounded like a bizarre question.

Eric smirked at her. "Not quite the way you mean."

"I'm human," Sidney yelled. "I want to be human. And I've got the best voice in this town. I'm not just a blonde bimbo. If I was like her," she pointed at Pipes, "that journalist would have come to me first. You slept with him, didn't you?" she shouted at Pipes.

"N-no," Pipes mumbled.

"I'm the best," Sidney stormed. "But I was overlooked because I'm not flashy. Liza and Amber stood in my way. Only that's changing right now. With Pipes—for as long as I need her—I'll get the notice I deserve. I'm going to be the biggest headliner in town once all this quiets down."

"Sure you are," Eric sneered. He turned to Marley. "She brought her rivals here to frighten them and threaten them. But then they couldn't be allowed to leave because they knew too much. Sidney's competition had to die, you see."

"Shirley Cooper was nothing to do with me," Sidney said. "I was just the excuse for another killing. A stupid street singer. He wanted to have her and then he wanted to kill her."

"Shut your mouth," Eric said. "You talk too much."

"Where is Erin?" Marley whispered to Pipes.

The other woman only shook her head and cried harder.

"Is she okay?"

"Quiet," Eric said. "You need to concentrate. We were worried in case Sidney had been careless, and someone would come here looking for the women. We decided to start leaving the bodies in the Quarter. That way all attention is concentrated there. We will continue until the danger is past."

Marley decided she should just keep her mouth shut. She only became more convinced that she, too, was never intended to go free again.

"Because of her," Eric nodded at Sidney, "at first the killing was essential to keep us safe. Strength came from destroying those women. Then the appetite for death reignited and it was all her fault. Sidney's. The lust for thrill killing had been quelled, but once the hunger returned, it had to be fed."

Marley listened quietly to this mad diatribe. How long did she have before they decided to dispose of her? And they would. Like the others, she was too dangerous to them as long as she was alive.

"So you killed anyone who Sidney decided was a better singer than her?" she said.

The shrieking that went up tore around the roof. "They were not better. They were lucky. Now it's my turn. First, anyone left who can harm us will have to go."

Who did she mean, "anyone who can harm us"?

She wasn't asking any questions, Marley decided. If there was any chance, she would do

470

everything in her power to stop more carnage . . . and the madness. That was the duty she'd taken on from Belle.

"Now," Eric said. "Let me show you why you're going to do everything you can to help us."

He dragged her across the dirty concrete floor to the locker in the corner of the room.

Marley visualized the inside of the dollhouse, the pipes she had seen that would be beneath this very floor.

All around her the walls sweated, and the ceiling. Rivulets of grimy moisture trickled down—the same as on her other visits.

Eric hauled open the heavy locker door and pulled Marley inside after him. Icy vapor roiled around them. She glanced back and saw the other two women follow.

Again Marley remembered the grids under the floor. Were they some sort of freezing system? Not that it mattered anymore.

The line of white, oblong containers, like top-opening ice boxes, stretched in front of them.

"See this?" Eric said, pointing out a red lever on a wall. "All I have to do is turn this and the air in here freezes within minutes. If you're unfortunate enough to be locked in here, it freezes your lungs."

"Did you design all this?" Marley asked. "It's brilliant." Flattery pleased a lot of people.

"This was done by my . . . my guide," he said, the corners of his mouth jerking down.

He threw open the first box. "They're in order by date of death," he said. "We're very organized here."

Marley looked down on a woman she recognized without knowing why. She was older and perfectly preserved—and perfectly dead. Marley held her breath. She didn't have time to get emotional or sick.

The woman had been in that room where she'd seen Erin in the dream. The hat the woman had worn rested on her chest. Her head was twisted at an unnatural angle.

"Meet Selma," Eric said.

Marley recoiled. "I thought Selma was your mother. I thought you were going to take me to meet her."

"I have," he said and giggled like a schoolgirl. "And here's Eustace."

The man had been bulky with a thick head of gray hair. His eyes were open and Marley had to look away.

"Not our parents. That's just a convenient story. These two used to own the house but they were empties. Made no impression on anyone, so when they disappeared no one noticed. A new family lived here instead. Us!"

"How old are you?" Marley asked impulsively.

"We reach our perfect age within days of our birth," Eric said. "We never change after that. That's how old we are."

This time it was Sidney who laughed. She pointed upward where Marley didn't want to look. "You'll like them," she said. "You really will. Look."

Unwillingly, Marley followed Sidney's pointing finger.

"They're next," Sidney said. "We're keeping them alive until they're going to be left in the Quarter. That way they're fresher—and they get plenty of time to consider what's happening to them. Torture is good for the backbone, and fun to watch."

Eric said, "Liza had already frozen before we dropped her off for her *show*." He laughed. "The police could get really curious about the condition of the body, if they've got enough gray cells between them to notice."

"Amber's next," Sidney said. "She won't use me again."

Marley did look up then and slammed her hands over her mouth to hold in a scream. Side by side, Amber and Pearl Brite, swathed from their feet to their necks in plastic bags and suspended in harnesses, swung gently from overhead hooks. Both were gagged.

Marley wanted to rush and get them down. Both women stared at her with terrified eyes.

"More of the same here," Eric said, walking beside the ice boxes and flipping open lids, waiting for Marley to draw level, and closing them again. The only male had been Eustace, the rest were young women—when they were still recognizable. Signs of the "hunger" Eric mentioned were everywhere.

"We've got to go," Sidney said. "Hurry up."

"Mother's gone," Eric said to his sister, completely confusing Marley. "She wasn't in her body when I thought I killed her. Bummer. Now we'll always have to be on the watch for the old bat."

"How could you make a mistake like that?" Sidney said.

"You know Belle," Eric said. "She always liked those little *travels* of hers. So she just traveled when I locked her in the box to suffocate."

"Her body—"

"Gone," Eric said. "I'm sure she thinks she's very clever."

Eric looked at Marley with a knowing grin. "Our father isn't human, only Belle. But she's supposed to be dead and she doesn't count anyway. Bolivar is our father, not our grandfather."

He used a heavy metal ring to pull a stone flag out of the floor. "Down," he said, giving Marley a shove.

She calculated her chances of disabling him and managing to deal with Sidney at the same time. She could do it, but best wait and keep looking for the best opportunity.

Soon the four of them bent over to walk along a tunnel with gravel beneath their feet.

Eric went ahead of Marley. As he passed, he grinned. "Don't feel bad. We'll make sure you come back to your friends."

Her skin felt several sizes too small for her body. *"Marley?"*

She almost stopped walking. Gray's voice came to her again. She answered. *"Where are you?"* and willed him to hear her. *"I'm coming. Where are you?"*

"The Garden District . . . " She felt them separate and wanted to shout out for him to come back. They had communicated. She would keep working at it.

"Come on," Eric said. He was really hurrying now.

Marley considered calling for Sykes. But if he came—and he sometimes dropped from the system—and stopped the Fourniers now they might miss finding other victims still alive. And she didn't have Pipes's little girl yet. Sykes was pretty cool, but she had also seen him lose it when he was really angry.

"Gray. I'm under the Fourniers' house in a tunnel. I think we're walking away from the house."

She focused on the center of her mind, but Gray didn't answer.

A gust of air whipped along the tunnel into her face and she turned her head aside. The disgusting odor she'd smelled on that creature was carried on that air—coming from the direction in which they were headed.

Pipes began to cry again.

They reached the end and Eric said, "Keep Pipes here, Sidney. And don't touch her."

He held Marley's arm and pushed her ahead of him up several steps to a door. A small, mostly white building stood there, its door recessed. There were no windows that Marley could see.

Eric reached past her, brought his face so close to hers, their skin touched. She shivered and he laughed—and slipped his tongue along her jaw.

Marley straightened her back and looked straight ahead.

He knocked on the door and a noise came from inside. One push and the door swung inward.

Eric had to force her to keep moving. She tried to whirl around in his arms, but he had her wrapped tight. His strength was a shock. Up they went to a raised room with silk-covered divans on all sides and lush hangings—and a table like an altar on a raised area in the center. An elaborate casket stood there, large and with the front open to show black velvet inside.

Marley stared. She saw an image hovering there, an image of the chinoiserie house. It faded, only to return with varying amounts of strength. It was like a hologram, not at all real.

"We have work to do, you and I."

She stood quite still while, from behind one of

the hangings, a distorted shape swathed in a hooded cloak appeared.

"Wait outside, whelp," it hissed at Eric who scurried from the room and shut the door.

Marley's fingers stiffened. She felt what she had been told she would if she was ever mortally threatened—but only if her death was imminent.

This was it, then. She flexed her hands, widened her stance and allowed her entire being to come to full alert. If there was to be a fight, she must be ready, watchful, able to find the points that could disable her foe.

"You have what's mine," the thing said. It pointed a long, curved talon toward the shivering image of the red house. "You have that. Now you will take me to it."

She stared, uncomprehending.

"You could invade my secrecy through what you stole, and then return to it. This time you will take me there."

Marley knew that if she would ever consider taking this creature to Royal Street and into the place where her family was, she could not.

"Come," he said. "Take my hand."

She swallowed to stop herself from retching at the sight of the repulsive claw held out to her.

And she didn't move. Couldn't move.

"Do as you're told," he thundered.

"I can't," she said.

"You can and you will. You did it when you

wanted it for your own purposes, now do it for mine."

"I can't, I tell you."

He swung toward her, grasped her wrist in cold, thorny, yellow-gray talons and pulled her closer.

The stench weakened her knees.

"What is it?" he said as he must have seen her expression of horror.

"Nothing," she choked out.

He made a wailing noise, clutched at his body and convulsed, but gripped her arm tighter. And the cloak slipped to the floor.

48

He had to get inside the Fournier house.

A yellow sheen showed through a gap in draperies at a side window. Hunched over, Gray crept up the sloping lawn and peered in. The light came through an open door from somewhere deeper in the house. This was what he preferred. If possible he would always choose to go from dark to light areas to give his eyes time to adjust.

The windows were the sash kind that opened from top to bottom—and they were locked, dammit.

He grasped the top of a frame and pulled, and the entire window lifted away effortlessly.

Gray frowned. It shouldn't have been that easy,

but he put the window aside, hauled himself up and inside the room.

He'd been there before—on the occasion when he'd entered through the front door.

Quickly, he crossed the room, making sure no one passing outside would see him.

His spine tightened, not in the way it did when Marley was near, or a premonition started, but an old-fashioned sensation of being watched. He turned around slowly.

A bamboo screen behind one of the purple chairs wobbled ever so slightly.

Gray pulled his gun and dropped into a crouch. "Come on out," he said quietly.

The screen wobbled again.

"Now!"

A wave of sniffles erupted. Gray took a second to realize his enemy wasn't a big, bad guy and rushed the screen. He snatched up a small girl huddled there, put a hand over her mouth—as gently as possible—and lifted her out.

"It's okay," he said. "You're fine. Safe, honey, you're safe. Are you Erin Dupuis?"

Very carefully he took his hand an inch away from her face.

"Of course I am," she whispered with a fierce frown. "Who do you think I am?"

Gray tried a little grin and shrugged. "Of course. I should have known."

Her body shook. The sharp comeback had to be

a reaction to fear. The kid would do well. "Who are you?" she said. "You're big."

"I'm Gray," he said, seeing no reason to lie. "And big is good when you need to get some things done."

She considered that. "I can't find my mom," she said very quietly. "I can't find anyone. Guess how I got out of that room?"

"What room?"

She tutted. "The one way upstairs where they locked me up, silly."

"Of course," Gray said. "How'd you get out?"

"Picked the lock." She smirked a little. "Licorice taught me. He's in the band at the Cage, but he used to help people when they got locked out of their houses."

Sure he did. "Good for you, kid. I want you to do exactly what I tell you. You're going to let me put you out through the window, then you go hide behind the bushes by the gate and you just wait there. Can you do that?"

"My mom's here," she said. "Somewhere."

"And I'm going to find her," he told her, hoping he was right. "Now, do what I've told you to do—fast—so I can get on with it."

He lifted her, but when he went to put her through the window, she clung to his neck. Gray wasn't used to children, but he didn't dislike the feel of the trusting little arms. "What is it?"

"I think they're down in that place. In the place

under the floors. I saw the stairs in the pantry."

He thought so, too, but reinforcement didn't hurt. Gray hugged Erin, lifted her outside and leaned to set her on the ground. "The only people you come out of hiding for are me or the police. Got it?"

"Got it," she said and immediately scurried off into the darkness.

"Gutsy kid," he murmured and wasted no more time finding his way into the hall, behind the left staircase and along a corridor toward where he figured the kitchen must be. He didn't hear a sound or see any evidence of another soul.

Finally he paused and pulled out his cell phone. He couldn't risk talking but he could text. The message he sent was to Nat Archer and it was specific enough that he knew his old friend would grind his teeth to nubs with rage. And later he, Gray, would suffer. But he had to do this his way.

He kept moving all the way to the bottom of the steps into a concrete reinforced area camouflaged beneath the house and lawns. The silence gave him the creeps.

Now where?

"Go. Don't wait. She needs you now."

He spun around, but didn't see any ghostly face. What he heard was one of the whispery voices that had spoken to him in Marley's workroom.

"Go where?" he muttered.

Whispers seeped in on all sides and rose to an ear-battering crescendo.

"Speak one at a time," he said, wincing.

He saw the locker and ran to wrench open the door. Bright light hurt his eyes and he flinched at the sight of two bodies hanging from hooks. He stared, and saw living eyes looking back at him. As fast as he could, he cut harnesses suspending each of two women, lifted them down and tore off gags. He released them from plastic bags tied at their necks.

"Thank you," one of them croaked. An African-American with scratch marks on her lovely face, he recognized her as Pearl Brite.

"I want you up those stairs and outside," he said, taking his knife to the bonds at their wrists. "Pearl and . . . ." He didn't recognize the other woman.

"Amber," she said. "They went down there." She pointed to a flagstone that had been removed from the floor at the far end of the room.

"Okay," he said. "Outside now. The police are on their way. Do *not* show them how to get down here. I can't risk any slips."

He didn't wait to watch them go or give more than a cursory glance at a precise row of what looked like white, top-loading ice boxes.

The hole in the floor led to a tunnel where gravel had been spread underfoot. The tunnel only went in one direction and he ran, ignoring the sound his feet made—until Eric Fournier and Sidney came around a corner, their eyes staring. Eric dragged Pipes Dupuis behind him.

"Get out of here," Eric screamed. He looked wildly about and yelled, "No, no. Get down on your face and don't move."

Gray looked at him steadily and broadened his stance.

"On your face, punk," Eric howled. "Get down."

Sidney flattened herself against a bricked-in wall. She breathed loudly through her open mouth.

"You're wasting my time," Gray said.

Eric released Pipes and fumbled with his jacket. He didn't seem the type to have a gun but Gray wasn't trusting that instinct.

"Right," he said. He gave Eric an openhanded blow to the face and caught him by the back of the collar as he went down, whimpering. "Pipes, get going. Erin's safe."

"Oh, oh, no," was the best Sidney could do as Pipes stumbled past Gray on her way out.

Holding Eric a foot off the floor and at arm's length, Gray spun Sidney around and picked her up the same way. He brought their heads together with a *thwack* and felt their bodies go limp.

His own amazement seeped in. That kind of strength was nothing he'd ever thought of having. Dropping the unconscious brother and sister, he ran on with a vague thought for the way the window had shot from its tracks on the way in.

Strength wasn't something he'd ever questioned—he had it—but not like this.

An image flashed, quickly, and was gone. The children in the foster home laughed when they were feeling bad because he, Gray, could make them laugh. The people supposedly caring for them hated it. They hurt the kids and Gray made them laugh.

He did it by . . . telling them what they were thinking and being right. All these years and he hadn't recalled that.

And he was so strong for a little kid that the adults fought to get him on that kitchen table and tie him down before they took their knives, or whatever weapons they chose for the occasion, to a part of his body they could hide under his clothes.

He'd reached the end of the tunnel and there were several steps up. He could see the sky far above, but at the top of the steps a white building picked up a sheen, even though he could see moss staining its walls.

Without pausing, he reached the door and pushed gently. It swung inward slowly and he recoiled from a bestial, inhuman howling that burst over him.

Moving as carefully as he could force himself to do, he hugged a wall and edged around until he saw the whole place. In truth he only saw Marley bent forward with an unspeakable creature attached to her back and shrieking at her.

Long, covered with a spined yellow-gray hide that had torn free of underlying flesh in many

484

places, the beast had its claws around Marley's neck. The side of its belly had burst open and parts bulged through the hide.

Its tail thrashed, but thick legs shook as if they would collapse.

"Take me there now," the creature yelled at Marley. "Now. I can't wait anymore. I have to go."

The thing had a long, broad head and when it opened its mouth, a double row of thin teeth, like long, backward-curving needles, dripped slime.

Gray smelled the foul odor again. Now it was overwhelming.

He worked his way carefully up two steps and started around the room, behind divans, making for the rear of the monster.

Marley yelled. She didn't cry or scream, she gave a great, full-throated yell, reached back to push her fingers into the thorny hanging folds beneath the thing's jaw and forced her hand up with enough effort to shake her whole body.

The creature staggered backward, pulling her with it, and she attacked the other side of its neck, pushing in, grinding her fingers back and forth.

Gray rushed and grabbed hold of the talons at Marley's neck. He yanked, and the legs flew wide, letting Marley spin away. But the weight of the lizardlike animal slumped. Its head fell forward and Gray let it go.

He glanced at Marley in amazement. She had immobilized a sort of immense dragon. It lay twisted on the floor of an unreal-looking white stone and silk-draped chamber.

"Come here," he told Marley. "Please."

She came, her face serious, and stood at his side. They put an arm around each other. "Who is going to believe that?" Marley said.

"Do we believe it?"

"Oh, yeah. I believe it. It kills with its teeth. The only reason I'm not dead is because it wanted me to take it to that red dollhouse I'm working on. He said it's his only way to go home to somewhere called Embran—deep in the earth."

"Uh-huh," Gray said. "Why am I glad Nat Archer's not here? He'd be trying to say we invented the damn dragon."

"Look," Marley said. "He's . . . rotting."

"He was already rotting when he was trying to use you like a witch's broom."

Marley found and held his hand tightly.

More and more rapidly, hide shriveled. What must have been internal organs dried up and crumbled. Within minutes all that remained was a heap of crusted tissue, and the teeth and talons and dust.

Except for the figure revealed by the destroyed form.

"What the hell do you think you're up to, Fisher?"

Gray registered Nat's voice behind him, but couldn't look away from what he was seeing.

"It's him," Marley said, moving even closer to Gray.

"Bucky's outside with two unconscious people," Nat said.

"Detain them," Gray told him. "And shut up. I sent you a message. You weren't supposed to try to find me."

"The latest recruit to your fan club is worried about you," Nat said. "She sent me looking for you. These fans of yours are getting younger, pal."

"Erin Dupuis," Gray told Marley.

Staggering to his feet and reaching out to take up and use an ebony cane, Bolivar Fournier rose from the destroyed carcass of something Gray could only think of as a dragon. While they watched, the remains completely disappeared.

"My God," Nat muttered.

Bolivar turned slowly toward them, his face serenely arranged. "I don't recall inviting you in here," he said, planting his cane with shaking hands and a resounding crack. "You can leave now."

Marley pointed at the cane. "Remember the rubber piece from the warehouse," she said. "It was from his cane." The bottom of the stick was pale, pointed, and missing its protective cap.

"Nat," Gray said. "You can take this one in, too—if he doesn't die on you first. We've got witnesses to some of his crimes."

Bolivar laughed. He focused on Marley. "Give Antoine my best, but make sure someone gets a message to Judas that the Embran will be back— eventually. Enjoy your little triumph—for as long as it lasts."

49

"Will this ever really be over?" Marley said. They had finally been allowed to leave Nat and his henchmen.

They had Gray's Volvo and headed for Faubourg Marigny.

"In time," Gray said. "But I think I've had it with Embran for one night."

Marley grumbled to herself and finally said, "Yeah. Right."

"Did you notice how Nat and company all avoided the big question?" Gray said. "How do you put nonhumans on trial?"

"Two of them are part human. Supposedly." She had difficulty finding any humanity in Eric and Sidney. "What are they going to do when that comes out?"

"Not our problem," Gray said.

Marley sighed. "For how long, I wonder? Bolivar said another like him would take his place. I wonder if Pascal knows who Judas is."

"You don't know?" Gray cleared his throat. "Judas was what they called him after he married the first one who came from Embran and the trouble started. His real name was Jude and he was the first dark-haired one. He's the Mentor."

Marley caught her breath. "You should have explained all this."

"We haven't had time for long chats," he pointed out.

"No," she muttered. "Where is he?"

"You're asking me? Sykes talked about that book, too. But I don't think I'm going to be the one to sort it all out, not that your Mentor is likely to come racing back now you Millets are okay. That's my take, anyway. How many dark-haired Millets have there been?"

Marley's throat dried out. "Sykes is the second one. That's why he can't take over as head of the family when the time comes. That's why my parents are off looking for an answer to the curse."

"One dark-haired man makes a mistake so it's a curse forever?" Gray said.

"We can't be sure. The Mentor broke the tradition and the bottom fell out. You can't blame the family for being suspicious," Marley said. "I'm going to be in the doghouse tomorrow. There are going to be more questions than I want to think about."

"You told your family to go to bed. You told them you're safe and you told them you need to recover before you talk to them about everything. They'll understand."

"No, they won't. They don't. But I can't face them now."

Marley looked at Gray. Streetlights highlighted the shadows in his face as they passed. Rain fell again and the windshield wipers squealed.

She turned toward him. "All I want is to be with you."

The corner of his mouth turned up. "That can be arranged."

She felt afraid, deep inside. Excited, aroused, but uncertain enough to struggle with tumbling thoughts.

"What is it?" Gray said, glancing at her.

"What will you do now?" she asked. "If you don't think you can finish the article you started, you could write about the case—like Gus suggested."

"No, I couldn't. I'd have to lie or no one would believe it. Anyway, I'm part of it all now and I'm not into personal exposés."

I'm part of it all now, she thought, concentrating on the nuance of each word he'd said.

How could I be anything else?

Hearing him connect with her, she looked at him sharply. *Can you hear what I'm thinking?*

Yes. Weird, huh. I tried when I was looking for you. I thought I heard you call out for me.

I did, Gray.

"I want to kiss you," she told him aloud. "And I want us to be completely honest with each other."

He groaned. "Always the serious one. Can't we just kiss and all that stuff?"

"All that stuff?"

She got another mind-destroying grin. "*All* of that stuff," he repeated.

"What will Gus think about us going back to your place?"

"He's in bed and Gus is happier than he's been in years. He thinks you're too good for me, but he's crazy glad you came along."

They arrived in front of the cottage and Gray pulled in to park at the side.

Marley made a move to open her door, but Gray reached across to stop her. His hand landed over hers on the handle, and they both sucked in a breath.

"Do you think it will ever go away?" he said. "This private energy field of ours?"

"I don't know."

Gray laughed. "I hope not."

She sat still, looked straight ahead in the darkness.

Gray put a hand on the back of her neck and she shivered. "Where do we go from here?" he asked. "Bonded. That's what we are, right? So what will that mean?"

Her heart beat harder. "It means there can never be anyone else for me. I have no choice."

"Do you wish you did?"

She gave a short laugh. "It doesn't work like

that. What I feel for you now I will always feel. Of course, you are different. You do have a choice."

He reached across her again and released her seat belt so he could pull her into his arms. "I have no choice, Marley. I don't want one. That's not what I meant. What does your family expect from us—or from me? Will they make it difficult for us? I know how much they mean to you."

She really laughed this time. "The main reason they're probably chomping right now is because they want to get their hands on us. A Bonding doesn't happen very often and it's exciting for everyone. A new chance for life." She blushed scarlet in the darkness and hid her face.

"Mmm," Gray said. "I can understand them thinking about that. First I get you all to myself, though. Can we go away somewhere? Get married and go somewhere?"

Married?

Yes. I want that. It's what people like me do.

I think you're similar people to me. We Bond.

Any reason we can't do both? If you won't do it for me, will you do it for Gus?

"Listen to us," she said and giggled.

"We should make sure it doesn't become a habit, this nonverbal communication. We could make enemies."

"I didn't think men were very keen on getting married," Marley said.

"Garbage. Propaganda."

"Okay. But you get to arrange it. I wouldn't know how."

Gray snickered. "I think Gus will arrange it—with the help of Willow and her gang. What Willow doesn't know, she'll find someone who does for advice."

They smiled, felt their smiles even though they couldn't see them. And they fell silent.

Eventually Gray said, "You have to keep your word. You said you were going to kiss me."

Marley bit her lip. She knelt on her seat, took his face in her hands and kissed him deeply.

When their lips finally parted, Gray said, "I love you so much."

"Not as much as I love you."

"A million times as much as you love me," he said.

"Uh-uh, I love you—"

Gray kissed her again, shutting off the rest of what she was going to say.

They went into the house and upstairs to his bedroom as quietly as their breathing, kissing and muffled exclamations would allow.

"I want to undress you," Marley said, surprising herself, but thrilling herself, too.

He held still, or he did most of the time, while she took off his clothes, lingering over each part she exposed. She found a few of the very pale, raggedly healed wounds he had suffered at the hands of strangers, kissed them and didn't comment.

"My turn," he told her when he was naked.

Gray had exquisite patience and stripped her so slowly her knees grew weak, and every place they touched shot an electric charge that clamped them together and eventually brought them into a tangled heap on the bed.

Under the covers, mouth to mouth, body to body, their hands roaming between gasps, they forgot about the past, didn't think about the future, while they passed the night in sweet, hot lovemaking.

"Did you see that?" Gray asked once.

"Mmm, what?"

"Sparks," Gray said, and they laughed while they came together again.

There were sharp bursts of color. "We make our own light show," Marley said.

After that they didn't talk much for a long time.

Center Point Publishing
600 Brooks Road ● PO Box 1
Thorndike ME 04986-0001 USA

(207) 568-3717

US & Canada:
1 800 929-9108
www.centerpointlargeprint.com